DAUGHTER

of

SAND

and

STONE

MORE BOOKS BY LIBBIE HAWKER

Tidewater

The Sekhmet Bed

The Crook and Flail

Sovereign of Stars

The Bull of Min

House of Rejoicing

Storm in the Sky

Eater of Hearts

Baptism for the Dead

DAUGHTER

of

SAND

and

STONE

LIBBIE HAWKER

LAKE UNION
PUBLISHING

Text copyright © 2015 Libbie Hawker

Published by Lake Union Publishing, Seattle

www.apub.com

Amazon, the Amazon logo, and Lake Union Publishing are trademarks of Amazon.com, Inc., or its affiliates.

ISBN-13: 9781503947634
ISBN-10: 1503947637

Cover design by David Drummond

Illustrated by Lane Brown

Printed in the United States of America

For my nieces, Agatha, Maia, and Aubrey. May you grow up to be warrior queens, each in your own way. And also for Paul.

PART ONE

ZENOBIA BAT-ZABBAI

260 CE

1

BORN TO KNOW THE SCENT OF BLOOD

On the last day of spring, the moon is just past full and still visible, pale and round in the late-morning sky. The women of the great chief take their embroidery, their gossip, and their games to the shaded rooftop where the breeze is cool. This is the season when the winds come from the east—from Eran and from India beyond, slow and languid and heavy with the odors of spice: the bitter taste of golpar; the bright bloom of coriander; the low earthy hum of rose; and cinnamon, sweet and compelling as a lover's voice.

These are the odors of wealth, of gold. And gold is the odor of blood.

The wind carries the rich smell of the ancient oasis, the place called Tadmor. It is a pool of yellow-green water sunk in a carpet of green vegetation so bright it startles the eye amid the endless expanse of desert. Tadmor breaks the high ranks of dunes and the flat pans, the dry basins with their hard, cracked floors and outcroppings of stone, all of it the same listless dun, the same gray-gold. It is a sanctuary, ringed with date palms, those swaying old sentinels that have dropped sweet fruit to caravanners for countless centuries, the palms offering up their friendly bowers of deep, damp shade. Beneath the perfume of the lush things that grow in the date palms' shadow, the breeze lifts the scent of the pool itself—a bitter sulfur that fills the colonnades and alleys of the nearby city of Palmyra.

Now and then a stronger wind sweeps through the city streets, through the avenues of white limestone and painted walls that spread below the chief's palace like the weave of a fine new rug. The wind flattens the veils of the women on the roof, pressing the thin fabric against the backs of their necks. The chains of gold discs hanging from their bright, flat-topped turbans chime, and their hands, as narrow and delicate as ornamental vases, flick the silken veils away.

These women—four of them, at any rate—are the very jewels of Palmyra.

Forty years of life and six spells in the birth chamber have left little mark on Berenikë, the great chief's wife. Her hair is still as black and glossy as hand-rubbed ebony. She is a tiny woman with a strong, sharp nose that speaks of her Macedonian blood. Her pointed features and black, shining eyes evoke a small songbird, all fear and flight. But when she turns a dark, level stare on companion or servant or even the chief, she is a sacred ibis, a thing of stately grace and divine confidence. When she moves, her claims ring true: that she is of the blood of old royal Egypt. When she speaks, her throat is full of the voice of Cleopatra, queen of kings, she who stood against the might of Rome.

As Berenikë sinks onto her cushions and takes a book of poetry from her servant's hands, the three young women settle about her. They are her daughters, her only offspring to survive the brutal ravages of childhood, and all the legacy left to the great chief. Nafsha, the eldest, is narrow-faced, but not without her own stamp of beauty in her onyx-hard eyes and regal bearing. Zabibah, second born, is as sweet and melting as a cake of honey, round and soft and biddable. And Zenobia—*ah*, Berenikë sighs. Zenobia is still unmarried at seventeen.

Berenikë's bright, birdlike eyes land on her youngest daughter. She studies the girl as Zenobia locks a length of blue silk into an olivewood embroidery frame and slicks a scarlet thread between her lips. She could as well sharpen a sword on that tongue as thread a needle.

Over the past two years, the names of eight suitors have been laid at Zenobia's feet—eight good men with caravans and established trade routes, men whose workers know the desert well and whose reaches extend beyond the eastern wadis into the far-off lands of silk and spice, silver and gold. The chief would have been proud to call any of the prospects a son-in-law, yet Zenobia has rejected every one.

The girl seems unaware of the cheerful gossip and quiet laughter around her as her sisters and mother, and her cousins and aunts— the courtly companions of Berenikë and her daughters—settle in the shade. Unlike Nafsha and Zabibah, who have been brought back to their father's palace for shelter while their husbands are off making war, Zenobia does not need the distraction of her family. Her face is calm and stoic as she begins her stitches, her mouth silent. *She knows the smell of blood,* Berenikë thinks, and somehow the girl's acceptance of danger is a comfort to her, despite Zenobia's infuriating rejection of so many fine suitors. Berenikë returns to her poetry.

Far below the great chief's rooftop, the blows of a craftsman's hammer ring. A merchant's voice rises in a shout, a coarse call to the men who unload the goods from his camels' packs. From one of the cistern plazas an ass brays a rasping protest as its panniers are laden with heavy skins of water. Even with nearly all the men away, Palmyra continues on its course.

This is a city of unsurpassed riches, its wealth as vast as the desert's sprawl. It is the golden hub around which the Roman Empire turns, creaking beneath its own lumbering weight. In a city such as this, where even the lowest-born craftsmen can afford silk, and the servants wear white linen from the south, a pampered girl may grow to comfortable womanhood and live out her years in happy peace. She may lay all day on a bed of fine cushions if she pleases, kept as well as the Egyptians keep their cats, the pet of a wealthy husband's home, as untroubled and safe as a kitten on a cushion.

But that sort of life is for the women of merchants—those whose bloodlines originate in far-flung lands, from the same distant places that yield up the spices and dyes that flow along the trade routes into Palmyra, and from Palmyra into the coffers of Rome. Zenobia is no coddled woman, no Egyptian cat. She can trace her line back to the very foundation of Palmyra—and beyond. She holds her chin high as she works precise stitches into the length of blue silk and looks down her aquiline nose at her work. She will not bow her head to any woman or man, so why, indeed, should she bow to a needle?

Zenobia's father is the great chief—the Ras, as the tribes say. His name is Amr Ibn Zarib, though the citizens of Palmyra affectionately call him Zabbai. In Palmyra he stands second only to the governor. For the Amlaqi tribe, he stands first.

In days long ago, generations before Rome seized control of Palmyra, four nomadic tribes tended the oasis and the beautiful city that grew up beside it. Although Rome did its best to blot out true Palmyrene culture—when has that sprawling empire left one of its conquests unaltered?—the tribes' influence can still be felt in the city today. Children learn the tribes' names as soon as they can say *mother* or *father*: Mattabol, Komare, Ma'zin, and Amlaqi. The tribes are as much a part of the city as the white stone of its temples and palaces.

Although traders from every land have settled here, now you can scarcely find a born Palmyrene who cannot trace his blood back to the great desert tribes. Some, of course, have purer blood than others, and blood counts for much in Palmyra. All the tribes are great forces, it is true. They work together like brothers, minding the city and the myriad trade routes that feed Palmyra like a trickle feeds a flood. The city could not function without the tribes' stewardship. Even distant Rome can't change that fact. But of all the tribes, the Amlaqi has always been the best—the noblest, the strongest, the most loyal and fair—as any Amlaqi will tell you.

A cynical Palmyrene—or one who hasn't a drop of Amlaqi in his veins—will tell you that there is nothing intrinsically better about this most influential tribe; it's simply a matter of politics. When it comes to playing games of power, games of quick maneuvers—Roman games— the Amlaqi have a certain taste for it that other tribes lack.

But whether taste or nature is to blame, only a fool would deny that the Amlaqi tribe holds Palmyra almost as tightly as Rome does. Their fondness for politics has made them the proudest and richest of the tribes.

An outsider might find Zabbai an unlikely leader for such a grand and influential clan. His origins were humble. He built his trading empire from the dust beneath his feet, grappling his way up from the outskirts of the tribe, winning allies and supporters by dealing fairly with everyone. As a young man, he worked as a guard in a caravan, protecting other men's goods—and soon his reputation for honesty and hard work earned him a caravan of his own. Zabbai grew his string of camels year by year and found work for any man who showed a desire for it. He even invented occupations for the street urchins who came knocking at his door, setting them to sweeping up dung in the animal yards or pulling burrs and thorns from the camels' tails—anything to give them a sense of utility and pride in their own accomplishments. He never cheated in trade, never rigged the scales to skim a few coins or an extra pinch of spice. When the wife of one of his caravan guards fell ill, Zabbai himself paid the physician's fee and sent she-goats to the family so the little ones would have plenty of milk. When a caravan went missing—led by a young shepherd who was not much more than a boy—Zabbai rode out into the desert to find the train himself, arriving in time to rescue it from a raider's ambush. When the goods were safe,

Zabbai, who might have berated the boy for his carelessness, instead embraced him like a father, weeping in relief that his life was spared.

Such things matter to Palmyra's tribesmen. Is it any wonder, then, that support for Zabbai grew? Before his first daughter was weaned, the kindly, brave merchant found himself borne up on a tide of popularity, pushed from one civic office to the next. In each new office, he had shown the same fairness and wisdom that had won the hearts of the Amlaqi tribe, until at last he was adopted by the aging Ras, whose sons had all been killed. When the gods took the old Ras, Zabbai became the Amlaqi chief, and never had the tribe felt more fortunate.

With his full beard and long-sleeved tunic, Zabbai appears Arab to any eye that looks upon him. However, his adopted father, the Ras, traced his descent not only through the desert nomads, but also the Seleucids—and he will tell any man willing to listen of his glorious heritage. The grandfather of Zabbai's grandfather was Antiochus IV Epiphanes, companion to Alexander the Great and founder of the noble family of Seleucids. Over the generations, Zabbai's noble line decreased in glory, as all bloodlines do sooner or later. But the fact that he grew up a simple merchant did not prevent him from honoring his heritage, from preserving his ancestors' noble Hellenistic ideals. The Seleucids were the guardians of all that was Greek and good; if not for their memory to inspire the soul, one might think the entire world had always existed under Rome's harsh sway. The memory of the Seleucids certainly inspires Zabbai. His ancestor Epiphanes fought at Alexander's side and aided him in founding Alexandria—which is, as all men know, a city of limitless knowledge. Zabbai has great respect for learning and good works, and so he bears the standard of his Seleucid blood with unapologetic pride.

Zenobia breathes deeply as the other women giggle. She feels the bite of spice on the wind and knows that danger is not far off. She was born to know its scent. Although she has seen only seventeen years and has no husband, as a daughter of such noble parents, her veins flow with the blood of desert warriors, Greek heroes, and Egyptian queens. How can she help but know when war is coming? War is her heritage. She does not shudder; she does not fear. No Amlaqi has ever feared a sword. Zenobia plies her needle and lifts her face to the wind. She narrows her black eyes at the smell of blood.

In the ruddy shade of a canopy made of red-dyed linen, the aunts and cousins gather around a game board, while Nafsha smiles coolly in their midst. The women are arrayed like the petals of a jasmine, delicate and bright. They laugh quietly as they make their pawns skip across the polished stone squares, click, click, a sound like beads of turquoise falling one by one along a ribbon of silk.

Nafsha's voice rises above the murmurs of idle gossip. "But of course, some of us are still unmarried." She cuts her sharp eyes toward Zenobia.

The younger sister lays her embroidery in her lap and stares back at Nafsha. Zenobia's eyes are faintly mocking. Having lived as the daughter of Zabbai, Zenobia wonders, why should she so lower herself to wed a mere merchant?

There was a time when you, too, stood high as a Ras's daughter, Sister, Zenobia says silently, gazing into Nafsha's thin face. *But now you are only a wife.*

Nafsha frowns. She glances away, as if she has heard Zenobia's thoughts. Nafsha has long since married Antiochus, a distant cousin of tenuous Amlaqi descent. She is now more the wife of her husband than the daughter of the Ras, and her marriage has meant a certain loss of status. It is a small and temporary loss, to be sure—but Nafsha feels any slight keenly. She will not cease to prod Zenobia until her youngest sister gives in and marries—and once more stands below Nafsha in the family hierarchy. For in the chief's family, as in all of Palmyra, a woman is only as powerful as the man who keeps her, and although Antiochus has a list of fine traits long enough to make any woman swoon, he is *not* Zabbai.

Antiochus is strong, kindly to his wife, and fair to his servants. He is even quite handsome, with fine Seleucid blood evident in gray-green eyes and a beard the color of new bronze. He is a rich man, the owner of several dozen camels and the head of a small army of traders who travel year-round to the most exotic lands to bring back a continuous stream of quality goods. Antiochus possesses a lovely, well-shaded estate near the amphitheater that any Palmyrene who has not grown up in the palace of the chief would covet. But he is not Zabbai, in spite of all the gods have blessed him with.

Nafsha may have stepped only one small and temporary rung down the ladder of life, but any step that does not take her higher gnaws away at her soul.

The other women of the household titter at the air of sudden tension between the sisters. Their hands freeze over the game board; bracelets tremble on poised wrists. They are waiting for the spat to come, as eager as kittens begging for a dish of cream. A confrontation between Nafsha and Zenobia always promises a good time.

Nafsha arches her kohl-black brows and turns her face coolly away from Zenobia. "But then, some of us don't know when it's time to put away a child's life and take on the duties of womanhood."

Berenikë looks up from her book of poems with a rebuke on her lips, but the wind sends the book's pages fluttering. They are of the thinnest papyrus and rattle together in a dry chorus until Berenikë's finger halts their frantic movement. She pins the pages down with the same air of natural calm command she uses to maintain the smooth flow of her household. The pages will not flutter because her fingers hold them; her daughters will not quarrel because her eyes silence them.

"Be quiet, Nafsha," Berenikë says softly. She has no need to raise her voice—her Cleopatra voice. "Zenobia, remove the look of impudence from your face and be humble as suits a virgin girl. Your sister is a married woman, and deserving of your respect."

Zenobia continues to stare at Nafsha, who has already turned back to her game, hiding her flush behind the drape of her veil.

"Zenobia," Berenikë says, only slightly sharper now.

Berenikë knows that her daughters have laughed together over her claim that she is descended from the great Egyptian queen—never daring to laugh when Berenikë might hear them, of course. She does not blame them for their incredulity. She knows that the famed beauty who outwitted Rome and ruled Egypt as a goddess on earth seems a thousand leagues from her—small, dark-haired Berenikë with her firm jaw and her Roman nose, who wedded a mere nomad many years older than she and lived in a mud-brick hut on the outskirts of Palmyra in the days before Zabbai's caravan—and his good reputation—made him rich. But such is Berenikë's confidence in her own blood that she has never felt the need to defend the veracity of her claims—even when she lived with a dirt floor and dust between her toes, when the shit of goats and camels was her carpet. In truth, Berenikë can trace her line back further still—to Dido, in fact, the legendary queen who founded Carthage, the city that has ever been a thorn in Rome's side. And on her father's side, her roots reach back to Julia Domna, the jewel of the desert whose rise as the emperor's wife soured many a Roman lady's wine not so long ago. Berenikë knows that when she speaks this way, her voice low and fierce and full of a certainty that she *will* be obeyed, even Zenobia will flinch.

The sound of her mother's rebuke makes Zenobia's skin tingle with an enticing thrill. When Berenikë speaks to her with her goddess voice, all her sisters' whispers fade away and Zenobia knows, down to the pit of her stomach, that her mother *is* a princess of Egypt, a rare and precious vessel that still carries the blood of the highest royalty.

All the more reason why I will never accept a husband whose status is so far below my own, Zenobia thinks. But she bows her head to her mother's command, just enough to avoid further scolding.

She returns to her embroidery, pursing her lips to drive away a mischievous smile. She feels the soft, sensitive gaze of her middle sister alight on her face. Zenobia looks up in time to see Zabibah lay down her own needlework—she had been stitching tiny indigo-colored flowers, each one encased in a precise hexagon, along the hem of a new yellow gown—and rise from her place at Berenikë's side. As ever, Zabibah has misinterpreted Zenobia's expression, projecting her own tender sweetness onto the hard world that surrounds her. She lowers herself onto one of Zenobia's cushions and drapes an arm around the younger girl's shoulders.

"Don't let Nafsha's chiding or Mother's glares bother you," Zabibah says. "Father will be home from the battlefield soon, and then he'll make you a match that will make your heart sing. A young, handsome, brave man—and he will be so fine that your head will go dizzy when you look upon him."

Zabibah herself is newly wedded to just such a man: Vakat, an Amlaqi warrior and the most trusted guardsman in their father's caravans. Vakat will run his own routes one day and carve out for himself a strong share of Palmyra's considerable trade wealth. Zabibah's happiness will only grow as the years pass. Zenobia is grateful to the gods and to her father for placing her sister in Vakat's care. If any woman deserves such a life of quiet contentment, it is the chief's middle daughter. Zabibah has no stomach for a life more complicated or trying.

Zenobia has always had a yearning for something more—for a life of glorious complications. Since she was a little girl, long before she was old enough to wear a turban, she has been fascinated by the interplay of the tribes, by the looming influence of Rome. She feels the pull and tug of politics running silently beneath every facet of her life—of every life in Palmyra—of every life in the world. It is an intoxicating current. It calls to her ceaselessly, and all she has ever wanted is to plunge into its depths.

She has tried. A year ago, just after she'd rejected her fifth suitor, Zenobia sat, perfumed and adorned, between her two sisters at a banquet in Zabbai's palace. She watched as the Ras received the honors of his guests one by one, straining to hear the men's conversations over the soft notes of cithara and flute and the clatter of conversation. Berenikë was a delicate ornament at Zabbai's left hand. She was near enough to hear everything the men said, yet Zenobia's mother only cast her elegantly distant stare toward the musicians or out into the garden where the dusk had begun to gather, affecting not to care about the intense, low-voiced words the chiefs of the tribes exchanged.

Zenobia had risen from her seat abruptly—Nafsha squawking in rebuke—and moved steadily down the length of the banquet hall, driving toward the empty seat at Zabbai's right hand as if it were her birthright. She was acutely aware of the guests' questioning glances, and of her own finery—her bright, layered skirts brushing her legs as she walked, the bangles on her turban swaying. She looked so *pretty*, she knew. Such a lovely, admirable, perfectly marriageable girl, if rather headstrong.

In that moment, crossing the hall under the curious eyes of tribesmen and their wives, Zenobia at last understood what she wanted from life. She wanted to be more than pretty, more than simply marriageable. She wanted to sit at Zabbai's right hand and hear the words of Palmyra's chieftains, instead of the soft, unchallenging music meant to entertain soft, complacent women. She wanted to delve into that thrumming, rushing, all-encompassing current of politics—to know the current's course, and to guide it, control it, if she could. She would never have that if she remained sitting with her sisters. She would never have it if she married a merchant, either.

Zenobia didn't make it all the way to her father's table before Berenikë's gaze sharpened on her daughter. Zenobia's newly named desire warred with her lifelong awe of Berenikë, and her confident stride faltered. She stood mute and still, her hands limp at her sides. Behind her, she could feel the entire banquet hall watching, and she sensed Nafsha burning with fury and embarrassment. Zenobia couldn't move.

She was like a dove ready for a temple sacrifice, too stunned even to twitch.

"Zenobia, my darling?" Zabbai said.

His voice was warm, as it always was for his daughters—for Zenobia especially. Zabbai had always shared a special bond with her, even allowing her to accompany him on trading expeditions now and then, when the destination was not terribly far from Palmyra. But before the eyes of the guests, the affection in his voice stung Zenobia. *Darling*, she said to herself, eyeing the empty chair next to Zabbai. That place at his side seemed to recede away from her, escaping rapidly down a long tunnel of impossibility. Zabbai would never call a son *darling*, and only a son could sit at his right hand.

Without answering, and with no explanation, Zenobia turned and glided smoothly from the banquet hall, her face an impassive mask. But once she climbed the stairs to the palace's second story, she groaned in humiliation and snatched up her skirts, running for the sanctuary of her chamber. She threw herself across her bed, weeping into a pillow. She knew just what she wanted—the desire was a fierce ache inside her. But fiercer still was the knowledge that it was beyond the reach of a female.

As she lay on her bed, she was more aware of the secret current than ever before. She could feel it scouring through the banquet hall, carrying every guest along on its unseen waves. She could sense it sweeping down the hill, into the heart of Palmyra, rushing on toward distant Rome. But she could not hear the words of the chiefs—those words that had the power to move the current, to bend it to use or will. All she could hear was the delicate, muted tones of the cithara. Lovely—very pretty music. But it was only music, and music didn't matter.

Sitting on the rooftop with Zabibah's arm around her, Zenobia shrugs and smiles to please her sister. But the ache has never left her. It has only grown over time; it has made Zenobia aware of a world beyond herself, beyond what she may, as the daughter of a chieftain, reasonably expect. She cares nothing for fine looks or a dizzy head. Fine looks will not bring her closer to the mysterious, compelling current.

She sighs and picks at her embroidery frame. *This* will bring her no closer, either—lounging on a rooftop, working at her stitches like a proper lady—or gossiping over a game board while her thoughts drift away, of no use to anybody. She knows already, young as she is, that the gods intend her for a greater purpose. She was born for something more—greatness, power. Why would the gods have put this keen interest in her heart, this yearning for politics, unless it serves some purpose? Why would they have made her so discontented with a lady's easy, unchallenging life?

If her destiny resides with a man—and when does a woman's future not depend on her father or her husband?—then Zenobia has no care for whether his good looks will make her heart flutter or her head reel. She cares only whether he will give her a place of honor at his table— and whether his table will draw men of power.

He must have more to offer than any merchant or guardsman, she tells herself, frowning at her needle and thread even as Zabibah chatters on. *I cannot be content with embroidery and games forever. It is not the life for me, and I swear it will drive me mad.*

Since that evening at Zabbai's banquet, Zenobia has sensed her future waiting just ahead, as one senses the presence of an unseen figure at the end of a darkened hall. Glory waits for Zenobia, silent and expectant, shrouded in shadows. She knows it—but she cannot reach it.

Let Nafsha be happy with her game board, Zenobia tells herself, sighing. Her own life will not be one of leisure. It must, she thinks fiercely, be worthy of her Amlaqi heritage, worthy of a descendant of Cleopatra, and of the other great queens to whom she can trace her blood: Julia Domna and Dido. Her life *must* be worthy of her ancestors. Anything less would be failure—and an insult to the gods who have made her.

Zenobia pats her sister's hand. She cannot speak of such things to Zabibah. Although she is a married woman, Zabibah is as soft and fragile as a little child. It is not in her nature to understand discontent. Zenobia will do whatever she must to shelter her sister from the hard edges and bruises of the world.

"I am sure you're right," Zenobia says for Zabibah's sake. "When Father comes home, Vakat will return, too—and so will your smile."

Zabibah draws a corner of her yellow veil across her face, hiding her deep blush, as giddy and shy as a virgin bride. It has been several days since Zenobia's two sisters arrived at the palace to take shelter from the battle, which, rumor has it, is frighteningly close—somewhere just beyond the northern fringe of Tadmor. Palmyra has no walls—trade on Palmyrene scale would only be impeded by walls. So even though their own homes are fine and sturdy, their husbands insisted that Nafsha and Zabibah await their return in their father's palace. Zabbai's estate, unlike the city itself, at least has a gate. If the battle should be lost and Palmyra attacked, the Ras's palace should be able to withstand assault. For a time, anyway.

Zabibah is not thinking of walls or assaults. She thinks only of Vakat, his kisses and his gentle touch. She has made sacrifices in the Temple of Bel, pleading with the god to bring Vakat home safely. Bel has always been good to Zabibah. With a childlike trust, she has complete faith in her prayers. And when Vakat returns, she will kiss him and kiss him until her mouth goes numb. Thinking of it, she blushes deeper and lowers her head.

Berenikë watches the exchange, as keen-eyed and assessing as ever. She raises her voice so that all the women on the rooftop might hear her words—the cousins and nieces, the servants who lounge and whisper in the shade of the potted palms. "All of our men will return soon, and the Tanukh will be vanquished—forever, I pray. May the gods grant that it will be so."

Nafsha and her cousins leave off chattering over their game board and bend their heads, a pious acknowledgment of Berenikë's prayer. For a moment the day's spirit of leisure is dampened as the women recall the reason for their men's absence.

It surprised no one, certainly not Zabbai, when the Tanukh chose this moment to rise up against the city. Palmyra's governor and the better portion of his soldiers have departed to rescue Valerian, the current emperor of Rome, who has been captured by the Sasanids.

Zenobia's mouth tightens in scorn as she muses on the fiasco. *One can count on a Roman to achieve any pinnacle of folly.* And emperors are far worse than common Romans when it comes to blundering and general uselessness. In recent decades Rome has seen a rash of assassinations, coups, and deadly plagues and a proliferation of emperors to match. None of the men Rome has raised to the purple have been strong or wise enough to rule an empire. Zenobia stabs her needle into the silk. But even for a Roman, Valerian's willingness to walk into captivity is a marvel of absurdity.

The governor of Palmyra is well known for his loyalty to Rome. In his attempts to free Valerian, he'd first sent gifts to the Sasanid king, but Shapur the Sasanid only spurned Palmyra's gifts. *Sasanids,* Zenobia broods, *are a haughty and ungrateful lot.* The incensed governor struck out three weeks ago to free Valerian by the sword, leaving Palmyra thinly defended.

What better time for the Tanukh to slink from behind their thickets of thorn and heaps of desert stone? They came scrabbling and biting at Palmyra's flanks, jackals harrying a flock of sheep while the shepherd's back is turned. Her father, Zabbai, so trusted and beloved by all the people of Palmyra, took charge of the men who remained in the city—merchants and caravan guards, craftsmen, and a scant handful of soldiers. He united them with the skilled desert warriors of his own Amlaqi tribe. But it is the peak of the spice season, and most of the Amlaqi have taken their caravans east. Altogether, Zabbai's ragged army numbers just under two thousand. They rode forth bravely to meet the Tanukh on the treacherous sands.

As the men paraded down the city's long, colonnaded Great Row they made a brave show, cheering and waving their swords. Zenobia watched with the rest of the women from the rooftop as Zabbai, mounted on his fiercest camel, led his string of men from Palmyra. She stood with her arm around Zabibah, who had wept to see both her husband and her father going off to war. Zenobia's heart ached for Zabibah and even for stoic Nafsha, who held herself some distance apart, watching her own husband's departure with dry eyes. Zenobia had found herself unable to tear her gaze from the sight of their father.

Zabbai's roots among the Amlaqi have made him a great trader, cunning and hardy. He is at home in the desert, where the dry sands and harsh sun have darkened his olive skin to the burnished brown of worn cedar and carved into his face the deep traces of a ready smile. His Seleucid heritage gives him a certain erudite grandness, a respect for all things civilized, orderly, and fine. A man like Zabbai will not suffer glorious Palmyra to fall to the Tanukh, who hunger after chaos and wild fear.

But though his heritage is worthy and his intentions good, Zabbai is an old man. His long beard is more gray than black; his hands tremble, and his steps are slow.

And yet who else can answer the challenge of the Tanukh? If they are not stopped, the wild tribe will fall upon Palmyra while the city is weak and helpless in the governor's absence and rape it of every bright and good thing it possesses. The Tanukh would scatter Palmyra's worth across the desert sands, dissipating its refined culture until there is nothing left of it but a fading memory.

The Tanukh are nothing more than animals, Zenobia thinks sourly. But she knows, as do all the Amlaqi, that animals of the desert can be deadly.

"Perhaps," Nafsha says lightly, breaking the silence that has fallen over the women, "when Father returns he'll bring back a Tanukh captive for our little Zenobia to wed."

Berenikë shoots her eldest daughter a warning stare, but Nafsha pretends not to see. Zenobia raises her brows. Perhaps her new status as a wife has made Nafsha a little bolder. Zenobia can recall a time when her eldest sister would have run and hidden from Berenikë's glare.

Nafsha's smooth hand reaches for an alabaster pawn. She taps it languidly across the game board. One of the cousins groans as Nafsha captures her game piece, and Nafsha sits back, eyeing Zenobia.

"Nafsha is so concerned with my virginity," Zenobia says, "I am beginning to think she would wed me herself. Alas, the only tool she might use to make me a woman is her tongue—and it is far too sharp for me to allow it beneath my skirts."

The cousins gasp in delighted horror and Zabibah stiffens in shock. From the cluster of servants in the shade of the potted palms, Zenobia hears a snort of stifled laughter.

But her comment has gone far beyond the limits of decorum. Berenikë stands with smooth grace, hands her book of poems to one of her waiting maids, and glides toward Zenobia.

Zenobia looks up at her mother, mouth open to make an excuse or apology. Berenikë's hand flicks out and catches her across the lips. It is a featherlight strike; Berenikë's knuckles and rings barely brush her daughter's face. Still, Zenobia flames with humiliation and remorse.

Berenikë seizes her daughter's wrist and pulls her to her feet. Her sewing falls in a heap on the cushion. Zenobia is dragged across the rooftop, out of the protection of the red canopy so that the full force of the desert sun beats against her exposed shoulders and arms. She squints as she stumbles after her mother.

They halt at the low wall of pale-yellow-gold limestone at the edge of the rooftop. The wall is carved with a motif of blooming flowers and curling palm fronds. Berenikë drops Zenobia's wrist and folds her hands placidly atop the wall, gazing down on the roofs and streets of Palmyra. She is Cleopatra now, calm and possessed, impossibly serene.

In the face of her mother's unruffled dignity, Zenobia's embarrassment only deepens.

"Nafsha is right about you," Berenikë says in her low, melodious voice. The quiet music of it betrays nothing of the anger she still feels, but her hard grip on Zenobia's wrist speaks eloquently enough. Zenobia pushes her bracelets up her arm so that she might rub the ache away. "You should have been married long ago. A husband would quell your haughtiness, and the gods know you need that."

Zenobia inhales sharply through her nose. She can think of no response that will not sound haughty—and therefore prove her mother's point.

"You've rejected every suitor your father has brought before you. Why, Zenobia?"

The girl weighs her words with great care before she responds. "I am grateful for the thought Father has put into choosing my husband. And I know that in allowing me to say yes or no to the men he suggests, he shows me more esteem than a daughter deserves."

"Then why have you rejected all of them? Nafsha agreed to marry Antiochus when she was fifteen, and Zabibah was sixteen when she accepted your father's choice of Vakat."

"Zabibah would have said yes to whatever man Father offered. She is sweet, but you know she has no will of her own."

"She has plenty of will. She tempers it with wisdom and obedience. You would do well to adopt some of Zabibah's traits. You will not be young forever, Zenobia, and your value as a bride decreases with each passing year."

The girl ceases to rub her hurt wrist and draws herself up. She is taller than Berenikë—though not by much—and is also imposing when she wishes to be. She has spent many hours in the garden practicing a commanding stare in the slick, polished electrum of her hand mirror. She knows just how to make her eyes flash with inner fire, how to draw majesty and disdain about her like a jeweled robe. She sets her burning eyes on her mother.

"Spare me your theatrics." Berenikë turns her own face away, a simple, small gesture that nonetheless conveys more stately grandeur than Zenobia can ever hope to master.

Zenobia feels herself deflate a little, like a water bladder that has suffered a leak. "My value will not decrease," she says rather lamely.

"Year by year. It is so. By all the gods, why is this a surprise to you? You're a bright girl; you know what it means to be a woman. Even a daughter of Zabbai cannot escape the truth. When your father comes home you will consider the next suitor he presents to you. And so long as the man is not lame, or known to be cruel or a drunkard—and Zabbai would never offer his daughter to such a man—you will tell your father that you will be pleased to—"

Abruptly, Zenobia spins away from her mother's words with fury, rejecting the dull and lowly life Berenikë proposes. But as she turns she catches again the heavy languor of spice on the air. Its richness fills her head, and she knows suddenly that her destiny is at hand—that the unseen figure in the darkened hall will soon step into the light and make himself known. Zenobia pauses. She holds herself completely still while the silks of her veil and her layered skirts swing about her. Her stomach curdles on the cloying draft of cinnamon.

She stares along the bright limestone slash of the Great Row. The road extends straight and precise to the west, its pale length scored by the violet shadows of colonnade pillars that stand like planted palms on either side. In the distance, where the road ends at the Western Gate, a cloud of dust billows up from the earth, as yellow as the golpar spice whose smell thickens the air.

Berenikë follows her daughter's gaze. "Have the men returned?" Her smoky voice trembles with relief—a rare concession to emotion, which Berenikë always takes pains to conceal.

But Zenobia does not answer. Her body shakes with the urge to flee, but she has no place to run to. She lifts the hem of her skirt, bunching the silk in hard fists. As they watch the procession in silence, the gods reach down Zenobia's throat and drag the words out of her.

"Something is wrong."

"Wrong?"

Berenikë moves close to her daughter's side as if seeking shelter. It is an alien and fearful thing for this daughter of Egypt to long for comfort when she has always held herself as firm and strong as a temple statue. Zenobia shifts her feet; she wants to withdraw from her mother's sudden weakness, but something in her goes loose and fluttering, and her limbs feel as insubstantial as water. She puts both her arms around her mother, not knowing whether she clings to her like a helpless child or whether she offers her own strength to Berenikë.

A murmur of voices lifts from the streets below. High on the palace roof, the two women can discern nothing of the words, but in the throats that cry out from the alleys and the courtyards with their covered wells, they hear the unmistakable sound of sorrow.

"Mother?" Nafsha has left the shade of the canopy and crossed the roof. Zabibah trails behind, clinging to her sleeve like a child. "Mother, what is it?"

The wordless cries creep nearer the sheikh's palace, moving across Palmyra with the slow, inevitable sweep of advancing dunes. Women come out onto the rooftops below, leaning over mud-brick walls to hear the news. And they, too, take up the cry, and the suffocating dune moves faster through the streets, until at last the words break against the palace walls. They pile there in heaps and then rise to the rooftop, terrible and clear.

"Zabbai is dead! Killed by the Tanukh—Zabbai is dead!"

Berenikë's face pales and her eyes flash with anger and disbelief. For a moment it seems she will shout and drive back the cries with her own denial.

Then her lips tremble. She sways and goes limp in Zenobia's arms. *"Nafsha!"* Zenobia shouts.

Nafsha runs to her youngest sister's side, dragging Zabibah behind her. They gather around Berenikë, holding her up, forcing her to remain on her feet, although she reels back from the wall, and her slight weight crumples against her daughters' bodies.

The wind is thick with spice and blood. A bitterness cuts through the smell—not the sulfur of distant Tadmor, but the hateful, blunt taste of tears.

2

AN URGENT ERRAND

When the mourners reach the palace gate, the women of the household go to meet the sad procession. Berenikë leans on Nafsha's arm, her steps stumbling and wooden. Her face is bloodless, as white and translucent as alabaster. Her eyes are blank with disbelief. Nafsha bears up with heroic grit, determined to remain a pillar of support for her mother. Zabibah weeps openly, pressing her red face with trembling hands. Silent, Zenobia follows a step behind, feeling with sick dread the pull of the current that moves Palmyra—that moves the world. It has caught Zabbai at last and swept him away, and now she fears it will carry her away, too.

The hallway that leads to the courtyard has never felt so long. It stretches out before Zenobia, a tunnel of too-bright tiles and painted frescoes that distort and warp each time fresh tears spring into her eyes. At first she blinks to keep her cheeks dry. But soon she can no longer hold back her sorrow. She knows that soon she must reach the end of the hall, where she will be confronted with the fact of Zabbai's death.

Zenobia will not allow her father's men to see her weep. Tears and wails are for the soft and sensitive—for Zabibah, for the household maids. Zenobia will be as stoic as the grown son her father never had. Since her baby brothers died and it became clear that Berenikë would have no more children, Zenobia has felt a peculiar duty as the youngest daughter to be the brave one, the proud, the uncomplaining—the one who, like a worthy son, can bear any burden.

She is not sure how she will bear this. She is afraid she will break in front of the men—fall to the ground and tear at her veils and her hair. She will scream her pain so the gods can hear it and know that they are cruel. But it's something she cannot allow any man to see, and so, step by step, she slows and allows her mother and sisters to pull away. Lets them be swept forward on the river of grief. Zenobia will forge her own path.

Eventually she stops; the others go on without her. She watches them, sees how frail they are in their sorrow, how their limbs move like dry branches in a winter garden, surprised by the gusts of this sudden and terrible storm. *I'm sorry,* she tells them silently, knowing they won't understand. Then she turns away and climbs a nearby stair.

She makes her way to her bedchamber and shuts herself inside, then leans against the door as if she can bar grief from entering. And then here, alone at last, the loss takes hold and she sinks to the white tiles of her floor, trembling and rocking.

"Zabbai!" she calls, as if expecting him to answer. Her voice is lost among the wails outside. They snake into her chamber, coiling over the carved lintel of her window, sliding into the shadows of her room. She can't escape this pain, but at least no one will see her weep.

Zenobia knows the moment when her mother lays eyes on the slain body of her father. Berenikë's scream, ravaged and high, seems to pierce the sky itself. Zenobia stills her sobs and forces herself to rise. She stumbles to her window and looks down on the courtyard.

She stares down, seeing nothing of the great crowd that mills on the pale paving stones—not even seeing her mother or her sisters. She can see nothing but her father's body. It looks so diminished, so small in its stillness, lying in a cradle of rough wool slung between the hafts of two spears. Coarse cloth is bound tight around his middle, no doubt covering the wound that killed him.

That is not Zabbai, she tells herself frantically. *That cannot be him. Zabbai never looked like that. He was . . .*

He was alive. And now he is not—now he is only a flat, waxen figure in the courtyard far below.

She nearly gives in to the temptation to sink down again, to weep and wail in privacy. But then she recalls that the funeral rites must be performed—Zabbai must be washed and dressed for his tomb. Zenobia will be expected in the garden, where the servants are, no doubt, already setting out kettles of perfumed water and clean silk robes with which to dress that still, cold body.

I cannot touch him. She knows at once it's true. If Zenobia touches him and feels his unmoving flesh beneath her hands, then Zabbai will never live for her again. All her memories of her father will be of his corpse, and nothing more.

Zenobia wipes away her tears with one sleeve. Then, moving as silently as she can, she slips from her chamber and flees down the upstairs hall.

When death is near, so are the gods, for they sense the thinning of the veil between heaven and the mortal world. Zenobia feels them crowding all around her. Their eyes are expectant, their breath close and hot, but she doesn't know what they want from her.

Bel, she prays, *Almighty Sun, giver and taker of life . . . guide me where you will. Only don't make me face Zabbai's body. Don't take his precious memory from me.*

She hears servants' voices on the stair: "Where is Lady Zenobia? Someone find the young mistress; she is wanted in the garden."

Zenobia darts for the nearest door. It resists when she pushes, and she flings her weight against its carved panels. It finally opens with a slow, rusty creak. The chamber inside is as dark as the inside of a cistern, but she pushes her way in and shoves the door closed behind her. It is only when she's inside that she realizes where she is. The warm, welcoming smell of camel hair mingles with the dry, sun-baked odor of desert sand. It is Zabbai's smell, and its sudden nearness makes Zenobia's heart surge with gratitude and love. Now when she weeps, the tears are not entirely those of sorrow. She can feel the living presence of her father all about her.

In the darkness, Zenobia feels her way along the shelves of Zabbai's personal storeroom—the place where he kept his trading goods, the fabrics and spices he gave to his servants to trade in the marketplace, the bangles he doled out freely to his wife and daughters. Zenobia's hands run over bolts of winter wool, so fine and neatly woven that they feel almost like silk. Her fingers trace the designs on carved boxes, and she wonders what might be inside—not because she is avaricious, but because they belonged to Zabbai, because it was he who procured them and saw fit to save them. She finds thin metal chains that might be golden necklaces—she can't tell in the darkness—and leather sacks filled with the rough, hard shapes of unpolished gems. Sticks of incense leave their sweet, comforting scent on her fingers, and exotic hides tickle her palms.

All around her, in the shelter of darkness, Zabbai lives again. She savors each texture and smell in its turn, recalling the face, the laugh, the embrace of her father. And she realizes, brimming with thankfulness, that the gods have allowed her to keep his memory.

You are kind, Zenobia tells Bel and the other minor deities, whose presence she can still feel. *You have spared my heart, and for that I thank you.*

At the thought of the gods, Zenobia's searching hands still. She presses her face against the plush fur of a hide and remembers that on the rooftop, when she first heard the mourning procession coming, she knew that her destiny was at hand. Today holds more import than the death of her father—and she realizes with mingled curiosity and fear that the gods have brought her to this storeroom for a reason of their own.

"What is it?" she whispers. "What do you want from me? What am I to do?"

But Bel makes no answer.

Zenobia steps away from the shelves stacked with trade goods—and trips over something hard on the floor. She hisses a curse as she staggers across the room, her heart lurching in fear. The blackness is complete, and she is certain she'll crash against one of the shelves and injure herself, or tumble over an unseen precipice into a black pit far below. But after a few frantic heartbeats, she rights herself and holds still, squeezing her fists tight to quell the angry throb in her toe.

When she feels she can move again, Zenobia turns carefully and tracks her way back through the darkness, shuffling her silk slippers along the floor. She finds the offending object with her sore toe and crouches to touch it.

It is a box—long and narrow and made of fragrant cedar. She finds its cool metal hasp and lifts the lid. The inside is packed with various small objects—little glass vials; rings; the smooth, carved figurine of what must be a camel. Her fingers tangle in a length of fine silk just as she hears voices outside the storeroom door.

". . . can't find Mistress Zenobia anywhere," one of the serving women says.

"Lady Berenikë will be angry."

A third voice says, "The young mistress is too headstrong. It's time she was married."

"Oh," says the first voice mournfully, "but who will decide her husband now? Zabbai—poor Zabbai! On top of everything else, he's left his youngest daughter unwed."

The servants go on discussing Zabbai's loss; they pass the storeroom door, and then their footsteps and the chorus of their sorrowful voices vanish down the hall.

Zenobia feels the silk, cool and reassuring in her hand.

"Is this what you sent me for, Bel?"

Zenobia's brow pinches in a frown, and she rises with the silk still bunched in her fist and finds her way cautiously back to the door. After a long pause to listen for more servants, she hurries back to her bedchamber unseen.

In her chamber, Zenobia lifts the storeroom treasure to examine it—and gasps. The silk trails from her hand, a long, fluttering streamer of imperial purple, a color as fine and rare as Zenobia's own blood. She stares at the fabric as it dangles from her hand and piles on the floor. The rich, red-violet folds stand out sharply against her pale floor tiles.

Finally Zenobia creeps to her bed. She folds the long, narrow band of silk neatly on her pillow, then climbs up onto her mattress and huddles at its foot, pulling her knees against her chest. She watches the silk as if it might be the cold, slow-breathing body of a resting cobra. Then, as she grows used to it, she eyes it with speculation.

"So this is what you want from me," she mutters to Bel.

The god does not answer—not explicitly. But the daring, reckless thrill in Zenobia's breast is answer enough for her.

***

Late in the evening, as the sun begins to redden, sinking toward the western hills, the wailing in the streets and in the courtyard of the great chief's palace finally dies away. A silence falls over the household, heavy and thick, a stifling, gray void of sound. Yet the silence is also a relief, and Zenobia sighs to hear it.

When she is sure that the funeral rites must be finished, she ventures outside her chamber door. She startles a weary-looking maid, whose eyes are red and puffy from crying. She is carrying an armful of bed linens and nearly drops them when Zenobia emerges so suddenly from her door.

"Mistress!" the maid squeaks. "We thought you'd run away."

"I've been inside my chamber the whole time."

"Why, I searched your room myself, mistress, but I never found you."

Zenobia wrinkles her nose. "Then you didn't look hard enough."

She means no actual rebuke—in fact, she'd hoped to make the exhausted-looking maid smile. But the young woman takes it for criticism. Her lip trembles, and fresh tears shine in her eyes.

"Now, now," Zenobia says quickly. "Don't weep. We are all sad today, but you can bear up. I have an errand for you—will that distract you from your sorrow?"

"An errand, mistress?"

"Yes." Zenobia casts a quick glance back into her chamber, suddenly fearful that the purple silk has disappeared, that it was only a dream brought about by her misery. But she can see one small, vibrant corner of it dangling from the edge of her bed. "Go down into the city and bring my seamstress to me. You know her, don't you?"

The maid nods. "I'll do it, mistress, straightaway. Only let me take these linens to Lady Nafsha's chamber."

An hour later, Zenobia drops her arms and the seamstress, whose eyes are still wide with wonder over being summoned so abruptly to Zenobia's chamber—and at a time such as this—winds her knotted string around one hand. She marks Zenobia's length from wrist to wrist on a narrow tablet of dark wax.

The seamstress's keen eyes flash up from her tablet, and Zenobia can practically hear the thoughts spilling through the woman's head. *A new gown? Now, when her father isn't yet laid in his tomb?*

There is no time to explain, nor does Zenobia have the heart for it. It seems now that she has done what the gods want, gone where they've directed, and they have abandoned her once more to her grief. Zabbai's loss weighs heavy on her heart—with each beat it seems to close more tightly around her, forceful and suffocating. But she will not cry in front of her seamstress, any more than she would in front of her father's men.

"When will it be ready?" Zenobia asks. Her voice is dulled by sorrow, but she allows no quaver of tears in it.

"Tomorrow, mistress, as you ordered. I shall work through the night if I must."

Zenobia moves briskly to her bed and pulls aside the pillow. She removes the length of silk from its hiding place. The seamstress gasps at the sight of it, one hand flying to cover her mouth.

"This is for the hem," Zenobia says. "Just like the robe of a Roman nobleman—you understand?"

She extends the silk toward the woman, but the seamstress sways, caught between a desire to touch the imperial purple and a superstitious fear of its symbolic power.

"Mistress," she mutters, "is it allowed? Purple, after all . . . I am unworthy."

"Someone must sew the robes of emperors and Roman nobility. Who, if not a seamstress?"

The woman hesitates an instant longer, then gathers her strings and her pins. She drops her wax tablet and stylus into a linen bag. Last of all she takes the silk, folding it with exaggerated care and tucking it behind her sash, until not a thread of it shows. "I will allow no one to see it until the gown is finished," she promises.

"That is wise. You may leave me now."

When the seamstress has gone, Zenobia pulls her chair well away from the window of her chamber and sits with her back to the view. Ordinarily Zenobia watches the vibrant reds and citrus-peel oranges of the sunset fade from the sky, but this is no ordinary evening, and she can no longer bear to stand at her window. The sight of its carved sill sickens her. It fills her head with the memory of looking down into the courtyard, seeing Zabbai's dead body. She refuses to allow the image into her mind.

As the terrible day gives way to the red evening, the household is subdued, the servants crouching in their small chambers like desert mice hiding in burrows below the roots of palms. Sorrow needles her relentlessly; Zenobia stirs from her chair and paces from the window to her bed and back again, moving in an endless rhythm, her neck and shoulders tight with the weight of grief.

As she paces, she thinks. The procession that had accompanied Zabbai's body to the palace's gate was large, but comprised mostly of citizens of Palmyra. They had joined in the march as the body was borne up the Great Row, raising their voices in cries of despair until the city echoed with the sounds of mourning. But only a few of that number were the Amlaqi men who had set out days before to face the Tanukh in the desert.

Zenobia is troubled by this realization. Where were the rest of Zabbai's men? Surely the Tanukh had not slaughtered them all. Are they scattered, Zenobia wonders, or pinned down at the spring of Tadmor by their enemies, unable to return home?

Surely she can't be the only person in Palmyra who has noticed. Yet with the governor gone and nearly all his troops with him, there is no one to ride out and bring the Amlaqi aid—or even to verify whether they still stand. The city is left with women, children, old men, and drunkards, and most of them are grieving Zabbai.

Does anyone even see what I see? Zenobia clutches her own throat, for it has gone tight with fear. *If the Amlaqi are scattered in the desert, then there is no one to stop the Tanukh if they still plan to attack Palmyra.*

As much as Zabbai's death pains her, Zenobia realizes she can hide in her chamber no longer. For one furious, despairing moment she wants to throw herself across her bed and bury her face in a cushion, wailing until her heart finally bursts and empties itself of the sorrow that overfills it. But she has no more time for mourning. The Tanukh gnaw at her thoughts like an alley dog with a sheep's bone.

All of Palmyra mourns now. And when we are in mourning, we are distracted—we are vulnerable.

Palmyra is like a goat tethered in a jackal's territory. It is only a matter of hours before it is attacked. Zenobia knows with a compelling certainty that the Tanukh will not leave such an easy conquest in peace.

Her pointed chin rises. *All his life, my father worked to make Palmyra great—a city as worthy of praise as Alexandria. I will not see it fall to his enemies now that he is dead.*

Zenobia forces herself to the window. She moves toward it with deliberate steps, firming her jaw against the visions of Zabbai's body that spring to her mind. She braces her arms on the sill and leans out, staring over the wall of the chief's estate to the city beyond. The sky's carmine glow touches the rooftops with flame. In the alleys and streets, everything is still. No children play in the squares, no women chat beside the cisterns. There are no men to be seen anywhere. Indeed, what men of any use are still left in the city? But not even a cripple hobbles down the Great Row; not even a brave old grandfather has mounted a bony donkey to take to the dunes and find the Amlaqi. There is no sense of urgency in the streets—only a shroud of quiet, of respect, for dead Zabbai and those who mourn him.

No one sees what I see, Zenobia realizes, trembling. *Or if they have puzzled it out, they can do nothing about it.*

She knows that she must act now, while the household is still subdued, before the halls and chambers come to life once more with the bustle of servants and their prying eyes.

Zenobia slides the ornate turban from her head and lays it on her dressing table. Its bright-blue veil pools like water on the tile floor. She loosens the bands of her embroidered girdle and lets it fall; it hisses softly as it slides down her skirts. The layered skirts follow, and then her loose tunic. She tosses the fine silks and linens onto her bed for the maids to take care of when they return to their duties.

Buried deep in the bottom of her carved chest, Zenobia finds the old linen skirt and plain robe she wore three years ago, when Zabbai allowed her to accompany him to the river port of Emesa, to inspect a shipment of dyes.

To a girl of fourteen, it had seemed a grand adventure to ride a camel out across the desert at her father's side and to sleep in a tent as the night winds beat against its sloped walls. From atop a high dune she saw the banks of the Orontes River spreading out below, as green as ripe olives and smelling richer than any spice-trader's wares.

Now the memory constricts Zenobia's throat. She swallows painfully and digs beneath folded skirts and old tunics until her fingers tangle in the coarse linen head wrap she wore on that long-ago journey. She buries her face in its folds, breathing in the warm, drowsy scent of Lebanon cedar and wiping away the tears in her eyes. She recalls how Zabbai laughed in pure joy as his camel snorted and swayed on the dune.

"I never grow tired of that sight," he called to her in his booming, glad voice, gesturing at the long, lush carpet of the river's banks, at the water that shone like electrum in the bright midday sun. He urged his camel into a lumbering run, whooping like a boy, while Zenobia, shrieking and clinging to her saddle's wooden tree, followed him down the dune's face.

She prays the clothing will still fit; she has not grown much in the three intervening years. Quickly she pulls the skirt over her hips; its belt ties without any slack to spare, but it will hold. The robe is not as roomy in the chest as she remembered, and it splits at the neck immodestly, exposing the top of the division between her breasts. But it cannot be helped; there is no time to find another garment.

As she lays out the head wrap on the lid of her chest, trying to recall how to properly fold the cloth, her chamber door opens. Zenobia spins, ready to send the servant away with a stern command. But it is not a maid who stands framed in the doorway.

Nafsha's eyes are swollen and red from weeping. She regards Zenobia dully, her arms folded beneath her breasts. "Why did you not help wash Father's body?"

"I needed to be alone. To mourn."

Her sister examines her face. "What were you doing, Zenobia? Mother noted your absence even in the midst of her sadness. She is not pleased."

Zenobia lowers her face contritely. "How is Mother doing?"

"Terribly. She puts on a brave show if any servants are nearby, but she's dismissed them all from her chambers and is on her bed crying. She can't be persuaded to move."

"Poor Mother. She loved him so, and was always a loyal wife, even before he was wealthy. Leave her be. Don't try to make her stop. Let her weep until her heart no longer aches."

Nafsha clicks her tongue in annoyance. "Wise words from someone who wasn't even there to tend Father's body. What do you know of it?"

Zenobia dodges the criticism. "And our sister?" Her anxiety is sharp and sudden. For all her wishes to shield Zabibah from the world's pains and sorrows, Zenobia can think of no way to protect her sister from this—their father dead, his men scattered, the fate of Zabibah's husband unknown. She clenches her fists, a gesture that only makes her feel smaller and weaker, more damnably female than ever.

"Zabibah fares well enough," Nafsha says. "She's tending to Mother now. Still, I would know what you were doing while we tended Father's body."

"I've been occupied with important matters."

Nafsha scoffs and throws her hands up helplessly. In Nafsha's mind, Zenobia has always held herself apart as if she were a creature beyond human reckoning, something breathed to life especially by the god Bel, and tonight Nafsha can stand none of her little sister's airs. "What could possibly be more important? Our father is dead, Zenobia. Dead! You do comprehend that, don't you?"

Even better than you, Sister, Zenobia thinks. But she says only, "I wish there was something I could do for Zabibah. Mother's heart is broken, but she will mend with time. Zabibah, though . . ."

"Vakat was one of the men who brought our father home," Nafsha says. "He is uninjured, thank the gods, and tomorrow at dawn he'll help us lay Zabbai in his tomb."

Zenobia sighs with relief. She could almost smile to know that Zabibah's husband is safe, and that her kindhearted sister will suffer no more sorrows. But she has not missed Nafsha's pause, the significant silence hanging in the chamber. "And . . . Antiochus?" Zenobia asks hesitantly.

So the girl is not entirely incapable of thinking of others, Nafsha tells herself wryly. But she will not allow Zenobia to see her approval—nor her worry for her husband, Antiochus. She tosses her head as if unconcerned. "There is no word of him. Vakat told us that the Tanukh drove between our forces like a wedge, and now the tribe is scattered out across the sands. No one who was with Father and Vakat could say whether Antiochus still lives."

A frown that looks very much like unselfish worry crosses Zenobia's face. She takes a few tentative steps toward Nafsha, and Nafsha, her cold façade cracking before such unexpected warmth, stumbles forward, too, her sharp chin trembling for the briefest moment before she regains control of her emotions. Zenobia clasps her sister's hands. Nafsha's grip is strong, but she is clearly reluctant to let go.

"Antiochus is well," Zenobia says. "He must be."

"I pray that it is so."

"As do I, and not only for your sake, though the gods know your happiness is enough reason for my prayers." Zenobia smiles a little sadly. "I know we quarrel, Nafsha, but you are my sister, and I love you. Surely you know that—and I believe you love me, too, for all our disagreements.

"But listen: With Father dead, your husband is the Ras of the tribe now. You are Zabbai's eldest daughter, and as Father never had a son, it's your Antiochus who must now lead the Amlaqi."

Nafsha's eyes widen. "Of course." With all that happened today, succession was the last thing on her mind. Then she blinks, at last taking in Zenobia's strange clothing. She drops her sister's hands and steps back warily. "What is all this? Why do you wear such a strange robe?"

Zenobia picks up the head wrap and winds it quickly about herself, covering her hair and crossing its ends beneath her chin. She tucks the loose corners into the robe's collar at the back of her neck. She's pleased that the proper way to wear the garment has returned so easily to her memory. "I'm going out."

"Out? What in Bel's name do you mean?"

Zenobia glances out the window, across the rooftops of Palmyra to the sands beyond.

Nafsha follows Zenobia's gaze. Then she grunts in disgust. "Oh, don't be such a fool! The desert is bad enough, but Vakat tells us the hills around the city are crawling with Tanukh, worse than fleas on a dog!"

"Somebody must find your husband, for Palmyra's sake," says Zenobia.

"Ah yes," Nafsha says, her voice rising to nearly a shriek, "a seventeen-year-old girl is exactly the right one for the task!"

"Hush! Don't disturb Mother."

"Don't disturb Mother, you say! As though it will disturb her not at all when her youngest daughter flies out into the dunes and ends impaled on a Tanukh spear."

Zenobia sniffs. "You're always so gruesome, Nafsha."

"You are not leaving this palace. Father left two guards to keep us safe. I'll send one to find Antiochus—if he can be found at all." Nafsha frowns, but lifts her chin as if to brace herself against Zenobia's certain protest. "You will certainly go nowhere until we've laid Father in his tomb. You shirked the funerary rites so you could lurk about in your chamber, but you will stand beside his tomb when we seal it."

"Father left only two guards?" Zenobia again stares out the window at the blaze of the desert. With a sick swell in her gut, she wonders how many Tanukh wait in the hills, how many more precious hours of peace remain until Palmyra comes under inevitable attack. *Not enough.* "Listen, Nafsha," she says briskly, "you must keep the guards here—both of them. For all I can tell, they're the only fighting men left in Palmyra. They should arm any servants who are fit to sling a stone, even the women, and tell everyone to do exactly as the guards say, just as if they were the Ras themselves. Get them all up onto the rooftop where they can see—"

"Stop it, Zenobia! Take off that ridiculous garb and dress yourself properly. I will send one guardsman out to find Antiochus, and you will stay here and help me care for Mother until dawn comes and we can carry Father to his tomb."

"I tell you, both guards must stay here and protect our household. The Tanukh will fall on the city before the sun rises, and we have only a pair of guards to defend us!"

"What do you know of it? You, an unmarried girl, no more than a child?" Nafsha waves furiously toward the window, pointing as if she could command the distant dunes to recede with one imperious hand. "Our tribe is out there—my *husband* is out there, fighting to protect us. That is a man's purpose—it's what men do. Don't meddle in things that are not meant for a woman. The gods will curse you if you do."

Zenobia rolls her eyes scornfully, and Nafsha growls in frustration.

"Arrogant as always," Nafsha shouts. "First you thought yourself too good to marry any of the suitors Father gave you, and now you mock even the gods! Truly, Zenobia, your gall knows no limits. One day you'll overstep yourself, and then you'll wish you'd learned humility. *And* you'll wish you had learned to keep to a woman's place."

"Be that as it may. I am going."

Zenobia strides toward the chamber door, but Nafsha catches her arm as she passes. Her grip is as hard and cold as bronze. Zenobia jerks her arm but cannot pull herself free. She will not further reduce her dignity by shrieking at her sister or tearing at her long, black hair, though she is sorely tempted.

"I am the wife of your Ras now," Nafsha says, her voice as low and confident as Berenikë's. "You will do as I say."

"Only the gods know whether Antiochus yet lives," says Zenobia steadily. "And so only the gods know whether you are the chief's wife."

Nafsha breathes in sharply as if in pain. Zenobia feels a tight knot of self-loathing seethe in her chest. She hates herself for wounding her sister with such blunt, cruel words, but she will do and say what she must to win her way free.

Still Nafsha keeps her hold on Zenobia's arm.

"Let me go and find your husband, Nafsha."

"I'm asking you," Nafsha says, her voice hoarse, "to please remain in the palace. For our mother's sake. Two deaths in one day will mean her death, too."

"I won't be killed."

"Are you a prophetess now?" Nafsha gives a short, mocking laugh. "Shall we garland you in flowers and carry you in a litter up to the Temple of Bel? How grand, to know the future with such certainty!"

Zenobia's jaw juts out and she presses her lips tightly together. She will not speak of her private certainties. Nafsha is practical and steady, trusting only in that which she can weigh and measure, like a block of limestone beneath her hand. Should Zenobia tell her that she knows—*knows*—that the gods have planned a greatness for her beyond what any woman in their family has yet achieved, perhaps even greater than Cleopatra? How can Zenobia die out there in the dunes on this night, falling prey to some beast of a Tanukh, if she is to take upon herself a glorious destiny? But no—she will never speak of this. Nafsha would scorn her, and perhaps rightly so. And yet Zenobia cannot alter her own heart. She feels the surety of her own greatness deep in her bones.

"Take care of Mother," Zenobia says. "If the gods are good, I'll bring Antiochus back. If not, at least I'll bring back word so you will no longer wonder."

At the sound of her husband's name, Nafsha's grip loosens. Her dark eyes are stunned and glassy. For a moment she gazes into an unseen distance. Then she recalls herself and sharpens her stare like a sighting hound's. "If you try to leave the palace, I'll send the guard after you. He'll bring you back in a wool bag before you even make it to the Great Row."

"Let him try to catch me, then," Zenobia says, and dodges out of her chamber.

Nafsha's shout of rage follows her down the palace hall.

***

The shortest route from her chamber to the stable is through the palace kitchens, and so Zenobia flees into their depths, as alert for the sounds of pursuit as a hare in the desert. She pauses at the kitchen's outer door, rising up on the toes of her sandals as she stumbles to a halt. She does not know how long she might be away, or whether she will have access to water—if she can approach the spring of Tadmor at all, with the Tanukh infesting the hills. There are a few small seeps and wells scattered across the desert, sunk in the secret places between the dunes, but Zenobia does not know how to find them. She realizes she must spare precious minutes to gather water and food.

She finds a small grain sack near the wax-sealed clay jars that hold the servants' rations of bread. She shakes the bag out, then peels away the ring of a seal and stuffs several pieces of bread inside. She adds a handful of sticky dates from another jar, then knots the sack closed.

It takes longer to find waterskins, but she locates them at last in a tiny closet, behind a row of woven-palm bins that hold all manner of tools of the cook's trade. Fighting to quell her rising panic she slings two skins around her neck, and then, as an afterthought, pulls a small bone knife with a narrow, hook-tipped blade from one of the bins. She slides it into the belt of her skirt and rushes from the kitchen to the courtyard.

Under a golden, setting moon, wrapped all about in the purple shadows of early evening, the courtyard seems an alien place, and frightfully large. All the servants are tucked away in their chambers, mourning. Zenobia ducks beneath a bower of roses and holds herself still in their fragrant shelter, wary for Nafsha's alarm. But nothing stirs in the courtyard save for the leaves of the palms and the jasmine vines.

She steps out onto the garden path, moving as swiftly as she dares, fearing to run lest the slap of her sandals alert the servants. Zabbai's stable hulks beyond a stand of shaggy date palms, its pale stone walls conspicuous against the darkening sky. Zenobia edges behind the palms and eyes the palace through the curtain of their dry, hanging fronds.

The palace stretches high above the dim, rounded shapes of the garden. A few of its narrow windows gutter with the soft orange glow of oil lamps. The light is cast out onto the sills, where it flows like trickling water over lintels embellished with geometric patterns and the stone petals of carved blooms. But the palace remains quiet. The entire household is stunned to stillness by the sudden shock of death.

Zenobia leans against the stable door. It creaks beneath her shoulder, and the camels within raise their voices in greeting, hoping for an extra ration of grain. She hasn't anticipated this chorus of growling moans, and she quickly shoves the door closed behind her, hoping to trap the cacophony inside.

"Hush!" she whispers, but the camels go on groaning, their mouths like black caverns in the dimness of the stable.

She must be swift. Soon the noise will rouse the household servants from their stupor, and either they or Nafsha's threatened guard will put a stop to Zenobia's plans.

She deposits her supplies on the dusty floor and drags the nearest saddle from its rack beside the door. It has been years since she saddled a camel herself, on the trek to Emesa with her father. She must do it all from memory, but it seems straightforward enough.

At least the camels are resting on the ground, lying on the thick calluses that pad their chests. Zenobia folds a thick wool blanket across the closest camel's hump, then wrestles the wooden frame of the saddle into place. It is light, but its forked arms make for awkward handling. The camel loses patience with her fumbling and snakes its head back to snap at her. Zenobia swats its nose, scolding, and the creature subsides with a grumble. It turns its great head away with ponderous dignity, flicking its ears as if to say that it would not deign to look at a flea such as Zenobia, let alone bother to bite her. A tight, triumphant smile comes to her lips despite her urgency, and she works faster, looping a thick woven strap across the camel's chest and another beneath its ropy tail.

She fills her waterskins from the covered cistern in the stable's corner, then ties her supplies to the saddle frame and takes up the camel's lead rope. Zenobia tugs and cajoles, pulls and curses, but the camel remains resolutely in place, its long legs folded neatly beneath its body, chewing its cud while Zenobia flails at the rope in hopeless futility.

Then she recalls the dates in her bread bag. Zenobia waves the sticky morsels beneath the camel's nose and it ceases its imperious chewing and stares at her. Zenobia takes one backward step, then another. The camel gives her a look of pained desperation, and with a groan it lifts its haunches high into the air, followed a moment later by its forequarters. The great, lanky legs unfold, exposing rough knees and wide, strong feet that step toward the dates eagerly. She allows the camel but one small date, slipping the reserve into the pocket of her skirt for later use. She quickly ties the camel's girth tight about its belly, and then with a confident command she leads it from the stable and into the dusky courtyard.

The air has begun to cool; the intense fire of day has dissipated rapidly from the earth, replaced by a brisk, windy chill. The palm fronds rustle, and, through their rattling hiss, Zenobia cannot be certain that the palace is truly as quiet as it seems.

"It is time to be off," she tells her camel, and gives it the command to cush.

The belligerent thing stares down at her from its great height and blows through its lips, making an obscene flapping sound. A spatter of strong-smelling saliva falls on Zenobia's cheek.

"Foul creature," she says, wiping her face with the sleeve of her robe and jerking hard on the camel's lead.

The beast throws its head so high that Zenobia is nearly pulled off her feet. She gasps and winds the lead around her hand, staring up at the camel's head. Its long, pale shape stands out stark against the rich dark blue of the evening sky.

She must calm the thing before it begins to growl again. Out here in the courtyard, beyond the confines of the stable, its voice will surely be noted. Zenobia reaches up and strokes the underside of the camel's neck, smoothing her fingers down the line of dark fringe that runs from its throat to its narrow chest, murmuring soft words.

The camel drops its head, and she offers it another date. This it accepts with a twitch of its furry lips, and when she gives the command to cush again, her voice very near pleading, the camel obliges, dropping to its knees and lowering itself so that Zenobia may climb aboard.

Her skirt pushes up well past her knees as she settles into the saddle's padded seat, exposing her thighs to the night air. Zenobia shivers in the cold. She remembers only now that she wore loose trousers beneath her skirt when she rode to the Orontes with Zabbai. She blushes to think of anyone seeing her this way, her legs bared so shamelessly. She'd give her finest gold necklace for a pair of riding trousers, but who is nearby to trade with her? There is nothing to be done, she tells herself firmly, and she has no time for modesty.

"My bottom shall match my top," she says to the camel, tugging at the neck of her revealing robe. Then she says firmly, "Hut-hut!" and the camel's hump lurches forward as its haunches lift once more. The sudden movement throws Zenobia toward the creature's neck, and she stifles a scream as she clutches frantically at the saddle's wooden horn. When her weight slides inevitably toward the hard paving stones of the courtyard, she leans back with all her might, bracing herself against the force of gravity. Just as she is certain she will tumble from the camel's back and crack her face against the stones, the beast straightens its fore-legs in one smooth motion, and Zenobia, trembling, gazes about from the lofty height of her saddle.

"Well done," she whispers to her mount—and to herself—tugging the hem of her skirt farther down around her thighs.

She turns the camel's head toward the palace gateway and urges it into a lumbering trot. It grunts but obeys her word, and she wills her body to loosen, to settle into the strange, side-to-side loping sway of its gait. They skirt the courtyard, keeping as far from the palace as Zenobia can manage. The arch of the gateway looms in the shadows ahead.

Over the shuffle of the camel's feet, she can just make out the sound of voices near the gateway—one male, one female. Zenobia's brows lower. *Nafsha.* The camel seems to sense her darkening mood, for it gives a quick barking growl, a sound she feels shuddering through the saddle's frame. The beast picks up its pace without being urged.

Two figures move from the arch of the gateway, small and pale in the dark. Night has stolen the color from the world, leaving in its wake nothing but shades of violet and blue, but even without the gleam of her signature saffron-yellow robe, there is no mistaking Nafsha. She comes toward the pathway, hands outstretched as if to stop Zenobia's flight. Behind her, the broad figure of a man moves with the brisk, sure steps of a soldier.

So her sister has rooted out one of the guards after all. *I will not be stopped by him or anyone else.* Zenobia leans forward in the saddle, kicking the camel's ribs with her heels, and stings its shoulders with the bight of the rein.

"Swiftly now," she cries, *"run!"*

The dark garden rocks around her as the camel gathers its long legs for the sprint. Nafsha and her guardsman halt in dismay, and Nafsha shouts, "Wait!"

In the next moment the camel sprints toward the arched gateway, and Zenobia clutches the saddle horn, holding her breath to fight back a whoop of pure, tingling excitement. The deep-black shadow of the gateway envelops her, and as she speeds beneath it she can hear the camel's footfalls magnified in the close space. She hears, too, Nafsha's shouts and the guardsman's sandals as he gives chase. Then she is clear of the palace wall, descending the slope of the hill at breathtaking speed, and gritting her teeth as the shadowed doorways of stone houses whip past on either side of the road.

She knows she will have a few minutes' head start; the guard must saddle a camel of his own if he thinks to catch her. *But gods grant that he stays put,* Zenobia prays, casting a pleading glance toward the high Temple of Bel. *Someone must protect my family and my father's faithful servants if the Tanukh come. Please, Mighty Bel, make the guardsman stay.* The temple's vast rooftop is lined with tiny pyramids of bronze. In daylight, they shine almost as bright as gold. Now, in the light of the moon, their jagged silhouettes remind her of teeth tearing at the starry sky. Zenobia clenches her jaw. *Gods, grant me safe passage through the desert, too,* she prays. *Guide me to Antiochus, you divine lords of Palmyra, you rulers of the dunes. And you, gods of my Seleucid forefathers—Ares, Athena, give me strength and wisdom!*

She leaves the slope of the hill. The road from the palace joins the Great Row at a sharp angle; she tugs the camel's rein, and it wheels gracefully in the center of that broad avenue, then lengthens its stride, stretching its legs to devour the road.

"You are as light as a feather," she tells the beast, and grins in spite of her tension.

Zenobia's body rocks and flows with the camel's movement; the sleeves of her robe ripple and flap in the wind. She passes the dark curve of the amphitheater, empty now of audience and players. Beyond it, the governor's palace stands dark and silent, awaiting his return from the land of the Sasanids. Columns stream by faster than she can count them, their pale lengths gleaming in the starlight, while overhead the stars themselves blur into a fast river of sparkling light between the twin banks of the colonnade.

Every now and then, Zenobia glances back over her shoulder, expecting to see the guardsman pursuing her on a camel of his own. But the Great Row remains empty, save for the handful of old men who stagger from wine houses or the odd donkey cart moving slowly in the shadows of the pillars.

"Useless louts," she shouts at the men as she passes. They should be riding out into the desert, not she.

When she arrives at the Western Gate, the grand archway that is the head of the Great Row, Zenobia pulls at her camel's lead. It slows and then stands swaying, blowing hard through its nostrils, eager for more speed. The city's entrance is a gate in name only, an ornament to welcome foreign merchants to Palmyra, for the city itself has no defensive wall. Zenobia wonders whether it would be better to leave the Great Row, find some winding path through the alleys out into the desert. But here on the outskirts of Palmyra the streets are like the Labyrinth of ancient myth; their twisting and winding will befuddle this palace-raised chief's daughter, unfamiliar as she is with their secret ways. The path through the Western Gate is straight and true, and beyond it, nestled among the dunes, Tadmor is evident as a dark shadow beneath the night sky.

Zenobia waits at the Western Gate for as long as she dares, and finally concludes it is unmanned. *At any rate, Nafsha can't have sent down word to stop me at the gate. There hasn't been enough time.* She pulls the ends of her headcloth high about her face, tugging again futilely at the hem of her skirt, and guides her camel toward the gate.

As she draws near, a man steps from the shadows of its high arch. "Halt for inspection," he calls. His voice is rather high, and Zenobia notes the narrowness of his shoulders, his silhouette as lanky as a year-old colt. A mere boy—no doubt Zabbai scooped up the best gate guards and took them into the desert, and this beardless child was the only one left to keep the watch.

Not that there is much point to watching. Without soldiers to patrol the city's perimeter, anyone who wishes to invade Palmyra can simply bypass the Great Row and stroll right through the alleys. It is doubtful anyone would even notice to sound the alarm. True, the streets are twisting and confusing to the eye, but it would be only a matter of time before the invaders found their leisurely way through. The thought of it makes Zenobia swallow hard, and she chews at her lip in apprehension.

The boy draws near. He reaches for the camel's lead rope, but Zenobia jerks it away from his hand. "A woman leaving the city alone, at this hour?" he says.

Zenobia pitches her voice low, hoping she sounds older than her seventeen years. "I am Iza of the tribe of Amlaqi. I carry a message to the new Ras Antiochus, from his wife, my mistress and cousin, the lady Nafsha. Stand aside. My mistress will brook no delay."

The boy chuckles. He squares his thin shoulders in an attempt to seem authoritative. "It is far too dangerous beyond the city. The Tanukh—"

"Do you think I don't know about the Tanukh, you insolent boy? My mistress's errand is urgent; otherwise, she would not send me into such danger."

The boy's eyes wander from Zenobia's sharp glare down to the neckline of her robe, then lower still to her bared thigh. A foolish grin splits his face, and Zenobia hisses and kicks out at him. The toe of her sandal narrowly misses his ear.

"Ill-tempered harlot," the boy spits. "No one even knows where Antiochus is. I heard as much when the troops returned with Zabbai's body. If your mistress would send you into the sands alone, then she is a fool. Or she thinks so little of you, you are expendable to her."

"*You* do not know where Antiochus is, perhaps," Zenobia says with a haughty sneer, "but I am not as dull as you. Now stand aside or I shall ride over you. I have tarried long enough."

The boy seems about to speak again, but a ragged cheer rises from the Great Row. He and Zenobia both turn to see a handful of drunkards milling on the side of the road in the distance. They are raising their hands to urge on a large shape that speeds down the center of the Row. Its long, loping gait can belong to no other creature than a camel.

Zenobia drums her heels against her own camel's flanks. It leaps forward, knocking the boy into the dust, and throws itself through the vast archway of the Western Gate. She clings to the saddle with sweating hands. Then the gate falls away behind her in a rush of cold, deep blue, and her camel gallops out into the desert, raising a cloud of dust from its pounding feet.

3

BAT-ZABBAI

She rides for nearly an hour, as best she can guess by the movement of the stars. She is no navigator, of course, and has no skill in crossing the desert under guidance of the nighttime sky. Still, as Zabbai's daughter she was given the finest education, including the barest tenets of astrology. The courses of the stars, their constellations and trajectories, are not entirely a mystery to her.

As she rides, watching the stars to gauge time's progression, she prays fervently that the boy at the Western Gate found some way to delay her sister's guardsman, that the rider she saw was not after her, and that she will find Antiochus before the Tanukh find her.

As soon as she is out of sight of the Western Gate, Zenobia guides her camel over the crest of a dune and slows its mad dash. Even in starlight, the dust raised by its feet would have been a betraying banner. She hopes the height of the dunes will shield her progress from any soldier—and that the guard who pursues her is not particularly keen-eyed. But the dunes tower over her like the walls of temples, watching her with the faint scorn the gods always have for the efforts of small, weak mortals. She shivers in the cold night, and now she almost hopes that the guardsman will catch up to her. It would be a relief not to feel so terribly alone.

She moves north between the flanks of the dunes, heading in the direction of Tanukh territory, giving the green-black fringe of Tadmor a wide berth. She is certain the oasis must now be overrun by Tanukh awaiting some secret sign to charge Palmyra and sink their teeth into its soft, unguarded throat. As she travels, she keeps to the low places, the depressions between the sliding hills and the tracks of dry wadis.

Along her route she occasionally catches the faintest whisper of voices in eddies about her, lazy and indistinct, like the last vestiges of a whirlwind dispersing in a cloud of dust. But she can make out neither words nor accent, and cannot say whether the men speak the harsh dialect of the Tanukh or the cultured Aramaic that is the common tongue of Palmyra. When she turns her camel toward the sound, hoping she might spy its source before she reveals her own position, the whispers drift around her, rolling and pouring like *fesh-fesh*, the flowing water sand of the deep wadis, directionless and borne away on the fitful evening breeze.

She glances up at the stars again and notes how steeply they have fallen along their plush, black paths. She realizes that she must get her bearings, or she will wander fruitlessly until the sun rises. And by then, it will be too late for Palmyra.

She rounds the shoulder of a dune and breathes a prayer of gratitude; a great shelf of bare rock juts from the sand as proud and tall as a palace. One of its faces is sharply sloped, but she thinks she might maneuver up its side with patience and the gods' grace.

"Come, Feather," Zenobia tells her camel. He is her only company, here in the desert, and she feels he deserves a name. She has also decided that he is male—the king of camels, in fact—though she isn't sure she could tell the difference between a male and a female if she'd been asked.

She guides the king of camels up the slick rock as far as he can climb, which is not far. From Feather's back she is elevated just enough that she can make out something of the vast terrain.

Sweeping away to her right, the sands stretch in ripples of shadow and starlight all the long way to the distant mountains. She can barely see the black clefts of the wadis, thin as a cat's whiskers, the steep-sided gorges that afford access through the mountain ranges to the eastern trade routes beyond. To her left, the limestone temples and palaces of the city are visible as a pale smudge along the crest of Palmyra's highest hill. Even in the dark of night, the carpet of Tadmor looks lush and rich where it spreads between her vantage and white, waiting Palmyra.

She turns Feather's head once more toward the north, but as he picks his way carefully down the face of the rock with abrupt, jarring steps, a form blacker than the night rises from the crest of the nearest hill. Over the sudden pounding of her own heart, she hears the blowing of another camel and a low, soft chuckle from its rider.

Zenobia looses one hand from the saddle horn and clutches desperately at the handle of her bone knife.

"I implore you not to run again, young mistress," the rider calls.

She relaxes by only the smallest measure. His tongue is Aramaic, not Tanukh. She is in no grave danger from the guardsman, but if he succeeds in dragging her back to Palmyra before she finds Antiochus, the city will certainly fall.

"Don't come any closer," she says as loudly as she dares. "I am on an important errand, and I won't be delayed."

"You're on a fool's errand."

"You dare to insult the daughter of the Ras?"

"The Ras is dead, gods keep him. I have been sent by the wife of the new Ras to—"

"Nafsha hasn't any idea what she's about. The Amlaqi are scattered and the governor of the city is gone, just as the Tanukh would have it. Yet all Nafsha can think of is controlling her little sister. As ever."

The guardsman kicks his camel forward. It moves carefully down the slope of the dune, the feet as wide as serving platters sliding through the sand. "Mistress Nafsha is reeling from the death of your father and fears for the life of her husband," the man says gently when he draws near. "She would not lose her beloved sister, too. Won't you please return to the palace with me, Lady Zenobia? It is safe there."

Zenobia's camel scrambles the final few feet down the flank of the stone outcropping. She takes the rein tightly in her hand and says, "If Antiochus is not found soon, no place in Palmyra will be safe."

The guardsman edges still closer, and Zenobia tries to wheel her camel away. But recognizing his herd mate, Feather groans a greeting and fights her rein, stretching his long neck toward the other.

"Ah," the guard says, "they are good friends. What a happy sight."

She kicks at the stubborn thing's ribs, but Feather only growls in protest.

"Make them be silent," Zenobia hisses. "The Tanukh could be anywhere."

"They are not close enough to notice these two old gossips. If they were, we'd have heard their camels long before now. Or their horses. Some of the Tanukh prefer such mounts, though I do not care for them much myself."

Zenobia rolls her eyes. "You are a worse gossip than any camel! What do I care for your thoughts about mounts? I must find Antiochus and turn him back toward Palmyra before it's too late."

The guard watches her for a moment as she struggles to turn her camel's head away. Finally he says quietly, "Does it grieve you at all that your father has been killed?"

"What a thing to ask," she flares. Then she remembers herself and lowers her voice. "Of course it grieves me. I have never known anything so terrible. But I shall mourn when I have the leisure for it. I cannot coddle my own broken heart while Palmyra is in danger. Zabbai always worked to preserve the good of the city—its beauty, its culture. Should

I see all his work destroyed by an envious tribe of desert brutes? Should I sit idly by while my father's legacy is ruined?"

The guard bows his head. Zabdas has worked for Zabbai since he was just a skinny whelp. He was, in fact, one of the lucky urchins Zabbai took in from the streets, and his affection for the dead Ras is nearly as great as his sorrow. Thanks to Zabbai's care, Zabdas grew from a luckless orphan into a capable man, first caring for the camels of the great chief's caravan, then guarding Zabbai's goods on the long, hot treks from Palmyra to the shipping docks at Emesa on the green Orontes River. Now he tends to the chief's own safety as a palace guard—a position he felt honored to accept. In spite of his many years of loyal service, Zabdas feels a failure. Beloved Zabbai is dead, and Zabdas was not at the old man's side to protect him.

When Nafsha called on him, Zabdas was eager for the chance to redeem himself before the eyes of the gods and save the chief's youngest daughter from her own headstrong folly. But now, looking at her stern face in the dim light of the moon, he knows that he will not take her back to Palmyra before her work is done. Her mission is true. She acts out of selfless love for the city, and for her father's legacy—not out of girlish hotheadedness.

"I mistook you, young mistress, and for that I am sorry," Zabdas says, bowing to her from his saddle. "I should have known that a daughter of Zabbai was no fool. And you're right, of course—the Amlaqi must return to Palmyra."

He offers a conciliatory smile, and Zenobia sees that he is young—perhaps only five or six years older than she. She can see little of his face in the shadow cast from his flat-topped turban, but she does make note of his beard. He is not clean-shaven in the Roman style, which is so popular with the city's ambitious young men—the ones who seek favor with the governor—but neither is his beard long and full in the style of the tribesmen. He wears it trimmed short, the black hairs bristling along a strong, square jaw. It is a perfect concession between the two styles and marks him as neither for nor against the Roman ways.

Canny, she thinks, appraising with a flick of her eyes his broad shoulders and the sure, quiet way he holds his camel's rein. *And cautious.* He is more intelligent, perhaps, than most guards, and certainly more concerned with the politics of Palmyra.

But she has no more time to spare for this guard with his not-quite-Roman ways. The stars are moving overhead, and she is no closer to finding Antiochus.

Zenobia pulls hard on Feather's lead. "I must be off. Return to my father's palace and tell Nafsha—"

His hand darts out as fast as a cobra striking and snatches the rope from her hand. "You may be right," he says, "but it's still dangerous to try—"

Before she can think about it, Zenobia jerks the bone knife from her belt and slashes at the guard's arm. The blade is white and cold in the starlight, the hooked tip glittering with a wicked sheen.

She misses.

The guard's growling laugh sounds not unlike the prattling of the camels he so loves. "Mistress! Your humble servant begs you to spare his unworthy life!"

"Let me go, you fiend! You don't know what you're doing in stopping me. You'll doom the city!"

His laughter leaves him at once. He is serious and shadowed, and though she cannot read his face, his wide shoulders stoop toward her slightly, the smallest bow of acquiescence. "You are right, mistress— about the danger to the city. I knew it the moment I heard of Zabbai's death. In truth, I was going to ride out myself, as you have done, to find Antiochus—or whatever is left of the tribe. Had your sister not found me when she did, I likely would have met you in the stable." His dark-shrouded face turns down as he examines her camel's chest strap. She need not see his face to know that he is grinning in mockery. "I could have saddled your mount for you, and done a better job of it, too. Your strap is twisted. No wonder he is so peeved."

"He is no more peeved than I." She glances away in embarrassment, then says, "So he *is* a male."

The guard laughs again. "Can't you tell the difference?"

"It's not as if the females wear veils!" Zenobia tosses her head. "You say you understand the danger, yet you keep me here while precious time slips away. You chatter at me as if I were a laundry maid and not the daughter of the chief!"

"I admit I would feel more urgency if I did not know where the Amlaqi were," he says, his voice infuriatingly lazy, "but seeing that I *do* know—"

"You foul creature! All this time you've kept the knowledge from me? Tell me where they are!"

"You passed them not far back, a few minutes' ride to the south and east. I heard their voices."

"I heard voices, too, but I couldn't tell whether they were Tanukh or Palmyrene. I was . . ." She hesitates to admit her fear, but she reasons that he'll quickly guess it and laugh at her if she doesn't come clean. "I was afraid to ride too close, in case they were Tanukh after all. I wanted to catch sight of them from a distance first, to be safe."

The guard does not acknowledge her fear, for which Zenobia feels grateful. "I rode near enough to be certain," he says. "I only pressed on after you because you're reckless enough to gallop off into the desert alone."

Zenobia gives him an icy stare. "I thank you for the information. And now I must be on my way."

Just as she finally succeeds in turning her camel's head, a steely hiss whispers in the darkness. Zenobia sees a long blade in the guardsman's hand, a pale slash against the looming shade of the dunes. She grips her rein in terror, afraid he means to harm her, but instead he offers her the sword, hilt first.

"This will do you more good than your little kitchen knife," he says. "Take it, here. Hold it while I untie the scabbard. I can't fix the scabbard to your saddletree while the blade is sheathed."

Zenobia hesitates, then kicks her camel nearer to him and takes the sword. It is as long as her arm, curved slightly at the end, yet it is as light as a silk veil when she tries a tentative swing.

Zabdas holds up a hand to stay her, then maneuvers his camel closer to her side. He leans across her bare thigh to tie the scabbard in its place, and under cover of darkness he does not stop himself from a lingering look at her bare skin. The unsheathed blade reflects the shimmer of the stars, and the light just illuminates the soft, bronze-brown hair along her shin, like the hazy glow on an evening horizon.

"I suppose I should know your name," she says when the guardsman straightens in his saddle.

"If a Tanukh comes at you, draw the blade and swing it hard at his face." Gently, he takes her wrist in the darkness. Her pulse leaps beneath his fingers as he guides the sword into its sheath. "And my name is Zabdas."

"I thank you for the blade, Zabdas. And now I truly must be off."

"Not alone. I'm coming with you."

Zenobia grits her teeth. This laughing, scornful man will be more likely to mock her than follow her. Yet he is obviously skilled in finding his way about the desert, and there is no doubt that he can use a sword far better than she. *I will be wise to tolerate him,* she tells herself firmly. "As long as you don't try to take me back to Palmyra, you are welcome."

"You are too gracious, mistress." Zabdas gives his camel a brisk command, and it trots away between the dunes. "Come along," he calls to her like a nurse to a reluctant child, and Zenobia trails along behind, kicking her camel forward so she will not lose sight of his mount's narrow rump in the desert night.

Zabdas goes swiftly through the sands, and Zenobia furrows her brow, concentrating on the work ahead. The high flanks of the dunes seem to close about her, towering overhead like banks of dark-gray storm clouds. Zabdas's camel moves along a deep-shadowed, twisting path, and as Zenobia hurries after him, her palms sweat and her arms tremble. A ripple of nervous fear creeps up her spine. The helpless, vulnerable sensation that she is being watched makes her skin go clammy and raises the hairs on her arms. From the shoulders of the dunes she feels fierce desert eyes upon her back, her neck, and her exposed, pale thighs.

The whisper of voices reaches her once more, and she opens her mouth to call out to Zabdas, to ask him whether they are near the Amlaqi camp. But in the moment she draws in a breath, she passes a dark depression where another path—a thin parting between two hills of sand—intersects her own. It is a cleft as black as onyx, and as she moves across its opening, a deeper blackness stirs.

Between one beat of her heart and the next, a man rises up from the shadows, his hard hand reaching for her like a leopard's paw outstretched toward some small and helpless prey.

Zenobia screams and rips the sword from its scabbard. She takes in what few details her eyes can glean in the pale starlight and the rising rush of her own fear. Dark, coarse robe; loose headcloth; black beard; small, gleaming eyes. *Tanukh.* And that reaching hand—that claw that seeks to sink itself into her bared skin, to tear her from the saddle.

Feather bellows, lurching, and Zenobia drops her rein. She clings to the bronze-capped saddle horn with one hand but, thank the gods, keeps the sword's hilt in a white-knuckled grip. Zabdas's instructions flood into her head, chasing away all thought and all sensation—everything save for the biting fear and the sudden, hot energy that thrums along her tingling limbs.

She swings the sword as hard as she can directly at her attacker's face.

The blade crunches into the Tanukh's body. A gurgling scream rebounds from the walls of the dunes, and a moment later Zabdas's camel shoulders past Zenobia's own. A second blade flashes in the cold starlight, and Zabdas leans from the saddle as he drives his sword into the Tanukh's chest.

Zenobia's attacker crumples to his knees, gives one slow, rasping exhale, then falls forward, his arms outspread.

"*Oh!*" Zenobia wails. Her hand loosens on the hilt of her blade. Its bloody tip droops toward the earth.

"Don't drop your sword," Zabdas barks.

Her hand tightens, responding to the command of its own volition.

Zabdas looks around the dunes. "If you drop it, there will be no time to cush your camel and retrieve it."

For several long moments he holds still, sword at the ready, watching the surrounding desert and listening for any breath, any slither of sand, that might betray the presence of more Tanukh. But the desert remains quiet, save for the occasional, distant hum of men's murmuring voices. The low sounds move past them, as intangible and ill-defined as morning mist over the green shadow of Tadmor.

From his camel's rigging, Zabdas produces a loop of light cord. He fashions one end into a slipknot and, leaning from the saddle and using the wet-dark point of his sword to guide the cord, snares the dead man's ankle. He jerks to tighten the loop, then winds its end around his saddle horn.

Zenobia stares down at the Tanukh. Her breath burns in her chest, and her whole body quivers. A swell of nausea rises in her gut; she swallows hard to drive it away. "Is he dead?" she whispers, watching the sand darken around the Tanukh's head and shoulders.

Zabdas laughs. Even in the dark he can see that the girl is pale, yet she still sits on her camel straight and unbowed. No tears shine on her cheeks. "It is rather hard to go on living when so much of one's blood is on the outside. No man could have survived the blow you gave this one, mistress."

She stares at the guardsman in shock. Her black eyes are huge and round. "I? But you stabbed him in the heart!"

"To end it quickly. Your cut to the side of his neck was the fatal one."

She gasps, covering her eyes with a cold hand. The sword is a hateful weight, and she longs to cast it to the ground. Yet because of it she still lives, still has her virtue intact, and is free to complete her mission and save her city. She forces herself to grip the hilt tighter. Her fingers ache and her knuckles burn, as though the skin might split.

"Sheathe the blade," Zabdas says gently. His camel steps close to her, and he once more lifts her wrist to guide her trembling hand. Zenobia is grateful for the strength of his arm. "But first you must clean your sword."

Too weak with shock to stop him, Zenobia watches as Zabdas wipes her blade on the folds of her bunched skirt. Then he helps her return the sword to its scabbard.

"Thank you," she murmurs. Tears sting her eyes, but she swipes them away with a quick motion. She will not weep for the Tanukh man. She is no sheltered woman of the Palmyrene elite. As an Amlaqi, she knows full well what men do to women when the heat of battle is upon them. She knows what this one would have done to her had he succeeded in pulling her down.

But she has never imagined herself taking a life. Nothing in her seventeen years has prepared her for the shock of it—the finality or the cold, quick ease with which it was done. Only a few heartbeats ago the Tanukh had been a living man, and now he is nothing but a flat shadow on the sand, his life spilled out in a red-black gush. Zenobia pales and hunches in her saddle. It is terrible that death might come even in the shape of a girl screaming on the back of a camel, swinging a borrowed blade with wild desperation—that even she can deliver to another being this grim and hasty fate. She feels small and alone. The merciless cold of the desert night bites through her robe, and she shudders.

Zabdas retrieves her camel's rein and returns it to her. "Not far now, mistress. The Amlaqi camp is close. Are you shaken?"

Zenobia looks up into Zabdas's face. The faint light bounces off the shoulder of a dune just enough that she can make out his features at last. Above the close-cropped beard, Zabdas's mouth is a line of tight concern. His nose is large and bold, and a scar slices beside it, running down the length of his left cheek into the trimmed black hair of his upper lip. His eyes are large, and he watches her face with a keenness that seems almost patronizing. She wants to take him to task for his impudence, but beneath the intensity of his gaze Zenobia detects a certain softness, an expression of regret.

Does he think it a mistake to have put a blade in my hand? she wonders. *Does he think me too weak and womanish to defend my own person?*

Zenobia sits up straight and meets his eye with a direct, haughty stare, the kind Nafsha uses in the halls of the palace. "I am not shaken, only somewhat tired. It has been a difficult day and a long night, after all."

Zabdas bows his head, but there is a certain charm in his voice when he answers. "As you say, mistress."

"Show me the way to the Amlaqi camp." She casts an uneasy glance over her shoulder. "I suppose," she adds, willing her voice not to tremble, "we need not worry about another attack."

"We must always be alert, but if there were more Tanukh hiding with this one"—he gives a jerk on the cord, and the corpse shifts heavily at their camels' feet—"they would have attacked when it became clear we are only two. Stay close beside me now. The going is easier here, with room for us to ride abreast."

Zabdas's camel groans in protest as they set out, for now it drags the weight of the dead Tanukh. Zenobia looks back at the body. Its arms have shifted upward and out, spread like the wings of a flying bird as it trails along behind them. The ends of the man's headcloth ripple with the movement. Where the fabric is not blackened with blood, she can see that it has been embroidered in finely stitched checks that glimmer in the starlight. Goldwork—stolen, no doubt, from a Palmyrene. No Tanukh could be wealthy enough to buy such finery. Facedown, the Tanukh cuts a deep track in the sand and darkens the ground with a wet stain.

My doing, Zenobia thinks soberly. She cannot name the strange sensation that coils in the pit of her stomach. It is queasy like horror, but sparks, too. That feeling—the sparking—is closer to pride than fear, and Zenobia wonders at it. *Is it possible to feel both proud and appalled at the same time?*

Zabdas turns toward a low-banked dune. The voices are louder here, and he can make out occasional words now, Aramaic and clear. He glances at his young mistress. Her chin lifts as she catches the familiar music of the tongue of Palmyra. The sound lifts her heart, he sees, and tears finally threaten her eyes, but she draws deep and steady breaths to ward them away. Zabdas pretends not to see.

They crest the hill and Zabdas reins in. The camp of the Palmyrene force spreads below them in a shallow bowl. The men are ragged and depleted, a mere scattering of warriors crouching in the sand beside their cushed camels or leaning against their beasts' warm flanks in an attempt to steal a few brief hours of sleep. There are perhaps two hundred in all—maybe not even as many as that—and in their huddled stillness they look baffled and utterly worn down.

How can so few stand against the Tanukh? The pit of Zabdas's stomach sinks like a stone dropped into a cistern. He cuts his eyes toward Zenobia, searching for the right words to encourage her in her duty.

Then somebody gives a warning shout from within the camp.

Zabdas holds up a hand. "Peace," he calls. "We come from Palmyra."

A pair of soldiers makes their way up the hill with swords drawn. Their steps are slow, and not only because of the soft sand that gives beneath their feet. As they draw near, Zabdas notes the caution and exhaustion on their faces. They are young—not much older than the gate guard who had been left to mind the city. This conflict has likely been their first taste of battle. *Bad luck,* he muses, not without sympathy. *I would not cut such young teeth on foes as hard as the Tanukh. Pray Bel they are not ruined on the idea of battle forever.*

"Halt," one of the boy soldiers says warily. "Don't come any closer."

Neither Zabdas nor Zenobia have moved from the crest of the hill. Zabdas scowls down at the camp. "What is the meaning of this? Bivouacking in a depression with the Tanukh so near—do you all wish to be slaughtered?"

"The Tanukh aren't near," says one of the soldiers, as cocksure as only a youth can be, even in the extreme of exhaustion. His eyes pass over Zenobia, lingering a moment on her bared thigh. Zabdas grunts a warning and the youth shrugs, then looks away.

"Do you truly think the Tanukh are not near?" Now Zabdas urges his camel forward a few steps. He turns his mount so the soldiers can see what he drags behind.

"Gods," one of them whispers. "Look at that wound."

Zabdas gives Zenobia a curt nod. "The woman killed this one not a quarter of a league away. The rest of his tribe can't be far off. Who's in charge of this sorry camp?"

The two men glance at one another, and Zenobia holds her breath until at last one of them says, "Antiochus."

"Thank the gods," she breathes. She has found her brother-in-law. With that certainty, weariness falls over her like the stifling weight of a wool blanket, and all the fears and sorrows of the preceding day and the long desert night batter against her bones. She sags in the saddle. But before she can give in to her exhaustion, she feels Zabdas turn toward her in the darkness. An expectant pause hangs in the air between them. He is waiting for her to speak, she realizes with dull surprise—waiting for her command.

Zenobia forces herself to sit tall and proud, as proud as the queens whose blood runs through her veins. "Take me to Antiochus."

The soldiers blink up at her in surprise. Clearly they had expected Zabdas to issue the commands, to take the lead. One of them raises his brow at the broad-shouldered guardsman, but Zabdas makes an impatient gesture with his rein. "You heard my mistress. Lead her to Antiochus at once."

The soldiers pick a careful path through the tattered camp. As they move among the men, the sight of a woman riding astride a camel rouses soldiers from their crouched, silent stupor—to say nothing of the spectacle of the bloody harrow that follows Zabdas through the sand. Men rise to their feet and follow until, by the time they reach the place where Antiochus leans against his slumbering camel, nearly the entire camp trails Zenobia and her guard.

Antiochus, who had been sleeping, starts and struggles up. He shakes the sand from his robes. "What is the meaning of this? Who comes? Are you a messenger from Zabbai?"

Zenobia cushes her camel and slides to her feet. Her legs and groin ache from hours astride, and the small of her back has cramped fearfully. But she strides toward Antiochus with her face set, determined not to cry out at the pain that wracks her body with every step, nor to allow that pain to show in her face.

She bows low before her brother-in-law.

"Zabbai is dead," she says in a clear voice. Her words carry over the sandy bowl of the encampment, and the gathered soldiers mutter and moan. "He was killed by the Tanukh when your forces were divided. His body has already been returned to Palmyra. You, Antiochus, are now the Ras of the Amlaqi."

Antiochus peers at her in the wan starlight. The head scarf conceals most of her face, save for her eyes and nose, and weariness has muddled Antiochus's perception. "I know you," he says uncertainly.

"Yes." She speaks out over the crowd, tugging the ends of her scarf down so that all might see her face clearly. "I am Zenobia bat-Zabbai, sister to the wife of Antiochus. I have ridden across the desert so that I might bring word to my brother-in-law that the tribe of Amlaqi is his."

The crowd ripples around Zabdas as he makes his camel kneel, then dismounts, standing ready to call out his support, to verify the woman's words. But he has no need to speak on her behalf. Zabbai's name is powerful. The girl's words are repeated in a hundred awed whispers: *Bat-Zabbai*. Daughter of the chief.

Antiochus reaches tentatively for Zenobia's shoulder; she turns at his touch and gazes into his face. The new Ras is not more than ten years her senior—young to lead a tribe as great as the Amlaqi. And yet by all the laws of Palmyra and the tribe, he must lead them now. His face is drawn and pale, framed by the dark wrappings of his turban above, and the Seleucid bronze of the beard below.

"Sister," he mutters so the soldiers cannot hear, "why in all the gods' names have you come yourself? Palmyra is a hard ride away. Would this task not be better entrusted to a man?"

"There are no men," she says, staring back unblinking into his gray-green eyes. "None fit to ride. Palmyra is left with grandfathers, drunkards, and little boys. All is just as the Tanukh have willed it: The governor is gone, Zabbai is dead, and the Amlaqi are scattered in the desert, crouching like hares in fear of the hawk's shadow. The city is weak and undefended, Antiochus. Only a fool would believe that the Tanukh do not plan to attack. You must return to Palmyra tonight."

"We had thought to root out the last of the Tanukh here . . ."

Zenobia shakes her head impatiently. "A few may remain in the dunes, but the rest are doubtless already massing to take the city. They may be in the streets by now, for all I know."

"When the Tanukh split our forces, we had hoped that Zabbai—"

The sorrow Zenobia has pushed down surges within her now. She chokes on the bitterness of her pain. "There is no use hoping. I tell you, Zabbai is dead! I saw his body myself. You are the Ras now, Antiochus. The tribe moves at your command. I rode all this way through the dark of night to find you—to plead with you to return to the city and defend us from the Tanukh."

He nods, his eyes distant and strained like the eyes of a gazelle staring beyond a pack of hunting hounds, searching hopelessly for an escape. "I do not know how to fight the Tanukh," he admits in a hoarse whisper. Zenobia puts him in mind of his wife, and he confides in the girl before he can think better of admitting such weakness. "They are more terrible and wily than ever I thought. With Zabbai gone and the governor far from home, how are we to stop them?"

"Gods keep me!" Zenobia returns his whisper with tight fury. "Even *I* killed a Tanukh, Antiochus. Fight them the way you fight any other man: swing your sword."

Antiochus's eyes sharpen on her, and Zenobia nearly steps back, suddenly mindful that this is the Ras of the Amlaqi whom she chastises.

"If it were as simple as swinging my sword, I would have no worries," he growls. Zenobia flinches when his voice rises. It cannot bode well for Antiochus's men to hear their commander speak of his uncertainties, but she has no way to silence him. As the men hear their chief's words, they seem to bend from Antiochus, straining outward like untrained horses that shy from their handlers. "These Tanukh move through the dunes like the shadows of jackals," Antiochus says. "They know the desert far better than we. We Amlaqi have spent too many generations within the city. We've lost too much of our desert lore. We are no match for them."

Zenobia's face burns with desperation and anger. "If you think this, then Palmyra is already lost."

The girl turns away in disgust.

Zabdas ushers the soldiers back from the fallen Tanukh, as Zenobia strides into the circle of trampled sand and stands over the body of the man she has slain.

"Men of the Amlaqi," she cries, "men of Palmyra. The Tanukh have led you into a snare. Your city lies undefended. Your wives and children sit waiting for Tanukh blades to fall upon their necks. Some"—she resists the urge to glance toward Antiochus—"think that Palmyrenes are softened by city life. Some think we have lost the ways of the desert, that the greatness that is ours by blood right has been diluted by the influence of Rome. No one believes this more than the Tanukh, who with our chief gone, think to lay us low.

"But I am bat-Zabbai! I am the blood of the Amlaqi, and I know that I am as much of the desert as any Tanukh thief."

She seizes the cloth of her skirt, spreading the garment wide like the wings of a felled bird, so that all the men can see the dark stain across her thigh. The blood has dried. It is stiff beneath her fingers.

"I struck down this man, the one you see before me. This is the blood from my sword—Tanukh blood, smeared across the skirt of a woman. I ask you, if a woman of Palmyra can wield such a blow against our enemy, then have the people of our city grown weak? Has Rome stolen away our courage? If a woman of the Amlaqi can fell an enemy, then there is nothing the men of our tribe cannot do!

"The Tanukh are keen in the desert, I know, and they have never lost their old tribal cunning. But I say that the Amlaqi are better. My father taught us all how to be worldly—wise and refined, men and women worthy of our city and its power—but the tribal fire still burns in our hearts, as hot as the midday sun. I am bat-Zabbai, and my father gave to me, as he gave to all of us, a great inheritance.

"Yes, I am a daughter of stone—of the Western Gate and the Great Row, of the colonnades and the temples. But I am also a daughter of the sands. In my father's palace I may dress myself in silk and jewels, but the dunes are like my mother's bosom to me. On the rooftops of Palmyra I feel the dry, hot wind in my hair, I smell the sulfur of Tadmor, and it is as good to me as the breath of Bel."

She steps toward the grouping of soldiers, reaching out her arms in an imploring way, as if she longs to wrap each man in a sisterly embrace.

Even Zabdas finds himself leaning toward her, yearning for the blessing of her hand.

"You are all the blood of Zabbai," she cries like a goddess in the darkness, "because he loved you—because he loved Palmyra. You are my brave brothers, my strong and fearless brothers, and you are all of the desert, too, as surely as I am.

"All that stands between you and your desperate city is the desert. You need not fear to cross it now, for wherever a Tanukh goes, the blood of Zabbai goes twice as fearless and twice as strong.

"Will you ride with me now, my brothers? Palmyra waits for you!"

As her voice dies away, the night rings with the steely call of swords pulled from their scabbards. A wall of raised blades flashes before the girl, their edges glimmering in the starlight. They sway like the palms of Tadmor when the wind rushes through, and the men lift their voices in a thrilling, pulsing chant.

"Bat-Zabbai! Bat-Zabbai! Bat-Zabbai!"

Antiochus steps into the circle beside Zenobia. He leans close to her ear.

"You've stirred them to life, Zenobia, and put steel in their spines." He looks down in shame for a moment, but his gratitude strengthens him. "You've accomplished what I couldn't do. I'm not afraid to admit it."

She glances up in surprise.

Antiochus smiles. "Zabbai's daughters are women to make any tribe proud. How does my wife fare?"

"Nafsha is her usual stubborn self. She grieves for our father, and she frets over your safety, but she is holding our household together. I promised her I'd bring back word of you."

"Then we must hasten to Palmyra," Antiochus says. "We have lost too much time already. The fire is in us!" Now he raises his voice, too, so that all his men might hear. "We shall race for the city, hide along its fringes, and give the Tanukh a surprise they are not apt to forget!"

The men shout their eagerness.

"But first . . ." Antiochus kneels. From the sand at her feet, he gazes up at Zenobia, earnest and hopeful.

Silence descends on the camp. The girl's face flushes in embarrassment and awe.

"Give me your blessing, Sister-in-Law. Let bat-Zabbai grace me with her father's approval. Let the strength and wisdom of the old chief pass into me from my brave sister's hands."

Zenobia's head and breast are full of the tight, loud drum of her own heart. She used the last of her strength to inspire Antiochus's men, and now her legs are as untrustworthy as a newborn foal's. Seeing the Ras kneeling before her, feeling the men's expectant eyes upon her, a swell of nausea rises in her gut. But the men begin to chant her name again, and Zenobia smiles. She once more lifts the hem of her bloodied skirt and bends to kiss Antiochus on the brow.

At once the camp swirls into activity. Men run for their mounts, shouting commands and jests, scurrying across the sand like ants whose nest a child has poked with a twig. In the midst of the tumult, Zabdas feels a hot flush steal over his face and scolds himself. *Don't be a child. And worse, don't be a fool. The daughter of the great chief is not for a man such as you.* He stoops over the body of the Tanukh, calmly removing the loop of his cord from the man's foot. But he steals one more glance at the fierce-eyed girl as he coils the cord in his hands. Her face is truly pale now, white as a sheet of Egyptian linen. She takes a step toward him, and her feet stumble in the deep sand. She staggers and thrusts out a hand to catch herself on Zabdas's shoulder. The touch of her hand is like fire against his skin.

"Mistress," he says, his voice thick with worry.

"I'm all right."

"You are not. You're exhausted."

"I just need a little sleep."

"What, here?" Zabdas stares about the bowl, at the camels rising and milling, the men rushing through the darkness. "I think not."

"If we can only make it back to Palmyra . . ." She leans on his arm and his heart lurches and pounds.

But he eases her to the ground, and she kneels there, sagging over her own lap, eyelids fluttering. All the might has gone out of her. She is as dull and useless as a cracked clay pot.

"There." Through her exhaustion, Zenobia hears the guardsman's voice, distant, strangely muffled by the pounding in her head. With effort, she looks up. Zabdas has tied Feather's lead rope to his own saddle, and approaches as if through deep water, the outline of his body wavering and rippling, his movements slow. Or perhaps it is only Zenobia's taxed senses that cannot keep pace with Zabdas, for before she even realizes he is at her side, the guardsman lifts her from the ground.

She makes some small noise of protest at the impropriety and his presumptuous boldness, but he hushes her and shifts her weight in his arms until she is cradled like a babe against his chest.

Zabdas eases her onto his saddle, then climbs aboard behind her. He tucks in her legs and arms until they both sit securely, and, although Zenobia grits her teeth at his touch, his hands are gentle and move with respect.

She is hardly aware of the shift and lurch of the camel rising, and the sounds of Antiochus's camp recede into the night even before they have climbed the closest dune. She plunges into the shelter of a heavy, determined sleep, the kind that only those who are well and truly worn can know. She does not dream, but even in the merciful blankness of her slumber she is dimly aware of the camel's gentle sway below her, and the warmth of Zabdas's chest at her back. He drives away even the chill of the desert night, and Zenobia bat-Zabbai smiles as she sleeps in his arms.

4

A Hem of Purple

Dawn wakes her, filtered and green, rustling and moving. Zenobia lies with heavy-lidded eyes, watching the emerald shade sway amid dapples of light. Wherever the light touches, the sand flames as golden as a temple fire, and Zenobia blinks at the brightness of the glow between the shadows.

She breathes deeply, carefully, feeling her ribs and back ache in protest. The air is sweet with the rich, damp odors of vegetation and water, and the sulfur scent of Tadmor is strong. Pain beats at her flesh even as she holds still. She knows she will be as stiff and hobble-legged as an old grandmother when she finally dares to stand.

Zenobia pulls rough folds of heavy, woven wool away from her chin. The fabric has trapped her sleeping breath against her face, humid and thick. The cloth is redolent with the earthy, warm scent of her father's stable, and she realizes with a frown that she rests beneath her own saddle blanket. The blanket from Zabdas's camel is spread beneath her, protecting her from the chill of the early morning sand.

Her bladder is painfully full; Zenobia will be forced to move, and soon. *Better to get out from between the camels' blankets, no matter how I ache,* she tells herself, trying to work the motivation into her stiff, unwilling limbs. At last she tosses her covering aside in one swift movement and rolls to her knees. The pain in her legs and back brings an involuntary cry to her throat. She tries to stifle it, but Zabdas, standing tense and still among the thick green underbrush, hears and turns.

"You're awake."

"How long did I sleep?" She straightens slowly, wincing. The tight muscles of her back protest against her breath, and so she stands panting until her back loosens.

"Four hours or so. With the burden of you on my saddle, I thought it better to come to the oasis than to return to Palmyra—at least until I can determine how the night's campaign went."

Zenobia recalls in a rush of fear that Tadmor may well have been the haunt of Palmyra's enemies throughout the terrible night. She looks around wide-eyed, but save for the palm leaves swaying in the gentlest of morning breezes, the oasis is perfectly still.

"They're not here," Zabdas says. "Otherwise you wouldn't have slept so soundly. I would say you slept peacefully, but that would be untrue. I've never heard a woman snore like you, mistress."

Zenobia finds she can draw herself to her full height after all. She forgets her aches as she flings her head in defiance. "I do *not* snore."

Zabdas shrugs. "I am loyal to the chief's family and would never lie to a daughter of Zabbai."

She feels his grin on her back as she turns away. He is still watching her, even as she steps into the thick of the brush. Zenobia glares at him from behind her curtain of leaves.

"Turn away! I must attend to private things."

He gives another of his infuriating chuckles as he turns his back. Zenobia can do nothing but grind her teeth and hike her skirt around her waist. *First he heard me snoring, and now he sees me like this,* she seethes. *He is one palace guard who will never respect me again.*

When she is finished, she gathers her dignity about herself and steps from the concealing brush. Zenobia makes herself walk to the guardsman's side, even though she is braced for more mockery. She folds her arms and follows his gaze.

The edge of the oasis is but a few strides from where they stand; out across the final stretch of desert lies Palmyra, an expanse of white limestone glowing golden in the sunrise. Here and there the bronze-crowned brow of a temple or palace sparkles in the new light.

"And so if the Tanukh are not here in Tadmor . . ." Zenobia begins. She trails off into silence.

Zabdas finishes the dark thought for her. "They must have moved on Palmyra in the night."

She swallows a lump in her throat as large and hard as a lemon. "Do you suppose Antiochus and his men made it back in time?"

He is silent for a long while as he considers the city. Zenobia steals a glance at Zabdas from the corner of her eye. In the light of day, softly blurred by the gracious shadows of the spring, his face takes on a liveliness, a depth of feeling, she had not seen by starlight. She watches as worry darkens his expression, then vanishes, replaced by a smoldering, angry determination. His brown skin is smooth, but his trimmed beard grows high on his cheeks so that his jaw seems jutting and hard. His eyes beneath the dark, lowered brows are a startling green, as green as the shade of the oasis.

Seleucid eyes, she thinks vaguely, and recalls her sister Zabibah's silly chatter about a good-looking husband to make her head dizzy. *Not this one,* Zenobia tells herself firmly. *Even if he were of the purest Seleucid blood, he is nothing but a guardsman and no fit match for me.*

"Surely Antiochus returned in time to stop the Tanukh," Zabdas mutters, not wholly certain whether he speaks to the girl or to himself. "If those sons of jackals had taken the city, we would see fires . . . smoke from the temples. The palaces, too, but the temples most of all. They would burn everything they could, starting with our gods."

"The city seems calm. Though how can we know from this distance?"

He nods. "It is time we returned, before the sun is well up and the desert grows any hotter. Pray that we find Antiochus and not a horde of Tanukh in control of the city when we ride through the Western Gate."

They start for Palmyra in trepidation, sharing the bread and water from Zenobia's supplies in silence. But by the time they have closed half the distance, it is clear their fears are unfounded. When they are still well beyond the unwalled fringe of the city, the ringing of timbrels and the notes of joyous song lift and scatter over the shifting sands. Through the arch of the Western Gate, Zenobia can see silk banners of the brightest dyes unfurled from many rooftops, stirring lazily in the final weak breaths of the morning's wind.

She kicks Feather into a brisk trot and pulls ahead of Zabdas, guiding her mount between the towering legs of the gate and onto the Great Row. All along the Row, between its stately pillars, the road is thronged with women in their brightest gowns and children leaping in coltish play. The road has been strewn with petals from rooftop gardens, and, although they have begun to wilt and brown beneath the crush of so many feet, the air is still sweet with their perfume. From beyond the pillars, in the streets and alleys between shops and homes, Zenobia hears the name of Antiochus on every tongue.

Zabdas draws level with her and catches at her camel's rein. He slows both creatures and offers Zenobia a laugh. It is friendly this time, not arrogant. "It would not do to trample the people in the midst of their revelry, mistress."

"Oh, Zabdas—he made it back in time!"

"All thanks to bat-Zabbai."

She makes no reply but turns her face proudly toward the heart of the city. Around her the celebratory songs continue, and Zenobia rides through the crowd straight-backed and bold-eyed, as if it is she they cheer, and not the new Ras.

"What will you do now?" Zabdas shouts over the din.

"I must return to my father's palace. I hope I'm not too late to see him laid in his tomb."

In the courtyard of Zabbai's great house, they cush their mounts on the paving stones. Servants come running to take Zenobia's rein and lead Feather off to his stable and a well-earned meal of grain.

"He likes dates," she calls after them, stretching the deep, sharp ache of too many hours spent riding from her back and legs.

Zabdas likewise surrenders his mount and stands yawning in the bright morning light. The palms and jasmine vines are still now; the breezes of the morning have subsided, and the day promises a fierce and terrible heat. Zabdas yawns again.

"Did you sleep at all last night?" she asks him.

"Of course not. I'd be a poor guard if I had. I kept watch over you all the night long—not that there was much night left by the time we made Tadmor."

The girl turns away from him quickly, but not before Zabdas catches the flush of color on her cheeks.

"Perhaps you ought to go now and rest," she says.

He gives her a small bow even though she is still turned away from him. "If you wish me to leave you alone to face Nafsha's wrath . . ."

"I have faced her wrath many times before and lived to tell the tale." When she is certain her face is composed again, she turns back to him. "I thank you for your good and attentive service, Zabdas."

"As I told you, mistress: I am loyal to the chief's family."

Zabdas sets out for the tiny guardsman's quarters beside the palace gate—not much more than shelter from the sun and a camel-hair mattress—and Zenobia moves toward the palace with dragging steps. In spite of her brave words to Zabdas, she knows that Nafsha will be stalking the halls of their father's house like a leopard, waiting for the chance to spring and deliver a fearsome bite. Zenobia stares up at the high limestone walls, shining bright white in the sun of early day. Their intricate carvings of linked hexagons and desert roses are all but blotted out by the glare, the fine detail of the well-worked stone lost in the intensity of the light.

Nafsha burns as hot as that very sun inside the palace's walls, Zenobia thinks with dismay. *I would rather face a Tanukh warrior than her anger.* But the smile she tries to force fades away almost at once, and she knows it is not true.

At least she has news about Antiochus—assuming he hasn't come to the palace already, though Zenobia suspects the new Ras has been preoccupied this morning, attending to all manner of duties in the wake of the battle. She prays that her news will be enough to soothe Nafsha's rage.

The household servants bow deeply as she crosses the threshold, but below the edges of their loosely wound head scarfs, Zenobia sees the horrified stares they cast at the great smear of red-brown staining her skirt. The servant women straighten and flock together, milling as nervously as sheep before a shepherd's trained dog.

"Where is Nafsha?" she demands. She supposes it's best to face the leopard in her den as quickly as possible—best to dodge those snapping jaws and flashing fangs now—and then get on with the day's business. There is much yet she must see to, if she is to claim the destiny the gods intended for her. Last night's ride out into the desert was a diversion from her path. A duty and a necessity, yes—but a diversion all the same. Now she must return to the work at hand. Despite all that has happened in the night, she still must attend to her future.

One of the women points upward at the beaten silver tiles of the ceiling, indicating the upper chambers. "She is in, mistress."

"Then Zabbai has not yet been carried to his tomb?"

The woman shakes her head. The soft folds of her linen robe, undyed but well-woven, shiver as the servant shifts her slight weight from one foot to the other, clasping and unclasping her hands. "We could not take him out at sunrise, for there was fighting in the city. Our poor lady Mistress Berenikë is still felled by sorrow—she has not left her chambers since Zabbai's death—and Mistress Nafsha would allow none of us to descend the hill and learn what news we could. We've heard the singing and celebrating, but we don't know what it's all for—only that *something* happened in the night. Please, my lady—you have come from the city, have you not? Won't you take pity on us and tell us the news?"

Zenobia smiles. "There is nothing to fear. The Tanukh made an attempt to take Palmyra in the night, but our brave new chief, Antiochus, repelled them. The Great Row is alive with celebration! Were it not for the fact that my father is not yet buried, I would fill our halls with music and order a hundred sweet cakes from the kitchens."

The servants sigh as one.

"I am glad to hear it, mistress," Bayaha says. "Each of us has family in the city, you see, and we have been fearful for their safety since we heard the fighting." She bows again. "Won't you please let me bring you refreshment . . . perhaps a clean robe . . ."

"I have no time," Zenobia says reluctantly. "I must speak with my sister now—alone. Be sure no one interrupts us, unless my seamstress returns to the palace. I have set a special task for her, and I will see her at once, the moment she arrives."

Zenobia climbs the narrow staircase to the upper chambers, her sandaled feet tapping on the bright-glazed tiles and echoing through the halls of the palace. She quells a shudder at the knowledge that Nafsha must surely hear, must know that Zenobia has returned. *She is doubtless sharpening her tongue on a whetstone even now, making one bitter stroke for every step I take.*

She does not tap the ornate bronze knocker against the cedar door of Nafsha's chamber, but pushes her way into her sister's room without announcement.

Nafsha is sitting on a stool by her window, staring out across the rooftops of Palmyra. At the sound of the door's hinges, she jerks and spins. An embroidery frame topples off her lap. The blue silk that is stretched across it remains untouched, save for a few desultory pale-red stitches. Her face is haggard with fear and loss, but when she sees that it is Zenobia who stands before her, her dark eyes brighten and all traces of fear melt away, replaced by gratitude and relief. She flings herself from the stool and runs to Zenobia. She enfolds her youngest sister in her arms as hard and strong as a carpenter's vise.

"Bless the gods. They brought you back to me." Tears quiver in Nafsha's voice, and Zenobia wriggles and shrugs until she is free. She has never seen Nafsha behave this way, clinging and clutching as Zabibah would do.

"In the name of Bel, Nafsha. What's come over you?"

"I felt certain you would be killed. The guardsman I sent after you—"

"Zabdas found me; have no fear of that."

Nafsha's eyes travel down Zenobia's soiled, rumpled robe and widen at the sight of the stain. "Is that blood?"

Zenobia turns slightly away, as if she might hide her skirt from Nafsha's scrutiny.

"Well," her sister goes on, the accustomed brusque authority shouldering through her moment of vulnerability, "the guard can't have done his duty well, by the looks of you. I shall see that he is dismissed from service at once."

Zenobia ignites with a fury so strong even she is taken aback. "Zabdas is all any guardsman should be, and a good deal more! I won't see him dismissed—not on my account."

Nafsha opens her mouth to disagree, or worse, to issue some command with finality, and Zenobia speaks quickly to divert her anger. "I bring good news, Sister."

Yesterday Zenobia was the daughter of the chief, with standing that surpassed Nafsha's own. Today she is only a fatherless girl, unwed long after the age when she should have had a husband. Now her eldest sister is the wife of the tribe's leader, and the time for looking down her nose at Nafsha has passed. Zenobia knows she must be wise and careful. If there is to be any hope of remaining mistress of her own fate, she must show her sister the respect she is entitled to. She thinks of Zabdas with his close-cropped beard, the delicate balance he walks between the Arabic tribes and Rome. She reaches for her sister's hand and extends this promise of happy tidings like a flag of truce between them.

"Well?" Nafsha prompts. Her mouth goes pale at the edges; her eyes brighten with desperate eagerness.

"Antiochus is well, and he has returned to the city as a conquering hero."

Nafsha squeezes her eyes shut, sobbing quietly with relief. Two tears like seed pearls fight past her matted lashes and rest on her smooth cheeks. "Oh gods, thank you—thank you!" She embraces Zenobia once more. "And thank you, Little Sister. I've been waiting to hear news of Antiochus. I was glad the city was saved, of course, but until I had some word of him . . . All will be well now, I know it—if we can only see our father safely into his tomb."

"Antiochus will surely come here soon to give you the news himself. This palace is his now—yours."

"Yes," Nafsha muses. "It's strange to think of it, that I am the mistress of this house—the house where we were children together. When I married and moved to Antiochus's home, I never dreamed that one day these halls would be mine. At least not for many years to come. When our husbands—Zabibah's and mine—sent us here, to be with you and Mother while they went off to fight the Tanukh . . . I'd grown so accustomed to my own home that I felt like a guest here, awkward and out of place. And now, so suddenly, I must run it as my own household."

"You will have Mother to help you. You won't turn her out, surely."

"Of course not! Don't even say such a thing. I'd never dream of it."

"Though I suppose she won't be much good until she's come to grips with her sorrow," Zenobia says thoughtfully. "Poor Mother. She's always been so fine and delicate, and she loved Father dearly. But I can help you until she's up to the task again. I know more than you might think, when it comes to overseeing this household. The servants and—"

"Oh no," Nafsha breaks in. "Mother will stay as long as she pleases, but you are a different sack of grain altogether. You will go directly to your husband's household, Zenobia, and I won't hear any arguments. It's long since time."

Zenobia clenches her teeth, and though a scowl ripples just beneath the surface she forces her face into a picture of serenity. "You haven't any right to marry me off, Nafsha. You are not my father, and you are certainly not a brother. You must give up all hope of sealing my fate for me."

"My husband is the Ras now, and he certainly may marry you to whomever he pleases. But don't fret, Little Sister—I will be sure Antiochus finds a good husband for you, and soon, too. As soon as Father's tomb is sealed."

Zenobia's scowl wins out over serenity and she gives a noisy sniff. "It's useless, Nafsha. I have already decided whom I'm to marry, and I will not settle for a lesser man."

Nafsha clicks her tongue. "Really, Sister. You can't simply go about proclaiming you will do this or you will do that. You are no longer a spoiled little girl sitting on the chief's knee. You are seventeen years old. It's time you gave up these childish fancies and settled into proper womanhood."

"And what is proper womanhood?" Zenobia snaps. "Shall I be meek and helpless like Zabibah? Shall I quail whenever my husband shouts?"

"Not all husbands shout, and well you know it. Though if you keep up this foolish stubbornness, I'll be sure Antiochus finds you the most disagreeable, loudest-shouting husband in all of Palmyra."

"Ah—shall I be at the mercy of my spiteful sister's husband? Is that proper and womanly enough?"

"I am not spiteful, you mean-spirited she-camel! I'm doing what is best for you—for our whole family. If you weren't so arrogant, you'd see that for yourself!"

Zenobia steps away from her sister and throws up her head in defiance. Her head scarf comes undone and slides down her back. The coil of her thick black braid frees itself from its pins and swings like the lashing tail of an angry mare. She will not protest against Nafsha's words. She *is* arrogant—she knows it well. But why ought she be humble? It was she who rode out alone into the desert and slayed a Tanukh warrior—and she who still wears her enemy's blood like a badge of victory. She roused Antiochus from his stupor and stirred his men to action. Zenobia saved Palmyra. Arrogant she may be, but her pride is well deserved.

The sharp rap of the bronze door knocker startles them both. Nafsha wheels toward the door, her face pinched with annoyance. "Who in the name of the gods . . ."

But Zenobia sails smoothly past Nafsha. "Enter."

"You have no right to issue orders to servants in my chambers," Nafsha begins. But when Zenobia's seamstress enters, Nafsha falls silent.

The woman bows her way in. Across her arms is draped a length of golden silk, as bright as threads of saffron. It is so fine that it floats as the seamstress moves, drifting in the air like a wisp of transparent cloud. "Your new robe, Mistress Zenobia."

Nafsha turns a questioning look, dark and impatient, on her sister. "When did you order this made?"

Zenobia bites her lip. "While you washed Father's body." It's shameful to admit now—and Nafsha will never understand that there was truly no other time when Zenobia could have commissioned a gown. And so much depends on the new silk robe.

Nafsha nearly spits in disgust. "Not only arrogant, but selfish, too. Truly, Zenobia, you have outdone yourself, and no mistake."

"But there was no other time I could have done it," says Zenobia calmly. "I needed it finished before my husband returned."

"Husband?" Nafsha shakes her head. Then, as the seamstress holds the fine silk up between her hands, displaying it against Zenobia's complexion and squinting one eye critically, Nafsha's gaze falls to the robe's hem. It is ringed by a band of dark silk, as regally purple as an emperor's toga.

Nafsha gasps. "Purple? But that's only to be worn by Roman nobility." And as she speaks these words, Zenobia's intentions come clear. Nafsha's dark brows lower. "Zenobia, you *cannot* marry the governor."

"Why?"

"In the first place, he has a wife already."

Zenobia shrugs. "Many men of the tribes take more than one wife."

"But the governor is not of the tribes."

"He most certainly is. His mother was Amlaqi."

"But he is all Roman. You've heard the gossip about him—you know he's besotted with Rome, far more than any tribesman ever was. But even if he were the most Amlaqi man the gods ever made, *why*, in the name of all that's good and pure, should he want *you*?"

Zenobia only shrugs and lifts the silk in her hands, considering it. Then she nods briskly to the seamstress. "It will do nicely. Take it to my chamber and tell my women to lay out my jewels and uncover my standing mirror. I will try it on when I get there." She gives her fuming sister a casual grin. "I am beautiful—you need not deny it just to be petulant. I know it's true. If he doesn't want me for that reason alone, I'll make him desire me in other ways. I intend to be the wife of the governor of Palmyra, Nafsha, and there is no use squawking at me over it. My mind is quite made up."

"We'll see what Antiochus says to that."

"Whatever he says will make no matter. I *will* achieve it; no one can stop me."

Nafsha's voice is quiet with a kind of frightened awe. "Do you truly think that you can do whatever you please? Do you think the gods so favor you that nothing ill can ever befall you?"

Zenobia says nothing. She only stares levelly into Nafsha's eyes.

Nafsha gives an involuntary shudder. "You are my sister, Zenobia. For all our quarrels, I don't wish any ill on you. But you must turn away from this arrogance and humble yourself. The gods don't like to see anyone so self-content. They will punish you for this hubris if you do not stop—and I shiver to think what your punishment may be."

Zenobia rolls her eyes. "You're as dramatic as the players down at the amphitheater. If the gods don't intend me to marry the governor, then they will not allow it to be. But if they do intend it, and if it comes to pass, then why should they punish me for doing their will?"

"But why have you set your heart so on the governor? I don't understand. He's so old . . ."

"Not *so* old."

"He is much older than you, and already married! What are you playing at, Zenobia?"

Zenobia firms her jaw and faces Nafsha squarely. In the tight lines of her young face, all the history—all the proud, reaching splendor of the Amlaqi and the Seleucids—shines like a cluster of stars. "All his life, our father fought to make Palmyra great. We have no brothers, and so it is left to us to carry on Zabbai's legacy. I will marry a man who is powerful enough to continue our father's work—a man who understands what Zabbai lived for, who loves Palmyra as much as he did. I will marry a man who would have made Father proud, and none other."

"There are plenty of men in the city who would have made Father proud, and who love Palmyra well. Plenty of men who don't have a wife already. You're not doing this for Father's sake—don't think I can't see past your deception. You're set on the governor because he will give you higher status, and for no other reason. Don't disregard my warning, Zenobia. Your arrogance taunts the gods."

Zenobia draws herself up to her full height. Even in her shabby and ill-fitting robe she already feels as finely draped as a governor's wife. "If the gods will that I shall marry someone else, then let Antiochus come here to the palace and make his decree. If, however—"

Outside Nafsha's window the low din of celebration in Palmyra's streets surges to a clamoring roar. The sisters stare at one another, Nafsha's face blank with confusion, Zenobia's lighting by the moment with a fierce inner fire. A swell of victory and pride rises in the younger woman's chest. In one fleeting heartbeat, the spell is broken, and the sisters hurry together from the chamber and down the halls of the palace, clattering up the stairway that spills them out onto the rooftop. Zenobia leads the way to the edge of the roof. She leans across its low wall, welcoming the fierce blow of the sun on her face, feeling the shouts in the street shivering along her skin.

Far across Palmyra, at the end of the columned and petal-strewn Great Row, the tiny dun forms of camels sway, rank upon rank, and the men atop them wave their arms in victorious salute. There are scores of men—hundreds—and everywhere amid that crowd is the flash of crimson cloaks, the red capes of real soldiers. The governor's army has returned.

"What is it?" Nafsha pants. Beads of sweat have already sprung up on her neck, and she lifts a hand to shade her eyes.

Zenobia answers without tearing her eyes from the procession. "My bridegroom comes," she says. She looks down upon the parade as if she can see the governor already, and lifting a hand in greeting, she smiles.

5

A Proposal of Marriage

The courtyard is lively with the sound of women at work. The wet, heavy folds of laundry slap against the flat stones beside the cistern, and the laughter of pouring water echoes, cool and inviting, between the high, carved columns of pale stone. Lucius Septimius Odenathus, governor of Palmyra, lowers himself into his high-backed chair and holds his body still, listening. From the long, narrow window, recessed into the limestone, a patch of soft morning light spills in. It sets the long table's smooth, well-rubbed cedar top glowing. The beam aligns perfectly with a stack of wax tablets and several books of papyrus leaves bound between board covers. Vorod, his deputy, who has shepherded Palmyra in Odenathus's absence, has placed the books and tablets in a neat, orderly row. In the dimness of the room, the light seems to hover on the day's work. It draws Odenathus's eyes to the tablets and his thoughts to the immediate, the mundane.

In the shadows behind his chair, the remembered glories of the Sasanian campaign wait like a servant poised on its toes, ready to be summoned. Odenathus is not quite prepared to consign these memories to the past and tuck into his accounts and columns, his reports of income and tallies of trade. Someone must lead Palmyra, he knows. The gods—and the luck of his high birth—have decreed that it should be him, but Odenathus has only ever wished to lead his army. Even worn out as he is—for it was only a week ago that he returned to his city—his very bones ache for the joys of the campaign. He longs for the peculiar pleasures of the march, sweeping across the land, secure in the knowledge that none will stand before him. His stomach craves for the hot rush of blood when battle is joined, the thrill of power that throbs in the veins and speeds a man to ever-greater glory.

The governor stifles a quiet groan as he shifts on the chair's silk cushions. He stares at the stack of accounts as one might stare at a basket of asps. Despite a long sleep in his soft bed, wrapped in Fairuza's familiar, perfumed arms, fierce pains still pierce him in half a hundred places. His soul might crave for the glories of the battlefield, but his body is nearly too old for fighting. He stretches one leg beneath the table and feels the ever-present ache in his knee leap and burn before it finally subsides. Gods, he thinks, he is nearly too old for riding, too— and for the rigors of diplomacy.

Throughout their long days of negotiation, Shapur, emperor of Eran, made him sleep on a hard pallet in a crude room, complaining all the while that it was the finest accommodation he could afford, because Palmyra has diverted the wealth of the world through its own already overflowing streets. Each morning Odenathus smiled coolly to Shapur's face, self-possessed as though he had slept like a babe, even though he had tossed on that damnable pallet throughout the cold Eranian nights.

And in the end, even after all Odenathus's fine and careful diplomacy, the captive emperor Valerian died while still in custody.

Odenathus narrows his eyes at the untouched tablets. *Shapur, emperor of Eran, if you please.* No doubt when Shapur finally realized that the Palmyrene force was too strong for him, Emperor Valerian met his end in a bowl of poisoned broth—it was like a Sasanid to thwart an honest victory in such an underhanded way. Or perhaps Valerian had simply expired after too much ill use. One cannot be sure, but it hardly matters. The emperor is dead, and Valerian is only the most recent in a long string of failed Roman rulers.

The Roman Empire itself, however, remains intact—thanks in no small part to Odenathus. When Shapur sent Odenathus packing with Valerian's pitiful corpse, the governor did not return to his own city straightaway. Instead, fueled by the fury of his ruined diplomacy, he laid an ambush at the Orontes, shattered the largest part of Shapur's forces as they returned from harrowing Antioch, broke the Sasanid grip on that great city, and restored it to Roman rule. The eastern half of the empire is saved, and better still, Shapur felt Palmyra's rebuke, which was richly deserved.

A suitable reward will be forthcoming from Rome, I should think, Odenathus muses contentedly. Even though he failed to bring the emperor home in a single piece, Antioch is worth much more to Rome than yet another emperor. But Odenathus must wait until the Senate approves Valerian's successor. Word from Rome will arrive soon, he knows. Odenathus is no stranger to Roman politics, Roman ways, and Roman rewards.

Outside, the rhythmic slap of wet cloth against stone makes a lulling sort of music. The laundry maids work in the sunny patch of yard that surrounds the cistern. He cannot see out into the garden from where he sits, but he enjoys hearing his household going about its pleasant, banal business. Idly, Odenathus wonders whether Fairuza is there in the garden, overseeing her women from the palm shade. From time to time she does that, watching the laundry girls or the gardeners, her stern Sasanid eyes a constant reminder that they work for Lucius Septimius Odenathus—that in the governor's house there is always more work to be done.

Fairuza. He almost thinks, *poor girl,* but catches himself. But he will not allow himself to pity his wife, even in his own thoughts. Fairuza has earned many things from Odenathus: respect, admiration, gratitude. Even, in some small and distinctly un-Roman way, love. But the one thing she will never deserve, or would desire, is his pity.

Girl, Odenathus broods, and his mouth curves in a small, distracted, self-deprecating smile. *I should not even think of her that way. It has been seventeen years since she gave birth to our son, and yet it seems I always see her just as she looked on the day I received her from her father, a quiet, wise-eyed girl of fourteen watching me from behind her Sasanian veils, as shrewd and focused as any ambassador.*

His marriage to Fairuza had been intended to seal a peace between the Sasanids and Palmyra, between Eran and Rome. And for eighteen years, it had worked. But then word came that Shapur had captured Emperor Valerian. Odenathus had been strolling in the garden with Fairuza, her small, cool hand on his arm and her low voice filling his head with its soothing rhythms. At the news Fairuza had looked up with an expression that had taken Odenathus aback. Her black eyes were ravaged with turmoil, her cheeks suddenly hollow and pale—for a brief moment she had worn a look of failure and self-condemnation.

It was the first and only time Odenathus had seen Fairuza anything but composed. He had turned to her with words on his tongue: *You are not to blame for the actions of your countrymen.* But she had stared at him, tight-lipped and chin lifted, daring him to speak words of pity, daring him to judge her weakened. Odenathus left his comforts unsaid.

Now, though, with Valerian dead and Antioch freed, with the blood rush of battle only a whisper, Odenathus is forced to confront the problem of Fairuza squarely. Surely the Sasanian alliance is well and truly broken. The woman who has served as a token of peace in his household for eighteen years will be seen by all of Palmyra as a symbol of deception.

It isn't her fault, Odenathus tells himself. The wet cloth beats against stone; the women laugh and sing. *Fate has been unkind to her. Fairuza is not to blame.*

87

But now that the Sasanids have turned traitor, she is a liability.

He refuses to think of it. He pushes the ugly, unfair tangle aside firmly before it can sink a dagger of pain into his heart.

Such dark thoughts drive the governor finally to his task. Odenathus lifts a book of accounts and scans it. The tally of imports and tariffs is perfect, as ever, marked in the unforgivingly precise hand of his deputy, Vorod. The spice trade has remained healthy while he was away; Odenathus lifts another tablet from the stack. His eyes run over the cuneiform, the scores like the tracks of birds in Orontes mud. Supplies of silk are low. A drought in Seres has depleted the colonies of silkworms. Vorod recommends—

Odenathus's eyes catch and return to the last line. He reads and rereads; the meaningless words repeat inside his head. The bold, hard lines of Fairuza's face rise like a rebuke before his vision.

Odenathus sits back, pinching the bridge of his nose. Vorod's tablet is heavy in his hand. He allows it to sag to the tabletop, where the wax sticks slightly in the growing heat. Vorod has done well in his absence. Vorod always does well, running the household—indeed, all of Palmyra—better than Odenathus can himself.

Perhaps I ought to ask Vorod what he thinks is best done about Fairuza.

As if the thought has summoned Vorod, the bronze knocker of the chamber door sounds: two sharp, efficient raps that can only come from the hand of Odenathus's deputy.

Odenathus turns away with relief from the accounts and from the problem of his Sasanid wife. Vorod eases the door open and pushes aside the folds of a long red drapery that hangs before the door, a muffle for voices as a surety against eavesdroppers. The deputy bows and his narrow-set eyes dart to the stack of tablets that gleam in the shaft of light.

Vorod suppresses a grimace. The governor ought to be nearly halfway through his work by now. Accounts, contrary to the beliefs of governors and emperors, will not keep. Cities will not keep. They both need constant tending, constant monitoring, as a mother goose tends to her unruly brood. But Vorod leaves aside his concerns for a moment. He can see at a glance that Odenathus is in no mood for a scolding, and, anyway, Vorod has a more urgent task to lay before the governor.

"My lord," Vorod says, "the Ras of the Amlaqi seeks your counsel."

Odenathus's brows furrow for a moment as he struggles to comprehend the announcement. *The Ras of the Amlaqi is dead.* It was nearly the first news he heard when he rode through the Western Gate.

Then he understands. "The new Ras—of course. Admit him."

Odenathus is pleased to see Antiochus stride into the room when Vorod stands aside. The young Amlaqi is tall and sure of stance, imbued with a quiet dignity that is never haughty, a fault Odenathus feels too many of his tribe possess. The governor has always liked this Antiochus. If he must lose Zabbai to some inscrutable folly of the gods, there is no man he would rather see take Zabbai's place.

He rises to clasp the young chief's arm. Antiochus's grip is strong, but even today still trembles faintly with the excitement of battle. Odenathus squeezes his forearm with a hard hand, savoring the pale echo of his own campaign's thrill.

"I have heard that it was you who turned away an attack by desert raiders," says Odenathus.

Antiochus ducks his head in acknowledgment. His thick beard cannot hide his smile.

"That was well done." Reluctantly, Odenathus releases his grip, and the memory of battle fades. "You have Palmyra's thanks. I suppose you have come to discuss a reward . . ." He will not begrudge it. He will be as lavish with the sheikh as he hopes Rome will be with him.

But Antiochus shakes his head. "Palmyra is secure. That is all the reward I need, my lord. I've come today to present my prisoner's case before you."

"Your prisoner?"

"Jadhima of the tribe of Tanukh. We took him late in the fighting. It seems he is a leader of sorts among his people. Not a Ras exactly—a battle chieftain, you might call him."

"And he wishes to present his case before me? That is . . . irregular. Don't you tribesmen typically handle these conflicts in your own ways?"

"We do. But he simply refused to accept my judgment. He insisted on Roman justice. He says all the Amlaqi are biased unfairly." Antiochus gives a half grin. He *is* biased, he knows. But he is certain that the governor will agree with him and will not permit Jadhima's brutal revenge. *Such a hearing is a waste of the governor's time,* Antiochus thinks, *but let the Tanukh see that in Palmyra we live by justice, not at the point of a sword.*

"Very well," Odenathus says. "Bring the man in."

Antiochus goes to give the command to his men, then returns to the chamber and stands waiting.

Odenathus watches the young man in silence for a moment, noting the natural firmness of his shoulders, the back that Antiochus has no need to coax into straightness. Doubtless his knees never ache, no matter how long he rides. Odenathus is envious. If any man were to ask him, he'd admit it readily—although no man would dare. This young hound Antiochus is strong, and now that he is the Ras, the world is at his feet.

The governor's thoughts sour. Faced with such vigor, it is easy to forget that he, himself, is governor of Palmyra, and expectant of a great reward from Rome. Of course, Antiochus has stepped into a role nearly too large for any man to fill. Odenathus can't resist picking at what is surely Antiochus's rawest wound, if simply to balm his own painful knees.

"I was sorry to learn of Zabbai's death," Odenathus says, watching Antiochus's face carefully.

The Ras flinches at the mention of Zabbai's name. He still burns with the exultation of his fight against the Tanukh and has not yet fully turned his mind to the tasks that lie ahead of him. Now he must take up the mantle his father-in-law dropped, and he can only pray—rather desperately—that he will wear it well. The gods have seen fit to test his mettle straightaway with Jadhima's demands for vengeance.

"A great loss to the tribe," Antiochus says, "and for the whole of Palmyra. It has been a week since we laid Zabbai in his tomb, but still I don't know what we'll do without him."

Odenathus would further plumb the depths of Antiochus's confidence, but the sounds of feet in the outer hall silence him. Both men turn expectantly toward the door.

Vorod opens the door, and the prisoner enters the governor's chamber with two Amlaqi warriors at either side, plus one man fore and one aft. Each guard is dressed in the quilt-stitched silk tunics and heavily embroidered trousers of Palmyrene city men—yet their flowing dark beards and Arab scowls cannot be mistaken. Nor can the swords and daggers sheathed at their belts. In spite of their fine city dress, these are dangerous men of the desert, filled with instinct and fire. Today they have no love for the tribe of Tanukh.

Though any man of Palmyra's benevolent tribe would hiss and spit at the comparison, Jadhima is not unlike the Amlaqi to look upon. The proud carriage is the same, even in captivity. But where the current of desert slyness runs softly beneath the Amlaqi surface, tempered by the civilizing influence of city life, it ripples and surges at the surface of Jadhima the Tanukh. He stands glaring at the governor with an intensity on his face that looks very much like a sneer.

Odenathus locks his hands behind his back and steps calmly toward the prisoner. His footfalls are silent on the bright-dyed wool rugs. Even the pain in his knee vanishes amid the alluring tension of the confrontation.

Odenathus thinks, *This arrogant, scowling desert rat would have taken Palmyra while the city was undefended.* Although facing Jadhima here in his chambers, surrounded by armed Amlaqi warriors, is not the same as facing him on the battlefield, it's the next best thing, and he relishes it.

The Amlaqi guards fall back from the governor's advance, but Jadhima raises his bearded chin in defiance.

"And so you are a captive of Palmyra, Jadhima of the Tanukh. And your tribesmen are always so pleased with their ability to evade justice. I wonder how this has come to pass." Odenathus allows his acquired Roman accent to peer through the Aramaic words. Often some reminder of the governor's close ties to the empire can be useful in the face of tribal recalcitrance.

The man answers in the tribal tongue, the Arabic syllables as sharp and short as belt knives. "I am not too prideful to admit that your lap-dog Antiochus took me in war. At least he fights like an Arab, even if he wears a Roman name."

No man can rule Palmyra and not speak the language of the desert nomads. Their language, and their influence, are as essential to the place as the green spring of Tadmor. Odenathus is amused by this Jadhima, with his impudent eyes and tangled beard, and so he will not make the interrogation harder on the captive than it must be. He takes up the conversation in Arabic. "If you admit you were taken fairly, then why do you insist on troubling me? I do not rule over dunes, nor over a pack of snarling dogs, as do you and your Ras. Palmyra is mine, Jadhima, with all its wealth and all its power. I am a very busy man, and you impose upon my time."

"If in fact you are a man, then you will agree with the righteousness of my case. Antiochus will soon take my head, and I do not fear death. But let the woman die with me, as she deserves."

Odenathus lifts one graying brow. *My Arabic is not what it once was, perhaps. I cannot have heard correctly.* "Woman?"

Jadhima clenches his jaw; the thin muscles at his temples pulse beneath the band of his turban.

Antiochus breaks in before his captive can answer. To the governor's surprise, the words are in Latin, heavily accented by the Ras's unpracticed tongue. Odenathus watches the captive carefully as Antiochus speaks. Jadhima's eyes give no flicker of understanding.

"After we took Jadhima prisoner," Antiochus says in his careful Latin, "he heard my men talking. The Tanukh, you see, managed to wedge between our forces out in the high dunes. That was when Zabbai was killed, the gods rest him well. We thought to remain out there, searching for the Tanukh forces . . . but they had already set their sights on Palmyra."

Ah, Odenathus thinks. *The young sheikh does not care for his prisoner to know just how close a thing this battle was.* "But we did not know of his death. Had not a woman come riding out to find us, we would have been too far away to defend the city when these sand fleas made their attack."

"Who was this woman?"

"Zenobia, the youngest daughter of Zabbai, my lord. As it happens, she is my wife's sister."

"Ah." Odenathus fingers his shaven chin. "And there is your bias."

Antiochus nods. "I'll not deny it. But even if she weren't my sister by marriage, I would not wish to see her destroyed, just to satisfy the tender feelings of this piece of dung." His eyes, gray-green as the leaves of olive trees, slide toward Jadhima with contempt.

"But why should he call for this woman's death?"

"Before she found our camp, she was attacked in the dunes by a Tanukh man, and Zenobia nearly took off his head with her sword."

Odenathus cannot hold back a laugh; Antiochus returns the governor's delight with a wary smile.

"The attacker," the Ras goes on, "wore a distinctive headcloth embroidered with golden checks. We all saw the body, and my warriors made mention of the headcloth within Jadhima's hearing. As you well know, it is unusual for a Tanukh to wear such finery. It seems the man who attacked Zenobia was Jadhima's brother. Jadhima knew it by the description of the headcloth."

Odenathus moves again toward Jadhima. He presses so close to the Tanukh, the man's body trembles with the desire to step back. But Jadhima will not allow himself to retreat. He will not show any more weakness than he must, with his hands bound and Antiochus's guards hemming him on all sides.

"So a woman bested a man of your tribe," Odenathus says in Arabic.

Scornfully, Jadhima turns his face away from the governor's words.

"You would punish a woman for being brave? For defending her virtue?" Odenathus continues.

"She is a murderess," Jadhima hisses. "By the laws of Palmyra and of the tribes, her life is forfeit. Even out among the dunes, we know how proud Palmyra is of its justice. If you have a shred of honor, you'll send my brother's killer to her death."

Odenathus regards Antiochus with amusement. "Perhaps I ought to bring the woman here, question her motives, and judge her for myself."

Vorod, still standing beside the rich red drapery of the doorway, clears his throat. "My lord, as it happens, the woman in question waits in the hall."

The governor and Antiochus share a surprised glance.

"How can this be?" Antiochus says.

"She arrived minutes after your prisoner did," Vorod replies, smooth and unflappable as ever. "She begged an audience, but I told her she must wait her turn. She gave me her name: Zenobia bat-Zabbai. That is the woman of whom you speak, is it not, Ras?"

Antiochus nods blankly.

"By the gods, then," says the governor, "show her in."

Zenobia sweeps into the chamber in a cloud of jasmine perfume, trailing the golden wisp of her veil and the tinkling chimes of her fineries. Her flat-topped turban shimmers with drapes of electrum discs, which dance on chains so fine they might be threads woven by some miraculous, glittering spider. Her eyes light with a brief flash of triumph as she watches the governor gaze upon her face, the neckline of her robe, and her small waist in its tight-cinched indigo girdle. The new saffron-yellow gown drifts about her body as she moves, and when Odenathus's eyes travel down its length to its purple hem, his face goes thoughtful and still. Zenobia quells a smile.

She clasps her hands and sinks easily to the floor, kneeling straight-backed and graceful on the governor's plush Sasanian carpet. "I hope, my lord, you do not find me too bold in coming without being summoned."

Jadhima the Tanukh snarls and lunges at her, reaching with his rope-bound hands, but the Amlaqi guards hold him back, barking warnings like a pack of Roman mastiffs. Zenobia, unperturbed, glances up at the struggling captive with a dismissive sniff, then turns her dark, liquid eyes on Odenathus.

"How did you know, young woman, that I would wish to speak with you?" Odenathus struggles to hide a grin of open wonder.

"I did not know it, my lord," she admits. Her voice is still pitched high, thanks to her youth, but it has a certain incipient darkness to it, a low richness that will mature in the coming years to the smoky tones of a priestess or a queen—a woman of great natural power. "I'd heard talk among the servants that my brother's captive wished to see me punished for the crime of defending my virtue and my life. When I saw my brother's men leading the prisoner to your estate, I thought perhaps my testimony could be of use to you. I wish only to serve Palmyra however I may."

"Please rise," Odenathus says, extending his hand. "There is no need to kneel."

She takes his hand lightly in her own. Zenobia's skin is soft and warm, but Odenathus can detect no shy, girlish tremble. She stands as smoothly as she knelt, holding his hand without shifting any of her weight onto his arm.

"This Tanukh says you killed his brother."

Zenobia looks first to Antiochus, her two fine, sharp brows arcing in surprise, then to the captive. "Did I?"

"Indeed," Antiochus says. "He calls for your blood, Little Sister."

She tosses her head, and the discs of her turban catch the light streaming in from the window. The morning sun flashes on her brow. "I could hardly have allowed myself to be assaulted, could I?" She turns a coy look upon Odenathus. To his surprise, her next words are in perfect Latin. "The Tanukh hunger for blood even more than the gnats on the banks of the Orontes. They are about as strong as gnats, too, if a woman can kill one of them."

"Not just any woman, I think," Odenathus says, and Zenobia smiles at the compliment. "Tell me why you have come. Truthfully, now. It is not to assist me with your brother's captive."

"Yes," Antiochus breaks in, frowning. "Do tell. I am sure we all are thoroughly baffled."

Zenobia considers the young chief for a moment with a dark, side-long glance. Her lips purse in thought. Then she says to Odenathus, this time in flawless Greek, "I have come to petition you, my lord governor, in the matter of my marriage."

"No Greek," Antiochus demands, annoyed. The daughters of Zabbai were carefully schooled in all the tongues of trade, but Antiochus has been forced to learn his languages in the streets. He is good with Latin, and of course speaks the patois of city and tribe with ease. But Greek has always evaded him, and Zenobia knows it well.

She continues as if the sheikh has not spoken. "I am seventeen and in need of a husband. My father is gone now, and cannot make a good match for me. If I do not find a suitable man soon, my brother-in-law here will marry me off to some old fat caravanner and be done with it."

Odenathus strokes his chin once more. He watches the seething Jadhima carefully, then considers Antiochus, whose brow is furrowed in a frown as he stares helplessly at his young sister-in-law. The girl herself, standing between them, is poised, her head held high, like a hunting eagle perched and ready on a falconer's glove. He concedes to her unspoken appeal for privacy and answers in the Greek she prefers. "Antiochus tells me you saved Palmyra."

Zenobia gives one simple nod. She is not evasive, nor does she demur. There is nothing humble about this woman. The heroine of a city ought to be humble, Odenathus thinks—as any woman should be. But even so, he finds her unapologetic boldness alluring.

"A woman who saves a city from raiders certainly does deserve a husband who can stand as her equal," Odenathus says.

"I am glad you agree, my lord."

"So, then, if you fear your brother will not choose a suitable match, what sort of husband do you desire, Zenobia bat-Zabbai?"

The girl does not answer with her voice. Instead, she glances down at the hem of her own gown. Odenathus, too, is compelled to rest his eyes upon the brilliant band of deep-purple silk. It pools around her narrow feet like the shadows of the oasis.

Roman nobility, he sees. *That is what she wants.*

But there is only one man in all of Palmyra who can claim such exalted status. He looks up quickly, and her eyes also lift from the gown's hem to meet his own. Zenobia holds the governor's gaze, and her face is both confident and willing.

She says, "I hope you don't find me too bold in saying so, my lord, but in the week since you've returned to Palmyra there has been a certain amount of talk."

"Talk?"

"That perhaps a marriage alliance with Eran is no longer prudent."

"I see," Odenathus says quietly.

Zenobia gives a soft shrug. "Even with your marriage to a Sasanid—and one of their royal line—they still saw fit to mock your efforts on Rome's behalf, and to raid Antioch as well. Perhaps it is time you took a Palmyrene wife. I know a certain eligible girl. She's a daughter of the beloved Amlaqi chief and has learned much from him—about the city, about trade, about politics. She could be of use to you, a tribal counselor in your own home. She is descended from great queens, and, best of all, she saved your city. Palmyra loves her."

Fairuza, Odenathus thinks desperately. His heart lurches at the thought of it, at the reality of what the girl proposes. Yet here, after all, is the answer to his troubles. The story of Zenobia's heroism will soon leak out—such tales always do—and even if she had not risked her own life and virtue for Palmyra's sake, she is the daughter of Zabbai, a man who was loved even by babes in their mothers' arms.

It is not done in Rome, taking more than one wife. Even living in its far-flung reaches as he does, Odenathus has always tried to exist in harmony with the empire and its laws. But the practice of taking several wives is not unheard of in Palmyra. It is quite common among some of the tribesmen.

Rome does owe me a great favor, Odenathus thinks, *for Antioch and for Valerian. There is no doubt the new emperor will turn a blind eye to it. He may even be relieved if I do not continue in sole marital bond with the treacherous Sasanids. Palmyrenes will certainly judge no error. For them, it's not unusual—and this is their heroine, their brave, beautiful savior. My citizens will rejoice to see her married to me.*

And the girl is certainly beautiful—no man can deny it. Odenathus allows his eyes to travel once more down the length of her frame. The suggestion of new-flowered womanly curves, hinting through her bright silks, is as tempting as a bowl of cool, firm fruit on a hot summer day.

Rome owes me a great favor.

"You know, I have a wife already," Odenathus says.

Zenobia gives one slow blink, dismissing Fairuza. "Many men have more than one wife."

"If I agree to take you, you will be a second wife. You will stand lower in status."

"Out of all the women in the city, I will stand only below your first wife."

"Your sons will be last to inherit, behind the son she bore to me."

"We must all be content with our lot in life," says the girl who rode out alone into the desert, the girl who stands unrepresented before the governor to offer herself into Palmyra's highest marriage.

Odenathus wonders when this woman has ever been content with anything in her life.

"I shall teach my sons to accept what is theirs, and to expect nothing else," she says.

Odenathus gives her one crooked, doubting smile. But he turns to Antiochus and speaks again in a language the chief understands. "Tell Jadhima that he must go without his vengeance. And you need not trouble yourself with finding this woman a husband, Ras. It seems she has found one already."

6

SECOND WIFE

It will never do for the governor's betrothed to go to her marriage riding astride a camel. Zenobia is suddenly, almost painfully aware that with the attainment of the status she has craved for so long, she must also put away such hoydenish feats and don dignity like a fine robe. She would have preferred Feather's saddle to a litter. The aches from her nighttime ride have faded, and now she only remembers the tense excitement, the freedom of the night wind whipping across the dunes. But as solemnity dictates, she allows herself to be carried from her father's palace on a litter made of Lebanon cedar, albeit without the shouts and parading that would accompany another bride to her groom. Respect both for her father—the mourning period is not yet over, although he died three weeks ago—and for the governor's first wife dictates the celebration be understated.

She does not wear a new gown, as a Palmyrene bride should. The saffron silk with the purple hem has served its purpose better than any bride's robe could. Now it lies in a wooden chest, folded carefully between layers of scented linen amid her other garments and treasures, which are packed into panniers, strapped to the humps of a few camels who follow her litter—Feather is among them, of course—like a merchant's train striking out into the desert.

Zenobia does not look back at the walls of the palace, the only home she has known. Instead she watches the world ahead as she passes beneath the palace's outer gate. The litter slopes down the hill toward the Great Row. Since Zabbai's death, the palace has not been the sanctuary of peace and loveliness it once was. Those times seem far gone now, an era long past, like the glorious days of Cleopatra or Julia Domna. Now its halls are washed by her mother's tears, its windows shadowed by Nafsha's scorn. The palace belongs to Nafsha now—to her and the new chief. Zenobia is no part of it. She never will be again.

Instead, she watches the small, pale dot of the governor's estate grow larger between the distant columns of the Great Row. It is perched on a small rise of its own—just a little hillock, really, barely high enough to afford a view of the amphitheater's clean-swept bowl, the nearby bronze pyramids of the Temple of Nebo, and, across the Great Row, the columned baths, lending the welcome scent of water and crushed herbs to the dry Palmyrene air. Zabbai's palace is somewhat removed from the press of the city's throngs, but Odenathus lives in the very midst of the people, and Zenobia feels a stir of happy anticipation at the thought of this sparkling new life, this new home in the center of the world.

"You seem pleased with yourself."

The sides of her litter are draped with indigo wool, and she pulls one swaying length aside to find the guard Zabdas riding beside her. He smiles down at her from the height of his camel's saddle. His grin is crooked, almost reluctant.

Zenobia says, "Shouldn't I be?"

"I make no accusation, my lady."

"My sisters think I've no cause to be pleased."

"Oh?"

"Nafsha is scandalized that I'm to be a man's second wife, even if that man is the governor, and scandal always makes her furious. Zabibah wept for me, but I couldn't make out through her tears whether she was crying because I was leaving or because I would never have the privileges of a first wife. I don't know why they carried on so. It's not unusual, is it?"

Zabdas shrugs.

"If I'd been a first wife," Zenobia says, "and my husband took another bride, even Nafsha wouldn't bat an eye. They're making much out of nothing, and I told them so."

"And your mother?" Zabdas says.

"Mother has more sense than either of my sisters. She knows I played the governor well."

Zabdas blinks, startled at such boastful words from a girl of seventeen. Then he throws back his head and roars with laughter. "Indeed?"

She slits her dark eyes at him. "Men always laugh whenever a woman says she has political skill. But it's not such a difficult thing to master."

"Isn't it?"

"Mock me all you like, Zabdas the guardsman. But politicians are all men, and any man may be influenced when one knows what motivates him. The Romans think only their highbred sons may take up politicking. To them, it is a rigorous and mysterious trade—far beyond the capabilities of a mere woman. But I am not a Roman. I *observe*, as any woman might. I *think*. And therefore I can master even the governor of Palmyra."

Zabdas's mouth twists in a doubtful grimace.

"I go to him as a bride, do I not?" Zenobia waves one hand curtly, indicating her litter, the train of camels with their panniers full of goods. "You see the proof of my skill before your very eyes, and yet you still taunt me with your foolish grin."

"I? Never, my lady."

"This"—she waves one slender hand again, taking in the roadway that stretches to the governor's estate, even the city of Palmyra itself, as though it waits for her like a patient hound—"is nothing more than my inheritance. Nafsha may be scandalized and Zabibah may be weeping, but I go to my just place. Cleopatra did the same."

"The same?"

"She used her knowledge of men's hearts to achieve her ambitions. And Dido—she did, as well."

"Dido with her oxhide—oh yes." Zabdas chuckles.

"I am descended from them both. Great queens—and I will be great, too."

"Dido," the guardsman ventures, his short-bearded face serious now, "was compelled to take her own life rather than give in to the man she'd thought to manipulate. And Cleopatra lost Egypt."

Clicking her tongue in irritation, Zenobia lets the drapery swing between them again. She can hear the shuffling gait of the camel, its blowing breaths, and the creak of Zabdas's weight against the saddletree. He neither falls back nor moves to the head of her tiny procession, and after a moment, Zenobia seizes the blue wool with an impatient hand. She tucks it behind her cushions so that she can see Zabdas clearly, and stares up at him with eyes that say, *Speak then!*

"Do you have any regrets?" he asks her.

"Zabibah," she says at once. Her surety surprises her. "Who will look after my sister now that I'm moving away? Oh, I know she has her husband, but not even Vakat can be as good to her as I was. When I'm married to Odenathus, I'll have little time for my sister. How often will we see each other? I can't say. I feel as if I'm abandoning her." The words spill out of her. Zabibah was not a factor she had considered until now. It has all come to pass so quickly, and confronted with the reality of her future, it seems Zabibah's weeping eyes and trembling lips are all Zenobia can see. "Nafsha has no patience for Zabibah's soft ways.

If her husband shouts at her or makes her unhappy, who will Zabibah turn to?"

"Your sister is all you regret—nothing else?"

"Nothing."

"Do you love your new husband, my lady?"

Zenobia scoffs. "Love? What has love to do with a marriage?"

Again he chuckles at her, at the indignant flush rising to her sharp-angled cheeks and the falcon-fierce, suspicious stare. He laughs, too, at the naivety of her response. For all her valor and strength, she is still barely more than a girl—and one who has grown up sheltered and petted in the chief's palace. Zabdas turns his face casually toward the Great Row, but still he peers at her from the corner of his eye, shadowed by his turban.

She seems as cool and carven as a statue of a goddess, he thinks, *but any urchin child in Palmyra's alleys—any barefoot girl of the dune tribes—likely knows more about life than this fresh little bud of a queen.*

But then he recalls the body of the slain Tanukh, the darkness of blood staining moonlit sand. Sheltered and petted she may be, yet still she swung the sword. Perhaps, Zabdas concedes, there is more of Cleopatra and Dido in her than even she thinks.

Of course she screamed like a snared rabbit as she swung the blade at her attacker, and went pale and quivery when the deed was done. He would laugh, but some insistent weight in his chest forbids it.

"Sober all at once," Zenobia teases. "Is it a toothache, loyal Zabdas? An illness of the bowels?"

"It is not becoming for a lady of your station to mock her servants. Especially a servant as devoted as I."

"*My* servant?"

"Yes, my lady. I requested that I be sent along with your goods. Your mother was happy to grant my request—a reward for my good service in keeping you alive on your little foray into the desert. So here I am, packed off to the governor's estate like one of your chests full of gowns. I have a suspicion that this marriage may go harder on you than you anticipate. The governor's first wife is rumored to be even more difficult than you, and I thought you could use a friend in your new household." He adds under his breath, "But the gods help Lucius Septimius Odenathus."

Zenobia holds still a moment, rocking and shifting with the movement of the litter. Then the perfect, smooth shape of her young face breaks with a bright grin. She pulls the drapery free of her cushions and flings it between them. It flutters as it settles into place, but through that soft barrier, as shifting and permeable as water, Zabdas can hear her girlish laughter.

***

The marriage is done in the Roman fashion, for though she considers herself no Roman, Zenobia will not cause any more discomfort to her new husband than is strictly necessary. Odenathus is well known as a loyal man of the empire, and for him, only a Roman ceremony will do.

If he feels any discomfort at taking a second wife—in bold opposition to Roman edict—he does not show it. Only a diplomatic calm shows on the face of the governor as he waits for his bride to arrive among a small group of witnesses. None of the witnesses are Zenobia's family. They refused to participate in a Roman ceremony—Berenikë may admire her youngest daughter's political skill, but even she has her limits. Still, at dawn they did wash and dress her in the palace's garden, under the open sky, as the Amlaqi do for a new bride. Zenobia cherishes the memory, and lifts a wrist to sniff the perfumed oil Zabibah rubbed into her skin.

Her litter deposits her in the blooming, sweet-smelling courtyard. Her camels cush, and her servants stand milling nervously, glancing about the grounds of their fine new home. When Zenobia leaves the privacy of her litter, the neutral calm flees the governor's face, and

Odenathus stares at the young woman who has come to this new, daring marriage, with a hunger in his eyes that he cannot, and does not, conceal.

One of Zenobia's serving women comes forward with the burning brand, bearing fire from the hearth of her childhood home, and Zenobia turns to take the torch. The governor's eyes move freely over the smooth, slender arm of his bride. The fire tints her olive-gold skin with a warm, enticing hue. She steps forward to light the torch that Odenathus holds, and their eyes meet over the kindling blaze. Zenobia's look is full of both promise and challenge, but there's no hint of apology for the difficulty into which she has maneuvered her new husband.

Odenathus hands the newly lit brand to Vorod, who bears it out of sight to the kitchens. Then the governor accepts a golden chalice full of water from one of his men. It is inlaid with a row of fine lapis lazuli flowers. When Odenathus turns, and the pure water within splashes over the cup's rim, the dampened lapis blooms seem to glow in the sun.

Zenobia takes the cup from her husband's hands. Her fingers brush his, and she detects a strange, thrumming energy stirring beneath his skin. It makes her face heat as she raises the water to her lips. But the blush of her cheeks and the tension that coil in her stomach have nothing to do with a new bride's sweet anticipation. It is a flush of power she feels. As young as she is, Zenobia understands what the tremble in Odenathus's body means: he is hers; her beauty and youth have won him. Through the governor and his desire for her, there is nothing she cannot obtain.

She lowers the cup and speaks the words of their sealing in Latin, to please Odenathus, to please Rome. "Where you are Gaius, I am Gaia."

"Where you are Gaia," Odenathus replies in his hoarse but cultured voice, "I am Gaius."

It is done.

Zenobia turns toward her servants and stretches out an arm, waiting for all the hands of her household to lift her and carry her across the threshold, into her new life. But it is not her servants' arms that lift her up. Zabdas steps forward before the women can act. He picks her up as easily as one might lift a bit of silk. She throws both arms around his neck, pulling herself close to his body, tensing at the unfamiliar sensation of being borne through the air like a white-fringed seed on a warm summer wind. Her guardsman's neck smells of camels and leather, and his body is able and strong.

Zenobia shifts until her veil swings, hiding her face from the servants as Zabdas follows the governor over the threshold and into the cool, dark beauty of the palace. She is not fast enough to hide her sudden discomfiture from all those who watch. Among the onlookers is a small but stately woman wrapped in silks the color of a morning sky. She stands stiff and quiet in the face of this blow to her dignity. As the servants flutter around her, as the interloper's camels are coaxed to their feet and led away, Fairuza's eyes never leave Zenobia's face. The drape of the veil cannot disguise the color that rises to the girl's cheeks. Nor does Fairuza fail to note how near Zenobia draws to the young guard's skin, the way her slender rib cage swells as she breathes in his masculine scent.

The first wife of the governor narrows her eyes, but she holds her tongue as she follows the throng into the palace.

***

Fairuza knows when to speak and when to keep her own counsel. It is a skill she learned early.

Her mother had been a true *dukšiš* of Eran—a woman of great standing—a prized jewel in the court of her cousin, the king, and Fairuza had served as her mother's handmaid. Although her mother was beautiful and kind, as a small child Fairuza had resented the work. She would rather have been outside in the gardens, playing with the other little girls—not waiting on her mother's needs while the great men of King Ardashir's court, and their wives and concubines, discussed politics and the ways of the world.

But as she grew older and wiser, Fairuza came to appreciate her education. She learned swiftly at her mother's side, and by the time she was fourteen—and promised in marriage to Palmyra's governor—she had no patience for the flights and fancies of other girls her age. She had felt herself ready for the task that lay before her. She had been confident in her powers to win the Palmyrene's heart, to use all the wiles and wisdom of a *dukšiš* to influence her husband, and to bind him and Eran to peace.

It is only now, as she paces down the long hallway of her husband's home, that she understands what a fool she was. Now, at the age of thirty-two, her youth long behind her, she wonders whether she ever had any power in Palmyra at all. It is no surprise to her that Septimius Odenathus has turned his eye toward a young and beautiful woman—she will not allow herself to feel surprised. Men have their predictable tastes, every one of them—and even a *dukšiš* cannot stay young and appealing forever. It is not that she loves Odenathus—not precisely. But one cannot live and work for eighteen years beside any man without feeling some bond to him, some affection. One cannot bear a man a son—his only child—without hoping she might find a place in his heart.

The doorway to the new wife's quarters looms out of the shadows of the hall. It is red-lacquered and carved, and has been scrubbed and polished by the household servants until it looks as new and fresh as the second wife herself.

Fairuza hesitates only a moment as she stands watching the door. *Mother,* she thinks, giving in to a rare moment of vulnerability, *if only you still lived. If only you were here to guide me.*

Never—not once, in all the years she spent at her mother's side, fetching and fanning and sprinkling cinnamon into her wine—did she ever see her mother put out by another woman. She was always unflappable, serene as an alabaster statue in the face of every challenge.

Fairuza draws herself up. She gathers her blue silk robes about her body, a body that for all her years is still shapely and firm. The daughter of a *dukšiš* has nothing to fear from some nomad-bred trespasser, some sheikh's brat with sand between her toes. After all, it is Fairuza who has given Odenathus what all men prize beyond any other thing: a son.

Her spine steeled by that thought, she pushes open the door.

The new second wife is sitting quietly on a couch of flame-orange silk, hands folded in her lap, face painted with a calm half smile as if she has expected Fairuza's visit. The artful folds of her veil accentuate the supple length of the girl's neck, and its drapings frame her unblemished, youthful face.

Fairuza watches her in expectant silence. The girl makes no move—doesn't even blink—and at last Fairuza says, "You are to stand in my presence."

"Am I?" Zenobia replies, and remains sitting. She is gratified to see Fairuza's chest expand with a lengthy, indrawn breath. The first wife is struggling for control, Zenobia notes, although her breath is the only sign of it. The sharp angles of her Sasanid face are not unlovely, Zenobia admits without grudge, and they betray nothing of the anger she feels.

"Do you deny," Fairuza says calmly, "that I am the mistress of this household? You may have turned Roman custom on its ear, but since when has a second wife of the nomad tribes ever ruled a household?"

Fair enough, Zenobia thinks. *She has me there.* She rises to her feet.

Fairuza gives a tiny nod. "Thank you. It will go better for both of us if we understand one another—if we keep to our respective places. I have always run the estate of Odenathus with peace and dignity, since I was a girl younger than you. I will not see anyone beneath my husband's roof—servant or second wife—disgrace herself by inciting needless trouble."

Zenobia bristles visibly at the implication that she has no more standing than a kitchen maid or a seamstress.

But Fairuza continues before Zenobia can protest: "It is particularly important that you keep to your place, Zenobia, in light of the danger you've put this household in. You must not overstep. Thanks to you we are all precarious."

"Danger?" Zenobia tosses her head like a horse defying its bridle.

"Rome will not be pleased."

"Rome," the girl breathes, almost a snort of disgust. "What have we to fear from Rome?"

"Plenty. It is the greatest empire in the world, with resources and powers you cannot imagine."

"Distant," Zenobia says, waving a hand in dismissal. "May I sit?"

Fairuza makes the girl stand in silence a moment longer, then finally nods. Zenobia sinks back onto her couch in a sigh of silks.

"How many years has it been since Rome had a worthy emperor?" Zenobia says. "And in any case, they cannot do without Palmyra, all those far-off nobles and senators. Gods preserve us, what would happen if their shipments of dyes and spices stopped coming? If their complaints are to be believed, the very heavens would fall down."

Despite her wariness of the girl, despite the hollow sense of betrayal and loss settling into her gut, Fairuza cannot help but smile. She has heard Odenathus read from letters, as Zenobia must have heard her father read. Fairuza is well acquainted with the complaints of Rome.

The girl is encouraged by Fairuza's smile. She says with the brash self-assurance only the very young can possess, "The days of fearing the empire are long gone."

The smile slips away from Fairuza. "That, they are not."

"Valerian got himself captured by your people. And managed his own death into the bargain."

"All emperors are not like Valerian."

"Oh, indeed," Zenobia says, laughing, "Trebonianus and his son, killed by their own soldiers; Aemilian ruled only two months before he was murdered. Hostilian, dead of the plague—good for us that the gods struck him down early. No telling what disaster such a weakling might have led the empire into. The Goths killed Etruscus and Decius—and Decius killed both the Philips before him. Shall I go on? I can, you know, for a dozen emperors more!"

Fairuza cuts her off with a wave of one hand. "It's clear that you know your history well. But do not make the mistake, Zenobia, of believing that Rome will never produce a worthy emperor again. The empire has a long history, and more great men have worn the purple than weaklings or fools. It is only a matter of time before Rome rises again, and when it does, it will be steady and sure. When that happens, I shouldn't like to be in the empire's disfavor."

It has been a long time since Zenobia has had a discussion so enjoyable. Fairuza, she now sees, is more than the jealous harpy she'd thought to find in the governor's household. She slides down her couch, making room for the first wife, and gestures an invitation to sit. But Fairuza declines with one small shake of her head. When she remains standing, Zenobia recalls her mother, imperious Berenikë, with a pang of longing and regret.

"I cannot stay and entertain you," Fairuza says. "I have my duties to attend. I wished only to instruct you to keep to your place and watch your step, for the sake of my husband."

"Our husband," Zenobia says quietly.

"Consider the danger you have put Odenathus in, and be wary."

"Odnat is a powerful man. He can handle Rome."

Fairuza gives a tiny, disbelieving gasp—for which she instantly curses herself. *"Odnat?"* It is the Aramaic form of the governor's name, as un-Roman as anything can possibly be, and to hear her husband referred to in such a way—to hear him uncoupled from the empire he has always served—fills her with an unspeakable dread.

"Don't you think that name suits him better?" the girl asks, her eyes wide in a parody of innocence.

"Don't be a fool. *Odenathus* has declared his loyalty to Rome—and whatever *you* may think of recent emperors—you, with your seventeen years of wisdom!—*our* husband knows best. Our husband is not such a powerful man that he can afford to defy Rome."

Zenobia leans back easily on her couch. She herself is a defiance of Rome. "By capitulating to Rome, *Odenathus*, if you please, is only stripping himself of power."

"I'm sure he would be wise to take political instruction from the child of a desert chief. Pull back your veil, girl, and show me where you're still wet behind the ears!" She is breathing heavily, stirred to open anger by the needling of this arrogant little she-whelp. Fairuza hides her hands inside her sleeves so that Zenobia cannot see how her fists clench, how they tremble with sudden fury.

"It's true," says the second wife. "Odenathus holds the loyalty of Palmyra—not only the great merchants, with all the wealth Rome relies on, but the very desert chiefs you disparage. Tell me, Fairuza, do you suppose any caravan from the East can reach Rome without the cooperation of the desert tribes?"

Fairuza's stillness is answer enough. Zenobia presses on: "And I, as a daughter of those same tribes, am now a link to power, as you once were."

"Once?" Fairuza says. Her voice is low and breathy, like the hiss of a cobra. "How dare you! I am all that holds this alliance together—all that keeps Eran compliant with Rome!"

"How well that has worked of late. Shall we ask Emperor Valerian whether the alliance still holds firm?"

Despite her flippant and goading speech, Zenobia tenses. She knows she has pushed Fairuza too far—beyond what any reasonable woman might be expected to endure. She braces for the first wife to fly at her, to strike her face, to claw at her with sharp nails. But Fairuza only watches her in silence, her dark eyes flat and patient, assessing.

Voices drift through the window—buoyant, masculine laughter, followed by a pause, then the cheers of several men. Fairuza turns away from Zenobia and walks to the sill. She says, "Come here, girl," and Zenobia, used to obeying Berenikë's commands, responds before she can stop herself.

The window looks out into the long, walled expanse of the garden. A few palms cast a patchy shade over the dusty earth; flowering shrubs and vines spread between the twisting paths. A knot of young men is gathered at the far end of the garden, milling and shouting.

One of them, dressed in a loose silk tunic embroidered with Palmyrene hexagons, lifts a javelin to his shoulder, testing its balance while his peers dare him and kick playfully at his ankles. The dust of their jostling obscures his face for a moment, but there is no mistaking the black, wavy hair, or the deep set of his eyes. The boy looks distinctly Sasanid. Ignoring his friends, he throws the javelin. It embeds itself with a thump and a shudder in the center of a hair-stuffed target at the garden's far end. The young men let out a collective whoop of glee and pound the Sasanid's back.

"Your son," Zenobia says. Who else could he be?

"Hairan. My son," Fairuza confirms. "The only child of Lucius Septimius Odenathus. The next time you think to gloat over your own imagined power, Zenobia, think on Hairan. There is nothing that binds a man's heart like a son. Even a young, pretty face cannot compete with that sort of power."

"Do you imagine we are in competition?" Zenobia says lightly.

"Don't think for a moment that I believe you will get a son of your own," the first wife says, ignoring Zenobia's question. She watches Hairan trot down the garden to retrieve his spear. "It takes trying—plenty of attempts—especially for a girl of your age. I know what a young woman's tastes are, and Odenathus is not the sort of man who sets girls like you to dreaming."

Zenobia thinks fleetingly of Zabdas. She can feel the first wife's eyes on her face—a dangerous, all-seeing stare. *I should have been more humble. I should have given her what she wanted, and stood when she entered, and kept my tongue still instead of goading her.* She turns to Fairuza with a frown. "What are you saying?"

The Sasanid nods lightly toward her son. "Stay away from Hairan, Zenobia. I shall have my eye on you."

Something in Fairuza's cool, calculating demeanor puts Zenobia on edge. Perhaps Zenobia has gone too far in needling the first wife, for there is a predatory gleam in Fairuza's eye and a hardness about her mouth that makes the younger woman feel suddenly out of her depth. Nafsha's voice crowds into her thoughts. *One day you'll overstep yourself, and then you'll finally wish you'd learned humility.*

I must tread with care, Zenobia tells herself. *I mustn't ruin my status before I've even begun to enjoy it.* A rush of comprehension overwhelms her, and she blushes with shame at her own overconfidence. Fairuza, she now understands, has real power. Fairuza is dangerous, and Zenobia has made an enemy of the first wife.

Zenobia lowers her eyes at once, bending her neck to Fairuza. She realizes it is not enough merely to deny Fairuza's implied accusations. She must become the opposite of a prowling she-cat, a woman hot between the thighs for a man—any young man—so long as it's not gray-haired Odenathus. Zenobia must be as unlike a she-cat as night is unlike day. Otherwise, Fairuza's accusations—when they come—will be accepted as true. Fairuza has the son: Fairuza has the power.

"I am only for my husband," Zenobia says quietly. "I have no interest in other men."

"None at all?" Fairuza replies in a voice rich with suppressed laughter. "Not even your guard?"

Zenobia glances up sharply, eyes wide with unfeigned surprise. Before she can bring herself back under control, Fairuza has swept from the room, and Zenobia is left alone with the sounds of the young men shouting, the hiss of the flying javelin, and the pounding of her heart.

7

A Cut to the Thigh

Zenobia comes awake slowly. The palms overhead rustle with the last of the morning's wind. The sound is dry, nearly hoarse, like Zabdas's voice—his low, impertinent laughter. She shifts beneath the camels' blankets. They are lighter than she remembered, and softer, too. She breathes deep, drawing in their scent, searching for the dusty, animal richness of the stables, the warm, close smell of Zabdas's neck. But the smell is all wrong. It's a light, soft perfume she detects, spicy and floral, and the ground beneath her is not the cold, uneven sand of Tadmor. It is far too soft, too comfortable—a mattress.

All at once, reality seizes her. She is not lying in the shelter of the oasis at sunrise. She is in her new bed in the governor's house—her husband's house. What she thought was the rustling of palm fronds is only the trickle of the garden fountain. She squeezes her eyes more tightly closed. She wants to be in Tadmor again, with Zabdas watching over her. She wants to open her eyes and find the patchy light playing, blurring among the palm shade. Instead, she knows she will see only the limestone walls of her chamber, the Sasanid carpets of her floor.

She lies still, considering her body. The pain is practically nonexistent. She aches a good deal less than she did after her ride out into the desert. Some hours after Fairuza left, when the anxiety of her confrontation with the first wife had exhausted Zenobia and she was ready for sleep, Odenathus came to her to claim his rights as a husband.

She was calm. She has, after all, two married sisters and a mother who has always been forthright, if modest, in her speech. Zenobia knew what to expect. And Odenathus was gentle and considerate, praising her with soft words, doing what he thought appropriate to prepare her. It had hurt some when he entered her—but no more than a skinned knee hurts, and Zenobia did not tremble or weep. When it was over, Odenathus kissed her on the brow and departed, pulling his robe around his body, fading into the blue of her chamber's shadows before he'd even reached the door. This will be easy enough, she thinks. Odenathus is a burden she can carry.

She stirs and sits up, pulling her coverlet aside. Between her bare legs, the linen sheet is unstained. Zenobia springs from the bed and searches, smoothing wrinkles from the sheet with both hands. She shakes out her blanket as if the proof of her chastity might tumble out of its folds, like beads from a broken necklace. But her bedding is spotless.

"Oh, blast of wind!" she curses.

This means nothing, she knows. Not all women bleed the first time. Zenobia was a virgin—she could swear to the truth of that, with one hand on a statue of the goddess Allāt. But Fairuza will take her unstained sheet as proof that Zenobia was spoiled before she came to the governor's bed—proof that she is the harlot Fairuza wants her to be. And once that thought is planted in his mind, Odenathus will take Zenobia's cool composure at his visit as evidence for her harlotry.

"Couldn't I have shed one tear?" Zenobia scolds herself, muttering aloud in her distraction. "Couldn't I have trembled a little when he came to me, like a proper virgin?"

The chambermaids will soon arrive to change the linens. Zenobia is not fool enough to believe that they will refrain from gossiping about the state of her sheets—or that even the most sensible of them will not spill out all she knows the moment the first wife offers a gold pendant or a new set of earrings.

At the edge of her room, past the soft pile of her carpets, Zenobia's cedar boxes and woven palm baskets are still mostly packed, awaiting the arrival of fine new chests, bridal gifts from her husband. She rummages in one basket until she finds her embroidery kit, then draws a needle from a thin leather packet. She holds the needle up to a shaft of morning light that spills in over the windowsill. The needle shines with a muted glimmer. Zenobia draws it sharply across the soft, tender skin of her inner thigh.

Even though she knows the pain is coming, it still makes her gasp. The needle slips from her fingertips and pings on the hard, bare floor. She crosses to her bed and lies down carefully, trying to recall the position of her legs while Odenathus rode her.

She holds herself still, spread like a captive, until the blood of her thigh beads and runs. She counts the droplets and tries to think of Odenathus, but all she can feel, other than the tickle of her dripping blood, is the memory of Zabdas behind her in the saddle, swaying with the camel's gait, holding her as she slipped into the mercy of sleep.

**

When the maids come to freshen her room and serve her breakfast, they smile approvingly at the stains on the sheet, red and round and scattered like cast-off garnets. Zenobia only gives the women a dignified sniff. She has dressed herself this morning, so no one will see the cut on her thigh.

The women chatter as they go about their work, and Zenobia turns to the food with rising appetite. Odenathus's cooks are even better than Zabbai's. There are stewed figs spiced with cinnamon; bread covered with crumbling, rose-scented goat cheese; and strips of pigeon breast, lightly fried, so freshly cooked that the hot oil still bubbles and snaps on the golden-brown meat.

One of the maids bows a little as she spreads a clean sheet over Zenobia's mattress. "Your new cedar chests are to be delivered this afternoon, mistress, from the best carver in the city."

Zenobia nods. She cannot speak—her mouth is full of figs.

"And, oh—the governor will attend a performance this evening at the amphitheater."

At Zenobia's request, the maids hold up a selection of skirts and tunics, commenting on the fine hand of the fabrics and the beguiling cut of each one, but she rejects them all.

"Bring me something modest," she says. "Something suited to a newly married woman. I can't have half the men in Palmyra gaping at me, can I? I'm the governor's wife!"

At last the maids find a robe with a high neckline and no hint of transparency to the sleeves. Zenobia inspects it: wool. Fine-woven, to be sure, and as light as any wool can hope to be, but it is not as airy as even the coarsest silk. It is dark blue, thoroughly dyed with plenty of indigo. It will still be hot out by the time the performance at the amphitheater begins. Zenobia can already feel the discomfort, can picture herself sweltering in the long-sleeved wool, its deep color drinking in the final fierce heat of day. But dressed in such a garment for all the city to see, no one will believe any slander Fairuza might try to cultivate. Only a preposterously chaste woman would ever wear such a robe.

"It will do," she says. "And a turban with minimal adornments. Set them there, on my couch. Now clear breakfast away and leave me, all of you. I need to think and pray"—*and plan,* she says silently—"and I would be alone."

* * *

The great stone bowl of the amphitheater collects heat like a cistern collects water. The voices of hundreds of men and women pour down its stepped, sloping, limestone sides; the stamping of their feet as they search for seating and their shouts and laughter press all around; the smell of close perfumed bodies is thick in the evening air. The presence of so many people only intensifies the evening's warmth, and Zenobia, seated in Odenathus's private box near the foot of the stage, fans her face with a painted, pleated half-moon of papyrus. She would curse the indigo wool, save for the way Fairuza looked at her when she arrived in Odenathus's courtyard. The flick of the first wife's eyes over the robe's high neckline and unrevealing weave was enough to make Zenobia grin in triumph as she climbed aboard the palanquin that would carry the governor and his family to the amphitheater. Fairuza was studiously quiet on the ride, and Zenobia kept her eyes carefully, modestly, on her own slippered feet.

Now, though, as the amphitheater fills and the musicians begin to warm their harps and horns, she turns in her seat, craning her neck to see past the ledge of the governor's box. Perhaps she might catch a glimpse of Nafsha, radiant in saffron-yellow, cool-eyed despite the heat—or Zabibah, muttering shyly behind a painted fan of her own.

"They are not here," Zabdas says. He sits at the edge of the governor's box, one hand resting on the hilt of his dagger—on duty, as ever, protecting his charge.

Zenobia cuts a sharp glance at her guardsman. "How did you know I was looking for my sisters?"

"It is only natural," he says. "A girl like you—"

"*Girl?*" she sputters, but her eyes spark with amusement within the dark boundary of her lashes.

"Woman, then, if you prefer. It is only natural that a new bride should feel some loneliness, and should long for the comforts of her prior, familiar life."

"I am not lonely," she says.

Zabdas turns to her with such earnest curiosity that she is taken aback. "Are you not?" he says.

Zenobia is fiercely aware that Fairuza sits nearby, speaking quietly to the husband they share. She lowers her voice so Fairuza cannot hear. "No, of course not. What cause have I to be lonely? I'm surrounded by servants, and my husband is the most powerful man in Palmyra."

"I don't see what power has to do with companionship."

She flutters her eyelids in disdain at his foolish talk, and will not condescend to answer. But she is acutely aware of his shape, of the simple, masculine harmony of his body, the broad shoulders and the narrow waist, the hardness of his well-trained muscles.

In certain ways, Odenathus is not unlike Zabdas. He was a soldier long before he was a governor, and the strength of a glorious past still clothes him like a bright mantle, draping and concealing the form of a man who is sinking toward his twilight years. And he is kind—a good man, thoughtful and just. That she can say for him. Yet even now, sitting in the theater box with the first wife like a palisade between them, Zenobia can't help but recoil slightly from her husband's age.

Now that she has lain with a man, she begins to see what Zabibah meant when she spoke of finding a husband to make her head dizzy and her senses swoon. Her single night with Odenathus had been a duty, the final act she must perform in order to secure her place in the world. She is grateful that he was kind—relieved, even—yet there was no dizziness in the transaction. Not with Odenathus. Even so, her body has a certain alertness now—a peculiar wakefulness—as if it longs for what Odenathus gave her, but something better, something sweeter. She senses that with the right man, she might derive some real pleasure from the act.

All at once a sweet rush of tingling fire fills her limbs, and Zenobia cannot look at Zabdas, even from the corner of her eye.

There is a veiled corner of her mind that looks on her own discomfiture and aching need with distaste. It has been only a few weeks since Zabbai's death. Of course her family is not here—her mother and sisters are still secluded in the palace, observing their time of grief. She should be in mourning robes, too, hiding her face from the world—but a new bride cannot be seen to mourn, can she? It would cast a pall of ill luck across her marriage. Yet she cannot help but miss the comfort of a strong embrace, the chance to weep for Zabbai on a friendly shoulder. Perhaps her fluster and craving for a man is only the desire to be held, to be sheltered for a time so that she doesn't feel so unspeakably isolated in her loss.

But I am not *lonely,* she tells herself firmly. She will not give Zabdas the satisfaction of being right.

She casts her glance to the opposite end of the box, where Hairan sits on the other side of his father. The young man is quiet and studious; his dark eyes study the stage as servants dressed in bright-colored tunics sweep it free of the dust and stray bits of refuse that have collected there since the previous night's performance. Hairan's forearms rest on his knees, his hands dangling, and Zenobia can't help but notice the smooth, flat muscle of his upper arm, the skin along his thick wrist browned from the sun like a well-baked round of bread.

She has not noticed before how attractive Hairan is. When he threw javelins with his friends in the garden, he had been only a colt at play, someone to be watched with distant amusement. Now he is suddenly a presence, and she can't help but wonder whether his body, thrusting in the darkness, would feel better—more exciting—than his father's.

She recalls herself and blinks, turning quickly away from Hairan. *Gods spare me,* she thinks. *I am every bit the she-cat Fairuza thinks I am.* The moment she turns away from Hairan, she feels the first wife's dark gaze slide over her. *I will be perfect,* Zenobia tells herself. *Chaste, unfailing. I must be. I cannot give Fairuza the satisfaction of being right about me.*

It is to her annoyance—almost her despair—that she learns what the evening's performance will be: a troop of young acrobats,

Egyptian-trained, toned and tanned, performing in the scantiest of silks, both female . . . and male.

Zenobia sighs as the musicians strike the opening chords and the acrobats, their strong, beautiful bodies shimmering with gold dust that catches the light of the oil lamps, array themselves along the edge of the stage. Her dark-blue wool feels very hot indeed. It is going to be a long, wearying evening.

***

When at last they return to the governor's estate, Zenobia is flushed and fierce, as keen as a hungry lion in the dunes. The modest robe scratches her skin with its weave, and even that unpleasantness seems to enflame her. She throbs from head to foot.

To her disappointment, Odenathus shows no inclination to come to her bed. He kisses both his wives on their hands and makes his apologies, then retires to his office, where his deputy, Vorod—that dry, whispering papyrus scrap of a man—has more accounts waiting. Odenathus doesn't make Zenobia's senses swim, yet after the spectacle of the Egyptian acrobats, contorting and posing with their firm, supple bodies on golden display, she craves for her husband—for any relief to the dull, delicious ache inside her. She bids Odenathus and the first wife good night, then walks slowly to her chambers in the darkness.

The air has cooled completely now. The chill of a desert night seeps through the rugs in the hall and presses through the soft soles of her slippers. All at once the loss of her father stabs at her again, as piercing as the cold, and more profoundly than it ever has cut her before. The pain mingles with the heat within, a curious, clear poignancy as strong and deep as bone. She recalls Zabdas turning to her with his raised brows, his look of pure surprise. *I am not lonely,* she tells him in her head, and then insists for the benefit of the dark hallway: "I'm not."

But what, then, is this consuming sense of longing, if not loneliness? This yearning for a man in her bed, for arms around her, for the proximity of warm flesh? What is this sorrow, this knowledge that she will never see Zabbai again or hear him laugh as he rides his camel down the slope toward the Orontes? She would spit it out, if she could. The taste of this whole tangle of loss and lack and sharp desire is as bitter as the pith of a lemon.

She wants something to make her forget Zabbai—to forget Zabibah left undefended in a harsh, bristling world. She wants someone to drive away this desolation. She wants a man.

And so, when she opens her chamber door to find Zabdas pushing and straining against the great, oiled block of a new cedar chest while her maids stand about, calling instructions to him—"Now try it there, beside the window!" "No, just below the window!"—and tittering behind their veils as they watch the muscles in his arms and shoulders bulge, she finds the presence of her guardsman a godsend.

"Out, all of you," she says to the women, making a scattering gesture with her hands. They shuffle and whisper as they leave, casting glances back at Zabdas. It's foolish to send them all away so that she is alone with a man who is not her husband. But right now, she doesn't care.

Once the chest is in place, he, too, heads toward the door, but she lays a hand on his forearm to stop him.

"When did you come to my chambers, Zabdas?"

"As soon as we returned from the amphitheater, mistress. You were still speaking to Odenathus and the first wife. The porter told me your new chests had arrived and mentioned they were too heavy for your maids to move, so I thought . . ."

Softly, Zenobia shuts the door. Her chamber is alive with lamplight, flickering and moving, pulsing like an accelerating heart.

"Do you like that chest there, the largest one—or shall I move it somewhere else?" Zabdas asks.

It would be a lovely game, Zenobia thinks, standing back to watch while he shoves the heavy thing to and fro, working like a stallion harnessed to a chariot. But such frivolities are better suited to maids than to governors' wives. A woman of her stature has no need for coyness. She has the freedom to be direct.

"It's fine," she tells him shortly.

"I hope I didn't offend you."

"Offend me?"

"Back at the amphitheater, mistress, when I asked whether you were lonely."

"Ah." For a moment, one brief, sharp beat like the rap of a drummer's thimble against a drumhead, Zenobia is poised and unshaken. Then she feels her regal surety crumble as she gives in to the rising well of sadness and isolation. Her face sags and shows her desperate longing. "Oh, Zabdas!" she cries.

Startled, he steps away from her. He has never seen her this way, her rigid hauteur softening, melting like a block of beeswax in the sun.

"Oh," she says, reaching out her hands as if she might catch hold of him to keep herself from falling. But her hands close on empty space, and she hugs herself tightly. "I *am* lonely, Zabdas, and sorrowing—and afraid."

"Afraid? What have *you* to be afraid of, bat-Zabbai, the heroine of the city?"

"Fairuza, of course." Abruptly, she turns away from him, so he will not see the angry tears that sting her eyes. "She wants me to slip up. She is watching my every move—watching for my failure. She's jealous and scheming, and the moment I leave myself open to her attack, she'll sting me, just like a desert scorpion." As if to illustrate her point, Zenobia jabs at the air with her finger.

"Can you blame Fairuza?" Zabdas asks. "She's been loyal to Odenathus for all these years, playing the part of the good wife in an arranged, political marriage. She's given no one in Palmyra any reason to doubt or dislike her, and yet her husband takes another wife—much younger and every bit as beautiful. More beautiful, perhaps. What is she to do? Raise a goblet and drink to your health?"

Zenobia tugs at the waist belt of her robe, straightening it, pulling herself together. "If only I weren't so alone," she says, barely louder than a whisper.

"You do have me." Zabdas closes the distance between them in one eager stride, but he does not presume to touch her. "I told you—didn't I?—that you would need a friend. For whatever it's worth, you have me."

She turns and looks up at him. She has blinked the tears away, and now her eyes are steady and dry. "Why? Why do you care whether I have a friend? Don't read me wrong—I am not ungrateful. I only wonder . . ." She falters and her gaze slides to the floor. It is no false show of modesty; Zenobia finds herself gripped by doubt and humility, unaccustomed sensations. Combined with the turmoil of her desolation and desire, she feels untethered, like a tuft of wool floating on a breeze. As surely as Zabibah ever was, Zenobia feels at the mercy of an uncaring world.

"You are brave," Zabdas tells her. "I saw you in the desert, riding to save Palmyra. No man could have watched you that night, rallying Antiochus's men, and not come to . . . to appreciate you."

"Appreciate me?" Her smile is mischievous—a hint of her usual confidence returning.

In the quiet, dancing light of her chamber, she imagines that the world has constricted, falling in upon itself until it is only the shell of lamplight that surrounds the young heroine and her loyal guard. But just on the edge of their private sphere, her troubles still lurk—Fairuza with her watchful eyes, Odenathus and his expectations in a wife, and, most of all, her father's death. The reality of her situation catches up to her stride by stride like a leopard overtaking its prey. She feels these things moving in dark ripples, forming and breaking like a reflection in disturbed water. But they can't penetrate this tiny world, this glowing, golden place where she and Zabdas stand together. The desire she has felt all evening long rushes along her limbs with sudden force, making her gasp and shiver.

Zabdas senses the sudden change in her, the single-minded drive. He takes her by the shoulders, more roughly than he'd intended, but in her heavy-lidded eyes and parted lips, he sees at once that he's forgiven. Beneath the wool of her indigo robe, her body is firm and strong and curved like the graceful lines of a Seres vessel.

She touches his face, tracing the line of the scar that slashes down his cheek to his upper lip. Her hand is as soft as silk, the product of a lifetime untroubled by coarse labor.

"I dreamed of you," she murmurs, her voice a whisper of longing. "Under the palms. I dreamed of you watching over me. I dreamed of you holding me."

Before he can allow his better judgment to stop him, Zabdas has taken her by the nape of the neck, pressing her veils against her skin. He kisses her with such force that she gasps through her nose, and when she exhales, it is with the tiniest whimper—a vulnerable sound, a sound that comes from her most secret and carefully hidden self.

He would do more. She would do more—she nearly commands him, as his mistress, to be loyal and *do more*. But Zabdas masters himself and pulls away.

"Fairuza," he says.

It's all he needs to say. With obvious effort, Zenobia quenches her own flame. "I know. Gods damn her, I know!"

Zabdas laughs, though it has a bitter sound, even to him. "It was you who insisted on marrying the governor."

"If not for her, I might find some way to take a lover on the side. That's not so unusual a thing. Odenathus might not notice. By what my maids tell me, he's always so preoccupied with his duties. But Fairuza has her eye on me. She will see anything—everything."

There is a tickle on Zenobia's inner thigh, then a sensation of burning. All at once, she recalls the needle scratch there, and the blood dripping from the cut as she lay still and deliberate on her sheets. *Deception,* she thinks miserably. *I must keep my place with deception—for I am a she-cat, it seems. I would make Zabdas throw me across my bed and savage my body until this suffocating grief and lust are gone. If only Fairuza would not see the truth, I'd do it. I would do it if there were any hope of keeping my secret.*

Zabdas draws a deep breath. He wants to speak—to tell her that he doesn't care what Fairuza sees, or the governor. But he knows it would mean disgrace for Zenobia, and banishment or worse for him. No words will form, and he lets his breath out in one long, defeated sigh.

"The gods led me here," Zenobia says. "They want me to be the governor's wife. They require it. It's the destiny they've made for me."

To hear Nafsha tell it, Zabdas thinks sourly, *you led yourself here. You made this destiny, built it brick by brick out of your own lust for greatness and your own unshakable pride.* But Zenobia's reckless aplomb is the very thing he loves about her most.

Loves? *Yes,* he tells himself. *Love.*

Zenobia twitches her veil back from her shoulders. She is businesslike now, as straightforward as a camel seller in the marketplace. "My only hope of maintaining my place—and becoming something more, if I can—is to appear as chaste and devoted to my husband as Fairuza is. I must look even more perfect than she. You are my loyal friend, Zabdas, but my maids will gossip, and we must not be alone this way again."

Zabdas nods, unable to look her in the eye. When she dismisses him, regret and relief war inside of him.

It's not until he's crossed the estate, standing on the threshold of his little room in the guardsmen's quarters, that her last words strike him with full force. *Becoming something more, if I can.*

A foreboding chill creeps up his spine and raises the hairs of his scalp. Zabdas turns to look out across the garden, keen-eyed, expecting to see danger slink between the flower beds like beasts on the hunt. But the night is still, wrapped in its cloak of violet cold. Across the governor's estate, the lamp in Zenobia's chamber is still burning.

PART TWO

Septimia Zenobia

266–267 CE

8

A WIFE WILL DO WHAT SHE MUST

From the rooftop of the sprawling estate, Zabdas can see nearly all of Palmyra. It lies like a cat in the sun, pale and sprawling, self-satisfied and warm. The Great Row's surface is so trammeled by generations of traders that it looks like smooth, beaten gold inlaid into the earth, cutting as straight as a bowman's shot through the heart of the city. It is the winter season, when days are short, the light thin and blue-white. Far to the east, a soft-purple density suggests a bank of cloud or mist clinging to the long track of the Orontes. Winter—yet it is unnaturally warm, and the shade from the Great Row's soaring pillars looks as inviting as the cool depths of a stone cellar in the heat of summer.

Zabdas frowns and watches the tiny figures of men and beasts moving among the city's fringes—going out, coming in.

"What are you looking at?"

The moment he hears her voice, as rich and nuanced as expensive wine, he turns. His response is quick and unthinking, an eagle winging to the falconer's call.

"Septimia Zenobia," Zabdas says, bowing.

Zenobia gives a little half toss of her head, and the strings of gems that adorn her turban click and sway. "Don't bow," she says. "You know I hate it when you bow."

"You love it when people bow to you. Don't deny it—not to me. I know you too well."

"Yes, and that's just it." She drifts toward him. Before she reaches him, the dry winter breeze carries her scent to Zabdas. She smells of roses and the honeyed, coppery oranges of Rome, but mingled with her perfume is the scent of incense from the Temple of Bel. She stands beside him, her clenched hands resting on the rooftop wall. "Everyone else may bow to me until their faces turn purple, but don't *you* do it. You know me too well."

Zabdas shrugs helplessly. "How many times have we had this conversation?"

"Too many. You're as obdurate as an ass. You bow every time."

"You are Septimia—the wife of the *Totius Orientis Imperator*. Everyone bows to you. It would be conspicuous for me not to do it."

She clicks her tongue at his blunt, infuriating logic. "I ought to take you down to the marketplace and sell you to the donkey drovers."

"What good would that do you?" he laughs. "You'd be left without a bodyguard."

"And without a friend."

Her soft hand unclenches, and she reaches toward him, a gesture of simple affection. But she recalls herself before she can touch his wrist, and her hand falls back to her side. It has been six years since she married Odenathus—and since the kiss she shared with Zabdas in her lamplit chamber. She can still feel the force of his hand on the back of her neck, the slide of the silk veil against her skin as he pulled her mouth toward his. Never, in all her dutiful, chaste dealings with her husband, has Zenobia felt this way again—burning and cold all at once, powerful and weak, alone in a sphere of perfect light—alone, save for Zabdas.

Zenobia inhales sharply to drive the memory away. She says again, "What are you looking at?"

"I can tell you what I'm *not* looking at," Zabdas says. His voice is like the grumble of a shopkeeper's dog, gruff and low and full of displeasure. "Walls."

"I know." She sighs, staring out at the ragged ends of Palmyra, where its edges bleed into a haze of sand, discarded refuse, and the small huts of the poor. "But you know there's no time to build anything of use, Zabdas. When would we do it? And with what funding? Whose men would we employ—the soldiers we cannot spare? The merchants we so badly need to keep trade flowing? If Palmyrene goods stop coming, Rome will be like a hungry lion prowling outside our door."

They both fall into silence. Somewhere in the city, a camel coughs and groans, and from the nearest cistern, they can hear the thin, lilting voices of children singing.

At last Zenobia says, "I have been praying all morning in the temple, hoping for some inspiration, some answer to this problem—"

"I know you've been praying in the temple . . ."

She blinks at him, expecting an apology for the interruption, but he is still gazing out over the city, frowning. He seems unaware of his misstep.

He says, "I can smell the incense on your skin."

Zenobia flushes and turns her face away. Her veil swings to block Zabdas from her view, obscuring him in a yellow haze, breaking the strong lines of his powerful body into a vague, senseless blur of unrelated shapes. Sheltered and removed, she gathers herself to rebuke him. *You know we must not speak of that night—that kiss,* she thinks to say, or perhaps, *I still remember it, too.* But in that moment a baby cries down in the garden, and Zenobia jerks toward the sound.

"The nurses have him," Zabdas tells her. "Let them tend to your son."

She gives a small, self-conscious laugh. "I know it. And those nurses do their duty very well. I can't help it, though—reaching for him when he cries. My body just acts of its own accord. Isn't that strange?"

"It's how the gods made mothers," Zabdas says.

This time his smile is genuine in its warmth. He is glad. There are times when he looks on Zenobia's one-year-old son, little Vaballathus, and loves the boy as fiercely as he could love any child of his own blood. Yet there are times when he resents Vaballathus for not being his child. The boy's existence proves that even in Zabdas's daydreams, Zenobia can never be his.

How sour and curdled those months when Zenobia carried Odenathus's child had been. Until Zabdas saw her belly grow large beneath her fine, luminous silks, there was still a part of him that could pretend her marriage to Odenathus was only a matter of show—that the old governor still preferred the affections of his first wife and left young and beautiful Zenobia's bed cold.

But even if that had been true—even if Odenathus had no desire for her, and what man with eyes wouldn't desire her?—Zabdas knows that Zenobia would have never let such a situation fester. The wife of a great noble needs a son, and Zenobia is not the sort of woman to leave so important a task undone.

Whatever her feelings for Zabdas—assuming she ever felt anything at all—a wife will do what she must.

The child quiets in the garden, giving in to the cajoling of his nurses—or to their milk-heavy breasts. Zenobia turns back to the city.

"I have been praying at the temple," she says, taking up the stream of their conversation as if it had never broken off. "At times it feels rather an empty gesture, but I can't just sit here on the rooftop staring out across the desert, doing nothing. Rome in one direction, Eran in another, and no resources to even build a wall. What a depressing view this is, gods help us."

For generations nigh uncountable, Palmyra has been one thing only: wealthy. The proximity of the oasis has made the city impossible to skirt, a funnel through which all the silks and spices of the eastern lands must pass before their merchants can hope to reach Rome's distant but eager markets. Palmyra's location, and its control of the only reliable water amid leagues and leagues of unfriendly desert, has made it secure, save for the occasional raid by small, nomadic tribes. Rome has been steadfast since the legendary she-wolf first suckled her brawling twins—or so Odenathus has always insisted. Rome, a bottomless pool of wealth, ever hungry for goods and ever a friend indebted to Palmyra.

But now Rome is more like that babe down there in the garden, tottering and squalling. One day the empire is on the point of collapse, and the next it lashes out with its armies—and if only tariffs could make a wall, Zenobia thinks, Palmyra would have a wall two leagues thick and a hundred feet high, a palisade of silk scraps and baskets of cinnamon, with redoubts built of ingots of gold. The gods know Palmyra has collected enough tariffs—taken its due portion of every drop of fine oil and every crumb of turquoise that has passed through its permeable boundaries. But it is a city of wealth—and nothing more. A city that will find itself entirely without defense should Rome finally, catastrophically fall.

How did this change creep upon them? How did mighty Rome come to its current degraded state? Zenobia knows, in general terms; her father Zabbai taught her politics, and since marrying Odenathus, she has learned much from him and his dry, obsequious deputy. She can recite the string of assassinations and plagues, the Gothic outrages, and the military coups. In abstract terms, she can describe the imperial mess that now threatens her city. But the truth is: this crisis was already ten years old by the time Zenobia was born. Since Elegabulus, that strange, mincing whelp of an emperor, the empire has seen no fewer than fourteen Caesars—fourteen Augusti. In Zenobia's twenty-three years of life, eight emperors have worn the purple.

A whole and functional empire has never existed for Septimia Zenobia. As far as she is concerned, the good, sturdy Rome her husband clings to and supports so loyally is a thing of legends—as amorphous as a harpy or the fishtailed women of the sea.

How did Rome come to this, indeed? One might as well ask how the sky turned blue or the desert became dry. To Zenobia, it is not *how*, but *always was*.

But knowing that the danger Palmyra faces predates Zenobia herself doesn't mitigate the sense of impending, ever-present danger she feels. Its shadow hangs over her every day and darkens her dreams by night.

"Sometimes I wonder whether the gods played some monstrous joke on me," she says and turns from the sight of Palmyra. She gazes down on the heart of the estate, toward the gardens, drab in their sleeping robes of green-gray and wintry brown. Somewhere in that tangle of vines, her son is playing, innocent and unconcerned. "Why was it my fate to bring a child into the world now, when Palmyra feels so weak, when Rome feels so tenuous and the Sasanids so vicious? How can I keep Vaballathus safe?"

Zabdas hears the tremor of anxiety in her voice. He moves close to her, but one hand remains on the hilt of his sword, and he does not touch her. "It's not as bad as all that," he tells her.

But Zenobia shakes her head. "Odenathus has done wonders—gods know he has. The Sasanids have not let up in six years, and he has stood firm against them, even with Palmyrene troops, who are more suited to guarding merchant trains than to campaigning against Eran. He has even made sufficient excuses to Rome that the emperor has turned a blind eye to me—to his scandalous marriage. No one could have remained as steadfast as my husband."

Zabdas hears the words she leaves unspoken: *How much longer can Odenathus stand firm, as old as he is?* No man can fight on forever. And for all Odenathus's skill with strategy, for all his bravery on the field, he is Palmyrene. Palmyra is a city of wealth, not a city of soldiers.

A year after Odenathus's marriage to Zenobia, a revolt arose, spearheaded by the two sons of Macrianus, a horse master who had served loyally under Valerian, the emperor whom the Sasanids delighted so much in capturing. The Macriani were young and strong, and bubbled over with an idealism that even Zabdas found difficult to resist. The East could be its own empire, they had insisted. Palmyra should break with Rome, which was as helpless now as a fish on dry ground. Take up with them, the Macriani had implored Palmyra, and cast off the shackles of Roman control.

No one had known what Odenathus would do, not even Zenobia. From the earliest days of their marriage, Odenathus had kept Zenobia close, inviting her into his office, hearing her words as he would any wise counselor—she was schooled by Zabbai, after all, and her knowledge was of use to him. But the old man told her nothing of his plans for the Macriani. He simply rode out from Palmyra one day, and six days later he returned with both brothers' heads. He had thrown in his lot with Gallienus, the current Augustus of Rome. He had committed Palmyra unshakably to her Roman masters—for better or for worse.

The Macriani heads had bought Odenathus an astounding new title: *Totius Orientis Imperator*, the Lieutenant of the East. If not an emperor in his own right, he is the next closest thing Rome will allow. Perhaps, Zabdas muses, he would have done the same if he were in Odenathus's position. Gallienus seems more distracted and thinly stretched than any Caesar Zabdas can remember, yet any Caesar might make a valuable ally. In this uncertain world, controlled by gods with the most whimsical senses of humor, who can say? A title as exalted as the one Odenathus earned might have been worth the gamble.

Zenobia was certainly worth it—for along with the title, Gallienus had finally ceased to write letters that made vaguely threatening references to Odenathus's unlawful marriage. The emperor had given his tacit acceptance of Odenathus's Amlaqi bride. And that is a prize Zabdas would have risked anything to win for himself.

But a title makes a small and brittle shield—a dozen slain Caesars can attest to that. Yet Odenathus seems determined to ride out under that meager protection, garnering glory more avidly than any boy soldier with apricot fuzz on his cheeks. Zabdas wonders how much longer he can keep it up. The old man has already crossed the Orontes to break a Sasanian siege on Emesa, and wrested Carrhae and Nisibis from Eran's control. Twice now he has thrown himself against Tisfun, the very seat of Sasanid power, but each time the city's walls have repulsed him.

Walls, Zabdas thinks sourly. *It all comes back to the damnable walls.*

"My husband thinks to go out again," Zenobia says, breaking into Zabdas's morose reverie. "To Tisfun, to confront Shapur."

Zabdas groans. "I was just thinking about Tisfun—that folly. What will a third campaign prove?"

"I don't know. That Odenathus is still young—I believe that's all he's driving at now, for I can't think of what else he might hope to accomplish."

"He's not young, nor will he ever be again."

"I suppose I can't blame him." Zenobia folds her arms and leans one rounded hip against the wall. "What else is a man to do, if he's not swinging a sword?"

Below her, the city shifts and stirs like a sleeper in the grip of an unsettling dream. The voices of the children singing by the well lift again. The words of their song are impossible to hear, but the notes rise and fall with a haunting persistence.

"He can swing a stylus against a wax tablet," Zabdas says. "I suspect there is plenty of work to occupy our aging Lieutenant of the East. If he would stop leading our paltry army out on campaigns, we might have time to raise the funds and the labor force required to build a wall."

Zenobia sighs. She stares out across the city, but her eyes are misted and unseeing. Palmyra is a blur of white to her, like blocks of uncarved marble in the blue winter light. "Is it too late, though?" she wonders. "Even if we could build it before the Sasanids or some other enemy attacks, Rome is rotting from within—and Palmyra is within Rome."

"Stuck like a sandal in oasis mud," Zabdas agrees. "The heads of the Macriani sons saw to that."

"At the very least, I hope Odenathus might take Hairan along on this campaign."

Hairan. Just speaking his name unsettles Zenobia. She chews her lip as she ponders the boy. No—he is not a boy. He is Zenobia's own age and has been afforded all the training and opportunity one might expect of Odenathus's heir—yet Hairan has never accompanied his father to war, nor embarked on any independent campaign.

Hairan has never married, either. Perhaps this is why she continues to think of him as a child, as someone younger and frailer than she. In reality, he is as strong and striking as a charging horse.

Zenobia wonders whether his lack of a wife is by his own choice, or whether his mother has had a hand in his fate. Fairuza bore only one child, after all. Perhaps she longs to keep Hairan for her own, never relinquishing him to the care of a wife or to the dangers of battle.

Fairuza is still dear to Odenathus. It would take only a whispered plea from the first wife to keep Hairan at home. There was a time when Zenobia would have scoffed at such dishonorable weakness and selfish meddling—but now that she knows for herself the searing, soaring love of a mother for her child, she feels nothing but empathy for Fairuza.

"If Hairan goes along, Odenathus might show a little more care," says Zenobia to her guard. "He might hold himself back, be more conservative with his strategy. He might remain with Hairan well away from the heat of battle, overseeing instead of participating. He might even give up the whole idea altogether before he reaches Tisfun."

"What makes you think that?"

"His only other heir is a one-year-old baby. With Hairan on the battlefield, perhaps Odenathus will finally realize that Palmyra cannot afford to risk itself again and again. Perhaps he will be content to stay home and lie low until Rome sorts itself out."

"If Rome ever sorts itself out."

Zenobia shrugs, and as she moves a chance breeze stirs, filling Zabdas's senses with the scent of her: rose and orange, and the burnt, sharp tang of long, desperate prayer.

"Rome may never sort itself," she says. "Odenathus holds tight to the hope, but the only Rome I've ever known has been in perpetual shambles. Still, if I don't believe in the possibility, I might go mad from fear."

Now Zabdas does touch her—he can't help it. The thought of Zenobia afraid floods him with guilt and shame. He is her guard—if she feels fear, he has failed at the very thing the gods have made him for. His fingers brush along the warm knob of her wrist, softly, apologetically. She does not look at him, but her hand slides into his own, and for one brief moment, her fingers lace with his. They have not touched one another in six years, yet this brief contact feels as natural as breathing.

Then she drops his hand and folds her arms beneath her breasts. She pulls herself up, straightening her spine, and a luminous halo glows around her dark veils and the black curls at her forehead and ears. In the pale winter light she seems much taller and stronger than she truly is.

"I shall have to speak to Odenathus before he leaves again. I must convince him to take Hairan along."

"Do you suppose it can be done? Fairuza . . ."

"For six years I have been as kind and deferential to Fairuza as anyone could have wished. I have maintained peace in her household—*our* household. But this is my home, too, and Odenathus is also my husband. More to the point, Palmyra is my city—and more mine than hers. If she wishes to come at me like a lioness, then let her roar. I've more important worries now than Fairuza."

Zabdas smiles. "If she becomes too much to handle, I can always loan you my sword."

"Just like that time in the desert, is that it?" She gives one high yip of laughter, like a hound keen on the hunt. "And if I make a deadly swing, will you wipe the blade on my skirt for me?"

He remembers bending over her bare leg, the color of her skin in the desert starlight. He remembers the leap of her pulse beneath his fingers as he guided her hand and cleaned the blade. He longs to take her hand again but knows it will never do. Zabdas sobers as he watches her face and sees the humor fade from it by degrees.

"I will always be at your side," he tells her quietly. "To swing your blade, or to clean it, or to fall upon it, if you command me. I swear it by all the gods."

By the time she leaves, a figure of misty veils and rustling silks disappearing down the rooftop stairs, Zabdas feels the weight of his oath sink into his bones. The unusually warm sun is still high in the sky, but all the same, Zabdas shivers.

***

Zenobia finds Odenathus and Fairuza in the garden, strolling along one winding path as if the shabby winter foliage is every bit as delightful as the brief, brilliant flush that accompanies the presummer rains.

For a moment, Zenobia hangs back and watches them. Odenathus turns his head, speaking close to Fairuza's ear. The lowering sun makes his graying hair gleam with a soft, hazy light. Fairuza lifts the hem of her skirt with one hand while she steps over a fallen branch. The hand that holds her skirt has all the sharp definition and bony dryness of a woman aging, even if frequent washing in ass's milk—Zenobia has heard the maids complaining about Fairuza's demands for ass's milk—has kept dark sunspots from forming. Fairuza laughs lightly at whatever Odenathus has said, and her other hand tightens briefly in the crook of his elbow, a gesture of long familiarity.

A sharp pang springs up in Zenobia's breast. It takes her a moment, and a deep, calming breath, to realize it's envy.

In their six years of marriage, Zenobia has never shared such an intimate moment with her husband. Oh, he has come to her bed more times than Zenobia cares to count, drawn by her youth and beauty as flies are drawn to honey. She knows the lay of his flesh like a trader knows a map of the desert wadis—his territories, private and common, and the boundaries that shift year by year as his body ages and softens. He knows her bare skin, too—but knowing a woman's flesh is not the same as knowing how to make her laugh or drop her gaze like a shy girl. For all their nights in Zenobia's bed, she has never touched Odenathus with the simple, profound intimacy of a hand resting on his arm. She feels, suddenly, a growing sensation of injustice, a sense that she has been deprived of something vital for these six years.

She hurries up the path and Fairuza and Odenathus pause at the sound of her slippers on the paving stones. They turn toward her, Odenathus with a startled but pleased smile, Fairuza with wary stillness.

"Zenobia," Odenathus says. "How good of you to join us."

Odenathus has let his beard grow out in recent years. It is a sharp little brush of hair, as pointed as the beard on a he-goat's chin, and is colored like ground peppercorns and the finest salt spilled out together on a table. The look becomes him, Zenobia thinks. It lends him some small air of the youthfulness he seems to long for.

Fairuza watches the interloper in guarded silence. Although Zenobia has never held their husband's heart the way Fairuza has, she has never stopped thinking of Zenobia as an invader, a dispossessor, a thief. She cannot help it.

In her more charitable moments, Fairuza thinks she ought to make some allowances for the younger woman. After those first few days the wives settled into a studious peace, with Zenobia maintaining a respectful distance and yielding to Fairuza with grace whenever they'd come into conflict. Zenobia has even been careful to yield time with

Odenathus to Fairuza. The younger woman takes her meals in her own quarters, except when state occasions demand that they be seen together.

And in all the years she's been wedded to Odenathus, Zenobia has maintained a faultless front of modesty and goodness, the very picture of a chaste wife, apparently satisfied with her lot as second in Odenathus's household and affections. The front has been perfect, as free from cracks or breaches as a vein of solid limestone—and the gods know Fairuza has kept a sharp eye out for any fault in Zenobia's façade.

But Fairuza knows no woman would have maneuvered her way into such a marriage unless her ambitions are as wide and all-encompassing as the sky. Despite the peace that has held between them, Fairuza has never come to trust Zenobia. The fact that Zenobia has recently borne a son only makes the first wife warier.

"Walk with us, won't you," Odenathus says. But he does not offer his other arm for Zenobia to take.

She falls into step beside him, keeping her hands folded at her waist.

"I won't keep you from your leisure," Zenobia says to them both. "I meant only to speak to you, Husband, about your coming campaign."

Fairuza looks up sharply. "Campaign?"

This makes Zenobia pause before she speaks on. Has Odenathus not shared his plans with the first wife?

He has never hesitated to share his thoughts and plans with Zenobia—but, of course, access to the realm of politics is all she has asked for, and all she has expected in exchange for the frequent, complacent use of her beautiful body. It's the prize she sought to win since her first day as Odenathus's bride—learning, experience, and a true share of his power. She knew from the first that her husband's attraction would be the key to opening political doors, and so she has worked with focus all this time, cultivating in her husband a sense of partnership in the office, building his trust in her intelligence and sound judgment.

In the best Palmyrene style, this trade has been equitable, satisfactory to both parties. Odenathus has ever been a fair dealer. But true to Zenobia's own style, from the moment she obtained her place at Odenathus's office table, she has wanted more. She has tried to turn their partnership into something more—but Odenathus has never sought out her company for personal conversation, nor strolled with her in the garden, and she has learned over these six years that it takes more than a beautiful face and a youthful body to hold the heart of a man Odenathus's age. If she had known this when she was younger, Zenobia would have thought better than to marry the old governor. She wants to be more than an office confidante. She wants to take a man's arm and walk with him while they pretend the winter garden looks as fine as springtime. She wants to know that if she is lonely, she can send a servant down the hall with a message, and her husband will come and embrace her—not for sex, but for comfort in the long night. Who can she do these things with, if not her husband? But Odenathus's heart was claimed long before Zenobia swept into his office wearing her gown with its purple hem. She has been sentenced to a life of lonely power, and she has no one to blame for it but herself—and the gods.

She has told herself, again and again, that access to power is far better than access to her husband's heart. And she has convinced herself that she is content with her place and her lot—more than content. What woman wouldn't be? Who else in all of Palmyra, woman or man, has access to Odenathus's knowledge and strategies?

But now, watching him with Fairuza, the unconscious, affectionate way he brushes the first wife's fingers gently with his own, she wonders whether she would rather have access to his plots or rest her hand upon his arm. Would she rather be the confidante of a powerful man—or would she rather be a woman? She considers the question as they walk, recalling her sister Nafsha's old warnings to keep to a woman's place—and decides she doesn't know the answer.

"I am going to Tisfun," Odenathus tells Fairuza.

Fairuza flinches as if she's been slapped. "Again? But why? For the sake of all the gods, Odenathus, what good can that do?"

He pats her hand gently. "I know you have strong feelings about Eran. It's only natural. But—"

"It's you I have strong feelings about," Fairuza insists, a bit too forcefully in Zenobia's estimation.

She knows Fairuza has played a difficult role since the death of Emperor Valerian by the Sasanids. As far as the average Palmyrene is concerned, the first wife is a Sasanid impurity in Odenathus's household, the only flaw marring his rule. Fairuza has walked this tenuous line like an acrobat balanced on a high rope—a stunning display of grace, but one that has surely exhausted her.

Zenobia peers past Odenathus, assessing Fairuza's mood before she dares to speak. The first wife's face is tense with anger and disbelief, and Zenobia recalls her flippant talk with her guardsman about lionesses roaring. In reality, a lioness may do far more than roar: she may savage her prey with teeth and claws.

But there is nothing for it. Zenobia must risk her own skin for Palmyra's sake. Before she can change her mind she unleashes her audacious request. "I think you ought to bring Hairan with you when you take to the field."

Fairuza makes an explosive sound, like a man with the wind knocked from his chest. She reels back, as if Zenobia's words have physically pushed her, and turns on Zenobia with stark fury on her face.

"Oh, indeed!" Fairuza says, nearly shouting. "I've no doubt that you'd love to see Hairan go off to battle. My only son—and when he's killed, your brat will inherit the whole city!"

Odenathus clutches Fairuza's hand, trying to soothe her. "Now, it's only natural that a mother should fear for her son, but—"

"Hairan hasn't the experience for battle. It's not safe."

"Fairuza," Odenathus says, "this is so unlike you, to react so strongly. Come, let us talk this out sensibly."

"Not with *her*." She shoots a look like arrows at Zenobia. "She is only scheming, Odenathus—can't you see that? Plotting on behalf of her son."

"Zenobia has been a credit to this household since our marriage. You've no cause to mistrust her."

"I've every cause! What sort of woman wedges her way into a marriage—a marriage that maintains a fragile peace, no less? Have you never asked yourself that, Odenathus? Zenobia climbed you like the rungs of a ladder, and now she thinks to tread on my son—*your* son—just as glibly. I won't have it!"

Fairuza storms down the path, her slippers beating furiously against the limestone pavers. Zenobia shares an uneasy glance with Odenathus, then both of them hurry after the first wife.

Odenathus calls to Fairuza, catching her gently by the arm. "You've always been coolheaded, my love. Why this show of anger?"

Fairuza's face is tipped downward, and she shrugs away from Odenathus's gaze. As she turns, Zenobia catches the shimmer of tears on Fairuza's cheeks.

"All these years," Zenobia says softly, "she has lived with this pain inside of her. Fairuza, I know it's been hard on you, sharing your household with me, and the gods know you've borne it with more grace than any other woman could have done."

Fairuza glowers at her but makes no reply.

Zenobia says, "I understand your love for Hairan. But we've larger things to think of now." She stretches out a tentative hand, reaching for the first wife. "Can't we talk this over together? It's not as terrible as you think. Come to my chamber, and we'll have wine and figs. I'll make you see the sense of it. For there *is* sense to what I propose, I promise you, and if you'll only listen, I think you'll come to agree with me."

Fairuza makes no move to take her hand, and soon Zenobia's outstretched palm begins to feel naked and cold. Zenobia tries another approach. "I admire you, Fairuza. I'm a better woman because of your example—more patient and humble." *More cautious, certainly,* she thinks sardonically. But she says in an earnest tone, "I really think that if we'd met under other circumstances, you and I would have been friends."

It is the wrong thing to say. Fairuza's eyes flick down to the still-outstretched hand, and the heat of her disdain makes Zenobia's skin prickle.

"I would never befriend you," Fairuza says. Her tears are gone, replaced with haughty self-possession. "Tribal trash." She picks up her skirts and sweeps away, disappearing into the dark archway of the estate.

Odenathus heaves a sigh. "Poor Fairuza. This marriage has been hard on her—I know it has."

"I used to fear her," Zenobia says. "I thought she would ruin me with rumors or find some way to make you cast me off. It seems strange to think that I feared her, when now I can only pity her."

Odenathus gives Zenobia a long, searching look. Then, for the first time in their marriage, he offers her his arm. "Will you come with me to my office?" he asks. "I have much to do, much to plan, if I'm to take Tisfun this time. I would have your counsel in the matter, Zenobia bat-Zabbai."

By the time they reach the office, pushing their way past the great red curtain that shields the room against listeners, Zenobia's face is lit by a flush of victory. Odenathus's arm is warm; the quilted, embroidered silk of his sleeve is smooth; and an easy, familiar quiet hangs between them, the kind of amiable peace she has always imagined husbands and wives share. It feels as new as a fresh dawn to Zenobia. For the first time in her marriage, she is both his confidante and his woman—she does not need to choose.

Odenathus pulls a three-legged stool out from the table and beckons her to sit. The stool is of the Egyptian style, with a scooped seat and intricate patterns of ivory sunk into the black-oiled wood. Lovely and expensive—the finest in the city, no doubt. Zenobia wonders how many masons it might buy—how many stools might pay for a city wall.

Odenathus sinks onto his own chair, the one with the carved back and arms, sighing. He sighs often now. Old men do.

"You think I'm a fool to go after Tisfun again," he says.

Zenobia doesn't know how to reply. Another Tisfun campaign is foolish. Anything except hunkering down within Palmyra—preparing to defend the city should the tottering empire finally fall—is the height of folly. But should she say so now, when Odenathus has finally treated her like a wife? She considers how Fairuza might respond—Fairuza from before today, from the years when she'd been unflappable in the face of any challenge.

"I don't understand the strategic importance of Tisfun," Zenobia says carefully, "but I do understand that Palmyra is not Rome. We do not breed soldiers here, Odenathus—we breed merchants and gold counters.

"Naturally, not knowing why Tisfun must be taken, I cannot comprehend the sense of it. But if you enlighten me, perhaps I can stand behind you with more confidence."

He chuckles. "Gods, what a diplomat you would have made! Was it Bel who sent you to me, the great god himself? I recall it like it was yesterday: Antiochus with his prisoner, that Tanukh man calling for your blood, and you, a girl of seventeen, kneeling calmly on the carpet, telling me I ought to marry you."

"In this very room," she says, and can't help smiling. "I remember it, too."

The room is dark and still, its furnishings all of ebony and umber. Odenathus laughs again; the sound is like some bestial echo in a cave. It makes the hairs rise on the back of Zenobia's neck.

"Listen, Zenobia: if I can take Tisfun, then all of Eran is mine, and I have only one empire to worry about. Conquer Tisfun, and it becomes a part of Palmyra. Eran will be complacent enough if I can kill Shapur. Even conquered, Eran will be far more stable than Rome."

Zenobia hardly dares to breathe. "What do you mean, 'becomes a part of Palmyra'? Palmyra is a city, not an empire."

"It will be an empire after I take Tisfun."

Her seat feels very hard and cold through Zenobia's skirts. She twists her fingers together in her lap, watching her husband with fascinated caution. "Are you speaking of breaking with Rome?"

Odenathus rises from his chair. He paces to the heavy red curtain, his hands clasped behind his back, then turns and stalks to the window, silent and brooding.

"What was all that nastiness with the Macriani for, if you didn't intend loyalty to Caesar Gallienus?" Zenobia cannot keep a hard note of challenge from her voice.

"I did intend loyalty. Gods know I was sincere. But I was a fool to choose him, Zenobia. Gallienus has proven himself just as incapable of managing Rome as the emperors who came before him. All these years I've hoped Rome might rise again. But it's down for good—I can see that now. Have you ever been hunting? When a gazelle falls on its chest or its haunches, it still might rise. But when it falls on its side, the hunt is finished. I'd hoped Rome was only on its haunches, but after so many years watching it thrash and heave, I can't deny the truth anymore. It's down flat. I can stand by Caesar Gallienus and let gods-know-what happen to Palmyra, or I can break from him now, while he's tangled up with the Goths and too distracted to stop me."

Suddenly his beard makes sense. It's more than a bid to recapture his youth—it's an outward sign of his impending rebellion. Zenobia can't take her eyes from it. Her vision unfocuses and the trim point of Odenathus's beard becomes the head of a spear, silver and sharp in the dim light.

"On the day I married you, Fairuza came to see me in my chambers," Zenobia says. "I called you Odnat, just to needle her, but she corrected me at once. Odenathus is his name, she said—and you must always call him that. No one must ever doubt his loyalty to Rome. The loyalty of Septimius Odenathus keeps us all safe."

He is quiet for a long moment. He studies the windowsill, his face shadowed by thought. At last he says, "She wasn't wrong. I've played the loyal man all my career—all my life. And it is risky to break with Rome. But you've been present when Vorod has shown me the accounts. You know trade is breaking down. More and more often, Rome cannot buy. The routes from here to the empire's heart are plagued by brigands like they never have been before. Caesar cannot keep order. I can't sit back and do *nothing*, Zenobia. Palmyra is my responsibility."

"Make me understand this," she says. "You're proposing that you take Eran . . . and then make them loyal to you. How? Bel's sake, Odenathus—or should I call you Odnat now, after all?—you've fought the Sasanids for years! Why should they ally with you—especially if you sack their capital first?"

"It's a fair enough question. Anyone can see that what I propose is a gamble."

"That's putting it lightly!"

"But not as risky a gamble as you fear. I've fought the Sasanids for years, Zenobia—for longer than you've been alive. Even with my marriage to Fairuza—when I had no need to take up arms against them, still I've fought them, with words and maneuvers, with trade routes, with ambassadors. I know them well—I know that they respect a display of wisdom almost as much as a display of power. If I take their city but treat its citizens kindly, I'll win their cooperation.

"In addition, I have Fairuza—the Sasanid wife, cousin to their king—who has been faithful to me for twenty-four years. She can speak in favor of a joining of empires, and they will listen. Her family, her bloodline, is well loved in Tisfun.

"But most of all, Eran hates Rome far more than it hates me. Allied with us, the Sasanids will have the ability to restrict Roman trade, to control goods, wealth, even food, if we move quickly enough and take Egypt, too. We can do it all before Caesar Gallienus knows what's hit him.

"I've turned it over and looked at it from every possible angle. I'm confident, Zenobia. We can break from Rome, and Palmyra will be the better for it."

It isn't a perfect plan, but neither is it so badly flawed that it seems impossible. Zenobia considers his words in silence while Odenathus continues to stare out the window, running his fingers through his rebellious beard. She can hear her own heart beating, ringing in her ears as loud as a temple gong.

At last she says, "I can't stop thinking of the Macriani. It seems the gods presented you with an opportunity then, Odenathus, and you rejected it. You made your choice, and paid Rome's price with those boys' heads."

"The Macriani are the one thing I regret in all my long life. I've often wondered what Palmyra might have become if I'd joined their cause years ago—if I'd allowed them to live. But the deed is done, and I must go on as the gods will."

Zenobia's shoulders jump with an involuntary twitch. Odenathus's words are eerily close to her own, on that long-gone day when she argued with Nafsha, asserting her own future, her destiny.

I thought I knew so much, then, she muses. *Young people are so full of certainty, and how quickly certainty becomes folly!* She eyes Odenathus for a moment. *It seems young people are not the only ones too full of certainty.*

Yet here she is, the wife of the governor—no, not the governor, the Lieutenant of the East. She has shared in his designs. She has spent years living humbly in Fairuza's shadow, but the gods have been as good as their promise and have placed her in these lofty heights.

We cannot escape the gods' will, no matter how we plot or scheme.

"Who am I to say," she says, "that the gods don't intend this for you? Who am I to tell you that you'll never be emperor? If the gods will it, it shall be done."

A voice whispers in her head, and it has all the bitter warning of Nafsha's voice. *And if the gods do not will it, then Palmyra will be destroyed.*

Odenathus turns toward her. His beard shifts with the slow spread of his grin. The shadows in the room draw about him like a cloak, and Zenobia recalls the sensation she had, in her young, unmarried days, of a figure standing in a darkened hall, reaching toward her, offering her glory.

"Think of it," he says, his eyes alight. "Empress Zenobia."

Or Zenobia, impaled on Gallienus's spear, the Nafsha voice mutters in Zenobia's head.

But despite six years of living as a good, peaceful wife—of doing what a second wife must—Zenobia is still herself. She gives in to the thrill of the prospect and allows Odenathus's words to settle over her like a mantle of imperial purple.

"Very well," she says. "Let it be as the gods will."

"I knew you would understand, clever as you are—clever and ambitious."

Zenobia has the giddy, almost sickening sensation that she is drifting, floating high above her own body. Distantly, she hears herself say, "Not an hour ago, I was terrified of your campaign, and thought to find some way to keep you here, or at least keep you from trying to sack Tisfun."

"Oh?"

"I thought that if I could convince you to take Hairan along, you'd be too cautious to do anything reckless. But I suppose it's safe to leave him behind. That will please Fairuza."

Odenathus's hand stills at his beard. "I'm afraid that can't be done."

With a jolt, Zenobia is fully back in her body, the stool biting into her backside, her hands cold in her lap. "Why ever not?"

"Hairan—Fairuza's son—he is of Shapur's blood, too. No, he is to be my standard-bearer, riding at my side. What better way to keep Shapur and his men from doing anything rash?"

Zenobia shakes her head. "I don't like this, Odenathus. Hairan is inexperienced—"

"He is well trained."

"Training in the gardens and on the barracks grounds is not the same as *experience*. Fairuza has kept him so sheltered, he knows nothing of battle—nothing of war! He is your only heir of an age to rule! You can't risk Palmyra by taking him on your campaign. Oh, Allāt's teats," she curses suddenly, "you can't know how *ridiculous* it is that I'm saying all this now, Odenathus! I'd planned to convince you to take him, and now I'm arguing that you *must* leave him behind!"

Odenathus comes to her. He stoops and plants a soft kiss on her brow.

"Don't fret," he tells her. "Hairan is more capable than you or his mother think. And although it pains me to think of him dead—gods save us all from that—he is not my only son."

"Vaballathus is a baby!"

"But his mother," Odenathus says, smiling down at her, "would make a very capable regent."

Gratitude floods Zenobia, along with an unaccustomed affection for the old man, the like of which she has never felt before.

Anxiety still plagues her, like a cloud of gnats in a summer garden. But above all else, even stronger than her fear, she feels desire. Not for a man, but for power—for the title. She repeats the words in her thoughts, chanting them like a spell against demons. The flurry of anxiety retreats a little, enough so that she can breathe. *Empress Zenobia. Zenobia Augusta.*

As she takes her leave, wandering back across the estate to her private chambers, her sense of duty toward the city tangles with her lust, that all-consuming need to have more, to take more, to *be* more.

9

TRAITOR'S BLADE OR GODS' TIME

Two days later, a knock on her chamber door rouses Zenobia from a fitful afternoon doze, in which she dreamed of pursuit, of some unseen, vast animal harrying her through darkened hallways and clouds of incense smoke. The smoke—as purple as Tyrian dye—billowing like storm clouds, rising in pillars above her head.

When she sends her maid to her door, she half expects to find the dream pursuer standing there—a bull with the head of a man, or a creature with flaming eagle's wings. And so the sight of Vorod and two finely dressed women, so safe and ordinary, makes her blink in surprise. In the haze of clinging sleep, it takes her a few heartbeats to recognize her sisters.

"By the gods," she exclaims. "Nafsha—Zabibah! Come in." She moves aside, and her sisters glide into her chamber. "Send a girl from the kitchens," she tells Vorod. "Have her bring wine and nuts—oh, and dried figs."

Nafsha makes herself at home on Zenobia's couch, but Zabibah embraces her little sister, pressing cheek to cheek and uttering wordless cries of joy. At last Zenobia disentangles herself and leads Zabibah by the hand, seating her beside Nafsha.

Over the years she has received her sisters several times—though not as often as she'd like—and her mother only four times. Berenikë has retired from public life since Zabbai's death. She prefers to keep to the palace now, and, as the governor's wife, it would be unseemly for Zenobia to visit her family in their own homes. She has invited them all to Odenathus's estate as often as she could, but never before has any of her family paid a visit unannounced. Zenobia examines them, wary and still in the grip of her dream. Zabibah seems carried away with emotion, clutching her hands together beneath her chin. Nafsha's brow is crimped by a frown, and she regards Zenobia with a level, somber expression.

"What has happened?" Zenobia asks. "Naturally I'm pleased to see you both, but you've never just shown up at my door before."

Nafsha opens her mouth to speak, but the door creaks open—it is the maid with a tray of refreshments. The eldest sister holds her silence. By the time the maid has set out the bowls of nuts and the platter of figs, even Zabibah's rapturous glow is melting into a look of worry.

Zenobia takes the flagon of wine from the maid's hands. "Go now," she says quietly. "Wait halfway down the hall. Allow no one but Zabdas near my door. I'll pour the wine myself."

Zenobia fills her own cup well. She perceives that she may need it. She takes a long swallow—under other circumstances she might better appreciate the sweet Alexandrian vintage—and then says to Nafsha, "Well?"

"Antiochus sent me," Nafsha says. She is robed in flame-orange silk, a color that speaks of alarm and urgency. Combined with her pinched expression, the effect twists Zenobia's stomach with anxiety. "My husband has an urgent message. Zabibah insisted I bring her along when she found out I was coming to see you."

Zenobia favors her middle sister with a soft look, but she soon turns back to Nafsha. "I don't know whether to feel relieved or apprehensive. When I saw you both standing at my door, I thought perhaps Mother was ill. It seems not—"

"Oh no," Zabibah tells her, "Mother is quite well."

"And that's my relief," Zenobia says. She tries to give her sisters a small, reassuring laugh, but it comes out as rusty as a camel's croak. "Should I be afraid, then, of your news?"

Nafsha sniffs. "I don't know whether you're kept informed of your husband's plans, Zenobia. This may come as a shock to you." She glances around the room warily, though no one is present but the three sisters. "Septimius Odenathus intends to lead the Palmyrene troops to Tisfun—*again*."

Zenobia does not even arch a brow.

Nafsha says, "I can see that this is no news to you. At least *you* are not shocked. The same cannot be said for the rest of us."

"Really," Zabibah says, "what can he mean by it? He's already tried to take the city twice, and failed."

"He has his reasons," Zenobia says. She takes another long draught of wine.

"He ought to reconsider his reasons," says Nafsha grimly.

"Is that Antiochus's message?"

Nafsha tosses her head. "No, of course not. You know Antiochus is one of your husband's best men. Odenathus trusts him with all manner of information—that's how he came to know about Tisfun."

"Don't the two of *you* go spreading the word about Tisfun," Zenobia warns them.

A deprecatory grunt from Nafsha. "It's a bit late for that. Whoever Odenathus has told, word has already gotten out among the common people. There are plenty of men who are displeased—who think it's the height of folly. For what it's worth, I agree with them."

Noting Zenobia's flagging concern, Zabibah lays a hand on her wrist. "But that's not the worst of it, Little Sister."

"No," Nafsha agrees. "A few men in the city are frustrated enough that they've been talking of rebellion—even of violence. Odenathus has made enemies in Palmyra, and Antiochus thinks they're ready to boil over."

Zenobia sits up straight. "What enemies? Who?"

"I don't know," Nafsha says. "Antiochus has no names. Right now it's only rumor, but he's working to get to the bottom of it. You know he's loyal to Odenathus—following in Zabbai's footsteps, holding the Amlaqi to Palmyra—but there are plenty of men in the city who supported the Macriani, Zenobia. Men who wanted to break with Rome and were outraged when Odenathus took those boys' heads."

She almost tells them of Odenathus's plan. The words are pressing against her teeth, fighting to come out—but she clenches her jaw and keeps resolutely still. *Why?* She wonders. Perhaps because Nafsha will take the news wrong and will chide her for her unchecked ambition, for desiring the title of Augusta.

When she is in control of her words once more, Zenobia says coolly, "Please tell Antiochus to trust in the Lieutenant of the East. My husband always has Palmyra's best interests at heart. He will not steer the city awry."

Nafsha rises, without having touched the food or her cup of wine. "I hope you're right, Zenobia. In any case, you must tell your husband to be careful. Antiochus hasn't had the chance to see Odenathus since he heard the news—he's had to deal with the Tanukh again, and Odenathus is always locked up in this estate. Antiochus thinks it's wise to be cautious now—that's why he sent me with a message to you and not a messenger directly to the governor. The gods alone know who we can trust. Will you speak to your husband, Zenobia?"

"Of course," Zenobia says.

"Good. Whatever we may think of this reckless campaign, none of us would like to see you a widow."

***

At his mistress's command, that same day, Zabdas goes down into the city to haunt the wine shops and the dicing alleys, to lurk along the edges of the camel-racing circuits, listening to the bettors and drinkers for any hint of conspiracy.

Although he has never done this sort of work before, it feels natural enough. While his long years serving Zabbai's family have accustomed him to a certain degree of fine dress and high living, he thinks he can learn to like his disguise of a common tunic and shabby sandals. Zabdas has never been one to fear getting his hands dirty or bloody. He has to admit, it's a pleasant enough occupation, leaning in the brick alleyways, laughing over dice with other men, even if the alleys of lower Palmyra are filled with the thick, biting smell of refuse and days-old piss.

The only part he can't get used to is the lightness of his belt. In order to fit in with the company he keeps, he carries nothing but a simple knife, the type of blade a workman might use for every purpose under the sun: cleaning his nails, prising the wax-sealed lid from a jar of beer, cutting his meat, or giving a pickpocket a warning jab in the ribs. It's too utilitarian to be of much use to Zabdas—certainly it's not the sort of knife he's used to carrying, a blade that means business. He keeps reaching for his belt and closing his hand on air, trying to grip, just for the reassurance of it, a sword hilt that isn't there.

Finally he resorts to locking his hands together behind his back, as Odenathus is fond of doing, to keep himself from searching for a larger blade. It will only take one observant alley thug to spot the gesture, to see his secret yearning for the comforts of a real sword, to realize that Zabdas is much more than he seems.

For the first time in years Zabdas spends his days far from Zenobia's side. What a strange feeling, he thinks, to know that she is across the city, separated from him by all the length of Palmyra. She is rarely so distant that he can't catch the brief, clear music of her laughter or hear her cooing softly to her baby boy. And yet he still carries her as close as he ever did on their night in the desert, when he'd settled her on the saddle before him and ridden for Tadmor with her slight, fragrant weight pressed against his chest. As he strolls through the city, sniffing after treason like a dog unleashed, all he can see is Zenobia, her dark eyes grave, peering up from the edge of her turban as she tells him of the news her sisters brought, of the Macriani supporters who plot to destroy her husband.

I should let them do it, he tells himself. *What is Odenathus to me?*

But even when Odenathus is dead, by a traitor's blade or in the gods' own time, Zenobia will still be as far beyond his reach as a star in the sky. He cannot escape the sinking, cold certainty that he and Zenobia are destined to remain what they are: Ras's daughter and common guard, heroine and nameless sword—untouchable beauty and scarred, hopeless, helplessly besotted ox.

Some days after beginning his hunt, Zabdas is lounging in an open-fronted wine shop, pretending to relish a jar of beer that is as weak and bitter as goat piss—*by Bel, how did I ever survive before Zenobia led me to Odenathus's fine estate? Even Zabbai's beer couldn't compare to the governor's, but is this what passes for beer in the city these days?* He drinks with six or seven other rough men. Their stools are old, bulging reed baskets stuffed with camel-hair pillows—the pillows, no doubt, harbor fleas—and their table is a ratty piece of cedar plank, bored here and there by wormholes, its edges rounded and slick from decades of abuse under drinkers' hands and propped-up feet.

"Yer." One of his cohorts chuckles, sieving beer through a long mustache. "I heard the old lieutenant is going to march on Eran."

"What, again?" says another.

Before Zabdas can add his own thoughts, the man to his left says, "He never will. Twice is enough. Don't be such a fool, Darius."

"Getting too old for marching, anyway," says the first. He licks his mustache clean.

"Getting too old for anything, is more like."

"Certainly too old for that wife of his."

"What, the Sasanid cunt? She's about as dried-up as he is. A match made by the gods, I say."

"No," says Darius, the man with the mustache. "The young one— she as saved the city."

"Ah," one of the men breathes appreciatively. "Septimia Zenobia. Now that's a woman for you."

"I *wish* she was a woman for me," says another. He makes a grabbing motion with both hands, spaced about the width of a woman's hips, then pulls some imaginary delight toward his lap, violently and repeatedly, as if he aims to fuck the very air senseless. His friends howl with appreciation.

Zabdas, inwardly seething, has no choice but to join in their laughter.

When their coarse merriment dies away, Zabdas ventures, "What a foolish game, though, to march on Eran again."

"I told you, he won't," says the man to Zabdas's left. "Allāt take pity on me, you're all a pack of fools!"

Zabdas ventures, "But suppose for a moment he *did* march on Eran—not now, but sometime in the future . . ."

"Before he drops dead of old age? What of it?"

"Well, like you say: twice is enough. Isn't there any way to stop him?"

"Who cares?" one of the drinkers shouts. The man is on his third jar of goat piss. The stuff isn't savory, but at least it is effective.

The man to Zabdas's left eyes him for a long moment while the rest of the men go on talking and laughing. Finally he says, "Stop him, you say—stop Odenathus?"

Zabdas affects a gusty sigh. "Septimius O, the darling of Rome. You know, sometimes I think—" He breaks off, peering around the open room, watching the people passing the shop for a moment, the women on their way to market with baskets balanced atop their turbans, the men dragging carts and laden, protesting donkeys. He leans slightly toward the man to his left. "Sometimes I wonder what would have happened if the Macriani boys had lived."

"Ah," the man says. His voice is barely a whisper, barely a breath. "You know, fellow, I have a friend you might like. You ought to let me introduce you."

Zabdas, hoping his flush of victory doesn't show on his face, downs the last of his swill. In spite of its bitterness, he doesn't need to force a grin onto his scarred, calculating face.

***

Two weeks have passed since Odenathus first hinted at his plans—two weeks in which Zenobia paced the floor, waiting for nightly word from Zabdas, hoping each evening that he'd finally uncovered the nest of vipers who plot against her husband. She passed Antiochus's warning to Odenathus, of course, but the governor seemed unconcerned—or at least unsurprised. His refusal to worry has only increased Zenobia's anxiety. Odenathus is her key to the empire, for she certainly can't take Tisfun or stand up to Rome on her own. Night by night, Zabdas creeps ever closer to the Macriani sympathizers, yet each night he reports to Zenobia that he has not yet found them. They are always just around the corner, two steps ahead, shadowy figures disappearing at the end of some stinking, piss-soaked alleyway.

Finally, on a morning heavy with the dusty, compelling smell of coming rain, Zenobia leaves her chamber and pauses, captivated by the sounds in the courtyard—the grunts and stampings of camels, the rustle of servants scuttling about with urgent duties, and the voices of a crowd of men.

She gathers up her skirts and rushes through the halls, pushing past the stewards who carry bags of flatbread and waterskins draped around their necks like victory wreaths.

In the courtyard, under a sky gray-green with the promise of a storm, she finds Odenathus in quiet conversation with his deputy. His hand is on Vorod's shoulder, and he nods solemnly as he speaks. Now and then his free hand rises, tamping at the air for emphasis. Then it falls again to the hilt of his sword. Odenathus looks very bold in his armor—hard, polished bronze scales, with scarlet silk showing in the cracks of their joins. He carries the armor with a straight back and squared shoulders that belie his age.

Fairuza waits, staring, stiff with anxiety at the courtyard's edge beneath the rustling fronds of a great, swaying palm. Her maids shuffle about her, watching the preparations with wide, startled eyes. Fairuza's stare is as hard and cold as her husband's armor. She will not look at Zenobia, and deliberately turns her face away from the second wife with icy, silent dignity.

Zenobia makes her way to her husband's side.

"It's come, then," she says when Odenathus has dismissed Vorod. And she thinks, *Thank the gods he's getting out now, before the Macriani supporters can do whatever treason they've planned.*

"Yes." He smiles at her and nods with a confidence that makes Zenobia's heart leap with hope. He whispers: "Empress."

"Don't claim your fate before the gods have made it," she says. "Anything at all may happen." But she feels stretched to bursting, flushed with a strange, urgent heat, like a skin filled with boiling water. *It will come off as Odenathus has planned,* she tells herself. *The gods intend more for me. I've always known it, ever since I found that purple silk in Zabbai's storeroom.*

"Be good to Fairuza while I'm gone," Odenathus tells her. Then he grips her shoulder and pulls her close to kiss her brow. Zenobia can feel his hand shake. It's not fear. She knows Odenathus does not fear battle. It is simply age. He'll take Tisfun this time—the gods will see to it—and Palmyra will become an empire in its own right. But this must be his final campaign. He cannot withstand another—he must be content to fight his wars with diplomacy when this battle is done. He must hold his empire by the strength of his mind, not by the edge of his sword.

"I will be good to her," Zenobia promises.

She hears a strained female voice, its tones ringing with desperation and sorrow. She cannot make out any clear words over the clamor in the courtyard. She glances around, and sees Fairuza clinging to Hairan's neck, her mouth moving against his curly black hair.

Like his father, Hairan wears armor, and a sword at his hip that Zenobia doubts he knows how to use—not against a real opponent, at least. His strong, young arms hold his mother up, cradling her and rocking her side to side, until at last he gently pushes her away. Fairuza takes one final look at him, then sweeps her women into an agitated train and flees from the courtyard with one hand pressed to her reddened face.

Hairan makes his way toward Zenobia. His face is dark with embarrassment at his mother's display, and his smile is hesitant, almost shy. Cordially, he takes Zenobia's hand.

"Stepmother," he says, then laughs.

These past six years, Zenobia has spent so much of her life sequestered in her own wing of the estate, avoiding Fairuza and her handsome son. Hairan has been little more than a casual acquaintance to her. She has never noticed before what a charming laugh he has, boyish and light.

He says, "It's always felt so strange to me, that I must call you step-mother when we are of an age. But a dutiful son must always be respect-ful of his father's wife." Hairan gives her a little wink, and Zenobia can't help smiling in return.

"Be well," he says, sobering. "Please look after my mother, if she will allow you to. I know this campaign will go hard on her."

Zenobia glances after Odenathus, who has moved away to direct the distribution of the camels' packs, and then turns back to Hairan.

"I'll care for Fairuza in any way I can—I promise you that. But you must make me a promise, too."

"Anything," Hairan says, grinning. He is so amiable. Zenobia won-ders again why he never married.

"Remember that you are Palmyra's heir," she tells him. "If your father should fall, we need you alive and whole. Guard yourself, Hairan—even if Odenathus commands it, don't ride into danger. You must keep yourself safe, for the sake of your city."

"I . . ." He hesitates. A pink flush creeps up his neck; Zenobia can see that he's torn by conflict. "But how can I disobey Odenathus if he commands me . . ." He shakes his head. "He's the Lieutenant of the East, in addition to being battle leader *and* my father."

Zenobia draws a short, sharp breath, and nearly rolls her eyes with impatience. "Don't be so damned dutiful," she hisses. "Or if you must be dutiful, let your duty be to your city first."

She realizes she's upset him—knocked him right off his tenu-ous perch of confidence—so she pulls him close in a sudden, rough embrace. Hairan goes tense with surprise. She has never embraced him before.

"Oh, do as you think best," she tells him. "Only think on what I've said—promise me you'll at least think on what I've said."

Hairan pulls away and clasps her hand again. "I can promise you that."

The servants of the estate set up a cheer when Odenathus and his son mount their camels. On foot, Zenobia follows them out through the arched gateway, into the broad, well-swept road. A great crowd of mounted men raise their swords and spears, cheering Odenathus, who waves a fist as his camel trots down the crowd's length to take the lead. Horses, ranged in long strings behind the camels, fling up their sleek heads and shrill their eager cries. The camels are laden with the long drapes of scaled armor that will enclose both horses and men when the Palmyrene force reaches Eran. The cataphracts—the armored cavalry— are slow, but in their heavy curtains of shimmering scales, they are very hard to kill. It's the only advantage the Palmyrene troops hold.

Zenobia stands mute in the arch of the gateway as the river of men and beasts follows her husband down the road. Women and children on nearby roofs wave and weep and call out their husbands' names. Across the city, a roar of anticipation is already rising from the pillared shoulders of the Great Row, where the citizens of Palmyra wait to watch the brave parade. It seems word spread quickly through the streets when the soldiers assembled. Zenobia can't contain a frown as she listens to the crowd. She should have known about this departure long before any of Palmyra's citizens did.

The troops salute Zenobia as they pass. No one has forgotten her bravery so many years ago. *"Bat-Zabbai!"* they call as they trot past her. She acknowledges their shouts with a raised hand, but the troops are a blur before her eyes. She can't pick out a single face, nor distinguish an individual voice from the hundred voices that call her name. She sees only their movement, their restlessness, and, overhead, the lowering clouds, the threat of the storm to come.

***

The sun has nearly set, a thin, feeble spill of orange light below a dense bank of cloud, when Zabdas returns to the estate. He must be careful now—no direct routes, no swaggering in the open, for Bel only knows whose eyes may be on him, who might have followed him from the lower streets up to the gates of the governor's home. He hesitates in an alley across from Odenathus's walls, flattening into the shelter of a shadow, listening. The streets are quiet, save for the intermittent rise and fall of a woman's voice singing from a nearby home. It is a lullaby, repetitive and low. The air is muggy and dense, and a distinct chill edges the evening like a freshly honed dagger. There will be rain tonight— hard rain, maybe.

When he is sure he has not been followed, Zabdas slips from the alley and crosses the road. He taps on the cedar gate and gives the password, then dodges into the safety of the estate before the gate is even half open.

He makes his way toward Zenobia's chamber in the early, green-dark twilight. Tonight there will be no true sunset, none of the usual hot, vibrant fire. The clouds are too thick; the palms move with the vigor of the gathering storm. The certainty of foul weather fills him with a strange, rippling energy, as if the clouds move and roil and condense within his own fast-throbbing veins.

He is so distracted by the crackling air—by the urgency of his errand—that he opens Zenobia's door without pausing to knock. She lurches up from her mirror table, clutching a red robe about her, but not quickly enough to hide the smooth curve of one breast. The shriek that is about to burst from her throat turns to an exasperated "Oh!" when she sees that it is only Zabdas. Her small, narrow feet are bare, and her long hair, unbound, swings like a dark curtain around her hips.

"I am sorry, mistress," Zabdas says, dropping his eyes.

Zenobia strides toward him, tying the belt of her robe. "Don't be ridiculous. Do you have news?"

"Urgent news, I'm afraid. I'll spare you the minute details—no time. Suffice it to say that the traitors have planted seeds among Odenathus's own troops. They plan to attack him on the march."

"Sweet Allāt, no!" She reels back from his words, then catches herself and advances on Zabdas, her fists balled, as if she might fight his news with her own hands. "The fools! He means to win them precisely what they want—freedom from Rome! And they'd kill him before he even has the chance to give them their prize!"

"Perhaps Odenathus has already told his men what he intends, and the traitors realize . . ." Zabdas trails off. It's an improbable hope. The governor has always kept his plans close and his hand concealed, even from most of his own troops.

She is so angry, so filled with fury at the gods' twisted sense of humor, that she spits onto her Sasanid rug, like a city tough gambling in an alley.

"They won't do it," Zabdas says, catching her by both shoulders. "We'll get to him first—ride out to Odenathus—warn him. This will give him the chance to announce his plans to his troops, and the conspirators will see that he's on their side after all, that murder is not necessary."

Zenobia stills in his hands. The feel of her, clasped in his grip like some rare, delicate bird, fills Zabdas with a surge of wild power. The storm is riding inside him, ready to split him open with its thunder, and Zenobia is small and breathless in his hands.

"Riding out," she whispers.

"Into the desert. Just like before. Are you game for it?"

Her slow smile is all the answer Zabdas needs.

10

A Storm in the Desert

The rain blows from the west, driving through layers of thick wool, darkening the camels' hides and filling their riders' eyes with stinging droplets that blur all sight. Some five leagues east, where the desert flattens into a broad, sere plain, the storm has spent itself and is dissipating on the wind. There, at the storm's fringe, stars emerge through the moth holes of low, dense cloud, and then vanish again when the wind shuts their small, fitful windows.

But the two camels and their hunched riders have not yet reached the edge of the storm. They can only press doggedly on, racing the weather in hopes that with the grace of the gods they will clear the dunes and leave the rain behind.

Now and then, over the flat expanse in the distance, the moon breaks through the patchy, roiling clouds. When it does, its silver light paints the belly of the storm and washes the dunes with an eerie glow, reflecting from a six-inch haze of rebounding water, the droplets nearly as numerous as grains of sand.

"Not far now," Zabdas calls over the tumult from the rain.

He has said it more times than Zenobia can count. Palmyra is far behind them now, and it seems a hundred years since she was warm and dry. Three layers of wool hang heavily from her arms, plastered against her back, slapping her chest whenever Feather stumbles over an unseen depression. She is even wet beneath her turban; she can feel droplets beading and running on her scalp, trickling into her matted hair. She will soon grow used to even that unpleasant sensation. An hour ago she stopped shivering. Half an hour past, she realized she could tolerate the lash of the rain. It is nothing to her now but the chafe of coarse-spun wool. The fearsome roar of the rain seems no more intimidating than the sacred iron rattles in the Temple of Bel.

A sudden flash lights the world, sharp and incandescent. In its green-white flicker, Zenobia looks down from the crest of a dune and sees a tiny river churning far below—the foaming, twisting runoff, snaking through the low places of the dune fields, carries twigs and dried leaves and the bones of small, long-dead creatures on its torrent. Moments later, a bellow of thunder shivers the dunes.

Zenobia turns toward Zabdas. She can just make out the shape of her guardsman, stiff and determined in his saddle, a shadow deeper than the night's blackness. She hears the harsh, snorting breath of his camel.

"That was a longer time, between the lightning and the thunder," he calls out to her.

"Then the storm isn't advancing."

"Not to the east—not in our direction."

"Thank Bel!"

The camels need no urging. That is one blessing the storm brings— a small counter to its vast sea of frustrations. Although Zabdas knows the Palmyrene army can only travel by certain routes—those broad enough for many men and animals to navigate with ease—the wash of rain has obliterated most of their traces. More often than he'd like, he is forced to pause and stare, taking advantage of the occasional moonlight to suss out of sand and shadow the faint remnant signatures of

Odenathus's band. Are those dapples of black and pale-moon-silver hoofprints or a rock face half buried by the ever-moving desert? Is that deep track down the flank of a dune the slide of a scout's camel descending, or a rivulet cut by the rain?

"This is harder than I remembered," Zenobia shouts. "The desert wasn't so unfriendly the last time I rode about the dunes."

Zabdas laughs. "You call a Tanukh ambush friendly?"

She pats the hilt of the sword Zabdas has loaned her, tied once more against her saddletree. "I'd take a Tanukh over a storm any day. At least I can cut off a Tanukh's head."

Zabdas turns his camel north along a dune's crest, and Zenobia follows him closely, feeling small and exposed so high above the desert floor. Their mounts grunt in protest as the rain drives in from this fresh direction, and even Zabdas huffs at the new, cold sting against his face and shoulder. But he is almost certain Odenathus went this way. He sees a swath of pocked and pitted sand climbing from the trench between two hills. It is far too wide for any merchant's caravan to have made. It is nearly washed smooth by the rain. If they'd happened on it minutes later, Zabdas might never have noticed. He follows the swath in silence until the roar of the downpour slackens a little and he feels he can sit up straight without hunching under the sting of the rain.

"The rain is clearing up," Zenobia calls to him.

Zabdas turns to look at her. She is pale-faced in the fleeting starlight, and raindrops cling to her cheeks and her proud, pointed chin, glittering like diamonds.

"Am I right?" she asks, a friendly challenge.

"You are. I think we may be coming clear of the storm—barely. Provided the winds don't change."

"Will we catch Odenathus in time?"

"We must. An army can't move as fast as we can, especially not when they're burdened with all the horses and armor of the cataphract. And moving so many men through this weather—no, they will have stopped for the night, and within a league or two of this place. I have no doubt."

"Can you still follow the trail?"

"It's stronger here. The rain hasn't washed it all away. If I could have some damnable moonlight for more than a few moments, I might make out their campsite, for they must be high on the dunes. There's no bivouacking in the depressions—not with this storm. The water running down there could drown the entire cataphract."

They press on, riding the arcs of the dunes, searching for any sign of the Palmyrene army. After another hour, the wind slackens, and the rain ceases its roaring. It falls now with a subdued patter, murmuring in the darkness around the camels' feet.

They are close to the end of the dunes. The storm's ragged edge, like the knotted fringe of a Sasanid rug, hangs above them. The moon sails clear of its cover and the desert springs into smooth, shining relief, like a frieze made of polished electrum.

Zabdas gives a quick, rough cry. "There!"

Zenobia sees it, too—blocky lines of darkness spread along the ridge of a moonlit dune, and, occluded by the veils of rain, the suggestion of figures moving.

They kick their camels into a lumbering run. At least now there is enough light that they can travel at real speed. They dip into the depressions between the hills, their camels splashing through the frothy runoff, then scramble up again, the bivouac growing steadily larger on the horizon with every crest they gain. But when they have nearly reached the camp—when it is only two or three dunes away—they hear frantic shouts cut through the steady beat of the rain.

"Zabdas," Zenobia cries. "Something is wrong!"

"Come!" He races for the camp, shouting, *"Palmyra! Palmyra and Odenathus!"* so that no one will mistake them for enemies. Zenobia clings to her rein and saddle horn with numb hands, trying to press Feather closer to her guard's mount, suddenly desperate for his protection as a flood of apprehension scours her as thoroughly as the storm has scoured the dunes.

They break over the final rise and charge into a scene of total chaos.

Everywhere, men are shouting, flinging off packs and cloaks and struggling with sword belts. Cushed camels lurch to their feet, bellowing and throwing up their heads. From another direction comes the shrill screams of frightened horses piercing the cold night air.

"Where is Odenathus?" Zabdas shouts down to the men who struggle and shove among the heaped gear and tented cloaks of the bivouac. "Bel damn you, listen to me—where is the lieutenant?"

"Down," one soldier replies. His eyes flash in the moonlight, wide and disbelieving, and then he spins away, gone into the shadows with his short blade drawn.

"Gods!" Zenobia wheels her mount and follows the fleeing soldier, leaving Zabdas behind.

Never before has she ridden so urgently, leaning over the camel's neck, breathing through gritted teeth. Strange, clawed shapes seem to leap at her from the umbral camp, and she remembers the gold-embroidered headcloth of the Tanukh man, the one she killed with one swing of her sword. In her mind's eye, under the singular light of memory, the gold-checked cloth glints as bright as the midday sun.

Zenobia tears her sword from its sheath and raises it high as she rides. *"Palmyra!"* she screams. *"Palmyra and Odenathus!"*

She can hear the hooves of Zabdas's mount close behind, drumming fast against the rain-taut sand. Together they wheel their camels, dodging between piles of gear and half-assembled tents, circling a knot of skittish horses, their manes wet and knotted like frayed rope. Zenobia and Zabdas move as one, turn as one, both intent on the same goal like a pair of dancers entertaining at a feast. They push toward the heart of the chaos, delving deeper into the fray where the men are not fleeing or scrambling but fighting—fighting one another and closing in on a handful of rebels who in a moment will be buried beneath the press of angry Palmyrene loyalists.

Somebody shouts, "It's bat-Zabbai!" and a cheer rises, even as the clash of steel rings loud through the camp.

Zenobia has no time to flush with pride over the recognition. One word repeats mercilessly in her head, thundering alongside her frantic heartbeat: *down.*

Odenathus is down. We are too late.

The ring of loyal soldiers seems to boil, rising as their quarry falls before them. Zenobia bulls her way into the fray, shouting at the top of her voice while Feather growls at the jostling men.

"Alive!" she shouts. "I want them alive, the gods damn you!"

In another moment, Zabdas is there, his camel shouldering its way past Zenobia's own. *"Stand down,"* Zabdas bellows, *"by the order of bat-Zabbai!"*

By the time they beat a path through the chaos, six men lie dead on the dark, wet sand. Even in the dim moonlight, with the indigo shades of soldiers flicking and rippling over the scene, Zenobia can see the extent of their wounds, the ghastly fury that has felled them.

"Traitors," one of the soldiers cries. "They died traitors' deaths, as the gods would have it!"

One, though, is still alive. He struggles to his knees, then sags again, gasping.

"Hold him," Zenobia barks. Several men leap to do her bidding, and then she turns Feather away from the slaughter, trembling with rage. "Where is my husband? Where is . . ." She chokes, and must force the words out. "Where is his body?"

A throng of men lead her through the camp with their heads bowed. Their vengeance is done, that dark lust sated, and now they are silent, a grim funeral procession. A few young boys are bent over a long, flattened mass, fussing with a pile of camel blankets. At a word from one of the older men, the boys back away, nervous and bowing.

Zenobia stares down from her saddle. She now sees that the blankets are a shroud. The shape beneath them can only be Odenathus. When she can speak, she commands her camel to cush and then slides from the saddle. She is too stunned to feel the ache or tremor in her limbs.

She drops to her knees beside the blankets. "Gods," she whispers. And then calls, "Odenathus?" as if he might be dozing, as if she might wake him gently.

A hand seizes the edge of the blanket, and would pull it back—but she grasps the wrist in a grip so strong it surprises her. She does not need to look up to know it's Zabdas whose arm she holds. He withdraws his hand, and Zenobia, before her courage can fail her, draws the blanket aside.

Her husband's eyes are closed. The gods have granted her that mercy, at least. But his lips are still stretched in a terrible grimace, and his skin is as white as alabaster. She pulls the blanket down and stares with blank acceptance at the red-black stain across his chest.

"He took off his armor," she mutters. "Why did he do that?"

"He thought he was safe." Zabdas is crouching on his heels, close beside her. She is suddenly aware of the heat of his body, his minute, unconscious movements as he maintains his balance—how very alive he is, how very alive.

"Safe," she says with a bitter laugh. "He thought the whole plan was safe—foolproof—or as close to it as made no difference. I should have seen it was folly. I should have stopped him. But I wanted . . ."

Zabdas takes a deep breath, waiting for his mistress to finish her thought. But she keeps her counsel for a long moment, then bends over Odenathus's lifeless form and kisses his brow.

"Emperor," she whispers, so faintly that only Zabdas can hear it, "and empress."

Zenobia stands and brushes the wet sand from her skirt in a businesslike way. Her eyes are dry, her mouth grim. She turns to the waiting soldiers. "Bring me the traitor."

The soldiers march the battered, gasping man forward. He peers at Zenobia from an eye swollen nearly shut, and blood and saliva dribbles from his split lip. *He looks Palmyrene*, she thinks with dull surprise. Then she scolds herself for foolishness. *Of course he's Palmyrene. A traitor can only be one of your own.*

"What is your name?" she asks him. "And your family?"

"Maeonius," the man mutters thickly. "Of the family . . . of your own family, Septimia."

"What?" She steps closer, peers more sharply into the bruised and swollen face, but she does not recognize him.

"A . . . a cousin of Odenathus."

The shock of it steals her voice. She can only gape at him, warring with the anger that boils inside her. She wants to scream—she wants to tear at him with her nails. She nearly succeeds in mastering herself and walking away, but the cruel, blind, stupid, gods-be-damned *irony* of it redoubles inside her and surges up like bile in her throat. She slaps him, hard.

"You imbecile!" she shouts. "You and your conspirators. He would have given you what you want! He planned it—a break with Rome, and a new empire, just like those rotting, useless Macriani wanted. But you've killed him—his own kin—killed him!"

Her words crash upon stunned Maeonius like a wave. "I . . . I didn't know. None of us knew! How were we to know?"

Zenobia turns from him in disgust. A nearby soldier drinks deeply from a skin of wine—she can see the dark-red thread trickling from the corner of his mouth as he tilts his head back, taking long, insistent swallows. Zenobia takes the skin when the soldier lowers it, and she, too, drinks. The wine is not sweet, not good. But it fills her throat with something other than the cries that tear at it. She lowers the skin, shutting her eyes tight as she swallows hard. She would shut it all out, if she could—the rain, the fury, the hand that still stings from striking her husband's assassin. But she can hear the men moving, murmuring. She can feel them waiting.

Zenobia tosses the wineskin back to its owner. It is only then that she truly looks around her—and she sees there are two forms lying beneath the blankets. She had not noticed the other before.

She rushes toward the sad heap, reaching out trembling hands as if she can catch fate in her palms and reverse it, throw it back toward the gods, or mold it like clay into some other, less horrific shape. "No," she sobs as she falls once more to her knees.

She does not need to pull the blankets aside to know what lies beneath them. But she does it all the same, and looks with a clutch of fear—and a deep, icy stab of sorrow—into the open, unseeing eyes of Hairan.

There are still raindrops in his dark hair, and his expression, dulled by death, is startled, almost innocent.

"I'm sorry," Zenobia whispers, though whether to Hairan or to Fairuza, she cannot tell.

Then she closes her stepson's eyes and stands. She feels as numb as she'd been in the lashing rain and wind of the desert storm.

She walks away from the bodies, brushing past Maeonius without a second glance at the man. The soldiers part to make her a path, and as she steps into their midst her name is like a charm among them, whispered and repeating.

"Kill the traitor," she tells Zabdas as she passes, her voice as flat and cold as Odenathus's corpse.

Far away, in the cold night where the storm still howls and rages, thunder rolls over the dunes, as quiet as a sigh.

11

As the Gods Will

No good will come of pressing on toward Tisfun. Zenobia sees that at once. Even if Odenathus had shared his strategy for taking the city—and as far as she can learn, he had not yet disclosed the specifics of his plan to anyone—the army's morale has expired, dead alongside their beloved Lieutenant of the East.

"Traitors have a way of sapping an army's will," Zabdas murmurs as they plod back over the desert toward Palmyra. "It's why they're so damn despised."

"Never mind," she says dully. The sun is well up, halfway across its short winter path already, and the despondent army is still leagues from home. "We'll work out a plan to take Tisfun later, if that's the only way to break Palmyra from Rome. For now, let us see Odenathus and Hairan to their tombs."

Together, she and Zabdas ride to the crest of a dune. They sit in silence while their camels shift and groan, watching the long train wend its way through the tracks of the desert, beasts and men with their heads held low. Near the center of the army, two camels carry grim burdens—the bodies of the Lieutenant of the East and his young heir, wrapped in blankets and slung over the beasts' backs like sacks of grain.

Zenobia remembers holding her husband's arm—that one and only time in the garden—before he'd let her in on his plan. *He deserved better than this,* she thinks, *better than to return to his city thrown over a camel's back, bundled and lifeless.* And then, her eyes lowering of their own accord, she thinks, *I should have stopped him. I should have told him it was a reckless idea, that he was too old, that Palmyra was never made to withstand so much campaigning and fighting.*

But she remembers the way he'd called her empress—she can almost hear his voice now, its familiar hoarse rattle, speaking in the dim shadows of his office, and she can feel the hard bone-inlaid stool beneath her. She again feels the thrum of excitement, the desire for power igniting her pulse, just as it had when Odenathus disclosed his plan—and she knows, still, unshakably, that despite his death, her empire can be obtained. The gods have not altered her destiny—not one bit.

And she knows that even if she could have stopped Odenathus, she never would have tried.

"It will be as the gods will," she says to Zabdas, although he certainly has not questioned her choice to return to the city. She kicks Feather's ribs until he breaks into a trot, sliding and stumbling down the face of the dune toward silent, waiting Palmyra.

***

It is evening by the time they reach the Western Gate, and Zenobia, riding in the midst of the train near the bodies of her husband and stepson, hears the city grieving long before she rides out onto the Great Row. She remembers how it was when Zabbai was killed, how the sound had flowed like a tide of sands, the wails and cries to the gods piling up about the walls of her father's palace. Now she rides in the midst of that same tide, a speck borne helplessly on its fierce, uncaring current.

When the camels that carry the bodies emerge onto the Great Row, the air shivers with the high, ululating cries of women in mourning.

In the soft wash of predusk light, the city seems a flattened surface, the shop fronts and rooftop terraces crowding forward to stand peering between the pillars of the Great Row, and the pillars receding into the streets, drawing back in shock from the army's sudden, inglorious return. Depth vanishes; Palmyra is one mass, one weight, pushing in on Zenobia like a palm pressed hard against the slick, cold surface of a mirror.

The din of grief rings throughout the city, shaking every limestone wall. And so it is no surprise to Zenobia that when she and Zabdas and the silent bodies reach the courtyard of Odenathus's estate, Fairuza is already waiting.

The first wife is dressed in her most regal finery, bright-blue silk that looks almost luminescent in the gathering dusk. Her women gasp and press their fingers to their pale lips or pull their veils across their faces so their mistress will not see their tears. But Fairuza stands immobile, her face as hard as a marble statue.

Zenobia is scarcely aware of her camel sinking to the ground. She slides from the saddle and shakes her woolen skirts—they are stiff from the long night of rain and sweat, from kneeling in the sand beside the bodies. Her sleeves and bodice restrict her, squeezing her body like a vengeful fist, making her breath come shallow and short. She walks to one of the pack camels and lays a hand on its burden. The shape beneath feels more solid than a human body should be, as dense as Egyptian granite.

"Fairuza," Zenobia says.

But the first wife strides to the camel without answering. She looks up at the bundled blankets, the long shape of what they conceal, and with a sickly pallor, she turns to regard the second camel's burden.

"You did this," she says to Zenobia.

"No."

"You—so that your son could inherit Palmyra. You—for your own glory!"

"Fairuza, no! I tried to stop Hairan from going. I told Odenathus—"

"I heard what you told Odenathus!" Fairuza screams. Her voice trembles as it rises, wavering like the cries of the city women; the sound is an agonizing peal of loss. "You insisted that he take Hairan!"

Zenobia reaches out her hands, though she dares not touch Fairuza. "But later," she says, cringing at how weak she sounds, "when I knew what Odenathus truly planned, I begged him to leave your son behind."

"You liar," Fairuza shouts. Tears stream down her cheeks, and she tears at her veil, for her hair is tucked up beneath her turban. The blue silk rips with a sound like a ragged sob. "You murdered my son and my husband—you sent out your desert-rat assassins to take their lives!"

Vorod pushes his way through the crowd of gathering servants. The deputy gives Zenobia a narrow-eyed glance, impossible to read—sympathy or suspicion?—then takes Fairuza under one arm.

"Come," he tells the first wife gently.

"Zenobia murdered my son!" Fairuza keens. She tears her veil again and again, until it hangs in shreds around her face. "My son, my only son!"

When Vorod finally pulls Fairuza from the courtyard and the first wife's cries are stifled behind the doors of her chamber, Zenobia covers her face with her hands, not caring whether the servants see her weep.

"Leave, all of you," Zabdas shouts.

She presses her hands tighter and listens to the servants' whispers as they shuffle into the shadows of the estate. How many of them believe Fairuza's accusation?

When the courtyard is silent, Zabdas moves near. She can hear his slow, calm breathing, can feel the warmth of his proximity.

"What now?" he says.

Zenobia drops her hands. "First, we must bury them—my husband and his son. Then . . ." She gazes into the depths of the estate, as if she might see past the carved limestone and painted cedar doors, into the heart of Fairuza's private chambers, into the heart of her grief. "Then we must determine where Palmyra stands with regards to the Sasanian Empire."

***

Where does Palmyra stand? The answer is plain enough two days later when, having seen her son and husband buried and blessed by the gods, Fairuza begins packing her things.

She packs every fine possession Odenathus ever gave her—Seres silk and bright jewels, carpets, jars of the finest oils, carved chests and ornamental chairs, bedsteads, couches, vases, and bowls too beautiful to use for serving food. She sweeps through the estate, earmarking what is hers. A cadre of stewards bustles in her wake, incising her commands into tablets of wax with sharp, orderly marks.

She is fair. She leaves what rightfully belongs to Zenobia, or what is, by rights, the property of the city or of the estate itself. But anything that a reasonable person might call *hers*—every artifact and relic of the twenty-four years she spent at Odenathus's side—she quickly and efficiently claims.

At first, Zenobia is afraid to lose this crucial link to the Sasanids. She pulls Vorod aside and whispers desperately, "Can't you stop her?" For it is clear now that Fairuza intends to leave—to return to her family in Eran, Zenobia assumes.

But Vorod says, sensibly and without a hint of distaste toward Zenobia, "What good would that do, mistress? You are not her husband. There is no reason for her to remain with you."

"The peace with Eran . . ." Zenobia falters.

But the wry twist of Vorod's mouth silences her. There has been no peace with Eran for six years, and if Zenobia were to contrive some means of holding Fairuza to Palmyra, the woman would make for a resentful and ineffectual shield.

So Zenobia stands back as Fairuza disassembles the estate, never interfering as the first wife—first *widow*—strips the place practically bare. When she is done with her matter-of-fact inventory and the servants have set to work—wrapping and packing the goods, removing legs from tables and backs from chairs and calling for more camels— Zenobia drifts through a home denuded of memory. With the fine Sasanian rugs rolled and waiting in the courtyard, her footsteps echo down the bare halls. Each time she comes across some small possession that has been allowed to remain—the vase Odenathus gave her, or an ivory hair comb she'd left lying in a windowsill—she feels like a ghost, standing and staring at these isolated objects untethered from their proper context, drifting like flotsam down the dark river of the lonely estate.

In the early evening, when birds settle in the palm roosts, resolving their small, momentary disputes in their chattering voices, Zenobia walks with Zabdas in the garden. Here, at least, the landscape is unchanged, though Zenobia is certain that Fairuza would dig up every last rosebush and jasmine vine if only she could think of a way to transport them across the desert.

At the fountain, her little son, Vaballathus, is dabbling and splashing his hands in the water, his soft, round face intent on his play. The boy ignores his nurse's scolding, splashing a moment more, then darts off toward the flower beds, giggling.

"To be young and carefree again," Zabdas says, watching the boy run.

Zenobia gives a brittle smile. "Was I ever so happy? If I was, it was a thousand years ago. I've all the troubles in the world now."

"Surely it's not so bad," he says.

"There is no hope now of taking Tisfun—of putting Eran under our control. Not with Fairuza in such a state. She and Hairan were the keys to Odenathus's plan."

Zabdas shrugs uncomfortably. "I do not think there ever was much hope of taking Tisfun, unless by some gods-given miracle. I am not glad your husband is dead, but Palmyra may be better off this way, mistress.

"Remember our talk of walls," he continues. "Now we have the opportunity to stay here, to build, to create the defenses Palmyra will need if Rome falls, or turns on us—and either may happen, you know. The empire is like a rabid dog. It could bite the hand that strokes it at any time."

"I know. But we may need our defenses more urgently than we can build them, Zabdas. Fairuza is leaving—back to Eran, I presume. Where else would she go? She will take her accusations with her and turn her people more staunchly against Palmyra than they ever were before. And we have never been the best of friends, Palmyra and Eran."

They are both silent for a time. Somewhere in the garden, Vaballathus squeals with laughter.

"So now you think we need an immediate shield against Eran," Zabdas ventures.

"I think it may be prudent." She pounds her fist into her palm, a gesture that only makes her feel smaller and all the more helpless. "Gods damn me, I was sure—*sure* his plan would work."

"Odenathus's plan?" Zabdas regards her skeptically. "Why?"

Zenobia sighs. She tries to fight back the confession welling inside her—she can practically feel Nafsha's stare from across the city, judging her, warning her—but the truth presses and surges in her gut until she must speak or be sick with it. "Because it's my *destiny*, Zabdas! Because I've always known the gods made me for something more—more than just a wife, just a mother, just a woman. They made me for power!"

She gazes up at the sky, toward the city. Although the sight of it is blocked by Odenathus's walls, she knows it is there—*her* city, under her command, as Vaballathus's regent—at least until she marries again. And yet it is not enough.

Her face is gaunt with need, hollow-eyed and sharp-cheeked, and in the fading light of the garden, her profile leaps sharp and vivid into Zabdas's awareness. She looks determined enough to conquer anyone. She is as hard and unyielding as stone.

He recalls swearing to her that he would fall on his sword if she commanded it, and he curses the foolishness of such a pledge, even as he knows that his oath was true. He would—he *will*—follow her, fight for her, die for her. He will not tire until she does, until she has everything the gods have promised.

Is it only because he loves her? No. It is because it rings true when she declares the gods have made her for more. Why else would they have stitched her from the very stuff of destiny, as a tailor turns silk into a robe? They have fashioned her bones from courage and painted power on her skin. She would inspire any man to such dedication—and to equally foolish oaths and loyalty every bit as reckless.

"I believe the gods *have* made you for more," he tells her, and her grateful smile fills him with heat.

"Nafsha would scold me if she heard me," Zenobia says, almost laughing. "But I can't help it. We are better than Rome. Rome is nothing without Palmyra. Why should we remain yoked to them, vulnerable, ready to fall when they do? We could be so much more. Odenathus said he wanted empire for Palmyra—for us—and the words sounded so *right*. It *was* right, and it's right still."

"But now we must do it without Eran," Zabdas says. "I could see half a chance, if Palmyra had the Sasanids on our side. Their territory is vast, and their men know how to fight. But if we make enemies of Rome and Eran at the same time . . . Where can we turn? Who will be our ally? Palmyra is too small and not nearly militaristic enough to go it alone."

"I know," Zenobia says. She toys absently with the hem of her veil. "I've thought about that, too. But I do have an answer—I have a plan."

"I am waiting to hear it."

"Caesar Gallienus has his hands full with the Goths. He simply cannot manage the eastern half of the empire—he is spread too thin. No man can divide his attention in such a way—not if he hopes for success on any front. I'll write to the Caesar and propose a partnership."

Zabdas is so startled that he bursts out with a laugh. "Partnership?"

"Yes," Zenobia says icily. "Why not? I will suggest that we break the greater empire into two distinct factions: his Mediterranean states and the eastern vassal cities and trade routes, which are under Palmyrene control. Palmyra will be a sister to Rome—an empire in its own right, yet always subservient to her brother. *We've* enough money to fund the running of an empire—the gods know we do it already for Rome—but Rome has the manpower we lack.

"I will propose a more equal division of labor. Rome sends enough men that I can hold the East against Eran, and I keep both my empire and Gallienus's reliably fed, and furnished with all the spices, silks, and gold that Rome's upper classes can't do without.

"Gallienus can't turn his attention to Eran, and, with Fairuza turning her back on us, Eran is more a threat to our stability—and the stability of Rome—than ever before. With Rome's focus on the Goths, and peace between Eran and Palmyra definitively ended, Eran will turn its attention on us. Gallienus's alternative to my plan will be to abandon the Gothic front to defend Palmyra and all the trade of the East against the Sasanids, which he will not want to do.

"Now what's wrong with that idea?"

"Nothing," Zabdas admits, "to any sensible man's ears. But how long has it been since Rome had a sensible Caesar?"

Zenobia clicks her tongue. "If you can't see anything wrong with the plan—"

"Other than the fact that Caesars are fools—"

"—then I'll dictate the letter tonight, and thank you very much for your useful counsel, Zabdas."

Zabdas shrugs. The evening has grown cool, and he watches Zenobia rub her arms through her robe's sleeves, working the warmth back into her skin.

At last he says, "It will go as the gods will it."

Zenobia gives a terse nod of satisfaction—that has always been good enough for her—and calls to her nearby maids. "Send for a scribe to meet me in my room," she tells them. "Have the scribe bring clay tablets, not wax. My message has some distance to travel."

***

It takes more than a month for Caesar Gallienus's reply to make its way to Palmyra. The emperor's hands have long been full of Gothic treachery, and now, like toxic mushrooms sprouting around a rotted corpse, pirates have sprung up in Libya. He has no time to turn an ear to the prattling of a woman. He tells Zenobia so, in no uncertain terms, and appends to his note an admonishment for Zenobia to remarry quickly so that her new husband might take Palmyra's rudder and steer the city back to the proper course.

The proper course is, it goes without saying, toward Rome.

Zenobia reads the clay tablet three times in the silence of Odenathus's old office. She has furnished the room with a new table—Fairuza has long since left with the old one, as it was a gift from her to Odenathus—and a comfortable chair with a silk cushion, but as Caesar Gallienus's words sink into her mind, her seat feels as hard and uneasy as the old three-legged, bone-inlaid stool.

Zenobia picks up the tablet carefully, shoulders past the heavy red curtain that drapes the door—at least Fairuza left the curtain—and makes her way toward the garden. Vorod falls into step behind her, murmuring a question that Zenobia is too distracted to answer.

In the garden, the nurses watch little Vaballathus. The boy's laughter is a distant music in the estate these days, for Zenobia has been too busy with her daily analysis of Sasanid and Roman moods—to say nothing of Vorod's tallies and accounts, which grow more alarming by the week as Eran tightens its grip on the towns along the far eastern trade routes. She is dimly aware at all times, even, she thinks, in her sleep, that she longs for the boy. He is growing up without her. It seems that each time she sees him he's a little larger, a little quicker. In a blink he'll be a little man, already training with a sword. But she cannot leave Palmyra untended.

Zabdas is in the garden, too, lounging on the lip of the fountain, casually honing a dagger blade while Vaballathus toys with the pebbles at his feet. The guard looks up as Zenobia sweeps into the garden, into the sunlight that falls bright and cheery on a wide circle of paving stones. She halts in the brilliant light and pauses, her scarlet skirts and yellow tunic blazing, her golden veil rippling with the momentum of her furious stride.

Without a word, Zenobia lifts the clay tablet high above her head and dashes it on the stones.

It breaks with a tremendous crash, and little Vaballathus squeals in approval, clapping his chubby hands.

Zenobia gives her son a smile. "That," she says coolly, "is what I think of Caesar Gallienus." She turns on her heel and breezes away with her head held high.

Zabdas hurries after his mistress, and Vorod puffs along beside him. The deputy's eyes are wide and his cheeks are pale, but he says nothing. Zabdas asks no questions of the man.

Zenobia's chamber door is closed. Vorod hesitates, but Zabdas seizes the handle and pushes his way inside. The room smells of Zenobia— roses and oranges—with the faint undertone of spice carried on a chance breeze through her window: golpar, coriander and peppercorn, the sweet hint of cinnamon, a breath of saffron.

She is standing at her wall mirror, a great, still pool of electrum in a patinated copper frame.

Zenobia is peripherally aware of the men hesitating in her doorway. But she cannot tear her eyes away from her own reflection. She had thought to gaze into her mirror, watching tears of futile anger well in her own eyes as she railed silently against the gods—but when she saw herself, she stopped with a jerk and approached the glass disbelieving, slow and careful, like a priestess in a holy trance.

Never before this moment has she noticed how very much she looks like her mother, Berenikë. Is it only because she is now a woman—a mother herself? Or has this striking resemblance been there all along, and Zenobia has failed to see it? The similarities astonish her: the regal stillness of her face; the quiet power in the petite, womanly frame; the long neck and dark eyes, like those of a sacred ibis.

"Mistress?" Zabdas says, quiet and uncertain.

But Zenobia cannot answer. She touches her reflection, as if she might cup her own sharp cheekbone or lift her pointed, stubborn chin. She wonders, as she stares into her mother's face, about Queen Dido and Julia Domna—about Cleopatra.

When Zabdas questions her again—"Mistress? What will you do now?"—she responds with a single, breathless word:

"Egypt."

12

An Offering to Venus

Zabdas halts the train at the crest of the final hill. The slope falls away beneath his camel's feet, a thick carpet of grass rippling and hissing in the wind. The early summer rains have been kind to Anatolia; the hills are greener than the depths of the Euphrates River, greener than emeralds or peridot, and although the air is so thick with moisture that one could practically cup it and weigh it in a hand, it smells as rich and intoxicating as the best honeyed wine. The waves of grass seem to tumble and flow down the hill to meet the waves of the sea. The water, an astonishing and vast deep lapis blue, breaks into lines of white foam on the shoreline of Didyma, the home of the oracle.

"We're here, at last," Zabdas says.

Zenobia, reining in her camel beside him, laughs with pleasure and relief. For nearly eight weeks, they have traveled across the desert, across the Euphrates, through high, rocky mountain passes, and over barren plains, seeking the Oracle of Apollo.

Zenobia left Palmyra in the capable hands of the deputy Vorod, with the Ras Antiochus serving as the city's protector, and set out on her risky and secretive journey. She was accompanied only by her son with one nurse, a small contingent of soldiers, and Zabdas—all of them well disguised as simple traders striking out early to stake a claim on Anatolia's goods for the new season. Their plain linen, rough wool, and simple, rolled turbans have made them all but invisible, not worth the bother of close scrutiny. A good thing, too. The lands through which they've traveled pass unceasingly from Roman to Sasanid control and back again, like balls tossed between two jugglers at a feast. Neither Zabdas nor Zenobia have been sure from one day to the next whether they've ridden through friendly or unfriendly territory.

Unlike poor Odenathus, Zenobia's image is not imprinted on the face of a coin—and so it is unlikely that any Sasanid scouts might have recognized her, even if they had seen her. Still, even the remote threat of the possibility has kept her awake for long nights in her trader's tent. The sight of Didyma is like a balm rubbed on her skin, instantly soothing. She can breathe, finally, thank the gods. Her task is half done, and the hardest part is nearly over.

The ride down to the gray stone city is serene. Surrounded by bright grasses and blooming flowers, with the sapphire sea like a great bolt of silk unrolled before them, it seems the gods have tiled the world in faience. Even the butterflies that flit amid the swaying, sunlit awns are as bright as polished jewels.

"It's a good omen," Zenobia says, waving to take in all the beautiful world. "The gods will favor me."

They had damned well better, Zabdas thinks drily.

Once her mind was made up to take Egypt—and the gods bless Zabdas if he knows how she is to accomplish *that* feat—Zenobia turned her thoughts to Apollo. Her Seleucid forefathers had loved Apollo best of all the gods, and it's the Seleucids that tie her to Egypt. She believes that if she can curry favor with Apollo, Egypt will come tumbling into her lap.

Despite his doubts about her plan, Zabdas raised no objection when Zenobia set her sights on the Oracle of Apollo at Didyma. If Egypt is to be taken at all, divine intervention will be necessary. Apollo, Zabdas considers, can do the trick as readily as Bel or Allāt.

In a quarter of an hour they've reached the city proper. Its broad marketplace is ringed by gray granite pillars, each one carved with the deep channels and precise lines the Seleucids favor. The market is loud with the shouts of farmers hawking the first fruits of summer, and mothers calling to their children and ladies to their servants—and over everything, like a god's steady breath, is the shush of waves on the shore.

In no time, Zabdas has found an inn—the right kind for traders of respectable but unspectacular wealth, with ample stabling for their beasts and small but tidy rooms, one for the men and another for Zenobia, Vaballathus, and the nurse.

But they haven't rested for more than two hours, and Zenobia is already harrying them up, eager to present herself to the oracle. Grown so used to their disguise, the way the simple robes make them equals, Zabdas nearly tells her to lay off, to let him rest, and almost shuts the door in her face. But her dark, piercing stare recalls him. Even in shabby wool, she is who and what she is. Zabdas sighs and nods.

"All right," he says wearily. "Let me get my sandals."

Vaballathus fusses as the party makes its way across Didyma on foot, pausing in the marketplace just long enough for Zenobia to buy sacred laurel leaves, which are tied at one end with a simple bit of linen twine. She also chooses a fine cut of goat's meat from a nearby vendor. She sends the nurse to a baker's booth for a honey cake to quiet Vaballathus's complaints. Then, with her purchases in hand—the meat leaves a thread of watery blood running down her knuckles—she leads the way to the Temple of Apollo.

Zenobia has never been to Didyma before, of course, but she has no need to ask directions. The temple dominates the town, a forest of columns sprouting from a terrace of steps, the peak of its gently sloped roof raised above even the grandest of the nearby homes.

They move through crowds of people, most of them draped in the simple, belted smocks favored by Anatolians. There are others here, pilgrims from throughout the Roman Empire, dressed in stolae or Egyptian kilts and capes, in the elaborate pleats and embroidery of the north, and even some in Sasanid robes. No one looks twice at a party of Palmyrenes—Apollo has his devotees in all corners of the world.

Zenobia hesitates only a moment at the broad foot of the steps that lead to the temple's yawning mouth. From here, the pillars and roof seem to stretch to an impossible height, so tall that they hold up the sky. Vaballathus has finished his honey cake and begun to fuss again, but when he looks up to the temple's imposing reach, even the boy falls silent. The great blocks that support each pillar are carved with the faces of Seleucid gods—Apollo with his spiked crown of sunrays, Medusa with a deep, searching scowl.

"Come," Zenobia says, and begins to climb the steps.

At the top of the terrace, where the pillars loom like the bones of mountains and the shadows between them are cold and dark, a white-clad priestess steps out of the gloom.

"I seek the word of the god," Zenobia says, "and his blessing on my designs."

"You have brought an offering," the priestess says. It is not a question; she eyes the laurel and meat in Zenobia's hands with dull unconcern, like a merchant taking stock of some disappointing wares.

"I have more than just this," Zenobia tells her hastily. She nods toward Vaballathus, carried in his nurse's arms. "If the god will favor me, I will dedicate my son to his service, and raise him to revere Apollo above all other gods."

The priestess considers Vaballathus—the boy's eyes are wide with wonder and fear—then glances at Zenobia's rough wool robe and unadorned turban. "The son of a lady merchant?"

"Who knows what great heights *any* woman's son might rise to?" answers Zenobia. "And for all you know, my son may be better positioned for greatness than he seems."

Zenobia jerks her head at Zabdas; the guard takes a coin from his belt purse and flips it toward the priestess, who snatches it from the air as deftly as a back-alley dicer.

"Very well," the priestess says.

She leads them past orderly rows of columns, which are barely visible in the shadows, and their footsteps echo back at them from amid the cool, blue depths of the terrace. When they stand on the brink of the sanctuary, Zenobia cannot stifle a gasp. A wide stairway descends into the body of the temple, through which runs a long tunnel of torchlight, reflected from row upon row of small bronze mirrors. The glowing passage seems to go on forever, boring into blackness like the shaft of some primordial cave. The air is heavy with the smoke of centuries.

The priestess takes a little papyrus vessel from a stack at the top of the stairs. She hands it to Zabdas, who inspects it in the orange light. It is a small boat, he sees, narrow and deeply cleft, cleverly folded so that it holds its shape without any findings.

Zenobia leads the way down the stairs and into the sanctuary. Although she knows the temple's roof is far overhead, she feels an ominous weight pressing down upon her, and she hunches her shoulders as she hurries along the length of the tunnel of light. In its grand, terrible dimness, the Temple of Apollo is much more imposing than the Temple of Bel in Palmyra—and that's to say nothing of its size. Through her apprehension, she congratulates herself on choosing Apollo as the patron for her designs. If she can win the favor of a god this great, then surely he will not allow her to fail.

At last she sees her goal materializing through a haze of dark smoke and flickering torchlight: the little, white-stone shrine that roofs over the sacred spring. She gives Zabdas a few quiet instructions, and when he has laid the small papyrus boat at her feet, Zenobia arranges the laurel leaves inside it, then tucks the cut of goat's meat into the laurels like an egg in a nest. She takes a slender torch from a basket snugged against one of the shrine's pillars, and lights it in the nearest lamp.

Kneeling, holding the burning brand before her, Zenobia gazes at her reflection in Apollo's sacred spring. She is lit from behind by the great tunnel of torches, and her offering flame flickers beneath her chin. In the dark mirror of the god's water, she is sharp-featured and glowing, isolated from reality with a separateness that is almost numinous.

She sets her offering boat on the water, steadies it for a moment with her hands, then lays her brand amid the offerings. The boat moves slowly toward the center of the spring. It rotates, the flicker of its flame shuddering upside down in the reflection, and Zenobia holds her breath, praying to the silent, unseen oracle.

Now, she wills the boat. *Catch fire—now!*

The brand gutters, dims, flares up with a strong, leaping flame— and then dies.

Behind her, she hears the nurse gasp, and Vaballathus whimpers softly. Zenobia sits back on her heels, staring in shock at the papyrus boat. In the darkness of the shrine she can just make out its pale, drifting shape. It swings sideways, then, as she watches with cold dismay, it tilts slowly to one side and slips beneath the surface. Only a few laurel leaves remain, floating thin and black amid the ripples.

"Get up," Zabdas says urgently in her ear. He pulls her to her feet with one hand on her elbow, and Zenobia is grateful for the support. Her legs have turned to water, and she can barely feel the steps she takes.

She allows Zabdas to guide her back down the tunnel of light, but when they reach the stairs, she breaks away and climbs them herself, stamping with a furious energy, her fists swinging at her sides.

At the top, the priestess calls out to her. "Were you successful, lady merchant? Did you dedicate your son to the god?"

But Zenobia only stares at the woman for a moment while Zabdas and the nurse file past. Then she turns and follows her people out of the temple, into the brightness of the day.

The blood from the goat's meat has dried on her hand. It itches and flakes away when she rubs it in absent, anxious thought.

***

"It's a clear message from Apollo," Zabdas growls. "You know it is."

Zenobia stalks down the center of the broad main street, seeing nothing around her, eyes glazed with anger. Beneath her breasts her arms are folded, tight and defiant. She refuses to respond to Zabdas.

"You cannot ignore an omen of that magnitude," he says.

He has to take quick strides to keep up with her. He never would have suspected that such a small woman could move so very fast. The nurse, Vaballathus on her hip, must scramble to keep her mistress in sight.

"Zenobia!" Finally Zabdas seizes her arm, jerking her to a stop.

She turns on him, hissing through her teeth like a startled cat. "Don't touch me!"

"Why won't you listen?"

"To you—or to the god?"

"Take your pick. Apollo and I are both telling you the same thing. It isn't meant to happen—you cannot take Egypt. The gods won't allow it."

"*One* god won't allow it."

"Apollo is not a god I'd choose to cross."

The nurse catches up to them, and Vaballathus reaches out his arms for his mother. His face is red, flushed with his fear of the temple and anxiety over his mother's suddenly foul mood. Zenobia takes the boy, pressing her cheek against his soft, dark curls. It calms her a little to feel his precious weight in her arms.

"There, there," she tells him. "At least we didn't have to dedicate you to Apollo. Imagine being shackled to that ungrateful deity for the rest of your life! And after we came all this way—eight weeks of travel! Through Sasanid territory, no less!"

Once Vaballathus and his mother are calmer, Zenobia passes the child back to his nurse. She looks up at Zabdas with the familiar, unshakable confidence shining in her eyes.

"One ill sign doesn't mean all the gods in the heavens are set against me."

"But the Seleucid god—the god that ties you to Egypt? The very oracle of that same god?" Zabdas shakes his head. "Tread carefully, Zenobia. This seems like a clear warning to me."

"Warning?"

"Not to reach too far. To keep to your rightful place."

She flings up her chin, skewering Zabdas with her haughtiest stare. "Nafsha's words. Keep to my place, indeed. I should have known you were Nafsha's man when all those years ago you came searching after me in the desert like her trained hound."

He scoffs. "Don't be ridiculous. You know whose man I am."

Zenobia bites her lip. She knows it's true. Zabdas has been hers, unfailingly, from the night they met, and she is unjust to suggest otherwise.

"We should return home," Zabdas says. "Palmyra needs us. Egypt does not."

She turns her face away from her guard. A breeze stirs, carrying the odors of salt and seaweed, cooling the flush from her cheeks. It feels good—soft and reassuring, a respite from the anger of the moment. Zenobia closes her eyes, and, as if she is an airborne seed, she allows the wind to move her. She takes a few stumbling steps, going where the wind directs her.

Zabdas grabs her arm again, just as she trips over a loose paving stone. "What are you doing?" he says roughly.

When Zenobia opens her eyes, she is looking up into the hills—into the emerald cascade of grasses that ripple like a banner over Didyma. She squints at their heights. There is a dark cleft—just there, almost at the top of the nearest hill. It is too straight-sided to be anything but man-made.

A hidden temple. It must be.

Zenobia turns to the nurse. "Take Vaballathus back to the inn. Feed him and put him down to sleep."

The nurse blinks at her over the boy's curls. "But where are you going, mistress?"

"Zabdas and I have business with a god."

"Which god?" Zabdas demands.

But Zenobia only shrugs and sets off toward the hillside. After a moment, she hears the steady thud of her guard's feet, running to catch up with her.

***

The trail that leads up the hillside is as thin as an old, discarded ribbon—barely more than a goat track. Despite the breeze from the ocean, the day is warm, and the dense humidity of the coast makes breathing nearly as much effort as climbing. By the time Zabdas and Zenobia reach the dark, rectangular entrance to the hillside shrine, they are dripping with sweat and gasping for breath. Zenobia's head pounds, and she recollects that she has not drunk water since the morning.

Slumping on a flat stone beside the shrine's doorway, she pulls off her turban and tosses it aside, shaking out her hair, allowing the wind to dry her sweat and carry her weariness away.

Zabdas braces his hands on his hips and heaves for breath. "The gods never meant people to live in such a place. These Anatolians must be more fish than human! How else can they stand to breathe this water? Give me the desert, any day." Complaints duly lodged, he turns to scrutinize the shrine, still puffing a little. "What is this place?"

"I don't know." Zenobia rises. Her hair blows around her, swirling like the currents of a dark river.

"Then why have we come?"

"I came to Didyma to seek the favor of a god. I will not return to Palmyra until I have it."

With that, she ducks through the shrine's entrance.

The interior is cool—it relieves the heat of the climb and the pounding of her head almost at once. The spill of daylight that comes through the doorway is blue, as if filtered through the finest indigo silk. Zenobia stares about the dim interior, trying to discern which god dwells here, which one called her to the shrine. The light is snuffed out briefly as Zabdas enters, but when it returns, Zenobia sees the small statue tucked into a niche in the back of the shrine.

The goddess stands, her weight slung dreamily on one hip, the pleats of her gown falling around her thighs, her hands palm up in a gesture of soft appeal. Curls frame her face, tumbling from the diadem that crowns her brow. She is carved of pure white alabaster. In the patch of light reflected off the sea, the stone seems to glow with an inner translucence, a pale-violet limn like a halo of sunlight on a flower's petals.

"Aphrodite," Zenobia whispers. *Yes—yes,* she thinks, *of course. This is good, this is right. Aphrodite, too, is beloved of my Seleucid ancestors. She was known by Alexander, by the Ptolemies, by Cleopatra—by all those who ruled Egypt.* And then, because it seems prudent to appeal to all aspects of any goddess who might be willing to help, she speaks the deity's Roman name, too. "Venus."

"Ah," Zabdas says. "The goddess of love."

"Perfect."

He stares at her in exasperation. "Perfect? How will a love goddess help you conquer a country?"

She does not explain herself to him. How can he understand? Cleopatra, her own illustrious forebear, was like Venus herself, like Isis, like all the love goddesses of all the lands. *She made Julius Caesar and Mark Antony love her,* Zenobia thinks, watching the goddess's alabaster face with awe. *Cleopatra ruled thanks to love.*

To find Venus here, waiting patiently for Zenobia's offering, is the best kind of sign—the very oracle Zenobia has been looking for. Did she not attain her own position of power thanks to love—by making Odenathus love her? *Well,* she corrects herself wryly, *Odenathus and I shared love of a sort.* It is good enough. It's the sign Zenobia has been looking for—the sign she traveled so far to find.

I will be like Cleopatra. I will take what is mine by right of my blood. This is what the gods made me for. This is my divine destiny. Aphrodite— Venus—Isis—you have willed it. Cleopatra's successor should have Egypt once more, and I have come to do thy bidding.

She cherishes these thoughts, admiring them like a child running her fingers over polished stones, enchanted and half disbelieving. But she will not speak this revelation aloud. She will not allow Zabdas to know her thoughts. She knows she will only hear Nafsha's voice speaking from his lips, telling her she is vain, that she reaches too far, that she should mind a woman's proper place.

Egypt is my proper place. It's Cleopatra's blood that runs in my veins, and so Egypt belongs to me.

Venus will ensure her success, but only if Zenobia propitiates the goddess. She steps toward Zabdas, and only then does she notice his silence, the intensity of his eyes on her face.

"Zabdas?"

In one swift movement, he takes her by the shoulders and presses himself close. The cave shrine is small, and Zenobia's back is against the wall. She looks up at him with heavy-lidded eyes.

"We must go home," he whispers.

"I won't give up on this—Egypt. It's mine by rights."

"Why won't you listen to me?" His voice is thick with emotion—with long years of frustration and the knowledge of the futility of his love. What a bitter joke, he thinks, that he should find himself here, in Venus's shrine, with the woman he loves—a woman who prefers power to the impulses of her heart.

Zenobia makes no answer. She cannot speak. The memory of their long-ago kiss leaps in her gut like fire, and the sudden blaze leaves her trembling. Zabdas's grip tightens; the nearness of him floods her, washing away, just for a moment, all thought of power and empire. He is like the storm in the desert, like water rushing between the dunes. He bears away Zenobia's ambitions on the current of his surging desire.

"Gods, Zenobia," he whispers, his breath stirring the hair that curls against her cheek. "You never loved Odenathus. Not like you love me. I know it—I *know* it!"

He swallows the great lump of pain that sits in his throat, the pain that has lain in his chest like a millstone since he watched her sleeping in the shelter of Tadmor and knew that he could never have her.

She tries to speak, to explain herself, but she can only say his name. "Zabdas."

"For the sake of the love I know you bear me," he says, nearly choking on the words, "why won't you *listen* to me? I swore I'd do anything you commanded, and the gods curse my foolish heart, I will. But don't throw me away, Zenobia. Don't throw yourself away, or your city. Listen to me! Why won't you . . ."

He falters, and in that moment Zenobia mouths the words *kiss me*. But she doesn't know whether she's finishing Zabdas's demand or commanding him silently to do her bidding. Her body is like molten bronze, hot and flowing.

She catches sight of the alabaster goddess waiting in her niche, and with great effort she forces her thoughts from Zabdas and back onto the proper path, toward destiny—toward empire.

She draws the dagger from Zabdas's belt.

He steps back in shock, looking first at the knife, then at her face, pale and distinct in the cave's cool twilight.

Zenobia says nothing but bundles her tangled hair in her fist. She uses the dagger to tear through the black curls. When she feels her hair swing loose above her shoulders, her eyes fill with tears. But no offering to any god is sufficient unless it involves some measure of sacrifice. She lays the frayed rope of black hair at Venus's feet.

Gently, Zabdas takes his dagger from her hand. "It's not enough," he says. "She is the goddess of love. You know what she requires."

Zenobia watches him, the blue light carving his likeness from the black of the shrine—his Arab nose and square jaw, the cautiously cropped beard, the green Seleucid eyes. The scar that holds him back from beauty. To Zenobia, he has always been the most beautiful of men, the very image of trust and refuge, of love.

"I can't," she says, her voice small with the pain of the admission, for she knows it will hurt him. "I can't, Zabdas, my only love—I can't be distracted, can't lose sight of my goal. If I turn from my path—"

"Then what?" He slams the dagger back into its sheath and rounds on her, glaring down with equal parts rage and desperation. "You might be spared reaping a bitter harvest? You might keep your city, and your son, and the man you love—and live a long, happy life?"

"You know it's not as simple as that. Palmyra still lies undefended, ready to fall the moment Rome does. Who will save my city, if not me? Vaballathus cannot do it. I'm his regent—I'm the only one. And how will I save Palmyra, if I don't do as the gods instruct?"

Zabdas squeezes his eyes shut, and the view from the rooftop of the palace comes back to him. Palmyra, defenseless, its frayed edges blending with the sands, all the people going out, all the people coming in. She's right—or, at least, she's not entirely wrong.

He flinches when she touches him—her smooth, slender hand creeping into his own. She runs her thumb across his knuckles, his skin as rough as sandstone, once, twice.

"Trust me, Zabdas," she tells him. "The way I trusted you when you put a sword in my hand, when I was just a girl of seventeen."

"You have my trust," he tells her, and he means it. "My heart—everything."

Zenobia's hand withdraws, and his fingers are cold where she held them. He longs more than ever for her touch.

"Come on, then," she says, stooping to exit Venus's shrine. "There is so much work to be done."

***

The next morning, as they prepare to return to Palmyra, a chorus of shouts in the street outside tears Zenobia away from her packing. She makes her way down the hall to the inn's common room. The name of Caesar Gallienus is on every tongue.

"What news?" she asks another patron.

But the man shakes his head. "It is all rumor," he tells her. "Don't believe a word of it."

Still, Zenobia listens as she squeezes through the crowd, jostling with men as they come in from the streets to spread the news. *Dead*, the men are saying. *Assassinated—another emperor assassinated; by the gods, you could set a water clock to it, or predict it like the change of seasons.*

Outside, Zenobia finds her soldiers saddling Feather in the inn's stable yard. "Have you heard?" she asks them. "Do you believe it's true?"

"Yes, mistress," one of them tells her, stopping his work to bow slightly. "The news is running too fast down the streets to be any common rumor. I believe it's so."

It is true; Didyma rumbles with the sound of hundreds of voices, all of them spreading the same news. Zenobia knows that there are only two things that can spread through a city so quickly: fire and truth.

And so when Zabdas appears in the stable yard with his full saddle-bags slung across his shoulders, Zenobia greets him with the news. She is confident as she tells him, "Caesar Gallienus is dead."

Zabdas turns an unsurprised glance toward the street, where Didymans clamor outside shops still boarded from the previous night, calling the exciting rumor out to their friends.

"So I heard," he says. "Who's to replace him?"

"I heard the men inside the inn tossing about the name Claudius. Gods know whether they're right, but I can't think of anyone else better placed to take over. Claudius seems likely enough to me."

"I don't know him." Zabdas tosses his saddlebags in the dust and brushes his hands together. "But what difference does it make? One Augustus might as well be another. They drop like petals off a wilted rose."

Zenobia says, "Claudius will have his hands full, taking up the war with the Goths where it left off."

"Much luck to him." Zabdas chuckles. "And to whomever his unfortunate cavalry commander may be. You know all the responsibility for putting the Goths in their place will fall on Claudius's commander. There's no job I'd want less in all the empire than planning and execut-ing a war for yet another unlucky Caesar."

Zenobia looks up at him, grinning in the shimmering dust of the sunlit stable. A single lock of her short hair curls against her neck—a bit of silky black that she's neglected to tuck beneath her turban. "Would you rather plan and execute a war for the lucky Queen of Egypt?"

Zabdas tilts his head. "I'm only a guardsman."

"But intelligent and wise. Wise enough that I will *listen* to you—I promise you that—as long as you swear to work toward my goals. To work *with* me."

"You know I will do whatever you command," he answers in a low voice. He lifts one pack and secures it to his camel's saddle. He does not look at Zenobia but feels her insistent stare.

She moves close to Zabdas and speaks so quietly even her trusted soldiers cannot overhear. "Rome will be more disordered now than ever. It's time, Zabdas. The timing is perfect, in fact. I made my offering to Venus, and now the goddess sets the stage for my success. For *our* success."

"News takes time to travel from the Gothic front to Didyma," Zabdas mutters. "Gallienus was long dead by the time you cut off your hair."

"Still, you can't deny the timing is uncanny."

Zabdas reaches for his other pack. He sighs uncomfortably.

Zenobia presses on: "By this time next year, I expect to hold Egypt."

"How will you do that with the Palmyrene army already stretched so thin?"

"I won't do it," she tells him. "You will."

"Think carefully before you issue me a command, Zenobia. For I will do what you tell me, even if I'm the worst possible man for the job."

She lays a hand on his cheek, running her fingers gently through his short, dark beard. "You're the best man for it. There is no one I trust more than you." She turns from him and pats his camel on its shoulder. The beast growls eagerly at her touch. "Start planning now, Zabdas. The seasons are turning," she says. "A year is a very short time."

PART THREE

ZENOBIA AUGUSTA

269–271 CE

13

WOE TO THE CONQUERED

The long halls of the Alexandrine palace echo with the ring of steel against steel. Zabdas thrusts his curved sword into the nearest Roman guard, and the man screams as the blade slides past his shield and punches through his collarbone, finding the one small, vulnerable gap at the top of his chain-mail tunic. The man falls, his steel-crested helmet crashing against the marble floor, and Zabdas spins and thrusts again at anyone dressed like a Roman. Another soldier drops to Zabdas's flashing blade; he whirls and strikes off the hand of another. The tall, elegant columns, carved in the likeness of placid-faced Isis, are spattered with scarlet blood.

Shouts in Latin thunder down the ornate hall as the Romans struggle to rally. Their words blend with the Aramaic of the Palmyrenes: the deeply accented Greek of far too many African mercenaries who sold their swords to Zenobia's cause, and the harsh, sharp syllables of native Egyptian, which crack in the ear like stones thrown against glazed pottery. The attack has been so sudden that between each assault on a

Roman guard, Zabdas can hear men shout from distant wings of the palace, *"Ambush! Ambush!"*

Timagenes appears from around a white pillar, his short sword dripping blood. He wears the sturdy Roman mail, but it is covered by a linen tunic striped blue and white—Egypt's colors—so that none of Zenobia's men will mistake him for an enemy and cut him down. The tunic hangs in shreds now, its bold stripes spattered with blood. Despite his political ties to the Romans who occupy Egypt, the man's dark complexion and short, wiry frame are entirely Egyptian. He throws a quick salute in Zabdas's direction.

"This wing is clear, General," Timagenes says. His Aramaic is strong but heavily accented. "I've sent my men back to clear the remainder of the palace." He grins—catlike, as Egyptians are. "The palace is as good as ours. And that means Alexandria is ours."

All of Egypt is ours—hers.

Can it truly have been so simple? Zabdas wonders. It had not taken him long to discover unrest among the native Egyptians, an anti-Roman sentiment that had simmered for generations, since the fall of Cleopatra, growing hotter by the year. Timagenes, a general of Rome's occupying forces but secretly no friend to the empire, was eager to help Zabdas arrange a takeover. Timagenes assured him the Egyptians would do anything to see another Cleopatra on the throne—someone dedicated to restoring the old ways, the old gods, and Egypt's long-gone glory. The country is desperate to throw off the unstable yet unbearably restrictive yoke of the Roman Empire.

Months of prior campaigns—securing first Emesa, then Antioch, and all the smaller villages between Palmyra and Egypt—had led to the taking of Alexandria, and had been far harder. To fund the campaign, Zenobia diverted a large portion of Palmyra's treasury to hire the African mercenaries. The very wealth that should have been sent to Rome has been employed to break the empire into pieces.

With each conquest, each new city taken, Zenobia's confidence has only grown. By the time Zabdas told her the plan to take Alexandria was ripe—that Timagenes and his rebel army were ready, the axe was poised to sever Rome's grip, and Egypt would soon be hers—she was almost nonchalant in her certainty. "Go and take Alexandria, then" was all she told him. And he had.

Nearly.

Zabdas glances toward the throne-room doors. Huge, towering, carved with winged beetles and plated in gold, they beckon him with silent promise. He and Timagenes stride toward the throne room together, but Zabdas hesitates before he throws the doors open. The gold leaf that jackets the carving is cool beneath his hand, leaching some of the battle heat from his blood, and the fate that lies within waits with a patient expectation that nearly makes him shiver.

Then he pushes the doors wide and hears Timagenes growl at his side.

The throne room is one long sweep of massive pillars, polished malachite, and glimmering, rose-hued granite. At the far end of the room, an ornate dais rises from the deep-green floor like an island emerging from the waters of Creation. It is carved with all the gods of the Egyptian pantheon, a clamor of deities picked out in stonework of vibrant colors—crimson carnelians and precious turquoise, jet-and-green agate, indigo lapis lazuli. Atop this pyramid of gods sits a throne, and on the throne sits a Roman: Tenagino Probus.

Zabdas understands Timagenes's anger. It must gall any true Egyptian to see a man as thoroughly Roman as Probus sitting on Alexandria's illustrious throne.

Together, Zabdas and his ally make their way down the long hall. Probus is silent, still as the pillars that stand as ancient sentinels. When Zabdas nears the dais he can see that the Roman prefect has passed his peak years. Age has begun to line his face, and his neatly trimmed hair is shot through with gray. He wears no mail; his helmet sits beside his feet, as polished and gleaming as the throne.

"Timagenes," says Probus. "I should have known you would rebel sooner or later."

"It's all of Egypt that's rebelling," Timagenes fires back.

Probus lifts one hand from the arm of the throne, a gesture of weary dismissal. "What difference does it make? Rome can do nothing now. The Gallic front is erupting in chaos, and the Goths—ah, but what's the use of talk? I've talked and talked to Caesar, warning him that the natives were agitating, that Rome's hold on Egypt was tenuous, but did he listen? Did he care?"

Zabdas almost feels sorry for the man. By all accounts Probus is a worthy opponent, cunning and dedicated—not some senator who rose to his prefecture by dint of lucky birth or wealth, but a soldier who proved himself capable in countless battles. It's disheartening to see a man as great as Tenagino Probus lounging in obvious defeat.

Probus's eyes flick over Zabdas, taking him in with one apathetic glance. He frowns at the quilted tunic showing beneath Zabdas's light armor, and the loose linen dust veil—speckled with Roman blood— hanging down beside his helmet.

"Look at you," Probus says. "Like you just stepped out of the desert. A Palmyrene, yes? I warned Caesar about you, too—you Palmyrenes. I told him you were taking over the East. Emesa fallen, then Antioch, and the gods know how many other towns. I told him, 'They'll have all the trade routes soon, and when they control them all, they'll come for Egypt.' It is so, isn't it? I was right?"

"You were right," Zabdas tells him. "I'm here to claim Egypt in the name of Septimia Zenobia, Empress of the East."

Probus grunts. Then he turns to Timagenes, his mouth twisted with distaste. "I hope this Empress of the East pays you well for your treason."

Timagenes bristles. "It is no treason—"

But he breaks off when Probus rises from the throne. The Roman's face is calm as he descends the steps slowly.

Zabdas's hand tightens on the hilt of his sword. For the first time since he led his men into battle under Zenobia's banner, he doesn't know what to do. This sudden uncertainty seems an ill omen, and he swallows hard to quell the nausea rising in his gut.

Probus draws his sword with a swift, sure movement, and even as Zabdas raises his own blade in response, he admires the man's poise and agility. As he prepares to kill Probus, he can picture him on the battlefield as a younger man—a man to admire, moving with masculine grace, with confidence and strength.

Before Zabdas can make the fatal lunge, Probus laughs softly. Zabdas pauses in confusion.

"Save it, boy," Probus says. "I won't die by your blade."

Then, as Zabdas watches in silence, Probus sets the point of his sword beneath his own rib cage.

"*Vae victis,*" Probus says, his voice unshaken, and drops with a sigh and a gush of red onto his blade.

***

Zenobia stares from the small window of the inn. The night has grown old. The docks of the nearby landing are silent now, though she can still smell the pungent, salt-and-refuse odor of the port. The shops of Alexandria have closed, but in the distance shouts and rowdy songs rise up now and then from a late-open wine room or a brothel. She hears two cats screeching, then a woman yelling for quiet. A few moments later, from several streets away, the cats begin their battle cries once more. All else is still, merchants' wares packed away, women and children abed on their wind-cooled rooftops, beggars tucked into alleys and stables to steal a few hours of restless sleep. Even the band of brilliant stars that streak across the sky, as white as spilled milk, have begun to fade.

Zenobia glances down at her linen gown. As she does, the wide band of her jeweled choker, like a mastiff's heavy collar, presses against her throat. Her wrists are twined with golden serpents, each a representation of the sacred cobra of Egypt.

Has this all been in vain? she asks herself. Not just the Egyptian finery, but her months-long march across the East, the diversion of Rome's funds, the risk of defying an empire? It has all gone so smoothly, so well, each city falling into her hands like a sweet parcel from the gods. And it has led to this—Alexandria, the crucial port, the capital of grain—the key to her empire.

Have the gods led me so easily across the East, only to chastise me at Alexandria? The night grows later, dawn creeps nearer, and still the signal has not come. *Perhaps this is the end, after all. Perhaps I have reached beyond myself. Perhaps my army has been defeated within the walls of the palace. Perhaps . . .* She falters in her bleak thoughts, tears stinging her eyes, blurring the stars into one wash of pale, silvery light. *Perhaps Zabdas is dead.*

Months ago, when their conquest first began, Zenobia remained in Emesa, the first of the cities Zabdas took in her name. There she had amassed a treasury and created secret caravans to transport it, so that her growing empire would never be without funds or supplies. It had been a torment to remain behind while Zabdas conquered in her name—not because she missed the moments of glory, but because she and Zabdas were apart. She never knew from one day to the next whether he still lived. It was only when his letters arrived, announcing that he had claimed another city for her empire, that she could feel the relief of knowing that Zabdas still lived.

Zenobia had her role to play, and Zabdas his. Necessity kept them apart, but her desperation to see him grew by the day. When his letter arrived that she should make her way to Egypt, that the country was ready to topple into the lap of the Empress of the East, she had shut herself in the private chamber of her Emesa estate and wept with relief. Not because Egypt would soon be hers, but because Zabdas's fighting would soon be done. She would see him again and know that he was safe.

Now Zabdas is hardly more than a stone's throw away, deep in the heart of the Alexandrine palace, and Zenobia has never felt more distant from him. What if he has already fallen? She can do nothing for him, crouching secretly in this waterside inn, dressed in useless finery. She cannot even hold his hand while he dies.

Through the mist of her tears, she sees an orange light glowing. Zenobia blinks, dabbing carefully at her eyes so as not to smear her Egyptian eye paint, and stares hard toward the palace.

One orange light—the fire of a single torch. As she watches, another appears. Then, as she counts the speeding beats of her heart, a third.

The signal. Venus—Isis—it's the signal!

As silent as a moth, she flits down the inn's steps and out into the stable yard. There her men have worked quietly, harnessing the Egyptian war chariot provided by the rebel Timagenes. They stand waiting, their eyes on the Alexandrine palace and its three flickering lights. When Zenobia appears from the dark doorway of the inn, all eyes turn to her. The men murmur and bow low; a palpable ripple of awe spreads through them.

"Do I look like a true Egyptian queen?" she asks one of the Egyptians, a confidant of Timagenes who has aided the cause in secrecy.

"You look perfect, Empress," he says, smiling broadly as he helps her into the chariot.

The driver guides the horses with caution at first, for the streets are narrow and dark, and, over the long campaign that has led to Alexandria, the Palmyrenes have grown used to operating covertly. When they gain the broad road that leads to the towering palace, Zenobia urges the man to drive faster. The stars provide enough light to see, and the way is wide and clear. She can pick out sleepy, tousled heads peering over rooftop walls, roused by the echoing beat of the horses' hooves.

"More speed," she tells the driver, and as the horses break into a run, she flings up one hand, waving to the Egyptians she passes, the starlight sparking from the golden cobras at her wrists. The white linen of her gown shines like the moon come down to the earth.

"*Cleopatra!*" she hears a man shout from a rooftop. And then a woman cries out, "*Cleopatra has come again!*"

The gates of the palace open wide for her. In the dark courtyard, she can see the shadowy, piled shapes of bodies—Roman soldiers, mostly, arranged neatly for carting away when the sun comes up. She hears cries of welcome, cries of acclaim—and all the words are Aramaic, the language of home.

"Which way is the throne room?" she asks one of the Egyptians soldiers.

He points, then gestures to some of his comrades. "Please allow us to escort you, Great Queen."

Zenobia considers the path the man has pointed out. It is broad enough, and flat.

"Not on foot," she says. "Any man who wishes to escort me shall follow my war chariot!" Then, with a great, buoyant burst of laughter, she rolls on, cleaving a path of starlight between the stern pillars and stone lions of Alexandria.

Eager Egyptian hands pull open the throne-room doors. Inside, the horses move slowly, their hooves clattering in a jittery dance along the slick stone floors. The throne room is filled with light, all its hundred lamps lit, and the golden throne—Cleopatra's throne, *her* throne—dazzles in the brilliant glow.

Zenobia halts her driver at the foot of the dais, and as she turns to climb from her chariot, a familiar hand takes her own.

She stares at Zabdas a moment, taking in his rough face; the long, pale scar; the blood that still soaks his tunic and his armor. And his green eyes—loving, worshipful, and proud. *Thank you, gods,* she prays.

"We've done it," she tells him. "*You've* done it."

Zenobia steps from the woven-leather platform of the chariot, and, holding her linen gown carefully, she ascends the dais of the gods. When she sinks gracefully onto the throne of Egypt, the hall lapses into silence, save for the drumbeats of the horses' hooves as her chariot is led away. Soldiers fill the hall—Egyptian, Palmyrene, even the African mercenaries. Palace servants begin to trickle in, shuffling among the columns but not daring to speak. Word has spread among them that they are not to be punished—that the new Queen of Egypt will not see her people harmed. They feel bold and curious enough to try for a glimpse of this new, unknown ruler.

Zenobia watches for a moment longer as the throne room fills with rebels and servants—common people, and true Egyptians, every one.

Then she speaks loudly so that every ear can hear. "It is true, what they say in the streets of Alexandria."

The silence in the hall breaks as the crowd issues a collective gasp, followed by a rising murmur. The woman on the throne speaks not in the Latin of Rome, nor even in the Greek of the long-dead Ptolemies. She speaks in native Egyptian. A thrill runs through them. Not since Cleopatra has any ruler spoken their tongue.

Zenobia waits for quiet to return, and then she speaks again. "I am Cleopatra returned. I descend from the great queen, who so revered the Isis Throne. And so, you see, I am Egyptian, too.

"As the inheritor of Cleopatra, I swear to rule my rightful homeland wisely, and with love and respect for all Egyptian people. Together we have cast off Rome's disagreeable influence. Now, together, we shall restore Egypt and her gods to their rightful glory!"

The throne room shakes with the thunder of cheers.

By dawn, word will spread, and in a day, all of Alexandria will be ready to declare its support for the incarnation of Cleopatra. Within weeks, the long stretch of the Nile will welcome the news, wrapping itself around Zenobia's finger.

As she accepts the bows of soldiers and servants, their oaths of loyalty and support, Zabdas climbs the dais and sidles close to her golden throne.

"The Egyptian tongue?" he whispers. "When did you learn it?"

"I haven't been idle up in Emesa, while you've conquered city after city, Zabdas."

"Don't feel too pleased with yourself just yet. You still have to deal with Caesar."

"As long as Caesar complies with my wishes, he has nothing to fear. If he gives me my empire, Rome will receive its wealth from Palmyra and its grain from Egypt."

"And if he continues to ignore your requests?"

"He can't ignore me. Not anymore."

"What if he responds with the sword, Zenobia?"

"He wouldn't dare. By holding Egypt, I hold every Roman cook pot in my hands. If he wants to keep all those soldiers on the Gallic and Gothic fronts fed, Caesar Claudius Gothicus had best step with care around the Queen of Egypt."

14

EXACT THE PRICE

The palace of Alexandria is like some splendid jewel, faceted and fired and set in the golden bezel of the Nile Delta. Each morning when Zenobia wakes, she lies in the luxurious stillness of her bed, a broad, claw-footed couch piled with linen throws and silk-sheathed cushions. She stares up into the vault of the ceiling, its white, limestone-and-marble heights as vast as a summer sky. Each morning she thinks, *I never could imagine any place finer than Odenathus's estate or my father's palace. But this—this is like the dream of a god.*

And it was here that Cleopatra dreamed—Cleopatra, a goddess on earth—yearning for a better, more sensible Rome.

We want the same, my ancestor and I. We share a common dream.

It is easy now, almost a year after the defeat of Alexandria, to tell herself such stories—to justify her ambition, to see righteousness where she chooses to find it. She sees it in everything, glinting on the edge of every facet, the soft, forgiving angles of her destiny.

Outside, through the door that leads to her misty, damp-smelling garden, the ibis birds are piping along the edges of the pond. She turns beneath her linens and listens. Those small, chattering voices are the same that Cleopatra heard when she woke in this very room, if not in this same bed. Cleopatra, too, looked up into the white ceiling edged with its bright-painted friezes and watched the morning light swell, warming the quiet chamber. Cleopatra also lay here and thought of Rome.

Zenobia thinks of Vaballathus nearly as much as she thinks of Rome. The boy is still too young, of course, for such a long trek—a journey to Didyma is one thing, but crossing the desert into Egypt, passing through the newly conquered Eastern Empire, is quite another. Besides, his presence would hinder Zenobia. She must remain keen and imposing. She spends long hours each day with her council, planning the distribution of her empire's wealth, planning how they will keep Rome quiet and complacent. It is better for her and for her son if they are separated now. She knows the boy is happy in the care of her sisters and mother. But she misses him all the same, his high, childish voice and the gentle music of his laughter.

There is a rustling outside the chamber door, and Zenobia sits up in the shaft of white morning light, letting the linens fall away. She remains naked to the morning air as her servants come in, bearing breakfast. How quickly she has adopted Egyptian ways! She has been in Alexandria barely more than ten months, but already it feels like home.

The maids place her tray on the table beside the widest window, so that she may watch the ibis wading as she eats. Zenobia does not bother to dress, but crosses the floor barefooted, her soles slapping the cool marble with a light, patting sound that resounds faintly in the pillared heights of the room. The maids bow their way out, holding up their palms in the Egyptian fashion, and Zenobia sinks onto her ebony stool with an amused, anticipatory smile.

Tucked amid the covered pottery dishes and the bowls of sweet and savory sauces is a piece of folded papyrus. It pokes up between a basket of flatbread and a stoppered jar of milk, like the flag of an impertinent enemy. Zenobia seizes it eagerly, inspecting the red wax seal—still intact and bearing the eagle of Rome.

She slides her breakfast knife beneath the seal, smooths the papyrus, and reads:

To the self-styled Queen of Egypt,

I would ask how you fare, but I know already that you are unchanged: still as bold as ever, and full of your outrageous demands.

I am in receipt of your last letter. You must know, of course, that Caesar was unimpressed. Your threats to choke off the army's food supply were as thinly veiled as you Palmyrene women always are. But that was the point, of course—to threaten Caesar.

While I stand in awe and grudging admiration of your bravery, I feel a friendly obligation to warn you against your own stupidity . . .

Here, Zenobia flushes with indignation.

. . . for our campaign against the Goths will soon come to an end. When it is concluded, do you suppose Caesar will allow your audacious offenses against his empire to go unpunished?

As I have told you before, someone must answer for the death of the prefect of Egypt, Tenagino Probus. But once that business is seen to, Caesar will be happy to install a new prefect to oversee Egypt in Rome's name. As you have been kind enough (so far) to allow shipments of Egyptian grain to move unhindered, perhaps Caesar will reciprocate your consideration by appointing to the position a Palmyrene man of your choice. If you will agree to this, you will be allowed to return to Palmyra unharmed, and there marry a man of your own choosing, who will be granted a high office under the new governor of the city, to be named by Caesar.

I must urge you to accept these terms, for Caesar grows weary of your playacting. If he must meet you on the field, Zenobia, he will not be so lenient. As one who has come to admire your will and ambition, I pray to Sol Invictus that you will make the right choice and yield quietly to Rome.

With friendship,
Aurelian, general of the armies of Caesar Claudius Gothicus

Zenobia reads the letter again as she spoons up her duck eggs and spreads bread with a smear of soft white cheese. *Aurelian, indeed,* she tells herself.

Within weeks of taking Alexandria, the first letter had come from the general of Caesar's armies. Why this Aurelian should take pains to write to her on the emperor's behalf, Zenobia cannot say. But as they've exchanged these salvos on papyrus—Zenobia never wavering in her demands for an empire, Aurelian giving not one foot of ground—she has come to enjoy the general's saucy notes. He, alone among all Romans, is no shrinking flower, and she feels almost relieved to know that the empire has not gone entirely to the dogs. Aurelian might be the only Roman left alive who is still worthy of respect. A pity the gods have pitted them against one another, but she is determined to make him an ally yet.

She rises, dresses hastily in a white linen robe, and winds her hair into a small knot at the back of her head. It has grown just enough that she may do so. She takes her bit of bread and cheese to her writing desk, and nibbles it while she composes her reply.

My good Aurelian,

What a thoughtful friend you are, to worry so over my future. But I wish to assure you that I have no need of another husband. I am ruling my lands quite handily on my own—not only Palmyra, which I need not remind you is the source of most of Rome's wealth—but also Emesa, Chalcedon, Antioch, Ancyra—all the lands I have conquered under my own banner while Rome continues to scrap in the mountains against a handful of Gothic barbarians.

Your letter admonishes me to fear Caesar's wrath. Why? This Caesar, like all who came before him, cannot hold one empire together. Even a woman can take from Caesar what he claims is his!

I shall not cede what is mine by birthright—by my descent from Cleopatra—to say nothing of what is mine by right of conquest. I repeat myself, as I have done so many times before: Let Caesar Claudius Gothicus proclaim me as Empress of the East. Let him acknowledge that the Palmyrene Empire is now a force unto itself—a force equal, at the very least, to Rome. If he sees the sense in my proposal, then we shall have peace and friendship between us, and, more importantly for you, robust trade in Palmyra's goods and Egypt's grain— neither of which Caesar can do without. If he persists in his foolish denials I shall be forced to don a thicker veil than a Palmyrene woman typically wears. It shall be made of steel, and I fear it will be so sturdy that not a grain of Egyptian wheat shall pass through it.

In short, my friend: I find your terms most objectionable. But you knew I would.

Awaiting your sensible reply,
Zenobia Augusta

***

"Are you mad?" Zabdas says.

He tosses the letter down on Zenobia's table and wipes his fingers on his tunic, as if the papyrus—or the words she has written on them—is foul.

"Oh, don't scold, Zabdas."

The breakfast tray has long since been removed, and now Zenobia sits on the edge of her couch, straight-backed and attentive, poring over another report from Timagenes. He has been upriver to Memphis, sounding out the city's mood. Zenobia lays the papyrus aside and claps her hands lightly, once, a gesture that says she is done with the conversation.

"Memphis is still besotted with me," she tells Zabdas. "In fact, Timagenes estimates that they adore me even more now than they did when I got rid of Probus."

"*I* got rid of Probus," Zabdas says. His arms are folded tight across his chest, and he stares, stony-faced, out the window. He sees nothing of the bright birds that wade in the pond or the banks of lilies and creepers that bloom in the shadow of the high limestone wall. "You would be wise to remember who does your fighting, Empress of the East."

"Zabdas!" Zenobia looks genuinely startled. "You know I could never forget all you do for me."

He gestures at her letter. "And yet you're aiming to get me killed—to say nothing of yourself. 'Zenobia Augusta'! You've named yourself empress without securing any kind of cooperation from Rome! You can't think Aurelian will let such an insult slide."

"Aurelian is only a general."

"A general who reports to the emperor. A general who does the emperor's bidding."

"And the emperor is Roman," Zenobia says, her voice heavy with scorn. "When has a Roman emperor accomplished anything? Caesar

Claudius Gothicus will soon find himself stabbed or poisoned, or have his horse cut from under him during a charge. Or the plague will kill him. Gods, what does it matter how he dies? He soon will, and we'll be on to the next emperor, and then the next. It's been the same endlessly repeating story since before I was born! Don't you think the East—our homeland—deserves better? A stable ruler?"

Zabdas shakes his head. "You know I do. But that's not the point—"

"What *is* the point, then?" Zenobia throws herself against the couch's backrest, scowling.

"Aurelian is the point," Zabdas says. "I've been listening carefully to reports from the Gothic front. It's going well for Rome, Zenobia. Finally, after Bel knows how many years of scrabbling for a desperate hold, the Roman army has found purchase. Little by little, they're pushing the Goths back. It is *Aurelian* who is doing it. That general you dismiss so easily is the very thing Rome has lacked since before you were born: a competent leader. Don't be foolish enough to think only I have noticed his competence. The Roman senate has noticed, too—mark my words."

A small, icy knot forms in Zenobia's stomach. She holds very still, pinned on her couch, staring at Zabdas. Her guardsman—no, her general—still stands with his back turned to her, watching the peaceful garden. A blaze of yellow sunlight surrounds him, casting a halo around him as if the gods have set him apart. She eyes the stiff, blocky shape of his shoulders, half hunched as if in expectation of some terrible blow. She watches his tense stillness for a sign of softening, hoping for some minute relaxation of his fear. But he is like a man cast in bronze, his form unchanging, his tension set.

"I can make an ally of him," Zenobia says at last. "Aurelian, I mean."

Zabdas turns from the window. The look he gives her—one eyebrow raised, mouth twisted—is eloquent with doubt.

"I can," she insists. "We have a . . . a rapport. If he is truly the leader you think he is, then I can sway Aurelian to our side, and he can become an advocate for me, and influence Caesar—"

Zabdas explodes with one great huff of laughter. "Influence Caesar? Zenobia, you don't understand what I'm saying."

"Tread carefully, Zabdas. I am no fool."

He reins in his passion with effort. "I know you're not. But I believe you're not seeing clearly now."

"Oh? How so?" Coolly, she slits her eyes.

"It won't be a matter of Aurelian influencing Caesar. Sooner or later—and you'd better hope it's later—Aurelian will *be* Caesar. Whatever your opinion of the senate, they aren't foolish enough to let a gem like Aurelian slip through their fingers. As soon as the Goths are beaten back for good—and they will be, with that man in charge— Aurelian will have Rome. If *he's* not already planning to assassinate Claudius Gothicus, somebody else *is*, so that the senate can shove Aurelian into a purple robe.

"If you keep toying with Aurelian as you've been doing, you'll have made an enemy of the most competent emperor Rome has seen for a hundred years. And when Aurelian takes his inevitable place as Augustus, I wouldn't like to be standing in your pretty silk slippers."

"You know as well as anybody that it's dangerous work, leading an army." Zenobia's voice is dry, half grudging. It's not that she hasn't already seen the situation for herself. But still she clings to her certainty that the gods have set her path. "Aurelian may die before his plans—or the senate's plans—can come to fruition."

Zabdas looks at her flatly. The light from the garden touches the edges of his beard with gold. "Are you willing to gamble your life on that?"

"I swore I'd listen to you." She sighs. "Now that I'm empress, I regret that promise. But I'm a Palmyrene, after all—a good trader. And a deal is a deal. What, then, would you have me do?"

"Don't send this letter, first of all, *Zenobia Augusta*. Aurelian offers you reasonable terms—better than any usurping woman can hope for."

She springs to her feet. The blood pounds in her face, and her nails bite into her palms, in the centers of tight-clenched fists. "I am *not* a usurper. I am of Cleopatra's own blood. This was her palace—her city—her nation!"

"And she lost her nation to Rome. No Caesar will ever see you as anything else. The fact that you are a woman is salt in the wound. Accept that you've done what no other woman could. Not even Cleopatra was a conqueror! You've conquered several cities and taken Egypt out from under Caesar's nose. Let that be enough. What more can you hope to achieve? What else *is* there, Zenobia?"

"You think I ought to accept Aurelian's terms," she says bitterly. "Go back to Palmyra, marry, and retire to a quiet life as some nobleman's wife. I've done that before, Zabdas! What else is there, you ask? A whole world! Everything—anything but consigning myself to that drab fate."

"What Aurelian proposes is fair enough," counters Zabdas. "You choose Egypt's new prefect—perhaps your brother-in-law, Antiochus—and your life is spared. It's better than you can hope for."

"I choose the prefect—and who chooses my husband?"

"You do, of course. You chose once." Zabdas glances down at the dark veins running through the pale marble of the floor. He dares not look up at her, for fear that the hope will show too clearly in his eyes. "You might choose again."

"If I did as you advised me, and accepted Aurelian's offer, I would not be allowed to choose whom I marry. You're a fool to think so, Zabdas. Rome will seek to keep me on a tight leash. Caesar will never allow *that* leniency."

She moves toward him, reaching for him with a sudden, involuntary need. The garden's light glowing on his skin reminds her of the luminescence in the shrine of Venus, and she longs all at once to feel his hands on her again, his breath against her cheek. When Zabdas takes her in his arms and pulls her against his chest, he gives a small, pained moan of confusion and despair.

"Aurelian would see me tethered to a loyal Roman," Zenobia whispers against his tunic. He smells of Egypt, of cool riparian greenery and grain drying in the sun. "I would never be free again—I would certainly not be free to love you. Are you sure that you would have me surrender to Aurelian's demands?"

"What does it matter?" Zabdas murmurs into her black curls. "You are free now, but still you will not love me. What difference would it make to me? At least if you give in to Aurelian's demands, you'll live." He can hardly force the words out. There is a deep, dark cleft inside him, years of thwarted desire splitting his heart like an axe blow.

Zenobia pulls back. She looks up at him with dark, searching eyes. For a long moment they are locked this way, held fast to one another by this intimate gaze. Then, deliberate and certain, Zenobia rises onto her toes and kisses him.

The taste of her lips floods Zabdas's senses, the warmth of her mouth burning away his fears like a fire burns pitch. Her hand rises quickly, grasping the back of his neck in a greedy gesture, as if she thinks she can take him as easily and with as much natural right as she seized Egypt. He clutches her just as frantically, holding her first by the arms, then by the waist, her warm, incurved back, and finally by her short, soft hair. His grip knocks the ivory pins from her curls, and the knot she'd fixed in her hair tumbles loose.

Her disarray seems suddenly ominous to him, as if she will break into pieces and disperse on a chance wind, blowing forever beyond his reach, and he clutches at her more desperately. His fingers move to her hips, biting into their roundness until she yelps against his mouth.

When he breaks their kiss to apologize, she bites his lower lip, and before Zabdas knows what he has done, he lifts her, bearing her slight weight across the room to the couch where scrolls of papyrus are neatly stacked, the notes from her Egyptian allies, the veiled threats from a newly dangerous Rome. Zenobia pushes the scrolls aside, and they scatter across the marble floor with a sound like a scandalized gasp.

Zabdas's hands tangle with Zenobia's in the knots of her Egyptian gown, the stylish, clever ties at the hip and throat, and they laugh and pant as they struggle to pull the linen free. At last it falls away, releasing her body from concealment, and she lies back on the couch—unashamed of her nakedness, just like an Egyptian.

Zabdas falls to his knees. He can see all of her now, every soft and vulnerable part. He can see, too, a strange fire in her eyes that is not ambition, not confidence. It is nothing but desire—not for power but for him. At this moment she is no empress.

As he lifts one foot with reverent care, kissing its pale arch, brushing his lips against the soft, dark hair of her shin, Zenobia's eyes well. She has pursued each desire, reached with a sanguine hand for every prize her boundless ambitions could conceive of. Only Zabdas—only love—has she denied herself. And why? First for Fairuza's sake and then for the sake of avoiding distraction, remaining focused like a falcon on her goals. It seems so pointless now, all that deprivation. She will deny this hunger no longer.

Despite the soaring pillars that surround them, the marble and limestone, the painted friezes—the ibis in the garden and the servants down the hall—despite the letters of state scattered across the floor, she is just a woman now. She has no enemies to threaten her, no ambition to drive her—and she is freer than she has ever been before.

***

At the noon hour Zenobia peered disheveled around her doorframe and told her servants to cancel her meetings. She had come up ill, she said, and could not leave her rooms. Then she padded naked back to the couch where Zabdas waited.

Hours later, they lie there still, weak with satiety, fingers intertwined and legs woven together.

"Do you still wish me to return to Palmyra?" Zenobia asks lazily.

"I ought to say yes," Zabdas replies. He yawns. "But gods help me, you know I won't."

"I don't want to go back," she says fiercely. She lifts herself on one elbow, her dark stare suddenly desperate. "I wanted you for so long, Zabdas, but I never dared . . . all my plans, you see, they'd have been ruined if . . ."

"Hush," he says, stroking her shoulder. "I know. All is forgiven."

"I won't marry some Roman noble, and I can't marry you—not after what I've done. And Vaballathus—what of his inheritance? If I take up with my general, Palmyra will never accept—"

"You needn't explain it. I know."

"This is why I won't go back—can't go back. The first time we kissed, that time in my chambers, I thought I was only giving in to my loneliness. But it was you I wanted all along. No other man has held my heart the way you have—not even Odenathus, for all his power."

"I once asked you what power has to do with companionship," Zabdas says, smiling.

"And I once asked you what love has to do with marriage," she replies. "I know now that love can exist outside a marriage, but only in a place that condones it. In Egypt, we can be what we are now. We can live and love as we do now. But if we return to Palmyra, we must revert to Palmyrene ways, and this love can never be. I can't accept Aurelian's terms. I can't give you up. I won't."

Zabdas's heart gives one great, straining lurch, and then he pulls her down on his chest, soothing her with his touch. "Nor I you," he promises.

"I don't want my life to be any other way. It's perfect as it is now. It's exactly as it ought to be. I would only have Vaballathus here if I could."

"We'll send for him when the desert cities are more stable—when it's safer for a boy his age to make the trip."

Zabdas toys with her hair, twisting his fingers through the dark curls. Then he gives an abrupt laugh that makes Zenobia sit up, a question plain on her strong, desert features.

"I was just remembering the shrine of Venus," Zabdas says. "You cut off your hair as an offering, but it wasn't your hair the goddess wanted."

"No," Zenobia says, smiling. "It was this—us." She pauses, reflecting. Venus made her desires known long before the shrine. In the shade of Tadmor, when Zabdas watched over Zenobia as she slept, and when Zenobia woke to see that his eyes were as green as the oasis—that was when the goddess first made herself known. But Zenobia has denied the goddess all along, until this day.

"I finally listened to the goddess," she says with a rueful laugh, "though I was a bit slow about it, wasn't I?"

"She's generous," Zabdas says soberly. "She granted you victory months before you gave her the offering she truly wanted."

"I shall have to—"

A sharp knock cuts off Zenobia's words. She frowns at Zabdas, hoping the messenger will depart, but a moment later an urgent voice calls out, muffled by the carved cedar doors, "My queen! Important news from Rome!"

A sudden chill steals Zenobia's breath. She watches as concern steals over Zabdas's face. She feels, with a sick thrill of premonition, his fingers loose themselves from her hair.

She wraps herself in the folds of her discarded gown. The walk toward her chamber door has never felt so impossibly long before.

She pulls the door open, and the messenger—a palace steward—averts his eyes from her half-robed body. He says quickly, "I've just received word, my queen. Caesar Claudius Gothicus is dead."

Zenobia's mouth goes dry. Where she should have words—questions or commands—she has only the painful racing of her heart. Her eyes unfocus and stare past the messenger, down the dim interior hallway. There is a niche in the wall and a goddess standing within it. Through the blur of Zenobia's vision, the goddess seems to take on a translucent violet glow.

She feels a stirring at her back. Zabdas has scrambled into his clothing, and he pulls the door wider. He scowls at the messenger's startled look.

"Who is called Caesar now?" he asks harshly.

"The general Aurelian, master," the steward says.

His duty discharged, the man turns to go. Zabdas lifts one hand as if to stroke Zenobia's hair again, but freezes and drops it back to his side.

We did not give the goddess the offering she wanted, Zabdas thinks. *Not when she demanded it—not in her time. Has she been lenient, and delivered us victory after all? Or has she only been waiting all this time to exact the price for disobeying her will?*

15

EMPRESS OF THE EAST

The poisoner comes in the cool of the evening.

The light in the Great Gardens is fading, taking with it the green-browns and dry grays of an Egyptian summer, leaving in their place a patchwork of shadowy blues among the half-dry ponds and the flower beds. The day's heat, as fiery as a kiln, ebbs rapidly, leaving what could be called a chill, if not for the thick humidity. A full year in Egypt, and Zenobia has nearly grown used to the dampness of the air—as used to it as a woman of the desert tribes ever can be.

She looks up as the poisoner advances. The woman is wiry and hard, with deep lines in her face that speak more of labor in the sun than of age. She wears a long cloak of heavy linen—heavier than is necessary for a summer night, even considering the drop in temperature. In the twilight, Zenobia can see that the woman's cloak is dyed a pale green. Zenobia raises one brow. By very old tradition—by native Egyptian reckoning—green is the color of death.

As the poisoner draws nearer, moving with a flowing, direct gait, Zenobia discerns that the woman is indeed a true Egyptian, with the typically dusky complexion; wide-set, piercing eyes; and small frame of the native born. She has eschewed current Alexandrian style, which favors Greek modes, and wears instead a gown of intricate pleats, its blue hem sweeping the grass below the swing of her cloak. Over her natural hair sits a thick, dark wig, blunt cut and beaded.

Zenobia speaks quick words of dismissal to her maids. They leave her at once, whispering behind their hands and casting uneasy glances over their shoulders as they go.

The poisoner stops several paces away and bows with her palms out.

"Please," Zenobia says in the old Egyptian tongue. She gestures to the stone wall of the pond, where she sits.

The poisoner's eyes widen below the fringe of her wig. "My queen," she says in a voice like old wood, cracked and pitted. "It is not fitting that I should sit beside you. Oh, but to hear you speak the mother tongue . . . ! Isis blesses me."

Zenobia insists. "You will hear me speak the mother tongue plenty, but only if you overcome your reservations and sit close. We must converse in low voices, you and I."

The poisoner hesitates only a moment longer. Then she bundles her cloak around her narrow frame and lowers herself onto the wall gingerly, as if she's afraid her negligible weight might crumble it and send the Queen of Egypt toppling backward into the water.

"I had heard that you speak our language well, as Cleopatra did, but I hardly dared to hope," says the woman. "Now I see that it is true. Isis blesses all of us." The woman nods and nods, the beads in her wig clicking in the gathering dark.

"Language is not the only interest I share with Cleopatra. What is your name?"

"Werenro, my queen."

A late-roosting bird calls in high, falling notes from a shadowy treetop. Zenobia looks up, gazing out across the length of the Great

Gardens. The pinpoint of an orange torch flickers and bobs on a distant path. She smiles.

"I sent for you, Werenro, because you are the best poisoner in all of Alexandria. Is it not so?"

"My family has practiced the art for countless generations, my queen. I can craft any poison—the slow and the quick, the silent and the spectacular."

The torch comes closer as Werenro speaks. Soon Zenobia can make out Zabdas's face, or a strange, theater-mask version of him, the fire ruddy on his skin, his eyes lost in pits of blackness.

Werenro breaks off describing her poisons. She watches Zabdas approach in wary silence.

"It's all right," Zenobia assures her. "The man is my own. I trust him with my life."

"Well, then, my queen," the poisoner says, tugging the ends of her green cloak tighter about her bony shoulders, "what is it you desire? I know better than to ask whom you want dead. That is none of *my* business. My business lies in finding the right substance for the task."

Even in the torchlight, Zabdas's harsh red-and-black mask manages a look of deep skepticism. "What is the meaning of this, my queen? Who is this woman?"

"Werenro," Zenobia says, as if that explains everything.

She turns back to the poisoner. "There is no one in particular I wish to kill—yet. I want only to learn. A time may come"—*soon,* she thinks sourly—"when such knowledge will be useful. Zabdas, sit here beside me. Hold your torch up—there. Listen while Werenro teaches us. You may find this instructive, too."

Werenro stands. She opens first one side of her cloak, then the other. For all the world she looks like a bat stretching its leathery wings. The lining is stitched with pockets and pouches, with small leather catches that secure colored faience bottles by their necks. While Zenobia listens, rapt, the poisoner explains the contents and action of each deadly phial.

It is a gruesome occupation, Zabdas thinks, watching the eerie intensity on the poisoner's face as she recites the details of her brews. Only the weak use poison. A strong man fights his enemies with a blade, or a bow, or even with his bare hands. Then he glances at Zenobia, perched on the edge of the pond. Her small frame seems to flicker in the glow of the torch, its dancing light illuminating, then hiding the linen-clad curves of her body, the golden snakes wrapped around her wrists, the narrow diadem nestled in her hair.

I have seen her kill a man with a sword blow. I have seen her draw a blade and ride into chaos, without a trace of fear. Yet she is a woman, after all. One woman standing against Rome—against an empire of treacherous men.

No wonder, then, that her thoughts have turned down such a dark and twisted path. The letters from Aurelian have kept coming. She shows them to Zabdas, every one. Rome's new emperor seems almost friendly, jocular in his warnings, pleasant in his threats. But Zenobia has decided. Contrary to accepting Aurelian's directives, she has redoubled her efforts, demanding her share of the empire in terms so outrageous that even Zabdas can't imagine she is serious.

She is desperate now, he thinks. *She will ride this wild horse until it plunges off the cliff.* And why not? What choice does she have? Can she ever hope to safely dismount?

At least she is not alone, Zabdas thinks as the poisoner holds another vial up to the torchlight. *She never will be—not as long as I live. If it comes to poisoning, to fighting with a woman's weapons, I will uncork the bottle and pour it into any cup she commands.*

The night deepens. The chill is forceful now; Zenobia's linen shawl is not enough to keep her from shivering. She asks one last question of Werenro, listens attentively to the answer, and then rises from her seat beside the water.

"That will be enough for now," she tells the woman. "I have learned much, and I thank you. I will call for you again, when I have more time for lessons."

Werenro bows, drawing her strange cloak shut.

"My steward will pay you for your time. He is waiting at the garden gate, and will escort you out of the palace." Werenro turns to go, but Zenobia recalls her. "I would like to purchase one vial now," she says. "The one that induces sleep, then stops the heart."

"Hemlock, my queen."

"Yes, that's the one."

"It has been my pleasure to instruct you," Werenro says. "Let me give you the hemlock as a gift—an offering to Cleopatra come again."

Zenobia accepts the gift with a small, regal smile. When Werenro has drifted off into the darkness, she turns to Zabdas with a sigh.

"Cleopatra come again," she says. "How right the poisoner is. I've staked my claim against Rome, and only the gods know whether it will end with an asp clutched to my breast." Absently, she runs her thumb over the tiny, smooth bottle in her hand.

Zabdas indicates the hemlock with a nod. "Save that for someone else. Aurelian, maybe. Cleopatra's fate is not yours." He lifts her chin with his free hand, watching as the firelight plays over her flushed cheeks. "Where is the girl who was once so certain of her destiny?"

"Not here," Zenobia says, turning away.

She walks away from him, following an aimless path through the dark, cold garden. He hurries after her with the torch, but no matter how fast he strides, she remains just on the edge of the light, a phantom forever out of his reach, vanishing in a blur of white linen.

"Wait," Zabdas calls out. "Let me stay with you—I must protect you!"

Clutched by fear, by a certainty that he will lose her, he breaks into a run.

Zenobia halts when she hears his pounding footsteps. The firelight leaps, and suddenly she is beside him. She is more than a mere presence, larger than life in his ring of torchlight, a force of personality that seems to tower over his superior height.

Zabdas gasps in surprise. "Gods!"

But the torch gutters down again, and she is herself—small and solid, bundled in her cloak, looking up at him.

"There is no backing down now," she tells him, her words barely more than a whisper.

"If there ever was."

"Do you regret the promise you made me, Zabdas—to be my loyal man, to stand beside me no matter what may come?"

He touches her cheek and slides his hand around to cup the warm nape of her neck. "Never."

Zenobia looks down at the phial in her palm. In the torchlight, she can see that it is enameled in red, as slick and shining as fresh-spilled blood. Resolutely, she closes her fist around it.

"Even if I could back down," she says bravely, with hardly a catch in her voice, "I wouldn't."

Zabdas hears the lie in her words, and senses an unfamiliar texture through their filmy veil. Is it regret he detects hiding in her voice? Surely not.

"I know," he says, to soothe her.

"*I* know," she replies at once. Zabdas is startled to see her smile—a quick curve of the mouth that looks very much like mischief. "I know what I'll do. Either the gods truly do support me, or they don't. If they *are* going to see me through this, Zabdas, I've got to show some commitment to their cause."

He laughs—he can't help it. "I think you've shown more than enough commitment to satisfy any god."

"They're testing me," she says. "Testing my faith in their designs. Or they played me for a fool and have abandoned me. Either way, I've got to drive ahead with all my might. There's no way out but forward."

Forward, Zabdas thinks. *There may be no way out at all.* But he only nods mutely.

Zenobia taps a finger against her chin. "It's no longer enough to ask Aurelian for his cooperation—or his blessing. I must reach out and take what I want, not accept it from any man's hand—or it will never be truly mine."

They start back toward the palace, walking slowly, the torch held low. It casts a great egg-shaped glow along the ground, stretching and receding with the rhythm of Zabdas's stride.

"You reached out and took Emesa," he points out. "And Antioch, and then *Egypt,* Rome's breadbasket, in the name of all that's sacred. Haven't you done enough reaching and taking? Haven't you proved your point to all the gods, and to the Augustus?"

"Evidently not," she says fiercely. "But I know now what I must do—how I must declare my intentions."

"The Augustus won't like it one bit, I assume."

Zenobia doesn't answer. Zabdas watches her from the corner of his eye. She holds her cape tight against the chill, which only seems to emphasize her small, slender frame. She looks suddenly fragile, Zabdas notes with surprise. Where moments before she had seemed larger than life, now she is pale and rare, like a fine, white piece of Seres pottery. But her stride is determined, undaunted—the sure step of a Ras marching into war.

He almost asks her, *What will you do when Aurelian strikes back at you—when he makes his displeasure known?*—as he must, sometime, somehow.

But before he can speak, he chances to glance down at her fist—the fist that holds the phial of hemlock. Zenobia tightens her grip on the bottle and strides on into the darkness.

***

Two weeks later, Zabdas receives a summons to Zenobia's office, a curtained meeting hall furnished with a long cedar table and more chairs than he has ever seen men to fill them. Zabdas nods to the guard at the door—one of Timagenes's men—and pushes his way inside.

The office is empty, save for the statues of gods gazing down from their stone niches, frozen in postures of power. Zenobia sits with her back to the door, her hair pinned up in the familiar black knot, her hands busy on the table, and her pale neck bent over her work. For one hot, forceful moment, Zabdas is gripped by the desire—by the need—to press his lips against that neck, to taste the soft skin, as light and fragrant as freshly sanded wood. But he glances up at the gods, at their dozens of eyes upon him, and he walks calmly to her side.

She is bent, Zabdas sees, over a pile of freshly cast coins, examining the bags that have come from the mint on the southern edge of Alexandria. A tablet rests nearby with an account of the mint's production, waiting for her mark of approval. As he watches, Zenobia lifts a few of the coins and slides them between her fingers, examining their quality. They make a slithering noise, like a nest of snakes made of clean, new metal.

Without turning around, Zenobia lifts one hand and extends her two fingers toward Zabdas. There is a coin gripped between them, a little orb of light balanced on her fingertips.

Zabdas takes the coin gingerly and squints at its bright face. It bears an image of Zenobia—carved with harsher angles than those the gods gave her, but such engravings are always a touch unnatural. Her proud chin juts beneath her strong Amlaqi nose; her eyes stare undaunted into the distance. On her head is a rayed crown, and, around the edge of the coin, the words *"Imperatrix Orientis"*—Empress of the East.

The coin is colder than the stone of a tomb. Zabdas wraps it in his fist, as if he could hide it from the world. "What is this?" he says quietly.

"A declaration," Zenobia answers. She turns now, looks up at him solemnly with one arm braced on the back of her chair. "I am done asking Emperor Aurelian for his cooperation. I am *telling* him that the East is mine, the way Romans have always declared their greatness—with coin."

She stares at him, unblinking, a moment longer. The only sound in the empty office is the faint stir of her breath.

This is her last stand, he realizes. *Her final reach for her destiny—for what she* believes *is her destiny.* If the gods do not stretch out their hands to catch her, Zenobia will now fall. There is no other possible outcome.

She has done it boldly, Zabdas knows. She has made her declaration in no uncertain terms. Whatever else the world might say of Zenobia bat-Zabbai, no one will ever be able to call her a coward.

"Well," Zabdas says lightly, "it seems you are empress."

She doesn't laugh, doesn't smile. "There is more."

"More?"

The coin seems to burn in his fist. He opens his hand, and sees that it rests tail-side up. But there is no tail mark on the obverse. There is another head. Zabdas raises the coin to his face and scrutinizes the image. It is a man—young, even youthful, with a short, curly beard and a bright expression. He looks, Zabdas thinks, a bit like Odenathus—the way Odenathus must have looked in his early and reckless days.

Then his spine shivers with recognition. He abruptly drops the coin on the table. It rings loudly in the silence of the chamber, rolling along its rim until it settles with a rising, vibrating note.

"Vaballathus?" Zabdas nearly shouts. "You declared your son emperor? Zenobia, what were you thinking?"

"He is the Emperor of the East," she says, sliding a handful of coins again between her fingers. "I am only his regent until he comes of age."

"But why put him at risk? Gods save me, he's only a little boy!"

Zenobia draws a long, shaky breath. She looks up at Zabdas again, her eyes wide with both certainty and fear. "Do you think that matters to Aurelian? If Rome strikes against me, Vaballathus won't escape this any more than we will."

If, Zabdas thinks with a bitter inward laugh.

"My son will be killed anyway, Zabdas! Aurelian will punish him for my audacity; you know how these Romans are! I might as well include Vaballathus in whatever fate the gods have planned for me. That way, if there is any hope that I have not been played for a fool . . . then my son will be spared along with me."

She closes her eyes, and tears suddenly slide down her cheeks. Zabdas takes her in his arms, lifting her from the chair and holding her close as her body shakes with silent sobs.

Her hand opens, and the coins drop from her fist like a shower of rain.

16

THE INDIGO LINE

The seasons roll through Egypt. The fields upriver, in the southern cities, flood with brown, silt-laden water. When the floods retreat, they expose lands freshly covered in fertile black silt. The crops are planted, and, eagerly, they grow. Reports from Memphis and Thebes are all of bountiful fields and healthy cattle—signs of the gods' good favor. And when the orchards have yielded all their fruit and the farmers prepare to welcome the flood once again, more encouraging reports arrive in Alexandria: the river is rising to just the right level, at precisely the correct time. The gods are appeased. They are pleased with the Queen of Egypt.

This signs of the gods' pleasure should be enough to soothe Zenobia's fears, but in the eight months since the striking of her coins, the tight sensation of waiting—of bracing for Rome's inevitable blow—has never left her. She has not forgotten the sight of her offering to Apollo sinking beneath the dark waters of the sacred spring. More often than not, she is preoccupied, pacing with her thoughts on the roof or in the garden, staring silently into the distance while she runs through one plan after another, contingency after plot, trying to weave a net of scenarios and compromises that will catch her empire if it should fall.

On a misty morning, when the thick Alexandrine air could almost be called crisp, Zabdas finds Zenobia on the palace rooftop. Down the great length of the Nile, the last of the harvests have been brought in, and the surplus has made its way north along the river to the harbors of the Delta. The Empress of the East leans against the rooftop wall, gazing down at the port, where ships bound for Rome are being loaded with grain.

As Zabdas watches from the head of the stairs, the salt-scented breeze tugs at Zenobia's hair, rippling the folds of her cloak.

Zabdas clears his throat, and Zenobia looks around expectantly. There is a strain about her eyes, the same air of tight anticipation that has been her constant adornment these months past. But in spite of the worries that gnaw at her, she smiles with real warmth when she sees Zabdas.

"Any news?" she asks.

He knows what news she seeks: word from Aurelian. In spite of the fact that Zenobia sent a sack of her coins to Rome shortly after they were minted, the emperor has remained eerily, dangerously quiet. He sends no more of his jocular letters.

"The only news I've heard," Zabdas says, "is that the Dalmatian front has calmed somewhat. The fighting is not as fierce as it once was. The Goths are all but beaten and will soon be driven back for good—or so my men say."

Zenobia makes no reply, but taps her chin with one finger, staring again out into the mist.

"You've heard nothing from Aurelian?" Zabdas asks cautiously.

"Nothing."

Even when the war was at its worst, the Augustus still found the time to slide one of his needling missives in Zenobia's direction. Zabdas wishes he could convince himself that this is a good sign—that Aurelian has acquiesced and will allow the Empress of the East to continue in her reign.

"I've done all I can," Zenobia says, not for the first time.

"I know."

"I've instructed Vorod and Antiochus to maintain clear routes to Rome at all costs, to keep the silks and spices flowing from Palmyra. I've been punctual and unstinting with Egyptian grain. I've proven myself an amiable and reliable friend to Rome."

"And an impertinent one."

Zenobia cuts him a sharp glare. "I hardly need the reminder, thank you, Zabdas."

He bows his head, accepting her rebuke.

"Gods." She sighs. "I won't back down—you know I won't. Aurelian must surely see by now that I won't. This is my empire, my title. I've won them, and I will keep them. Am I wrong to be so determined?"

Zabdas declines to answer, certain his mistress won't like his response.

"If only there was some word from Aurelian," Zenobia says, folding her arms beneath her breasts as if warding away the chill. "Something to break his silence."

There is word, but not the kind Zenobia would like. Zabdas decides that now is as good a time as any to present it to her. He reaches into his belt pouch and draws out a letter.

Zenobia's eyes widen when she sees it. For a moment, a strange, desperate thrill pierces her heart—an impossible mingling of hope and hopelessness. *Aurelian,* she thinks. He has deigned to respond at last, and whether his letter confirms Zenobia's empire or condemns her to death, at least now she will know—at least the long, unbearable wait will be over.

But then she notices the blue wax seal and the papyrus flapping open as the harbor breeze skirls along the rooftop. Zabdas has already read the letter. As she takes it from his hand she sees that the blue seal bears the imprint of a hooded falcon perched on a spear. The letter is from the tribe of Amlaqi.

"Nafsha?" she says. Her voice is high and frightened.

Zabdas nods once, tersely.

Sick with misgiving, Zenobia unfolds the papyrus and reads.

Dear Sister,

First, be assured that we are all well. Mother and Zabibah and Zabibah's daughter are well. My two sons are fine, and so are your brothers-in-law. Vaballathus, too, is healthy and happy, and thrives under my care. But it is for your son's sake that I write to you.

Twice now, Antiochus has received threatening notes concerning your son. They are not signed, of course, and although my husband has strived to learn their source, as of the day I write this letter, all of his efforts are in vain.

We have given Vaballathus guards both day and night. On most days he remains in the palace where I can keep a close eye on him. We will not rest until we know who is threatening your son, nor will we cease our vigil over him.

Antiochus suspects that the Tanukh are responsible for this threat. They are agitating again, stirring up strife in the desert around Palmyra. Antiochus thinks they will attack the city soon, and mean to use Vaballathus—if they can capture him—as leverage over you and Palmyra.

I want you to be aware. Send whatever aid you can to Palmyra, for the Tanukh are as real a threat as ever.

Your watchful sister,
Lady Nafsha

Zenobia's hands go so icy she can barely hold the papyrus. She relinquishes it numbly when Zabdas tugs it from her fingers.

"Do you think it's truly the Tanukh threatening my son?" she asks quietly.

"No," Zabdas says. "The gods know the Tanukh love trouble, but I'd be surprised if they even knew Vaballathus is in your sister's care. That doesn't seem like the sort of information the Tanukh would ever bother to learn."

It is true. The Tanukh have no reason to strike at Zenobia personally—and a threat against Vaballathus is certainly a threat against the Empress of the East. Vorod or Antiochus—or Antiochus's sons—would be the likely targets of Tanukh ire, not Antiochus's five-year-old nephew.

"It can only be Aurelian," Zenobia says. "The Augustus is targeting my son."

Zabdas tilts his head. "Or the Sasanids."

"Sasanids? Why? I've left Eran to its own devices since my campaign across the East. The Sasanids have no reason to come after Vaballathus or me. No—it's Aurelian, and no mistake. I never thought"—she turns away with a choked, bitter laugh—"in all my correspondence with the emperor that he'd be small enough to threaten a helpless child. If he were a real man, he would come after *me*."

"What better way to draw a mother out than to threaten her child?"

"Aurelian doesn't need to draw me out!" Zenobia swings one arm in a wide arc, taking in all of Alexandria—the bustling port with its ships bound for Rome and the markets and shops and shaded fora, filled with citizens going about their lives, oblivious to their queen's turmoil. "He knows where I am. He knows where I've been for the last two years!"

"What are you going to do, then?"

She jerks her cloak tight around her body and paces the rooftop, brow furrowed in thought. As she stalks away from Zabdas, a stray cloud of autumn mist rolls up from the harbor. It drifts between them, obscuring Zenobia from his sight, and as she melds into the dense whiteness, Zabdas feels a surge of desperate fear, as on the night when she'd held the bottle of hemlock in her fist and faded into the deep shadows of the nighttime garden. Then she reappears, striding back through the stray mist as she completes her circuit of the rooftop. The mist rolls away, out across the city.

"I'm going to Palmyra," she announces.

"What? Zenobia, no."

"Yes. The gods know I love Egypt, and the life we've made together here. I have done well ruling this land as I ought—it's my birthright, after all. And if the gods are willing, I'll go on ruling well when I return. Egypt may be the seat of my empire, but Palmyra is the root of my strength.

"Nafsha would not have written to me if the situation weren't dire—not only the threats against Vaballathus but the Tanukh agitation, too." She twists the sash of her robe, watching the harbor's ships with a distant gaze. "It's clearly troubling her, and if my levelheaded sister is troubled, then I should be doubly concerned."

Zenobia turns to him suddenly, and her words sound almost pleading. "It is serious, Zabdas—my son and my city are in peril. I'll go to Palmyra, ensure that my city is safe—and, gods help me, I'll see a wall built. The start of a wall, at the least. Vorod and Antiochus can see to its finishing."

"Zenobia," Zabdas begins, but she cuts him off.

"When I'm sure Palmyra and Vaballathus are both safe, I'll return to Alexandria. *With* my son. If the gods are good, it won't be more than two months, and I'll be home again—back to Egypt, and you—where I belong."

Zabdas presses his mouth into a thin, disapproving line. "First of all, I'm going with you if you leave Alexandria at all. Second, I don't like it. Whoever is threatening your son is doing it to draw you out. Yes, Aurelian knows you're in Alexandria. But would you rather fight your way through a swarm of loyal Egyptians, and then prise a stubborn queen out of her fortified palace, or fall on a small band trekking through the desert? This is a trap, Zenobia—a ruse to make you vulnerable, to isolate you, so that you're easy to kill."

"Do you think I don't see that?" She flares at him, her eyes sparking hot as a fire. "Of course it's a trap, Zabdas. I see that plainly. But what choice do I have? A Roman will not scruple to kill my son. Aurelian will put every last citizen of Palmyra to the sword—undefended Palmyra!—if that's what it takes to get what he wants."

"Then you can, at least, surrender," Zabdas says, and braces himself for a hot and hateful reply.

Zenobia only takes a deep breath, gazing away from him, out into the glowing white mist that obscures the sea.

At last she says quietly, "I have a better plan. I *know* my enemy has set a snare—and that gives me the advantage. I can get to Palmyra safely. I *must* get there safely." She takes Zabdas's hand. "Here is how we'll do it."

As she speaks, unfurling a plan that is so desperate and reckless it might succeed, the Empress of the East stares steadily out over the harbor, in the direction of Rome.

＊＊＊

Alexandria is four days behind her. Three of those days on a hateful ship, lurching over the waves, struggling to comfort Feather, who moaned and suffered in the hold, even while Zenobia retched into a clay pot.

Then another long day of swaying on her camel, from the predawn grayness until long after dark. A long day of grim solitude, of moaning wind and glaring midday light. One long day on the thin, dark track of the old caravan route, her guide and lifeline, cutting through barren stone and inhospitable thorns all the long way from the secret harbor where she came ashore, north to Antioch.

Never in Zenobia's life has she been so alone; the vastness of her solitude astounds her. As she rides, rocking side to side with Feather's steady gait, it seems Zenobia can see herself as if from a great, distant height. She is a single dark speck, creeping across an endless expanse of arid wasteland, as insignificant as an ant, even if she is the Empress of the East.

She knows that Zabdas and a force of fifty thousand Egyptians march a day behind her, but out here in the staggering openness of the desert, alone as she is, it is a comfort so small as to be nonexistent. When you ride alone, a day's distance might as well be a week's, or a year's.

But this is necessary, this isolation and its accompanying anxiety. She knows it is necessary. Disguised once more in the rough clothes of a trader, she hopes to pass without comment should she chance to meet anyone on the trail between the harbor and Antioch. Attention will be directed toward Zabdas's great army—and if Aurelian expects to find Zenobia marching toward Palmyra, she devoutly hopes he will assume she marches in the midst of her troops.

Throughout the long and lonesome journey, guilt has assailed her nearly as much as fear. She hates the thought of using Zabdas as a decoy. If Rome is lying in wait for Zenobia, they will certainly attack her forces with breathtaking ferocity. Zabdas is a fighter worthy of any foe, but it seems dreadful that he should draw Rome's eye and assume all the risk, while Zenobia rides free.

What if he is killed?

She has asked herself that terrible question a thousand times since leaving Alexandria. She has chanted it inside her head like a refrain— and sometimes, when the fear becomes too great to bear it silently, she speaks the words aloud, casting the question out to the sand and the stones, but the desert gives no answers.

For Zabdas to die—it is nearly the worst thing she can imagine. She would rather die herself, a hundred times over, than lose him. It seems a cruel trick of fate: now when she has finally let herself love him and found true joy in his arms, he might perish on the point of a Roman sword, while Zenobia rides on toward Palmyra. What will her life be worth, without him? What will her city be worth—her empire?

She thinks about the first time she lay with him, on the couch in her palace chambers, with the scrolls of her office scattered across the floor. She remembers how he lifted her blunt-cut hair in his hands.

Venus—Aphrodite—Isis! She cries out to the goddess as she rides, and seems to see the translucent alabaster face peering from every rock ledge she passes, frowning in the shadow of every distant dune. *I denied your offering for so long. Have I angered you, great goddess? Will you take love from me now, to humble me, to punish me for all my sins?*

When the sun rides low in the sky, touching the pale horizon with the colors of flame, Zenobia finds a concealed rock formation and sets about making her camp. She does it automatically, unloading Feather's panniers with quiet efficiency, setting up the small skin tent with a few well-practiced movements—she recalls the way it was done from the trek to Didyma nearly two years ago. She fills Feather's feedbag and secures his hobbles, then climbs to the top of the rock formation as the last sliver of sun falls, gold as a new-minted coin, below the horizon.

Zenobia takes a scrap of papyrus from her belt pouch. It is a map of the trade route, each landmark and bend of the trail carefully noted. She orients the map—Zabdas showed her the trick of it—and confirms that she is still headed in the right direction. That, at least, is some small comfort. Soon she will reach Antioch. This isolation will not go on forever.

As she returns the map to its pouch, her fingers brush a hard lump tucked into the girdle of her robe. She pulls it free—the phial of hemlock. She isn't sure why she brought it from Alexandria. She stares at it a moment with vague mistrust, as if it might become a serpent that will uncoil itself and strike her. But it remains what it is, death contained in a tiny, bright-red bottle. The faience of the phial glints in the sunset, and, with a determined frown, Zenobia tucks the bottle back into her garment.

She sits, hugging her knees to her chest, gazing back the way she has come. As night advances, the desert turns to a land of violet shadow. The track of the trade route is like a streak of blue dye dragged along the earth by a careless brush. She has borne one full day of riding that long track—one full day of anxiety. One day of the goddess's stern rebuke. How much longer can she bear it?

Somewhere along that indigo line, at the head of his army of fifty thousand men, Zabdas looks toward Antioch, toward Zenobia, while she stares back desperately, wishing for a distant flicker of torchlight, for any small glimpse of him to comfort her.

***

Two days later, Zenobia reaches the pitted, old walls of Antioch early in the evening. At the gate, she sighs with relief, then presents a trader's token, a small wooden disc strung on a leather thong and emblazoned with the sedge-and-bee device of Egypt. The token will allow her to pass without suspicion. Here in the East, trade never stops, and traders are as common as fleas on a dog.

"Egyptians," a gate guard mutters, in Greek, to the other. "Don't know how to manage their women proper-like. Imagine, a woman trading!"

"And riding out alone," the other guard says as he prods at her panniers. "No telling what might happen to a woman alone."

They share a leering laugh and raise their brows.

"You do realize traders are known for their competence with language," Zenobia says in the Greek they favor. "Even female traders."

The guards exchange chagrined glances. Then one whispers in Latin, "Mouthy Egyptian slit doesn't know what's good for her."

"I speak Latin, too," Zenobia informs them.

She kicks Feather into a trot and proceeds into the narrow, crowded lanes of Antioch.

Her stomach curdles with rage over the guards' impertinence. She knows her anger is out of proportion to their offense, but the stress of her long trek and her days of isolation have come boiling out of the pot. As she rides, she clenches her teeth so hard her jaw begins to ache—and it is only when she finds herself in the stinking morass of the butchers' district that she realizes she has missed her turn.

Zenobia backtracks through Antioch, willing herself to calm. She searches for the meeting place she has arranged with Zabdas—the home of a wealthy merchant, one Elek by name, a seller of fine pottery who is known to be both trustworthy and loyal to the Empress of the East. Zenobia has never met Elek before, but Zabdas has had cause to work with him in the past. Half a day before she left Alexandria, Zenobia sent a messenger on a fast ship, accompanied by an equally swift camel, bound for Elek's door. If the gods have been kind, Elek will be expecting his illustrious guest.

At last, she finds the place—a small but beautiful estate set far back from a communal cistern, where a few women pause to gossip, leisurely drawing water from the well. Slender palms rise above the estate's pink granite walls, their fronds drifting and rustling on the growing evening breeze. The gate is of old cedar, dark and hard, its tight-fitted planks carved with the interlinked coils of snakes painted red and blue.

The women glance at Zenobia as she passes, letting their talk trail off. They raise their hands to their mouths, shielding whispers. No doubt they are remarking on the spectacle of a woman trader, but almost certainly in kinder terms than the gate guards used.

The inner arch of Elek's gateway is tiled in blue and saffron yellow. She hesitates in there, but the guard bows to her straightaway and shoves the cedar doors open, waving her on, then whispers to a little boy in a short linen smock, who goes sprinting across the pale, dusty yard, shouting, *"Master! Master!"*

Feather cushes, and Zenobia slides from the saddle, offering her trusty camel a scratch behind the ear, which Feather rejects with a curt toss of his head. She stretches, arching backward and pressing her fists against her spine. She nearly groans aloud with relief—at being out of the saddle, yes, but also at having reached the safety of Antioch at last.

Elek appears from a doorway, a small, bustling man past middle age with the habit of wringing his hands like a fretting old woman. He bows deeply, several times. "It is an honor—an honor, yes—please, won't you come in, Em—" He catches himself, glancing around the yard, though even the little boy is nowhere to be seen. "Mistress," Elek amends, and ushers her inside.

"So my messenger reached you," Zenobia says.

"Oh, indeed," Elek replies, leading her through a cool, dark hall and into a sitting room, where a low, circular table is set with plates of food.

Zenobia's stomach growls audibly. Since leaving her palace, she has eaten nothing but flatbread, hard cheese, and dried fruit—poor fare for one grown used to the kitchens and cooks of Alexandria. The smell of roast duck and fresh cream so overwhelms her senses that she finds she must fight back tears.

"This is all for you." Elek gestures toward the table. "I only regret that I cannot offer you more, mistress. But you have my hospitality, humble though it may be."

She eats, but though she knows Elek's rich dishes must be delicious—she can smell the delicacy of the spices, can see the jewellike brightness of the fruits and the golden perfection of the roasted duck's breast—she tastes nothing of her meal. Zabdas is still out there, open to Aurelian's attack. Until she knows that he is safe, she can take pleasure in nothing. Still, she eats until her stomach aches, for she is aware that her situation is tenuous, and she knows it may be a long time before she sees such a fine spread again.

As night falls, Elek shows her to a sleeping chamber—his own, Zenobia surmises. It is as finely appointed as any in her father's old palace, decorated with the artful pots and vases that are the man's stock in trade. His servants have left a kettle of hot water and a basin at the foot of the bed. Crisp linen towels lie folded on the coverlet. These simple luxuries make her heart pound in her throat.

She washes the grime of her long, weary trek from her skin and then falls gratefully on the bed. She is asleep before she can even pull the coverlet across her body.

***

A whisper wakes her. Zenobia's eyes snap open, staring unseeing into a fathomless darkness. For a long time, she doesn't know where she is. Then, as her eyes adjust, the shapes of pots and vases materialize in their dark niches, like ghosts rising from their tombs.

Of course, she thinks, cursing her momentary confusion. *The trader Elek's estate.*

The whisper comes again: "Mistress!"

Zenobia rolls onto her side, searching the blackness. After she'd washed, she'd donned her traveling clothes once more, wanting to be ready to move on again at a moment's notice. Now the linen and wool garments scratch against her skin; they are thick and abrasive with their long accumulation of dust and sweat.

"Mistress!"

At last she can make out a small, bony shadow, its little smock emerging from the darkness like the shapes of the pottery. It is the boy from the yard.

"What is the hour?" she asks.

"Just before dawn. A man has come for you, mistress."

Zenobia sits up quickly. "A man?"

"A big, scowling man with a scar on his cheek. He's talking to my master now. Master sent me to fetch you."

She is on her feet at once. "Show me the way."

It is too soon, she thinks as the boy leads her through the bright-tiled halls of Elek's estate. Zabdas was a full day behind and could not possibly have caught up to her with such a large army in tow. The only way he might have closed the distance between them so quickly is if he was forced to abandon his forces and flee for Antioch alone.

No, she tells herself, pressing her hands against her roiling belly. *Do not think the worst. It will be well. The gods will see to it.*

But when she sees Zabdas in the same room where just hours before she had eaten such delicacies, Zenobia knows her fears are well founded. He is battered and strained, clearly on the verge of exhaustion. A dirty, bloody cloth lies at his feet, and a woman dressed in the simple garb of a servant—one of the trader's maids, Zenobia assumes—is tending to his left arm. Zenobia gasps at the sight of him; she sways and clutches at the tiled doorframe, and the little boy takes her hand to steady her.

The servant finishes her work and bows her way out, allowing Zenobia to see Zabdas's arm. A red gash runs down it from shoulder to elbow, freshly stitched by the servant's needle.

Despite her tension and fear, despite the knowledge that some-thing—everything—has gone wrong, the sight of Zabdas alive strikes Zenobia with a wave of relief and gratitude so strong that her legs nearly give way. Somehow, she staggers across the room, knocking over a chair in her haste to reach him. She falls into his embrace, sobbing.

Elek sends the little boy away, and has the grace to leave, too, so he will not see Zenobia bat-Zabbai, the Empress of the East, weeping in her general's arms.

When her chest no longer aches with her sobs, and she can breathe again, Zenobia draws back. "Your arm—oh gods!"

"It is nothing, truly," Zabdas says. "I've had far worse wounds. It will heal."

"What has happened, Zabdas? Tell me!"

He draws her down on a cushioned bench. "A Roman force—a big one. They ambushed us from among the red cliffs—you know the ones; you would have passed them late yesterday. They were shouting for you as they attacked, all of them calling your name. There can be no doubt: Aurelian has come."

Absolute calm settles over her. She has come, at last, to the gods' day of reckoning. In a blink, her eyes are free of tears, and she gazes at Zabdas with a steadiness that would surprise her, if she weren't beyond the point of surprise.

"What's to be done next, then?" she wonders aloud. She finds herself against a wall, without a plan for the first time that she can remember.

Zabdas scratches at his beard. "This changes nothing, I think. It only confirms our fears. Aurelian was indeed lying in wait for you. Now we have found him—or he has found us. I'm sure, by now, he has realized you're not with my army . . . what's left of my army."

"Is it as bad as that?"

"I won't lie to you, Zenobia. By the time I broke free and fled for Antioch, the Romans had taken out a third of my force."

She sucks in a breath. "Truly?"

Zabdas nods. "I left a few of my commanders to rally whatever troops are left, but we'll be a small force—not enough to defend Palmyra once we reach her city limits."

"We'll need more mercenaries, then."

"If we can hire them quickly enough."

"We must trust the gods that the swords will come if we offer enough money."

"But Zenobia, you have no ready money—at least, not as you are now, alone and on the run. Even if you had, Antioch is not known for its population of soldiers for hire."

"No," she says. She pauses, thinking. The wall that hemmed her in dissolves; a plan begins to take shape in her mind. "But Emesa is. If you can get your army to Emesa, there I can add to your ranks with hired swords."

"But it is so out of the way. It would be faster to make straight for Palmyra."

"I've a treasury in Emesa—a stock of gold and other goods saved in a small estate. I laid it away during all those months when you were busy conquering my empire. It's enough to buy soldiers—I know it is. And Emesa is near the river. Word and men both travel quickly over water. I'll send out the call—to the desert tribes especially—and enough troops will quickly arrive to see us to Palmyra."

Zabdas shakes his head, but after a moment he gives a shrug, surrendering to the plan. "I suppose we have no other choice." *Truly,* Zabdas thinks, *the detour and the necessity of conjuring ten thousand more troops out of Zenobia's hidden coffers adds only a small interruption to their plans.* He nearly gives in to an impulse to burst into panicked laughter.

Zenobia calls to Elek, who steps eagerly from the back room, again wringing his hands and asking how he may be of service.

"Tell your men to saddle my camel. I must be gone before the sun is up."

She stares up at Zabdas for a moment, taking in the sight of him, his hard, tenacious face and his steady eyes. They are strained and harried, but they are as green as the palms of Tadmor, and she loves him—she loves him.

Zenobia lifts onto her toes and kisses him, long and deep, filling her senses with the feel of his mouth, the sound of his breath, the warmth of his hand pressing the small of her back.

She doesn't care that Elek sees. Let all of Antioch see, she thinks. Let Nafsha see, and her mother, too; let Egypt; let dead Odenathus see from the shadows of his tomb. Let every god in the wide, cold heavens see. They can damn her for it, and for all her improprieties, if they will. She doesn't care who might witness this indiscretion. As she holds herself against Zabdas, she knows that she might never have the chance to kiss him again.

17

A Handful of Dates

She is a day and a half beyond Antioch when Zenobia first learns that the city has fallen to Rome.

"Took it right back, he did," says a man's gruff, uncultured voice in the market square behind her. "Imagine, the Augustus himself, in Antioch!"

Zenobia's hand freezes over a small basket of dried figs. She holds her breath, straining to hear the conversation.

"Not so hard to imagine," says another man. "Hardly the first time an emperor has been to Antioch, after all."

"Ah, but old Aurelian snatched it right away from her. Empress of the East, if you please! Palmyrenes are too soft on their women. If she'd been my wife, I'd have—"

"You can't keep your own wife out of trouble as it is, Marianus, and *she* isn't the Queen of Egypt, so stop this useless fantasizing."

"Zenobia ain't the Queen of Egypt anymore, either," the first man mutters. "Not now that the Augustus is here."

The stall keeper, a woman with crooked teeth and a pinched, lined face, narrows her eyes at Zenobia. "Going to buy them figs, miss, or just stare at them all day?"

She takes the figs, and a handful of sticky dates, too. At the baker's stall she buys a few days' worth of flatbread, and at another stall she fills her linen sack with strips of smoked goat's meat. All this she does without thought, answering the merchants' questions without truly hearing their words, handing over coin without bothering to counting it.

Mounted once more on Feather, she angles the beast's head east and strikes out onto the flat, dry plain. When she has gone half a league, she turns in her saddle to glare back at the village, then spits over Feather's side onto the gritty trail below.

It's not true, she tells herself. *They know nothing, these ignorant village fools.*

But the story is the same in each new village she passes. At every shepherd's well, where she pauses to water her mount and slake her own growing thirst, girls in rough-spun robes whisper in awed tones about the Roman army, about Aurelian's wrath and Antioch's fall.

News speeds toward Emesa faster than Zenobia herself. She dares not turn again in the saddle, for she knows if she does she will see her empire crumbling in her wake, eroding rapidly to nothing, like a dune's crest blowing away on a strong wind. It is a sight she knows she cannot bear.

"Aurelian," she mutters as she rides, and his name is a foul curse on her tongue.

Her spine is stiff with disbelief, and she cannot loosen to Feather's stride. She jars painfully along, hearing now and then her camel's grunts of protestation. She pats his hump and whispers her apologies, but she cannot relax, cannot let go of her anger, her fear, or her indignation.

The gods know, though, she should have seen this coming. Didn't Zabdas warn her that Aurelian, alone of all Romans, was no man to be trifled with? Her face heats with shame as she recalls her taunting letters, the towering hubris of her coins—and, oh, the pain of knowing that she forced her son into this. In her own cocksure, blind, foolish arrogance she has doomed Vaballathus, too.

When a brisk wind rises from the west, carrying the faint smell of smoke—from Antioch?—it sends a spray of loose, light pebbles rattling along the trail. In the susurrus of their movement, Zenobia hears her sister's voice whispering. *Don't meddle in things that are not meant for a woman. The gods will curse you if you do.*

"I'm sorry," she says, stroking Feather's sweat-slicked hide. She jolts in the saddle, her back unbending as a dagger's blade. "I'm sorry, I'm sorry . . ." But she doesn't know whether it's only to the distressed camel she speaks, or to her sister, or to her son—or to her lover, who may be dead already, scowling his disapproval down on her from the heavens. And the heavens are empty and distant, and nothing she can ever hope to obtain.

***

Zenobia makes Emesa two days after first learning of Aurelian's march. It is nightfall as she crests a small rise and sees the city before her, demarcated by specks of orange torchlight. She is too tired from the trek and too stricken by loss to feel any sort of relief. Feather, too, is exhausted. He plods with his head held low, and the only sounds in the desert night are the tread of his wide feet, and the harsh, panting rhythm of his breath.

Again, at Emesa's gate she passes for a lady trader. Although she has not visited the city for more than two years—since Zabdas conquered it for her—she remembers the way to her fine little estate. She rides through the streets unseeing and unhearing. She is unaware of the war songs in the beer houses or the tense bustle of women in the streets as they make last-minute preparations for the conflict they fear is coming.

The gods have been merciful to Zenobia in one regard: they have closed her ears, finally, to rumor.

The overseer of her small but rich Emesa estate is Qoyah, a Palmyrene and longtime friend of Zabbai's family. When his servants alert him that a trader has come in the night, Qoyah comes stumbling into the courtyard, his eyes squinted with interrupted sleep and his robe still half off one shoulder. He recognizes Zenobia before she has even dismounted, and his exclamation of surprise—tinged with instinctive fear, for only dire circumstances could reduce the great bat-Zabbai to such a state—echoes from the pillars and walls of the estate.

Feather sinks to his knees with a drawn-out groan. When Zenobia drops from the saddle, she clings to her exhausted camel, her legs too shaky and weak to support her. Qoyah runs to her aid, murmuring apologies for his audacity even as he pulls her arm over his shoulder and holds her tight about the waist, supporting her toward the warm interior of the house.

Inside, Qoyah barks instructions at the servants. "Light the lamps, you fools! Bring cushions and a coverlet. Yireheh, fetch me broth from the kitchens." Zenobia is aware only of an orange light slowly blooming, unfolding like a night flower to reveal a floor of patterned green-and-white tiles. It is a floor she remembers from the weeks she spent in Emesa as its conquering queen—a floor from which she cannot seem to raise her eyes.

Qoyah eases her onto a couch, then gently pushes her onto her back. He peers down at her with obvious concern creasing and carving the deep lines of his elderly face. He is sharp-nosed and bearded, like a desert tribesman, and crowned with the flat-topped turban Palmyrene men favor. He looks like home—not Egypt, but her true home—the home, she now knows, she never should have left. She had only sought to save Palmyra by taking Egypt and forging her empire. Yet now it seems such obvious folly that she goes numb with shame. Qoyah murmurs to her gently. Her eyes unfocus on his turban. He looks like her father. She whispers, "Zabbai," and her voice breaks with regret.

"Tell me what has happened, my queen," Qoyah says, patting the back of her hand. "Is it Antioch? I'd heard rumors . . ."

Zenobia's eyelids flutter. The cushions seem to pull at her, dragging her down into a black refuge of sleep. She wants to forget everything, to be spared the knowledge of what she has done.

But soon Qoyah is pulling her up out of that sweet blackness, supporting her shoulders, propping cushions behind her until she is half sitting. She feels the rim of a bowl at her lips, and drinks, tasting warm, rich, salty broth. She coughs and sips again. The broth seems to flood her with renewed strength, and she sits up straight and takes the bowl in both her hands. With her eyes closed, she drains it dry. Its warmth invigorates her, though the gods know it's a cruelty, not a blessing. For now the full import of what she faces comes crashing down upon her, and Zenobia flinches from reality, nearly buckling under its weight.

"What has happened?" Qoyah tries again. "The streets are alive with rumors . . ."

"True," Zenobia croaks. "All true."

She looks around her Emesa estate, taking it in for the last time— she feels the certainty of that deep in her bones. The high, vaulted ceiling, the intricate floral carvings arching over lintels and windows, the woven silk tapestries bright with dancing, triumphant designs—all fit for an empress, and therefore, hers no longer.

"Rome has come," she says, flat and matter-of-factly. There is nothing for it now but to face the truth. "Emperor Aurelian has come. He has taken Antioch, and he is moving from one village to the next, claiming them all in Rome's name. Taking them back. I fear he'll soon be at Emesa, too." She thinks for a moment, submerged in utter calm, then says, "Egypt is mine no longer. How can it be? Aurelian will soon take Egypt, too, if he hasn't already."

Qoyah is silent for a long while, staring into the pools of lamplight, his eyes distant with shock. At last he murmurs, "Antioch—have they sacked it, then? Like the Sasanids did? Will they destroy Emesa, too?"

"No," Zenobia says, and not only to reassure her deputy. She has no doubt that she speaks the truth. "Aurelian has not destroyed Antioch, only captured it. He's more intelligent than that. This Augustus would never destroy a functional, profitable city. What would he stand to gain from it but the cost of rebuilding? No, Qoyah—Emesa will be safe, ultimately. It is I who am in danger."

"What will you do, then, my queen?"

Zenobia thinks for a moment, calmly. She must face this disaster without quailing from it. No Amlaqi has ever feared the sword. "I should still have some days before Aurelian arrives. If I'm lucky, I may have a week or more. After all, Antioch is so great—he will need to set up administrators, appoint leaders . . . and do the same in the larger towns he seizes. It takes time to conquer—the gods know I am aware of that truth."

"What is next, then?" Qoyah asks. "I am your loyal man—I'll assist any way I can."

She gives him a grateful smile. "Now I must turn my hand to gathering a new army. Emesa has a good, strong wall, unlike Palmyra. We can defend this city easily. All we need is more men. I've a treasury here still, yes? Good. Then I'll empty it at dawn, and hire as many mercenary tribesmen as will answer my call. When Aurelian reaches Emesa, he'll find me well-armed here, and my Egyptian troops"—*what remains of them*—"closing on him from the rear."

Gods be merciful, she prays, her chest tight with desperation, *let that be strength enough.*

Qoyah leaves her for a few hours of rest and Zenobia drops back onto her cushions, her body throbbing with weariness. In the dull, persistent beat of her heart, she hears the rhythm of hope. It is faint and thin as a thread, but it is there.

I will hold Aurelian off here, she tells herself, and as her pulse pounds the words change from a desperate wish to a declaration of certainty. *Mercenaries will come, and while they are fighting, I'll slip away to Palmyra—the source of my strength, my true home. I'll raise the tribes, mobilize the cataphract, and even without a wall, we will stand strong against Rome.*

But she is granted only a few short hours of rest. A cry wakes her, a woman's terrified wail twisting through the streets of Emesa. The sound is distant, but the urgency in it pierces Zenobia's deep, exhausted sleep and jolts her to her feet. Qoyah has laid out fresh clothing. The robe and turban are simple, but of the Palmyrene style. She dresses quickly, then moves to the window and lays her hands on its cool, tiled sill. The courtyard garden is quiet, fragrant with the damp of the cistern. Beyond the estate's walls, a man's warning shout rises to join the crying of the woman.

Qoyah rushes into the room. "I've been on the rooftop, my queen. It's too soon to tell for certain, but—"

"Rome." Zenobia tugs on her woolen tunic, pulling it straight. "How did Aurelian get here so quickly?" She asks the question coolly, of no one in particular. Qoyah certainly doesn't know the answer. "He must have left small encampments scattered all throughout the hills beyond the trade routes," she decides. "He must be mobilizing them each in turn via messenger, as soon as he's certain I'm not hiding in the cities and villages he takes."

She sighs. "It is no matter. How he got here changes nothing. He is here now, and I am out of time. Take me to my treasury, Qoyah. Let me look at what resources I have. I may still be able to do something about this mess, though the gods know what can be managed."

Zenobia's wealth is stored in a cold, dark vault, a cellar below an outbuilding of her estate. Qoyah holds a little oil lamp high while a servant works at the bronze mechanism of the Greek lock. The vault has not been opened in two years—not since Zenobia was last in Emesa.

My first visit to this city was in victory, she thinks as she watches the servant struggle with the rattling, dirt-clogged lock. *And my next—my last—in defeat.* It's the sort of justice a poet would love, the kind of story that can play out only on the stage of an amphitheater. She would laugh at the irony, if only her throat weren't so damnably dry.

Finally the lock gives in to the servant's coaxing. Zenobia herself pushes the creaking door open, and the flicker of Qoyah's lamp multiplies, leaping and blazing among her riches. There is gold everywhere. Bags and crates of ingots line the floor; worked vessels and other fine implements stand ranks deep along the shelves, like soldiers waiting for deployment. Pegs driven into the corners of the vault are draped with chains—silver and gold and Egyptian electrum, and fine stones set in intricate bezels. There are casks of coin, and casks of the finest wine, stacked and ready, all waiting for Zenobia's use.

And staring at this wealth, she can think of no use for it now.

Aurelian is at her door. She cannot raise a force—and even if she could, what good would an army of mercenaries do her? She has no idea how many Romans are closing on Emesa—no idea how many men she will need to counter their strength, and not the faintest clue whether Zabdas's ragged, brutalized force is still intact, let alone capable of striking Aurelian from the rear.

Very probably, she thinks, sagging against the door of her useless treasury, giving in again to the despair of loss—very probably, Zabdas is already dead.

"It is over. I must get back to Palmyra," she tells Qoyah weakly. "Alone. It's my only hope to see my son before Aurelian reaches him first. Lock this vault. When I am gone—when you hear that I am dead—use my treasury to give Palmyra the wall it never had while I was alive."

Together, they make their way to the stable. Emesa is coming awake now, hours before dawn, ringing ever louder with alarm cries from the rooftops and shouts to take up arms. Zenobia finds that Feather has been stabled well. He rests on a bed of soft straw with his legs folded beneath his chest, slowly chewing his cud. His eyes are closed, his head extended. The little dun snubs of his ears droop listlessly; they do not even twitch at the cries of fear in the city.

"He's exhausted," Zenobia says.

Somehow this—the sight of her loyal mount, her steadfast companion of so many adventures, now pushed beyond the limits of even his brave heart—is enough to move her to tears. She ducks beneath the wooden bars of his stall and wraps her arms around Feather's neck, pressing her face behind his warm ear. She can smell the dried sweat on his hair and the dust of their long, terrible journey. She whispers his name, and when his ear flicks against her cheek, the tears spill from her eyes onto his silky, golden coat.

Dimly, she is aware that it's absurd to weep for a camel. She hasn't cried this way for Zabdas, or Vaballathus, or for herself. But she can't seem to stop herself. She chokes on her sobs, clinging to Feather. She senses that to part with him is to part with everything that she once was: Empress of the East and Queen of Egypt, oh yes—but also Septimia Zenobia and bat-Zabbai, the headstrong young daughter of the Ras, who first mounted this courageous animal and rode him to save her city from destruction.

"I can't ride him," she tells Qoyah through her weeping. "He can't possibly go on."

And I should not go on, she wants to say. *I should give myself up to Aurelian.* But she cannot make the words come. Palmyra is her home—its dunes and its bright-white limestone, its baths, its temples, the halls of her father's house—and she will reach it before Aurelian does. She will look on Palmyra again. She will hold her son in her arms before Rome tears away that last small scrap of her glory.

"I know a man with very fast camels," Qoyah tells her. "Very fast indeed."

Zenobia sniffles and looks up from Feather's neck. "Do you? Might I buy one tonight?"

He hesitates. "I think it can be arranged, but . . . but you should know, my queen, that the man is a Sasanid."

Zenobia does not pause. "Send a servant to fetch him. Tell him to bring his very best camel. I'll pay any price for it—the gods know I have enough in that treasury to buy the finest camel in the land. I don't care that he's a Sasanid. If he's willing to sell, I am willing to buy."

It takes only a quarter of an hour for the Sasanid to arrive, mounted on a camel that eyes Zenobia with a spirited swing of its head, growling at her eagerly. The creature does look fast indeed, with long, clean limbs and a narrow abdomen; it snakes its neck high and sniffs the night air, tasting Emesa's tension, and then roars a loud challenge to the city—to Rome.

"This one will do nicely," Zenobia says. The tears have dried on her cheeks.

The Sasanid gives her no unusual attention; he appears to have no knowledge of her true identity. And despite the fact that she is dressed again in Palmyrene garb, with loose riding trousers beneath her wool skirt and a flat-topped turban trailing a rough linen veil, he does not balk at doing business with an enemy of his homeland, especially not when he sees the gold she offers for his camel.

"She is a very fast mount," he tells her. "None swifter. But her stamina is not great. If you leave now, she will lose speed by late afternoon, and will not recover for a long while."

"How far will she take me?" Zenobia asks.

"As far as the Lesser Palms. Do you know it?"

Zenobia has seen the place marked on her map—a small oasis, not nearly as impressive as Tadmor, but with reliable water and a settlement on its western edge. She nods.

"I have a colleague there," the Sasanid says, "a man called Babak." The Sasanid fishes in his belt pouch and pulls out a small wooden disc on a leather lace, not unlike the trade tokens Zenobia has relied upon to pass through the gates of major cities. It is carved with the image of a bat. "Tell him Takhma has sent you, and he will give you another camel—fresh and ready to run, and almost as fast as this one."

"I thank you," Zenobia says.

Before she accepts the reins from Takhma, she glances back at the stable. Feather has clambered to his feet, and stands gazing at the scene with an expression that might almost be called jealousy. Zenobia's throat tightens, and she hurries to Feather's side once more.

Her old saddle rests on the fencing between the stalls. How shabby and insignificant it looks now, that seat where she swayed and rocked across the barren desert for so many days, driven by despair and buoyed by frail hope—a hope which she now knows to be futile. Her bag of supplies is still tied to its wooden tree. She looses its cord and finds, deep in one threadbare corner, the handful of dates she'd bought in the village where she'd first learned of Aurelian's march.

She offers the dates to Feather. His breath is warm against her palm, and his velvet lips accept her gift with gentle care. She strokes his long face as he chews, then kisses him between the eyes and turns resolutely away.

"Take good care of him," she tells Qoyah. "And remember that he likes dates."

18

REUNION

Shortly before sunset Zenobia gains the green fringe of the Lesser Palms, a cluster of foliage and merciful shade that makes Tadmor look as immense as the sea. The Sasanid's camel is every bit as fast as he claimed; the sleek, straight-legged beast left Emesa in a cloud of dust well before dawn. The camel seems fresh enough now to keep going toward Palmyra, grumbling at commands to slow and throwing her head against Zenobia's tight rein. She is tempted to press on, but the Sasanid surely knows his camel better than Zenobia does. Any ground she's gained will only be lost again if her mount suddenly flags in the middle of the desert.

A small village crouches just to the west of the oasis, clinging close to take advantage of a narrow ring of arable land. On the village's fringe, where green gives way to desert, the peaks of shepherds' tents rise like a tiny range of colorful mountains. The air is rich with the scent of fresh water, a soothing, compelling perfume that fills Zenobia with renewed strength of will.

As she rode out from Emesa, she'd considered her options—few and small now, but extant still. The Sasanid camel keeper was willing enough to take her gold, despite her obvious Palmyrene ties. And she has plenty more gold in her vault beneath the Emesa estate. As long as Qoyah can keep the treasury hidden from Aurelian, it may not be as useless as she had first thought.

It's long past time that Eran and Palmyra set their differences aside, she tells herself. She knows the Sasanids have always loved riches.

There is a corner of her mind, shadowed by the worry of all she has been through, that shouts to her, tells her not to consider an alliance with Eran, that she is too worn out to think clearly and she ought to press on for home. But as the smell of the oasis sweeps through her and fills her with a great burst of confidence, she gives the camel its rein and lopes toward the village.

She inquires of a shepherd family—the dirty little boys are ushering their wiry, matted sheep into a pen for the night—where she might find Babak the camel keeper. One of the boys grins up at her and points with his crook. "Stable on the edge of the oasis bank, down past the big blue tent." Zenobia tosses him a dried fig for his trouble, which immediately sets him to scuffling with his brothers.

She passes through the trampled grass of a common area. It is ringed by little mud-brick kiosks that must be the stalls of a marketplace during daylight hours. A few humble houses stand clear of the palms. Thin streamers of smoke, pungent with the scent of burning dung, rise from their flat rooftops. Women are gathered on the roofs, singing or gossiping as they bake the evening's bread in mud-brick ovens.

Zenobia draws closer to the blue tent. It is large, indeed, its peak high enough to tower above her head even mounted as she is. The tent's doors are drawn tightly closed, and there is not a stir or whisper from within, yet somehow it doesn't feel empty. There is a certain weight or ripple to the air, a sensation of people close by who are unseen but going about some tense, important business, like spirits passing through the realm of the living.

A clatter jars Zenobia from her thoughts and she jumps in the saddle. She notes a young girl tending pigeons in a small lean-to cote near the blue tent's periphery. It is the birds' wings that have startled her, beating against the walls of their cage with a sound like a bundle of staves dropped on a tile floor. The girl ducks back out of the cote and shuts the door, then watches Zenobia ride on in wide-eyed silence.

The camel locates the stable for her, drawn by the smell of grain. The camel keeper's children are just feeding their beasts now, using clay measures to pour the grain into a trough. A herd of camels crowds and jostles in an adjoining corral; the camels stretch their necks toward the evening feed and bite at one another's shoulders and rumps as they growl in anticipation.

"Good evening," Zenobia calls to the children in Greek.

The children look up. One, who has been lugging the sack of grain into which his siblings dipped their measures, lets his burden slide to the ground with a thump.

"I am looking for Babak," she tells them. "Do you speak Greek?" Then she repeats the name. "Babak."

The eldest whispers into a little sister's ear and she sprints behind the stable, her bony knees flying beneath a dusty but colorful skirt. A few moments later, a grown man appears—another Sasanid, by the looks of him, with deep-golden-brown coloring and heavy, tilted brows. He barks a few words in his language, and the children scatter like fowl before a farmwife, chattering as they go.

"Good evening, good evening," the man says in Greek, dusting his hands together. "What may I do for you?"

Zenobia cushes the camel and goes to him, holding out Takhma's token. Before she can explain herself, Babak takes the little wooden disc, raises one slanted brow, and glances at her in unconcealed satisfaction.

"You've come from Emesa, then?"

"I have."

"We've heard strange gossip . . . about Romans," Babak says carefully.

"It's more than gossip," Zenobia tells him. "Emperor Aurelian has come."

"Dark days," Babak mutters. He tucks the token into his belt pouch.

"I need a fresh camel. Takhma told me yours are the best, and that you will sell one to me. I will pay whatever price you're asking," she adds impatiently. "I've no time for haggling, so do your worst."

Then the spark of an idea occurs, flaring amid the weary mist in her head. Zenobia says, "I will pay you well—very well—for another service, too, to carry a message north and east, quickly, into Eran."

"A message, mistress?" The Sasanid takes a few steps toward her, interested but wary. "To whom?"

"I hardly know—whichever powerful man is closest to the border when you get there. But at any rate, it doesn't matter. To *any* lord or chieftain, any great man you can find. I have a proposition for Eran—one I hope your leaders will see the sense of."

An alliance between Palmyra and Eran. In exchange for all the gold that Zenobia still holds, a setting aside of their habitual enmity so that they might stand united against Rome. It is a gamble that frightens her in its desperation. It is the last gasp of her dying hope.

The Sasanid Babak seems to perk up his ears. "Mistress, if it's Sasanid leaders you want, you are in great luck. The gods themselves have sent you here, I should think."

"Why? What do you mean?"

Babak points toward the huge blue tent. As the sun sets, the peak of the tent takes on a warm reddish glow, and Zenobia is reminded uncomfortably of imperial purple.

"It happens that we have a great noble of Eran staying here tonight, in our humble village. No need to send a messenger—you can make the proposition yourself."

How strange, Zenobia thinks. She glances again at the tent, and feels once more its grave, patient stillness. As she hesitates, her body aching with the demands of her long journey, her thoughts impeded by a thick, foggy veil, her pulse begins to race again, and a knot of warning tightens in her stomach.

But she turns to Babak and manages a smile. "Very well," she says. "Please take me in."

***

Babak leads her toward the tent's tight-shut doors and shouts a few words of the Sasanid tongue. In a moment the door flap is snatched aside from within. Babak moves close, directly behind her, and Zenobia pauses. All her senses come to keen alert like those of a cornered animal as she perceives that Babak has moved to block her from any retreat. She shudders as a thrill of fear wracks her.

She sees in her mind's eye the dull glimmer of moonlight on embroidery and the flickering image of golden checks—the headcloth of the Tanukh who clawed at her those many years ago. Zenobia's right fist tightens—on nothing. She has no sword, no height from which to swing, and no Zabdas to stab the man in the heart and finish the bloody job.

She must go into this fight alone, armed with only her wits—what little remains of them after her days of flight through the desert. She turns to give Babak one long, cold look of scorn, then walks into the tent's lamplit depths. She will not be marched or dragged; she can, at least, go to her fate with dignity.

The interior is as sumptuous as a tent may be. The floor is made of Sasanian rugs, once fine enough for any estate, but threadbare and old

277

now. In places the intricate patterns, the images of bounding animals and floral motifs, are worn into indecipherable smudges from decades of treading feet. Nevertheless, they serve their purpose well. The carved frames of a few cots stand to one side, assembled but not yet covered by camel-hair mattresses or by the linens that lay stacked in a large basket nearby. A few lengths of red wool are draped from the tent poles, as if an attempt was made to separate the space into rooms, but then hastily abandoned. It seems that this tent and its owner arrived in the village barely before Zenobia.

She turns toward Babak, and sees for the first time the man who opened the tent's door—a burly Sasanid soldier.

"Who . . . ?" Zenobia's question trails off as she senses movement from within the tent and turns to see a serving woman, garbed in silk with her face half covered by the modest veils of her kind, emerge from the shadows and draw aside one of the red woolen hangings.

On a stack of cushions a figure is seated cross-legged, hands braced on knees as if on the arms of a gilded throne. Zenobia takes in the sight of the woman with a lurch of panic and recognition. She knows this narrow, hard-angled frame, the shape of the high cheekbone and the dry, stark lines of the elegant hand. The woman looks up, her eyes shining with terrible triumph, and Zenobia whispers her name.

"Fairuza."

"Bring our guest to me," Fairuza says. She speaks in Aramaic— the language of Palmyra, of the husband these women once shared. If her Sasanid servants do not know the tongue, it makes no difference. Fairuza's meaning is clear in the sure, quick gesture of her hand, the crook of one commanding finger.

Trembling, Zenobia sinks onto a cushion opposite Fairuza. The female servant places a lamp on the floor between them, and the light glows along the angles of Fairuza's face, sharpening her feline features and turning her stare into a leopard's predatory gaze.

"Well," Fairuza says. "Here you are."

Zenobia balls her fists and resolves to make no reply.

"How was the ride from Emesa?"

But at this, Zenobia can't suppress a flinch. How can it be that this woman already knows where she has come from, Zenobia wonders, her stomach quivering with nausea. Then she recalls the pigeon cote outside. Of course. The swiftest camel in the land can't outpace a bird on the wing.

What else does Fairuza know? How many allies does she have, how many spies? Zenobia quickly realizes there is no sense in keeping silent or in trying to hide anything at all from Fairuza's sharp, exacting stare.

"You know, then," Zenobia says, "that Emperor Aurelian has come."

"Oh yes." Fairuza gives a low, delicate laugh. "I know."

"Don't think that he'll stop at taking my empire, Fairuza. Once he's conquered all my territories, he'll turn on Shapur—on your own cousin. Eran will fall, too, as the Goths fell—as I am falling. Unless we make an alliance. Now."

Fairuza watches her in silence for a moment. The glowing red mask of her face is the very picture of dignified amusement. In the stillness, the wick of the oil lamp gives a small, whispering hiss.

"And why not?" Fairuza says at last. "Sharing power—it would hardly be the first time you and I have shared, would it?"

The breath freezes in Zenobia's throat. Does she dare to hope again—to envision a world in which Aurelian can be stopped, and she is free to return to her throne? Her heart pounds, and she feels a flush of gratitude light her cheeks, until Fairuza speaks on.

"But alas, Zenobia, as before, I got there first."

"What do you mean?" Zenobia stammers.

"I cannot commit Eran to an alliance with your . . . *empire*. I've already spoken to my cousin Shapur. You are too late. Eran has allied with an emperor already."

The meaning of Fairuza's taunt strikes Zenobia like a blow to the face. She reels back from the lamplight, clutching at her cheek, though there has been no physical violence. "You mean you've allied Eran to *Rome*? To Aurelian? Gods have mercy, why, Fairuza?"

"Don't take on so," Fairuza says casually. "I am sure it's only temporary. Once the Empress of the East is quelled, and her stolen lands are back under Roman control, I have no doubt that Aurelian and Shapur will be at knives once again. You know how men are. When this task is finished, only the gods know what will happen to the alliance."

It's plain from her tone that Fairuza doesn't care what will become of the alliance, either. It is all one to her. She will see vengeance done—the setting to rights she has burned for since her only son was killed and her place in the world destroyed.

"How did you convince Aurelian?" Zenobia demands, her old temper flaring. "You, of all people? I have no doubt that it was you entirely, Fairuza. This can only be a plot of your making."

In the flickering, leaping light, Fairuza's mouth curves into a savoring smile. She turns to her woman servant and issues a few sharp words in the Sasanid tongue, then returns her gaze to Zenobia's face. She translates her command quietly, for Zenobia's benefit: "Bring me the emperor."

A lump like a great, dry, choking stone rises in Zenobia's throat. She swallows hard, trying to force it back down, but it remains, and nearly steals her breath. *Aurelian?* She thinks. The edges of a dark tunnel seem to close around her vision as her panic rises. *Aurelian is here?*

But from an unseen partition of the tent, behind another long drape of red curtain, a high, childish voice murmurs, sleepy and protesting. All at once, with tears burning her eyes, Zenobia understands. It is not the emperor of Rome Fairuza has in her keeping. It is the Emperor of the East.

The servant ushers Vaballathus into the lamplight. Zenobia recognizes him instantly, although she has not laid sight on her son in three years, and a force tears within her, a great, thrashing, rising tide of love, of frantic need. She is desperate to clutch him to her chest, to keep him safe, to weep out her regrets and apologies into his soft, dark, still baby-curled hair.

Fairuza extends a hand, and little Vaballathus goes placidly to her, rubbing his eye with one fist.

"I'm tired," he says. The sound of his voice nearly rips a sob from Zenobia's chest.

"I know," Fairuza coos to him. "You've had such a long day, such a grand adventure." She strokes his curls, watching Zenobia's struggle for control with all the cruel delight of a cat toying with a broken bird.

"As you can see," Fairuza says, "your son is alive and unharmed."

Zenobia hears the unspoken *but* clearly, the cold threat, the heartless promise. "It was you," she says, the words thin and strangled. "The letters Nafsha received—you."

"Well"—Fairuza laughs again—"not me personally. Shapur has scribes, you know."

Then she turns to Vaballathus and whispers in his ear. The boy looks up at Zenobia's face, his dark eyes suspicious. Then, to her relief and overwhelming gratitude to the gods, recognition dawns on his soft, round face. He darts around the lamp and flings himself into Zenobia's arms. She holds him, rocks him, and sobs against his small, warm body.

When she has caught her breath, Zenobia peers up at Fairuza. She holds Vaballathus tighter still, and trembles as she thinks, *Fairuza has always believed that I killed Hairan—her only son.* Is she cold enough to carry her vengeance that far—to make Zenobia suffer as she has suffered?

Burying her face against Vaballathus once more, Zenobia knows it is a risk she cannot take. Reluctantly, with her arms locked around the boy, Zenobia says, "You have me, Fairuza. I am yours—your captive. Do with me what you will, only—in the name of every merciful goddess, let my son live."

19

A City Without Walls

Fairuza and her men take Zenobia and Vaballathus back to Emesa. The trek is so drawn out, with all Fairuza's fine tents and retainers in tow, that Zenobia, even through her haze of dread, wonders whether she truly covered the same distance in just twelve hours.

The only mercy Zenobia can find in the slow, anxious march is that she has ample time to hold Vaballathus close. For a whole day she clasps the boy to her chest, rocking with him in the saddle of a camel that is tied in the midst of the pack train, as if Zenobia and her boy are nothing more than faceless baggage. But she pays no heed to the insult. She strokes Vaballathus, whispering endearments into the pink curve of his ear, marveling at his face, covering his brow with kisses—striving to fit years of neglected love into the few short hours she fears she has left with her son.

That night, in the dark of their well-guarded tent, Zenobia cradles Vaballathus against her body and lies awake, listening to his sleeping breath, to the murmurs of his dreams, until the sun rises and fills the cold tent with its pale-gray light.

Before the sun is high on the second morning, Emesa appears on the horizon. The city is a dark, violet streak in the earth below a staring sun. Zenobia searches for remnants of smoke, for any sign of Roman pillage—but as they draw ever closer to the city, it is clear that Aurelian has left it unharmed.

She searches, too, for any sign of the Egyptian army and of Zabdas, hiding in the distant hills or regrouping his decimated forces somewhere on the lonely banks of the Orontes River. But she sees no indication of him, nor any sign that he has attacked the Roman troops, as he'd planned. She can only pray that he is alive—though by now she knows that the gods have turned their faces away from her prayers forever.

Zenobia holds her head high as Fairuza's train passes through the outer gate and plods toward Emesa's heart. She is conquered, as she knew she would be when she left Emesa. But she can still comport herself with dignity and pride, no matter what may come.

Her dignity cracks only a little, and only for the merest moment, when she realizes that they are headed for her own estate. The tiled gates rise up before her, beyond the figure of Fairuza, who is perched on her camel, straight and strong as a pillar, at the head of the procession. Then Zenobia regains control with a shake of her head. Of course Aurelian has taken over the estate. It is the finest palace in all of Emesa. One would expect nothing else of an emperor—or an empress.

The camels cush in the yard and Zenobia waits compliantly for the Sasanid guards to approach, to take Vaballathus from her arms. One offers his hand as she prepares to slide from the saddle, but she declines his assistance with a sniff. If she has gained nothing else from these mad years—first conquering all the Eastern lands, then fleeing down their length as they are ripped back from her grasp—she has at least learned the knack of mounting and dismounting a camel.

In spite of her scorn for the guards, Zenobia stands between them servilely as the throngs of Romans inside the estate's walls, lounging against its pillars, snap to attention. Somebody has alerted the Augustus, who dwells in the bright-colored halls that were, only a few days before, Zenobia's. A Roman guard, conversing with Fairuza some distance away, breaks off to pound the butt of his spear on the paving stones, then gestures for Zenobia.

As they lead her toward the palace, she looks around frantically for Vaballathus. But the boy is already with Fairuza, holding her hand, looking up at her veiled countenance as he speaks to her with an animated face. Fairuza smiles down at him warmly, and as the guards bear Zenobia into the shaded dark of her erstwhile palace, she can only pray that Fairuza will be merciful to the boy, whatever Aurelian may choose to do to Zenobia.

They find Aurelianus Augustus in the roomy office on the eastern side of the estate. Many times before, as her heady years of conquest were only beginning, has Zenobia been in this room—but always as the mistress, the queen—never as a supplicant who will live only at the whimsical mercy of a Roman man.

As the door swings open, her eyes fall on the long, ebony-wood table—how many times did she gather there with Zabdas and his commanders, plotting their next move?—and then on what the table holds. She recognizes the contents of her treasury at once—the ingots in their crates, the lengths of precious chain laid out for measuring and accounting. It is only then that she remembers Qoyah.

Zenobia forces herself to look to the head of the table, at the man who sits there. Aurelian is busy with some sheaves of papyrus, his small, pale eyes running over the contents, and does not deign to look up at his captive. He is older than she expected, with gray in his hair and ample lines around his mouth. A short-clipped beard—so much like Zabdas's that it fills her with a swell of grief—cannot hide the fact that his chin is receding. Above the heavy ridge of his brow, his hairline seems entirely too low. The effect is one of unbalance, as if Aurelian's very countenance tips toward Zenobia, scowling down at her in judgment of her many offenses. The red cloak of the Roman military is pinned to his leather-and-bronze breastplate, and flung carelessly behind so that it half drapes the back of his chair. But his arms are bare to the desert heat, even in autumn.

Somehow this one concession—this small and insignificant weakness—gives Zenobia the courage to speak. "Where is my overseer, Qoyah?"

Aurelian glances up from his papers. He takes in the woman with one long, somewhat startled look. He had expected her to be . . . larger. Broad and tall, with sharp definition to the slender muscles of her shoulders—like the marble statues of Diana the Huntress. But she is small of frame. Her face, despite its Arab angles, is feminine, and her arms are as thin as a child's.

All the same, there is a certain presence about her. No larger than an unmarried girl and dressed in a drab, shabby tatter of Palmyrene traders' garb, she nevertheless fills the room, watching him with an air of unchallenged authority. Even as a captive, she has the presence of an empress.

"Ah," Aurelian says. "Septimia Zenobia. Zenobia bat-Zabbai." His voice is a grating rasp, as if in his past he has suffered some injury to his throat. Or perhaps it is only the dryness of the desert that affects him.

She lifts her chin. "Zenobia Augusta." She throws the challenge in his face.

"I think not," Aurelian says, unruffled. "Not any longer." Then he nods to the guards who still flank her. "Leave her with me. She'll do me no harm."

"Won't I?" Zenobia says.

But Aurelian only chuckles as his men withdraw.

"Please," the emperor says, gesturing to the many chairs that line the table. "Sit."

Zenobia swallows hard. She had expected to be thrown at Aurelian's feet, to be made to plead for mercy, perhaps with Fairuza looking on. She is put off guard by this display of civility. She cannot hope to guess what comes next—what her fate might be. She pulls out a chair with shaking hands and sits.

"Where is my overseer?" she asks again.

"Qoyah? A good man. He's run your estate well. I assure you, he's perfectly unharmed—he'll go on running this place in my name. There's no sense replacing him when he's proven himself so adept. But you'll not be allowed to see him."

"I see you've helped yourself to my treasury." The treasury that would have paid for mercenaries, if only she'd had the time to find them. And a wall for Palmyra—it would have paid for that, too.

"A most impressive store," Aurelian says. "I will put it to effective use, I assure you. I have plans."

Zenobia burns to ask what Aurelian plans to do with her—and with her son. But she is determined to retain her dignity, and any such question would sound too much like pleading.

Aurelian smooths a hand over his papers and sighs. "I warned you, did I not, that it would come to this?"

"I don't recall you saying as much—not in so many words."

"But you are intelligent enough to read between the lines. Or have I misjudged you? I'd hate to think I have. Your letters were often my only entertainment, all those long years on the front."

Despite the peril of her situation, Zenobia cannot help a tiny half smile.

The smile gratifies Aurelian, although he knows he ought to steel himself against Zenobia's charms. A beautiful, delicate woman in distress has been precisely the bait that has snared many a great man.

"I can see that you enjoyed our correspondence, too," he says. "Oh, Zenobia, it is a shame to meet this way. I had hoped so fervently that you might come to your senses, return to Palmyra, marry like a proper woman, and that we might be—"

"Friends?" The word is bitter on her tongue.

"Allies. It's no use to me if the eastern half of my empire resents me. You could have held your people in loyalty to Rome. Odenathus did. You might have been the wife of the Lieutenant of the East once more."

"You would never allow me to marry a man of my choosing, or even of Palmyra's choosing. I am not a fool, Aurelian. You'd stuff some Roman puppet into the role, and into my bed. I, and my city, would be no more than slaves to you."

"Slaves? Never," he says. He raises his hands in a gesture of conciliatory offering. If only he could get her to see the sense of his proposition! But if he couldn't bring her around via letter, there's little hope that he can do it now. Still, he tries. He should not try—Zenobia has proven herself disloyal. Yet he finds that he can do no less, for one whose bravery he respects so thoroughly. "Wife of the Lieutenant of the East!"

Zenobia blinks slowly, her dark lashes dropping like veils over her eyes. "It's an unimpressive role, when one has already tasted an empire."

Aurelian sits back in his chair and watches her in silence. The chair creaks. Zenobia holds his small blue eyes with her own.

Finally he says, "I doubt very much whether I could find a man willing to marry you. Oh, it's not that you aren't beautiful, and you're obviously still young—"

"Do you think I'm vain?"

"Of course," Aurelian says frankly. "Only a woman of staggering vanity would declare herself empress. I might ask myself how you've dared to insult so many Roman emperors, one after the other, but the answer is staring me in the face. Vanity—arrogance—pride." He says it without any malice. Indeed, he means no offense. It is simply a matter of course, he thinks; the way Zenobia is, just as Aurelian is a man of prodigious insight and will—or so he believes himself to be. He does not seek to reduce or demean any aspect of her. Aurelian has always been just, has always respected worthy opponents. To honor Zenobia for who she is seems to him the only just way to treat her.

"Do you call it vanity to see that I can lead an empire better than any Roman," says Zenobia, "to know that I have the skill and power to rule well—and to take what is mine by right? To accept the empire the gods have given me, not only through right of my birth, but through the strength of my will?"

"I have heard tales of your sharp tongue," he says appreciatively. "And the gods know I've read your biting words often enough in your letters."

"What else have you heard of me?"

"That you are brave, and generous," he says without hesitation. "That you've never flinched from battle. That you will ride with your men, sword in hand, into any crisis." Here he pauses, and gives a rumbling laugh. He goes on, brows raised with blatant disbelief, "I've heard, too, that you drink unwatered wine with your soldiers."

Zenobia rises from her chair. One of her casks of fine wine sits beside the table. It has already been breached, she sees, the wax-ringed lid resting slightly askew. She flicks it aside with the toe of her sandal and snatches a golden cup from among the remains of her treasury. She dips the goblet into strong wine as dark as blood on sand, raises it toward Aurelian in salute, and drinks it in one long draught. It is both bitter and sweet, and leaves a lingering taste of spice on her tongue.

Aurelian looks on in stunned silence, watching her pale, exposed throat pulse with each swallow. Then, as Zenobia sets the empty cup back on the table, he breaks into raucous laughter.

"Gods! Don't you know that our women don't drink unwatered wine? There is not a Roman woman alive who would dare to drink that stuff in front of the Augustus."

"I am no Roman woman," Zenobia replies, and then refills and drains a second cup, just to prove her point.

"No," Aurelian agrees. "But you ought to be. You *will* be, if the gods are on my side."

She raises one brow and decides not to answer.

Her silence strikes Aurelian as a challenge. He feels the need to explain himself. "Do you know what I've done, Zenobia? It was I who threw back the Goths. Hunting them for more than a year all through Dalmatia like a hound after hares. Sol Invictus, it was hard work. I'm not as young as I once was. And then the winter in Thrace—we had to hold the Goths pinned in the mountains, in the snow. You've never seen snow, have you?"

"I've heard tell of it. We are not ignorant, we Palmyrenes."

"You can't imagine it unless you've seen it. The privation it creates—the way it covers all the world, every blade of grass. It even covers sound. It muffles all your senses, dulls you down. That winter in Thrace was as hard on my men as it was on the Goths.

"And then, in the spring, the plague that followed the winter. I felt sure I would die of that illness. It wrung me out. I suffered for Rome—all my men did—as much as our enemies suffered."

Aurelian pauses, running one finger along the edge of a papyrus scroll, deep in thought. Then he continues: "The work that followed my accession to the purple was no easier. Italia wanted clearing out. Three different clans were there, gnawing away at my empire, like moths nibbling at wool. A few moths are insignificant until the day you pull a cloak out of the chest and find it's riddled with holes, and good for nothing at all."

"Is that what I am to you? A moth?" Zenobia's careful smile is back, the wry curve of her full lips.

"You, and the Goths, and the Vandals, the Sarmatians—flitting about my empire with your incessant nibbling. I've already got one great rent in my cloth, the Gallic 'Empire,' if you please. I have worked too hard, Zenobia—suffered too much, and lost too many good men in the snows of Thrace—to suffer another hole in the fabric of Rome. I will not lose Egypt. I can't: How else am I to feed Rome?"

Perhaps it is the two cups of unwatered wine, but a buzzing fills Zenobia's ears, and a sudden flush warms her skin. She is seated at the table with Aurelian as an equal, and they share a wary but mutual respect. There is opportunity here, and Zenobia has never been one to miss opportunity.

She says, "Leave me in control of the East, Aurelian. You're stretched thin—you've as good as said it yourself. I will hold Egypt for you. You'll get your grain—I'll be faithful and ungrudging. I will swear it on any god you please."

Aurelian considers her for a moment, his long, sun-darkened fingers scratching at his beard in exactly the way Zabdas used to do. At last he says, "Do you know what they called old Emperor Valerian? *Restitutor Orbis.*"

Zenobia frowns. *Restorer of the World.* "Valerian? He who was snatched up by Shapur and then wilted away in captivity?"

"The very one."

She gives a little snort of amusement. There could hardly be an emperor less deserving of such a grand, imposing title.

"And Gallienus, too," Aurelian says. "He was also a Restorer of the World." He swears: "Sol Invictus. Gallienus was almost as inutile as Valerian, if such a thing is possible."

The Augustus leans forward in his chair. His hands press flat against the tabletop, as if by force of will he might push the whole lot, ebony table and ingots of gold, down through the carpets and tiles, through the desert beneath, and into the heart of the world.

"They will say it of me, Zenobia," he says, and his words have all the gravity of a solemn oath. "But when men call me *Restitutor Orbis*, it will be no more than the truth. I am going to restore Rome. I will mend every rent in the fabric of my empire. Not a stitch will be left undone. I will not have it any other way."

With dull surprise, Zenobia realizes just how much she admires this man. In her enemy, she has found a spirit of strength and ambition equal to her own. They could be the best of allies—the best of friends— if only they could work together.

She must try once more. Too much hangs in the balance for her to back down without one last effort. "I could be your deputy," she says. "Now that I have seen you for myself, I will swear my loyalty to you. Now that I know you're not like the others who came before you, those men who did not deserve the name Restorer of the World."

For a moment, the proposition hangs before Aurelian, shining in his mind's eye with a glow like the rising sun. Palmyra and Egypt secured to him, united and directed by their acclaim for this astounding woman. The freedom to turn his strength, undivided, to the Gallic front, without concern for the grain shipments, or the baubles and spices that keep Rome's upper class complacent.

But then he eyes her more carefully—the feminine face, the sensual lips, the dark fire in her wily eyes. How many times before have men been led to their downfall by women just like this one, delicate and beautiful, as captivating as a goddess rising from the sea?

At last he shakes his head. "No, Zenobia. You cannot rule. I will not allow it. You are a woman, and everyone knows a woman can't be trusted."

***

Since she received Nafsha's desperate letter two weeks ago, Zenobia has pictured her return to Palmyra countless times.

In the early days of her flight, when she still felt certain she could scoop Vaballathus up into the safety of her arms and drive the Tanukh back into their desert crevices, she'd seen herself returning as the glorious conqueror, the mirror image of the young heroine who had ridden back through the Western Gate the morning after Zabbai's death.

When Antioch fell, she pictured her return as a bold warrior queen, one who would inspire her people to victory against an audacious but ultimately routable foe.

As she fled from Emesa, she saw Palmyra as her last refuge, where she would go to ground among her own kind, welcomed by loyal citizens who would fight bravely at her side even if hope were small.

But even in her bleakest imaginings, Zenobia never saw herself return like this. She rides hunched in the saddle, her bound wrists resting on the peak of the wooden tree. Aurelian has heard the stories of the Tanukh man in the desert so many years ago, how Zenobia delivered the killing blow. Even though she rides unarmed, the emperor will not risk the chance that she might snatch a blade from some careless soldier who passes too close. Vaballathus sits before her, cozied up to her chest and chattering like a sparrow, for it's all one grand adventure to the little boy. This is not meant as any kindness to Zenobia, but as added insurance that she will try nothing rash. Her son's proximity is a shield to protect the Roman soldiers from her.

She is surrounded by Romans, ringed by men mounted on thin, desert-bred horses. She watches the horses' movements with a fierce ache, the tossing of their heads and the flicking of their tails. She remembers Zabdas in the desert, on the night they first met, laughing at the twisted strap of Feather's saddle and prattling about the superiority of camels. He is gone—she knows it. She can feel the weight of his loss pressing on her heart. She remembers Zabdas leaning across her bared thigh to tie the scabbard to her saddletree. She would do anything to see him again, to touch him one last time.

From her camel's back she can see over the soldiers' heads, and so she is among the first to know that they have reached Palmyra.

At first it is only a shadow of deep green on the horizon—the palms of Tadmor, materializing through the shimmer and bend of distance. Then the city itself appears, a streak against the earth as pale as a spill of salt.

Some two leagues away from Palmyra, Aurelian calls a halt. He converses with his commanders, and then with Fairuza's men. His Sasanid allies have accompanied him, intent on seeing the thing done, hungry to take whatever they can salvage of Palmyra's riches. As the emperor issues his commands to the Sasanids, Fairuza sits watching the city in silence, the late autumn wind tugging at her blue veil. Then she turns in the saddle to stare flatly at Zenobia.

A special prison tent is erected on a rise, guarded day and night, and whenever the sun is up, Aurelian rolls back one wall of Zenobia's prison and makes her watch as he breaks Palmyra by siege.

From her vantage, she can see the double ring of Roman troops encircling her white, shining city. A second force surrounds the oasis, so that any Palmyrene who might escape will find no shelter, no water, no hope in the merciless sands. Day after day, Zenobia watches the slow trickle of the Roman troops, the sun bright on their red cloaks as they flow in their endless, impenetrable circuits around the city, a glyph drawn in blood in the pale sand.

She does not speak to Aurelian while they sit together, watching. When the Palmyrenes rally and throw their weight against their red, enclosing cage—it happens twice—she does not cheer, or sit forward on her straight-backed chair. She does not allow her pulse to speed, nor hope to flare in her breast. She knows how this pageant will end. It is inevitable—it is destiny.

It takes only two weeks to break Palmyra. It is a city without walls, and so Zenobia can at least feel proud that her people held out that long. But it is nearly winter. The few fields and orchards at the city's edge have long since yielded the year's final crops. Without trade flowing freely, Palmyra will surely starve. No doubt, she thinks, her family has gathered once more at the Ras's palace—Zabbai's palace, her childhood home. Does Berenikë watch from the rooftop? Does Zabibah weep beneath the red linen sunshade? Does Nafsha stare out across the sands to Zenobia's prison tent, and sense that her little sister is there, looking back toward her, chastened at last for her lifetime of ambition? At least the siege ends quickly. At least Zenobia can feel certain that her family is safe.

When Aurelian's general brings word that the Ras of the Amlaqi has surrendered and is ready to swear the city to Rome in peace, Zenobia is at last allowed to turn her face away from Palmyra. *The Ras of the Amlaqi is my brother-in-law,* she wants to say, just to assert herself, just to prove that she is still a woman of standing. But her mouth is too dry to speak.

Aurelian rises from his chair. He finally lets the wall of the tent fall, and the sudden dimness of her prison is a relief.

"It is done," Aurelian says. He is relieved, too. Sieges are costly, in supplies and time—and the Gallic front is calling.

"Palmyra was never a military town." Zenobia sighs.

"There is no shame in falling quickly in a siege," says Aurelian. "It's wisdom, that. That Ras you left in charge of your city made the right decision, for Rome can summon up an endless stream of soldiers, if need be."

"I didn't mean that," she says quickly, peevishly. "Never think that I feel the least shame in my city, Aurelian. I mean only that we are not a place that breeds soldiers. We are unused to violence. And so I would ask you to be merciful to my citizens."

She is startled to feel his hand on her shoulder. His palm, as thick as a stallion's crest, is rough with callus and sand. But the touch is so gentle, it is almost reassuring.

"I will not harm a single Palmyrene. I swear that to you by the truth of Sol Invictus. You know I need your city, Zenobia. Rome needs its trade—its wealth. I will be worthy of the peace your city pledges me—lenient and fair."

She nods once. A single tear slips down her cheek—of relief, of defeat; she doesn't know which—and she turns quickly away. The emperor will not see her weep. "I am grateful," she says in a voice unmarred by her sorrow.

Aurelian turns to go, but Zenobia halts him with a question. "You promise leniency for Palmyra. But dare I ask—what of me?"

He is silent for so long that Zenobia's fleeting, fragile hope sinks, cold and dark, into her middle. A chill spreads from that place to her limbs, her heart.

"Then what of my son?" she insists.

But she hears no answer—only the swinging of the tent's door flap as Aurelian leaves her, and the snap of metal and leather as the soldiers outside salute the Restorer of the World.

Zenobia's hand flies to her sash. She traces the outline of the bottle—the little phial of hemlock that has traveled with her all the way from Alexandria. She wonders, can she use it on her own son? Is she capable of such an act? Can she take her child's life?

The tent is as dark as a tomb. Outside, the Roman soldiers are cheering. Zenobia presses the bottle against her flesh, and clings to her resolve with a grip like an eagle's talons.

20

Beads of a Broken Necklace

The Romans tell Zenobia that the city where they've come ashore is called Actia Nicopolis. Caesar Octavian built it, they say, in celebration after he'd crushed Cleopatra's throne—after he'd driven her to the kiss of an asp.

"Isn't the sea beautiful," the soldiers say, gazing down from the promontory at their ships, which rest in the water like a sleeping pride of lions. The water is as blue as polished turquoise, and the damp ocean breeze stirs the deep-green gardens of Actia Nicopolis with gentle fingers.

Zenobia sees none of it.

After eight days at sea, battling nausea and dehydration, Vaballathus grew weak and pale. On the ninth day, after a night spent cradling her son's thin, feverish body against her chest, Zenobia fell on her knees before Aurelian, kissing the hem of his cloak, pleading for mercy for her little boy. Aurelian turned the fleet at once toward Nicopolis.

On the fern-covered promontory just outside the city, the Romans work to raise the small tent that is to serve once more as her prison, and her son's inadequate sickbed. Zenobia would have preferred proper lodging in Actia Nicopolis—Aurelian could certainly commandeer it— but the emperor is sure Vaballathus is only seasick, and one night on land will cure him. Tents are faster, he says, than displacing half the city. The boy will be well in the morning.

Zenobia is not so certain. She kneels on the rocky ground, bent over Vaballathus, who tosses and murmurs on the thick cloaks the soldiers have piled for a mattress. His baby-soft cheeks are livid with flush, and his eyes are tightly closed.

Zenobia does not know how to care for a sick child. In all the long days since her capture by Fairuza, never has she felt so helpless, so useless— not even while watching Palmyra succumb to Aurelian's siege. She was never taught about medicine, nor even simple soothings. Should she chill the boy's fever away, or wrap him in blankets to make him sweat? She does not even know how to comfort him, for all the years of his small, fragile life she was occupied—ruling her city, then conquering her empire, then holding fast to Egypt—and Vaballathus was left in his nurses' care, or Nafsha's. Zenobia has never so much as kissed away the sting of his scraped knee.

Each of the boy's fretful moans batters her with regret. She wonders, *Was it worth an empire, to miss my child growing up?* And the fact that she does not instantly answer "no" only deepens her bleak self-loathing.

She holds Vaballathus's tiny hand in her own and feels the pain of the rocks biting into her knees until at last the tent is erected. Then she rises, stifling a cry at the pain in her legs, and carries Vaballathus inside.

All through the heat of the day, Zenobia does what she can for her son. She wets his lips with water and holds damp cloths to his brow. She rubs his feet and washes him when, in his weak and fleeting dreams, he soils himself and the cloaks he rests on. She bends to kiss him again and again, as if she might draw the illness from his body, breathe it into herself, and suffer in his place. In rare moments he wakes, and then she tells him stories and promises that as soon as he is well their adventure

will continue. Soon he will see Rome—*just think of it! Rome!*—and what
a lucky boy he is, to be on such a grand journey. What a brave boy, what
a strong boy, and oh, how she loves him.

Evening comes. The slack tide comes rushing back in, the waves far
below the promontory crashing like drums in a dark temple. The breeze
is cool and salt-scented. Under its soothing influence, Vaballathus seems
to rest easier, but Zenobia is not convinced that the worst is yet over.
She ducks outside her tent and speaks to her guards in the gathering
dusk.

"Which is the lady Fairuza's tent?"

The guards eye one another with suspicion.

"Please tell me," she begs. "Have mercy on a mother's heart."

"That one," one of them admits. He points toward a tent on the
edge of the encampment with a high, slender, yellow peak.

"Will you take me there?" Zenobia asks them. "I must speak with
her. I will not run; I swear it."

Fairuza's maidservant opens the tent's door. When the woman sees
it is Zenobia, she draws back in surprise. But Fairuza soon comes to the
door herself, narrowing her eyes at Zenobia's red, desperate face.

"Please," Zenobia says. "My son—he's desperately ill."

Fairuza's expression softens, barely.

Zenobia says, "You're the only other woman in this camp, save
for your maid. What can these soldiers do for him? I need your help,
Fairuza. I'll beg it on my knees, if you wish. I have no pride anymore."
Her eyes well with fresh tears, and she is not ashamed that Fairuza
should see. "Please help me. For Odenathus's memory—for Hairan's
memory. Vaballathus is Hairan's brother." Fairuza frowns, and Zenobia
chokes on her tears. "He's my son—my only son."

Fairuza flinches. The echo of her own words at Hairan's death
strikes her, body and mind, like a blast of fire. She takes in Zenobia
with one slow, searching look. The old woolen trader's garb is now so
worn and tattered that the former Queen of Egypt looks as fine as a

beggar. The dark eyes are shadowed by fear, and the mouth, once so arrogantly curved, is now turned down in despair.

Fairuza recalls holding little Vaballathus's hand in the courtyard at Emesa, watching him from behind her blue veil as he chirped and chattered about his adventure, the excitement of his camel ride. She'd thought then how much he looked like Hairan, when her own son was the same age. She'd thought how clearly she could see the stamp of Odenathus on his round, barely formed features.

Fairuza turns away from the tent door, and Zenobia gives one ragged gasp. But in another moment she returns, swinging a fine blue cloak about her shoulders.

"Come," Fairuza calls to her maid, and follows Zenobia and her guards across the campground.

***

The women work over Vaballathus for hours. By lamplight, they monitor the depth of his flush and watch the fluttering of his thin, blue eyelids. They wet his hair and take turns smoothing his curls while the other fans his skin with scraps of papyrus. They never speak of Hairan, or Odenathus, or the enmity that has festered between them for so many years. Vaballathus's hot skin and labored breath have eclipsed all the rest of the world, and they strive together like oxen in a yoke, each pulling with all her might, each in unconscious harmony with the other.

Zenobia slumps back on the floor of her tent, weary but bolstered by Fairuza's presence, and watches the Sasanid woman dribble honey water from her fingertips onto Vaballathus's cracked, dry lips. She thinks, *We might have been friends, indeed—if only the gods had softened her heart, or my pride, sooner than this.*

Fairuza sets the bowl of honey water aside. She looks up at Zenobia with a grave, drawn face. "I fear his fever is only growing worse."

Zenobia sighs in answer. What other response can she give?

"I'll go to Aurelian," Fairuza says finally, rising. "There must be an herb woman in the city—somebody who knows some medicine or spells."

But it takes Fairuza time to convince the emperor that the situation is dire, that this is more than a desert child's simple, natural intolerance of sea travel, easily gotten over—as Aurelian had first thought.

As Zenobia waits—first patiently, and then with increasing panic—Vaballathus's breathing grows harsh and gasping.

She nearly knocks over the oil lamp in her haste to clutch her son. She holds him tight against her breast, wailing her helplessness, as his little body stiffens, shakes violently—and then goes limp in her arms.

By the time Aurelian throws aside the tent flap, Fairuza close on his heels, Vaballathus lies on his bed of Roman cloaks with the waxen stillness that can only mean the soul has departed.

Zenobia rocks to and fro on the ground, her mouth wide and distorted, but her throat silenced by the force of her grief. The knot of her hair has come loose, and it falls about her shoulders like a cape of darkness.

Aurelian stands immobile, shocked by the boy's death. He had been sure it was only a case of seasickness, that the little soldier would brace up after a day of recovery on dry, unmoving land. A curious, needling pain strikes him in the center of his chest. It takes him a long moment to give the pain its proper name: guilt. In all his long years as a fighter, a general, and an emperor, Aurelian has caused countless deaths. But never before has he felt so deeply, fearfully responsible for the loss of any life.

There is a flutter beside the emperor, and a sudden emptiness. Fairuza has spun away. She is striding back across the camp, her vision blanked by tears, her breath painful and short. It seems she is witnessing it all again—her son brought back dead from his only foray into battle, slung like a bundle of rags over a camel's hump. She cannot bear the sight of Zenobia—not because they are old enemies, but because she is a mother grieving the death of her only child. Fairuza cannot bear the memory of her own grief, for it has never left her, but has only crept closer to her hollow, veiled heart.

With as much effort as ever he's shown on the battlefield, Aurelian shakes off the grip of his guilt and makes himself walk—one foot, then the other—toward Zenobia. He takes her under the arms and pulls her to her feet. She sags in his grip, weighing less than a feather, her whole being eroded by all she has lost. But when he gives her a gentle shake, she steadies her legs just enough to turn herself in his arms.

Then she falls against Aurelian's chest, keening.

The Augustus wraps her tightly in his arms, this woman from whom he has taken everything—even, at the last, though the gods know he never intended it, her child.

***

When her weeping has ceased—it amazes her that it can cease at all—Aurelian allows Zenobia to walk alone along the crest of the promontory. Oh, her Roman guards are not far off. She can hear them rustling in the ferns as they follow her, can hear their great red cloaks sweeping the dew-heavy grass. But she is beyond them, apart, alone with her gods and her regrets.

Her stumbling feet cleave a path through the hilltop greenery. The damp of the seaside air soaks her tattered robe. The stars are heavy in the sky, falling toward the west, where Rome waits, vast and inescapable.

She finds a patch of bare rock that juts from the wind-tangled grass. From its height, she can see the little harbor, black now in the hour before dawn. The city of Actia Nicopolis is dark, too—not a lamp burning, and the waves of the harbor trace silver lines along its shore. Zenobia watches the lines of seafoam break and reform. No matter how many times the sea mends its silver net, the threads snap again, and everything is undone.

She slips her hand into her sash. The small red phial is warm, heated by her body through so many desperate hours. She holds the hemlock in her palm and considers it with dull, aching eyes.

This city, the Romans told her, was built to celebrate the defeat of Cleopatra. Zenobia gazes down on Nicopolis. The bottle in her hand feels as firm and smooth as the flesh of a snake. Cleopatra took her own life, departing this world on her terms, rather than submit to the degradations of Rome.

Zenobia raises the bottle to her mouth. She pulls the stopper out with her teeth, and spits it into the grass. There is the faintest taste of bitterness on her lip—hemlock, said the poisoner Werenro, has a flavor as bitter as life.

Gods, Zenobia prays, staring up at the stars. *You have taken all from me—my city, my empire, my lover, and my son. You have punished me for my hubris, because I tried to make my own destiny, because I did not keep to my place.*

A wind rises from the sea. It stirs the tatters of her woolen robe; it sends her black hair flying like a tangled banner.

Zenobia tips the phial upside down. The hemlock scatters on the night wind, droplets of silver light, flying like the beads of a broken necklace.

I will suffer whatever fate is truly mine, Zenobia swears to any gods who might still see her, who might care enough to listen. *I will walk the road you have paved for me, and humbly this time.*

21

Golden Chains

Grass sprouts between the large, flat paving stones. Zenobia can't take her eyes off it—the endless stripes and patterns of green that pass beneath her feet. This is the one thing that surprises her about Rome: how green it is. How, in a city of towering gray stone and houses crowded cheek by jowl, where the air stinks of shit and commerce and blood—in a place where thousands of feet rush from shop to forum to brothel, trampling without a care—can green things still grow?

She cannot take her eyes from the road. She has walked the same road from the banks of the Tiber—that vein of filth, reeking of Rome's iniquity—all along the Triumphal Way. Creeping since sunrise, Zenobia has watched the road before her, never looking to the left or the right. She has heard the shouts and calls of the citizens and endured both their insults and, now and then, the refuse they've thrown. She bears it all with patience. This is her fate.

The sun is well up now, and Zenobia grows hot. Aurelian has dressed her in outrageous finery—a robe stitched with heavy gold embroidery, overlaid with a netted dress of precious stones—in an exaggeration of the old Egyptian style. The cabochons sparkle in every brilliant color. She is crowned by a soaring headdress of gold encrusted with emeralds, and even the Palmyrene veil that hangs from the back of her head is stitched with lapis lazuli beads, so heavy with riches that it cannot lift to trail in the breeze of her movement.

Even her chains are golden. As she waited for the sun to rise, wrinkling her nose against the stench of the Tiber, Aurelian came to her and clapped fetters on her wrists. Although dawn had not yet broken, he blazed with triumph, glowing in his deep-purple toga with its intricate, gold-stitched designs. His face was a stern mask of red paint, isolated and austere against the gray of the early morning.

Zenobia looked away in shame while Aurelian fit her chains in place, but when the sun broke over the eastern hills, the glint on her wrists caught her eye, and she stared at the golden fetters in disbelief.

Zenobia has no doubt she makes a striking image, covered in riches, the very picture of a Roman fantasy of decadent Eastern arrogance. Shackled, in a poetic twist, by her own wealth. But the day is growing warm, and her trappings are heavy. Zenobia sways as she walks, determined to stay on her feet, resolved that she should not stumble and fall before the jeering, mocking citizens of Rome.

At last—thank Bel—the road begins to rise beneath her feet. They have reached the lower slope of the Capitoline Hill, the final leg of the triumphal procession. Her humiliation is nearly at its end, and for that certainty, Zenobia feels no fear, no regret—only gratitude.

The wealthier citizens have gathered here, lining the broad avenue as it climbs toward the summit. They cheer Aurelian with shouts of *"Triumphator!"* and *"Restitutor Orbis!"* Zenobia raises her eyes at last to look upon the Restorer of the World.

Aurelian rides some distance ahead, at the front of his great procession. He stands tall and regally still in a chariot drawn by four horses. A wreath of laurels flutters on his graying head, and the imperial purple of his toga is so dark that it drinks the light of day.

Behind him, the most honored of his soldiers march. Their red cloaks make a brave display, rippling like a sea of blood, and they walk in step, so that their feet pound out a dull rhythm that beats inside Zenobia's head with the steadily increasing heat.

Just to Zenobia's fore, ranks of slaves carry the treasures of Palmyra for all of Rome to see. There are huge white vases of Seres pottery, nearly as translucent as alabaster in the midmorning sun. Men display leopard pelts and long banners of silk. Women with dark skin are draped in ropes of pearls, so that the treasure's fine, pale nacre may be better seen by all. Bare-chested children scamper along the edges of the procession, scattering pinches of cinnamon and golpar to the breeze. The air is perfumed with Palmyrene riches, scented with the extravagance of wasted spice. Palmyra's gods, the statues stolen from the temples, are carried high above slaves' shoulders, their gold-and-electrum bodies stiff with indignation.

And behind the wealth of her conquered city, Zenobia bears up under the weight of her gold.

You would be nothing without Palmyra—without my rule, and my husband's, and my father's, she silently says to the watching nobility. *Without our trade, you high-born senators and lonely wives would be no better than the dung that lines the Triumphal Way below this hill.*

They are captives, Zenobia sees. As much as she is the prisoner of Rome, so are they the prisoners of wealth—of Palmyra. Every citizen that mocks her is also a prisoner in golden chains. The sudden knowledge nearly makes her smile, despite her weariness and the terrible heat. She holds her head high on the long climb up the Capitoline, for she walks now among her equals.

But at last the procession reaches the hill's crest. The Temple of Jupiter rises before her, its stern pillars red-stained, its peak crowned by the glowering god. She sees again, through her reeling senses, the vision she once saw in a fitful dream, of purple smoke rising, and remembers the sensation of being hunted by an unseen pursuer.

Zenobia watches calmly as Aurelianus Augustus draws his four horses to a halt and descends from his chariot with straight-faced dignity. He glances back the way he's come, searching for Zenobia, ready to beckon her forward. But she is already moving of her own will, dragging the weight of her riches as she strides toward him.

Their eyes meet in silence—his, pale and fathomless in his mask of red, hers serene amid a flare of gold.

Aurelian gestures and they climb the steps of the temple together. The nobles of Rome hush, and all the city seems to hold its breath, waiting.

Zenobia knows what is expected of her. She kneels before the emperor and kisses his purple hem. The Capitoline Hill erupts with a clamor of cheers.

She turns her face up to him. *"Restitutor Orbis,"* she says, "am I finally to be killed?" She asks it calmly, without a hint of fear. And indeed she feels no fear—only the peace of inevitability.

"Would that please you?" Aurelian asks.

Zenobia does not answer.

Aurelian extends his hand and helps her climb to her feet. She does sway now under the weight of her burden, but she has learned to bear it with grace. Aurelian holds her hand until he is sure that she stands firm. Then he gives her the smallest fraction of a smile. "I can't bring myself to kill so admirable a foe."

Zenobia lifts her chin. "Is it only because I'm a woman—is that why you spare me? Because you think this woman is too soft to face her fate?"

Aurelian's laughter nearly cracks the crimson paint on his face. "Oh, Zenobia—no. You are much more than any woman I have ever met."

22

Keep to a Woman's Place

By the time Zabdas finds the estate, far on the outer edge of Rome, almost amid the herds of sheep and the olive groves, daylight is long since burned. The night is rich with the scent of growing things, of leaves just beginning to unfold, of shoots yet to burst from the dark sleeping earth of Rome's outer hills.

Zabdas finds the moist air pleasant now, and shakes his head in disbelief whenever he catches himself thinking so. Imagine a desert tribesman, a Palmyrene through and through, learning to breathe this wet air like a fish—and enjoying it.

He waits in the shadow of a tiny roadside temple—one seldom used, to judge by the long-dried, rust-brown stains on its altar and the scattering of mouse droppings on the floor. He watches the silent, vine-greened walls of the estate until the moon begins to rise. It is a full moon, bright and silver-white, rising steady and smooth like a bird taking flight from the marshes of Egypt. When there is just enough light to make out the contours of the wall, Zabdas slips from his shadows and glides across the road.

It is the work of a few minutes to climb the garden wall. The unkempt vines make it easy enough. Zabdas has spent weeks searching, waiting, listening. He is sure he has found the correct place—and equally sure that he will meet with no danger.

He makes the top of the garden wall and looks around. The large, fine home—gray stone, as all good Roman houses are—sits in the center of a broad, lush garden, its paths and beds emerging from the darkness moment by moment as the moon climbs higher in the starry sky. An olive tree grows near the wall, old and with sturdy, twisted branches. The first flush of new leaves soften its edges and whisper together as Zabdas takes hold of a branch, drops his full weight over the wall, and swings heavily into the garden.

His feet strike the pavers of a pathway with a thump. He hears a gasp, and catches, from the corner of his eye, the rapid, jerky movement of a figure starting up in terror from a nearby bench. Zabdas hadn't thought the garden would be occupied at this hour. He holds out his hands in a pleading gesture to calm the servant he has startled. He is about to speak, to beg for silence, when the figure says his name.

He stands speechless and stunned. He has spent weeks, ever since his arrival in Rome—after a long, miserable journey by sea, tucked into an airless cabin on a merchant's boat—searching for Zenobia. But now it seems unreal—impossible—that he is finally face-to-face with her, after all this time. She is dressed in the Roman style, in a long, loose tunic, and draped with the folds of a one-shoulder shawl. Zabdas almost doesn't recognize her. But there is no mistaking that face, the proud chin, the Amlaqi nose, the black fire of her eyes.

He can think of nothing to say, except "Yes, mistress. I am here."

Zenobia takes one hesitant step toward him. It has been so many months since she's seen him. The fear and desperation of their last parting return to her with choking force—to say nothing of her long certainty that he was dead. She takes his inventory, staring with starved eyes at his dark hair, his green Seleucid eyes, the scar on his left cheek.

She compares the sight of his beloved body against her memory—broad shoulders, strong chest, those hands that know just how to touch her—and yes, yes, it is truly him! Against all odds, in defiance of the gods themselves, Zabdas is here.

She flings herself across the path, into his arms.

"Oh, Zabdas," she says. "You can't imagine—you can't imagine what I've been through."

His hand brushes her hair, and she feels the warmth of his palm cup the nape of her neck. The familiar sensation so overwhelms her that for a moment she cannot breathe.

"You're all right," he murmurs.

But Zenobia finally gasps and says, "Vaballathus . . ."

"I know. I heard. My love, I am so sorry."

She breaks from their embrace, and, leading him by the hand as if they have never been apart, pulls him to the bench. They sink down together. The Roman night holds a pleasant chill, the kind that compels two bodies to huddle close together, to seek comfort in one another's warmth.

"I have also heard," Zabdas says, "that you've been punished for your rebellion with a marriage."

Zenobia gives one short, sharp laugh and spills out the name of her new husband. "Marcellus Petrus Nutenus. A senator, no less. I lead a very fine lifestyle—or am beginning to be allowed it, I should say."

"A rather old man, I've heard. No reason for me to fear him. Otherwise I might have been more cautious than to climb over your garden wall."

"Yes, he is old. But Petrus is kind enough, if rather neglectful. That suits me fine. He needed a wife, for propriety's sake, and a man of his stature requires a wife of some renown."

"Isn't Aurelian afraid you might have another son—one who can stake a claim on Palmyra?"

"There is no danger of that with Petrus, believe me," she says drily. "Aurelian knew what he was about. There will be no more sons for Zenobia bat-Zabbai."

At this last admission, she looks down into her lap, and Zabdas can see how it pains her. She is still young enough to be a mother, several times over, and the loss of Vaballathus has no doubt left a terrible, deep hole in her heart. Another child would help fill it—but as Rome turns its might to the Gallic front, it cannot risk a Palmyrene prince raised by a fearless, ambitious mother.

Zabdas shakes his head. He will not acquiesce to Rome's punishments, their fettering of his city and his queen. He stands, pulling Zenobia to her feet. "I've come to get you," he tells her directly.

"What?"

"I've come to take you back to Palmyra."

Her mouth falls open in dismay. "Zabdas—no."

He takes her by the shoulders, as he has so many times before, and Zenobia flushes at his touch. It would be so easy to say yes and flee this sentence of loveless drudgery, the future Aurelian has laid out for her, quietly breaking her bit by bit, turning her into a proper citizen of Rome. But . . .

"What do you mean, no?"

Her body is hot with desire for him—for the passion they shared in Egypt, and even for their moments of solitude in the green, whispering shelter of Tadmor, long before they were lovers. Her heart belongs to Zabdas—but her loyalty belongs to Palmyra.

"I will not risk my city's safety again," she tells him gently, looking up into his hard, scowling, beloved face. "For too long, I ignored the gods' desires and pursued my own. I told myself I was chasing my destiny, but in truth, my quarry was ambition—selfish gratification. I've suffered for my wrongs, Zabdas. But worse—the people I love most have suffered. My city, my family, my son. The gods have chastised me. I will not provoke their anger by crossing them again."

He gapes at her. He can find no words. Her face is silvery in the moonlight, pale and adored and unforgettable. Having found her, how can he part from her again? How can he leave her to this cruel, disappointing fate?

"You cannot regret the choices you've made, Zenobia."

She drops her eyes, turns her face away as if in shame.

Shame—how unaccustomed it is on her face, how unlike a woman of the tribes! He grips her shoulders tighter, and although she still refuses to look at him, her chin rises again, as if he transmits some of his desert strength into her, refilling the cistern of her pride.

"Regret nothing," he says again. "You have not crossed the gods— you have made your own destiny, carved it for yourself from the stone of the world. How many people can say the same? Who else can even aspire to what you've achieved, my love, my Zenobia?"

Love—to hear Zabdas call her *love* is sweeter than the best honey, sweeter than the scent of cinnamon on an evening wind. But Zenobia shakes her head. "I aspire to nothing now. Nothing. It is better if Palmyra forgets me—if the whole world forgets me, and never hears my name again. It is better that I learn to live in humility."

"Like a proper Roman woman?" Zabdas says, his voice rough with disgust.

"If that is what the gods want of me—if it is my true destiny . . ."

"Don't say this," he begs her, for her words are like steel in his flesh, sharp and cold.

"Nafsha once told me that I must learn how to keep to a woman's proper place." She looks up at him, at last, fills herself with one last look at her lover. "If I had listened to her, Zabdas, everything would have been different."

He stoops to kiss her—but she turns her face away.

"You're right," Zabdas whispers. "Everything would have been different. But I will never regret what we've done, Zenobia. We made the world our own—and we loved one another. And those two things, I would never wish to change."

It is the hardest thing he's ever done, to bid her good-bye and walk away—to climb the olive tree and clamber to the top of the garden wall. A dozen battles, a bloody war, and the creation of an empire at her command—every swing of his sword was simple as a song compared to leaving the woman he loves to her lonely fate.

As Zabdas descends the outer wall, climbing down the thick vines on legs that shake with every shift of his weight, he wonders where he will go now, what he will do. Palmyra is out of the question—it is sure to be thick with her memory; haunted by her small, striding, proud-backed ghost; and every breeze will carry the scent of oranges and rose water.

He stumbles to the broad road, his heart hollow and aching. Then he turns for one last look at his lover's fine, inescapable prison.

His heart is stunned to stillness at the sight. For Zenobia has mounted the wall—by the tree, or by some unknown staircase, he is not sure. The moon is full and bright behind her, a great ring of silver light, and she stands centered against it in silhouette.

She gazes out across the hills, toward the gray stone weight of Rome. Her chin is high, her shoulders unbent, and as he watches with his heart in his throat, the wind lifts her hair like a banner of victory.

She looks like what she is: a queen—a warrior—a wind in the desert, a fire that can never be quenched. She is the girl who conquered the dunes to bring her city salvation and the woman who conquered an empire for the glory of her own unforgettable name.

Zabdas smiles up at her sadly, and tells her in his heart, *Try all you might to learn a woman's place. You have found it already. It is in the desert, with the stars shining on your skin. It is on the back of a camel, with a sword gripped tight in your fist. It is on the throne of Egypt—it is in the reach of your empire—it is in my arms, and in my heart. You made your place, and it is yours by right, Zenobia, my love.*

Author's Note

I confess I am not a fan of ancient Rome. That's not to say I don't enjoy novels and TV shows and other forms of entertainment set in Rome. The Republic and the Empire both fascinate me, but I find nearly everything about them so incredibly unlikable, from their appropriation of other cultures to their use of blood sport as entertainment, and certainly their oppression of women (ancient Egypt proves that not all neighboring cultures found it necessary to turn women into second-class citizens). Therefore, I've always been drawn to the points in history where somebody finally said, "Enough is enough!" and took a stand against Rome.

Of course, not many rebellions got very far, or lasted very long. In spite of all its moral shortcomings, or possibly because of them, Rome was the undeniable superpower of the world for a very long time. It had a mighty fist, and it knew how to swing it. The Palmyrene rebellion, initiated by Lucius Septimius Odenathus but carried through its rise and fall by Zenobia, his wife, stands out among many other rebellions for its sheer audacity as well as its relative success.

The Palmyrene rebels staged their revolt well, taking advantage of a time of chaos, when a long chain of assassinations, plagues, and general misfortunes of war combined with economic instability to create a Rome that was nearer collapse than it had ever been before. Today, historians call this period the Crisis of the Third Century, and for Rome, it was a crisis indeed. In fifty years, there were twenty-six emperors. The Gallic Empire split from Rome in 260 CE, which only further destabilized an empire already pushed to its limits by the incessant attacks from the Goths and their allies in difficult, mountainous terrain. Persia (called by its ancient names of Eran and the Sasanid Empire in this novel) was growing in power, and the capture of Emperor Valerian was only one of many moves the Persians made to try to put Rome in its place.

During this trying era, Rome's rapid succession of emperors relied on grain from Egypt to keep their overworked soldiers fed. They relied just as heavily on the luxuries flowing from the Far East (via the trading depot of Palmyra) to maintain the status quo back home—to keep Roman citizens convinced that everything was well in hand, that there was nothing to worry about, and that life would go on as usual no matter who wore the imperial purple. Throughout the Crisis of the Third Century, Egyptian grain and Palmyrene trade goods were the two things Rome simply couldn't do without. Whoever controlled these crucial resources could demand virtually anything of Rome.

No specific reason for Odenathus's revolt has ever been discovered. It was unusual, as revolts against Rome went, for Odenathus seemed to enjoy many favors from his Roman overlords, probably due in part to his loyalty. He quelled at least one attempt by others to break Palmyra away and forge a new empire—and then he initiated a decisive split from Rome himself, shortly thereafter. It's possible that he'd always thought Palmyra should enjoy its own empire, but wanted to ensure that *he* ruled it, not some upstart rebels.

Whatever his reasons, Odenathus didn't get far with his revolt. He and his son Hairan were both assassinated early in a military campaign— by whom is not definitively known. And it's here, just when Odenathus is killed, that Zenobia makes her grand entrance on history's stage.

Some sources claim Zenobia herself engineered Odenathus's death in order to take Palmyra for herself, in the name of her son, Vaballathus. Other sources name a variety of assassins, from a cousin of Odenathus to a miscreant who was angry because Odenathus threw him in jail. The perpetrator is impossible to name with any certainty, as are the precise reasons for the murder. What is clear, however, is that key members of the army, who were apparently present when Odenathus was killed, immediately handed over control of Palmyra to Zenobia—indicating first, that she was relatively near when her husband died, and second, that she was regarded quite highly by powerful people within the Palmyrene militia.

This is the first glimpse we get of Zenobia in all historical sources: a young mother, freshly widowed, in the midst of a revolt against an unpredictable Rome—and she is smoothly taking control of her city-state's military. It paints an intriguing picture and raises a wealth of questions—so many, in fact, that Zenobia is surrounded by far more legend than fact.

The bold Palmyrene queen and her revolt against Rome made a popular subject for plays, operas, and novels throughout the eighteenth century. Many different cultures have attempted to lay some claim on the enigmatic warrior queen by working her into their stories—she appears in the Talmud, for example, dispensing some rather sarcastic justice to the Jews. The Arabs were very fond of her, and even after Islam changed the face of Arabic culture, she continued to be a popular character in traditional stories, where she appears in the guise of al-Zabba, a queen of exceptional courage and beauty. Al-Zabba tales are brimming with adventure; here, Zenobia is seen as a storybook heroine, putting herself at serious risk to achieve great things for her people. One story, in which she tricks Jadhima, the leader of the Tanukh tribe, into meeting with a mere woman, only to surprise him by cutting off his head, found its way into this novel, albeit with a very liberal interpretation of the source material.

As popular as Zenobia has always been in literature and tradition, it's surprising how little we actually know about her origins and her life. Concrete facts are few and far between.

We know that she was born in Palmyra, which is a part of modern-day Syria. We know that she often used the name bat-Zabbai to refer to herself in official Palmyrene inscriptions. The name is from the Aramaic language, the common tongue of Palmyra, and its use (rather than a Latin version of her name, as Odenathus and many of his courtiers used) seems to indicate stronger ties to her Palmyrene roots than to her Roman overlords. It also seems to indicate a certain flaunting of her preference, and a lack of regard for how Rome might have felt about her questionable loyalty. Bat-Zabbai means "daughter of Zabbai," so we can assume that her father's name carried some weight in her world. She was probably the daughter of a very prominent Palmyrene leader, and indeed most sources agree that her father was the sheikh of one of the desert tribes that helped found Palmyra.

We know virtually no other facts about Zenobia as a person. Even her role as a mother is rather vague and misty. We are certain that she was the mother of at least one son, Vaballathus—but sources are unclear on how old Vaballathus was during the Palmyrene revolt. He was either in his early twenties, or he was a toddler—no source focuses much on Vaballathus, which seemed enough indication to me that he was probably little more than a baby. It's not even clear how long Vaballathus lived. The *Historia Augusta* mentions that he was with Zenobia when Aurelian captured her, but makes no mention of him in the triumphal procession—about which more later—so the general assumption is that Zenobia's son died en route to Rome.

Odenathus had other children, including Hairan, his eldest son who died with him. No one knows whether Zenobia was their mother, or if they were the children of Odenathus's previous wife, a Persian woman whose name has been lost to history.

Speaking of mothers, nothing is known of Zenobia's own, but various Arabic stories give the name of her sister: Nafsha or Zabibah, depending on the source. I chose to give her two sisters in this novel. In some of the Arabic tales of al-Zabba, the sister plays an important role as foil or motivator, sometimes checking al-Zabba's behavior, helping to keep her on the proper path (even warrior queens should still behave like ladies), and sometimes as a figure in need of al-Zabba's valiant aid. Here, you can see where my depictions of Nafsha and Zabibah came from.

One fact we do know about Palmyra's warrior queen, but which I couldn't find a graceful way of squeezing into this novel, is that she was highly cultured, a great believer in Hellenistic ideals, and that she revered philosophy and the arts. She took pains to promote music, dance, literature, and free thought in Palmyra and throughout her empire as her reach expanded. I regret that I couldn't find a relevant way to explore this aspect of her personality in my rather fast-paced novel, as I find it fascinating. I like how this tidbit of history humanizes Zenobia in a touching way—I could just see her hosting wonderful parties where she conversed freely with learned men and displayed the very best music, poetry, and visual arts the Palmyrene Empire had to offer.

But it was the more adventuresome aspects of Zenobia's story that led me to write about her in the first place—the battles, the revolt, the rapid rise and fall of her empire—and so it was on those episodes that I chose to focus my narrative. Unfortunately, most of what we "know" about Zenobia's most exciting deeds comes from an unreliable source: the *Historia Augusta*.

The *Historia Augusta*, although hugely entertaining, is almost certainly a collection of propaganda, an anthology of ancient smear campaigns that has survived into our era. Zenobia's purpose in the *Historia* seems to be to discredit the (short) reign of Gallienus, chiefly by pointing out that he was so terrible at being an emperor that even a mere woman could do a better job of it. The *Historia* claims to present letters exchanged between Zenobia and Aurelian, in which Zenobia's correspondence is mostly a lot of thumbing her nose at Roman emperors in general, and Gallienus in particular. It's good stuff, but it's almost certainly apocryphal.

Most of the information I could find about Zenobia was equally open to doubt and free interpretation. She takes on a wide variety of characteristics, depending on the sources—always reflecting the ideal concept of femininity, according to the culture you happen to be consulting.

Nearly every account, including the *Historia Augusta*, emphasized Zenobia's chastity. The *Historia* claims that she had no interest in sex at all, except for procreation. That, of course, is the standard misogynistic claptrap of ancient Rome. I didn't buy it for a second, and resolved to provide my Zenobia with a passionate love affair just to stick a fork in Rome's eye—but I was intrigued by how many sources insisted that Zenobia was a perfectly chaste woman. Her reputation for chastity was so widespread that I wanted to give it a plausible explanation in my book: enter Fairuza.

As mentioned before, the name of Odenathus's previous wife is not known. She was Persian, though, which is interesting, considering how unpopular Persia was with both Palmyra and Rome. There is absolutely no evidence that Odenathus was married to two women at once, but when I realized I needed a reason for Zenobia to maintain a reputation of absolute chastity, the scenario of a double marriage solved that problem, and many others besides. Allowing Odenathus's Persian wife to remain in the picture, an active character in Zenobia's story, added plenty of tension to the plot, even though it was pure fiction.

Also pure fiction is the romantic relationship with Zabdas. He's another figure about whom almost nothing is known, save for the fact that he was one of the generals of Zenobia's armies (the other was called Zabbai—her father, or just a man with the same name?). Zabdas led admirable campaigns while the Palmyrene Empire expanded—the

Palmyrenes were actually better soldiers than I gave them credit for—but he was not able to withstand the superior numbers of Aurelian's forces.

My decision to make Zabdas into Zenobia's "boyfriend" came entirely from my annoyance with the *Historia Augusta*'s insistence on her chastity. There is certainly no evidence to support such a relationship between the warrior queen and her general, but there is no evidence that Zenobia enjoyed any romantic love at all—good Roman women didn't think that way. But the real Zenobia wasn't a Roman ideal. She was human, and nearly all humans fall for somebody at some point in their lives. Why not Zabdas, after all?

So little is established as concrete fact when it comes to Zenobia's life and reign. Even the events of her downfall and her ultimate fate aren't clear. We do know that her decision to conquer Egypt played a major part in sealing her doom. What, precisely, she *did* with Egypt remains up for debate: some sources indicate that she promptly cut off Rome's supply of grain. Other sources seem to indicate that she only threatened a cutoff. Either way, it was a risk Rome couldn't ignore. Without Egyptian grain, the Roman army would starve—and so, by taking Egypt, Zenobia bumped her own downfall right to the top of Rome's "to do" list.

Zenobia claimed descent from Cleopatra VII, via the Seleucid line. Whether she truly believed this, or only used it as a bit of clever propaganda to justify her conquering of Egypt, doesn't really matter. The claim was politically significant: Cleopatra was a famous opponent of Rome and the last Pharaoh of Egypt, and any kinship Zenobia could emphasize to the famous queen would only help underscore her opposition to Rome and further justify her seizure of Egypt's throne. But like Cleopatra, Zenobia's downfall was a direct result of Rome's desire—or desperate need—to control the bountiful Nile valley and the shipping routes that ran from Alexandria to Rome.

Almost as soon as he was appointed emperor, Aurelian went after Zenobia with a vengeance. Unlike the many emperors who had come before him, Aurelian was determined to *earn* the title of Restorer of the World, and for Rome, the world could not go on turning without Egyptian grain. Despite the rather jocular correspondence they'd shared (if the *Historia Augusta* can be trusted), Aurelian was only too happy to become Zenobia's enemy on the battlefield. He added the defeat of the Palmyrene Empire to his long list of important accomplishments, along with curbing the Gallic Empire and defeating the Goths, who had plagued Rome for generations. It must be said that Aurelian seemed to know what he was doing when it came to restoring the world. Once he took charge of the empire, the Crisis of the Third Century was on its way to mending, and Rome began to move toward order and strength once more.

No one knows for certain what became of Zenobia after she was conquered. Legend has it that she was paraded in front of Roman citizens in a great triumphal display, so that all the citizens could see how the Empress of the East had fallen. Draped in riches so heavy she could barely move, and fettered by golden cuffs and chains, she was made to walk before jeering Romans in order to display her own hubris—and, of course, to illustrate the ability of Aurelian, the new emperor, to secure both cooperation and vast wealth from the far-flung reaches of his newly restored empire. Many scholars feel that Zenobia's close association with Cleopatra would have led her to commit suicide, as Cleopatra had done, rather than submit so shamefully to Rome. Such a scenario is possible—perhaps some other woman stood in for Zenobia in order to provide the desired lesson to Rome's citizens. We'll never know whether the triumphal parade truly occurred, and, if it did, whether it was actually Zenobia who dragged the weight of Palmyra's riches through the streets of Rome. But the image of a conquered warrior queen marching in golden chains before jeering Romans is certainly a compelling one.

Some readers may take exception to the perceived theme of this novel. I suppose it might be easy to interpret this book as a meditation on a woman's "true place." In some ways, I suppose it is just that—although not in the way it might seem.

Throughout the process of researching this book, it struck me as increasingly ironic that no matter how many legends or stories Zenobia appeared in, she was always made to reflect those cultures' ideals of what a "proper woman" should be. She was a warrior—a conqueror—one of the few women of her era who was bold enough to attempt to forge an identity for herself that went far beyond the narrow strictures the world offered. And yet in memory, she is only allowed to exist within those same narrow strictures, not as the self-determining force she truly must have been. In making her "the perfect woman," history has stuffed her right back into the very cell whose walls she kicked over in her own day.

I wanted this book to be something of a reflection on the restrictive nature of Zenobia legends—on the identity she was allowed to have (and, more significantly, the identity she was *not* allowed to have) by the men who defeated her and wrote her histories. The very idea of "a woman's place" is a concept that exists to plague and restrict both women and men to this day. I hoped to turn it somewhat on its ear—so that in my book, even as Zenobia thinks she "learns her lesson" and is chastised, the powerful male characters around her—Aurelian and Zabdas—develop an entirely new appreciation for women, changing their concept of femininity because of their feelings about Zenobia. I hope readers will be able to look past the surface of this novel and see the deeper theme I attempted to inject into the story.

But above all else, I hope readers enjoyed reading it. I enjoyed writing it, and loved learning about a woman as fascinating and powerful as Zenobia. My main sources for research were the *Historia Augusta* and *Empress Zenobia: Palmyra's Rebel Queen* by Pat Southern. The former is amusing, and the latter will provide curious readers with an exhaustive, thorough analysis of Palmyrene culture, the politics of the time, and as many details of Zenobia herself as can be wrung from the scattered and sparse historical sources.

Thanks are due to my editor at Lake Union, Jodi Warshaw; to my developmental editor, Kristin Mehus-Roe; and my copyeditor, Michelle Hope Anderson, all of whom put in an extraordinary amount of work on this book. And thanks as always to my readers, whose support means more to me than I can ever say. I must also thank Mark and Michele Schrader, who were kind enough to put me up in their beautiful, hundred-year-old dairy barn turned guest house over Super Bowl weekend, so I could get away from Seattle's rowdy Seahawks fans long enough to finish this book.

And thank you, Paul.

—L. H.
Seattle, Washington
2015

ABOUT THE AUTHOR

Photo © 2014 Paul Harnden

Libbie Hawker writes historical and literary fiction featuring deeply human characters, with rich details of time and place. She is the author of ten novels, most of which take place in the distant past among ancient civilizations. She lives in the beautiful San Juan Islands with her husband. Find more information about this author at LibbieHawker.com.